'Simants uses her knowledge ⟨...⟩
secrets of a reality TV show se⟨...⟩
traditional crime plot to ⟨...⟩'
Sunday Times

'This novel has a lot to offer. It moves fast, the tension is high
and the two main characters are likeable in their different ways'
Literary Review

'Brimming with stone-cold secrets, shocking lies and twists
that hit like an Arctic winter. Simants has sculpted a
breathtaking thriller out of pure ice'
Janice Hallett, author of *The Appeal*

'Brilliant – creepily atmospheric and incredibly tense. The
characterisation is fantastic and it cuts as cold as the Arctic in
which it's set'
Harriet Tyce, author of *Blood Orange*

'Superb. Utterly claustrophobic and chilling,
the perfect icy read'
Jo Spain, author of *Dirty Little Secrets*

'Packed with chills and spills, *Freeze* is a terrifically
entertaining thriller with a unique and fascinating setting'
Allie Reynolds, author of *Shiver*

'This book has everything – weather that can kill you, an
under-equipped ship stuck in a storm, a cast of people who all
have secrets and elements of their past they don't want revealed'
Catherine Cooper, author of *The Chateau*

'As addictive as any reality TV show and utterly chilling'
A.J. West, author of *The Spirit Engineer*

'Chilling in every sense of the word'
Lisa Hall, author of *The Perfect Couple*

'A tour de force; a brilliantly handled, gripping locked-room thriller of great scope, with deeply human characters that leap off the page and brain-popping twists'
S.E. Lynes, author of *The Housewarming*

'A reality TV show set in formidable Arctic conditions offers a fresh and enticing setting. The book's expert pacing will keep readers guessing right up to the end'
Ally Wilkes, author of *All the White Spaces*

'A fast-paced and vividly written thriller full of darkness and suspicion. Superb'
Guy Morpuss, author of *Five Minds*

'Simants gets under the skin of her characters with such humanity, yet never fails to deliver the twists and tension. A wild ride of a thriller in an incredible setting'
Emma Styles, author of *No Country for Girls*

'Biting and atmospheric, *Freeze* is the ultimate locked-room mystery, where the breathless intensity increases as the temperature plummets. Frostbite-inducingly chilling'
Sam Holland, author of *The Echo Man*

Also by Kate Simants and available from Viper

A Ruined Girl

FREEZE

KATE SIMANTS

This paperback edition published in 2023

First published in Great Britain in 2023 by
VIPER, part of Serpent's Tail,
an imprint of Profile Books Ltd
29 Cloth Fair
London
ECIA 7JQ
www.serpentstail.com

Copyright © Kate Simants, 2023

Typeset by CC Book Production

1 3 5 7 9 10 8 6 4 2

Printed and bound in Great Britain by
CPI Group (UK) Ltd, Croydon, CRO 4YY

A CIP catalogue record for this book is available from the British Library.

ISBN 978 1 78816 6997
eISBN 978 1 78283 7435

For Mo and Sid.
Please don't repeat any of the bad words
in front of Grandma or Auntie Faye.

PROLOGUE

She stands in the black night wearing only pyjamas, the mist parting around her as it rolls across the open hillside. There is silence, except for her own breath and that faint rasping by her feet. Maybe she could still save him. But she can't even bring herself to look.

If only she'd done what she was told.

If only she'd stayed on the other side of the wood, in view of her tent.

If only the new friend she'd made that afternoon hadn't seen those hazel trees. Their long, perfect branches, easy to snap, exactly the kind they needed to finish the den. Sticking straight up, beckoning like fingers, drawing them in.

In quiet, stalking footsteps, she and the other girl had gone further away to that other camp, just beyond. That's where they found the boys, the smell of their barbecue, their laughter. Older, but not old enough for the beer they were drinking. Their freedom, their easy way with the man they had with them, their chests bare.

Her fingers still held tight to the bark of that thick pine when he turned.

The hazel twigs forgotten.

And when that one boy saw her, if only she'd looked away more quickly. She didn't know what happens when they see you looking at them.

But she knows now.

She made the new friend promise to say nothing. The adults would only worry. They finished the den, but without enthusiasm – the silly fun of it having evaporated, leaving behind only an awkward awareness that they were too old for dens. Then they went their separate ways, back in time for tea. And by the time her family's campfire had burned all the way down and she'd zipped up her sleeping bag for the night, she'd almost forgotten about the boys, their party.

But not quite. Every time she closed her eyes, she saw his face. That bounce of black hair, the easy smile. Not like the boys at school. And she did try to ignore it, but something had changed. A circuit had lit up.

And so when she heard them out there, passing the shower block, she went on her own.

She thought they hadn't seen her when she went inside the squat building, but he was there after she washed her hands and went back out. Waiting by the door, alone now, this black-haired boy. His eyes soft. The kind of forehead that bulges above the eyebrows. A fine, angular nose. Head tilting, half amused.

Not that she knew then how his face would stick in her mind. How she'd see it every day for the rest of her life. In the dark of her room, in the shadows of nightclubs, in the rear-view mirror of every car she would ever own. Imprinted in her mind as if he was right there in front of her. Over and over again, until she learned to fear closing her eyes.

He said he hadn't mean to startle her, but it didn't stop him smiling. He couldn't sleep, he said. Couldn't she sleep, either? Maybe a walk would help.

So she went with him.

If they hadn't wanted to build that den, none of it would have happened. She'd be back in her tent, asleep, warm. Safe.

And this boy would be safe, too. This boy on this rocky patch of ground, halfway up the hill behind the woods. This boy who she'd thought was kind, but who wasn't. This boy – much more like a man than she had first realised – who thought she wouldn't fight back.

A new voice had told her what to do. She flexes her sticky fingers, recalling it sounding in her head. Quiet, calm – hers but not hers. Saying, *Stop. You cannot win like this. Wait until he understands you're not struggling. Choose your moment.*

So she did. She stopped fighting until she knew she could win. She didn't scream. No one came and no one will know. No one but her, and him.

A shiver goes through her now, half-pain, half-cold. She looks down and sees her legs and they are a surprise, glowing bare white. She blinks away the sense that they do not belong to her any more, that none of her body does.

She has lost a sandal.

There is a single dark track threading the length of her thigh, smearing out at the crease of her knee. Blood, she thinks, without feeling. She is bleeding.

But it's not just blood. Another wetness that she understands for a fraction of a second and then – no. She makes the choice not to acknowledge it.

She has lost a sandal.

She is bleeding.

Something hurts.

That is all.

The scream of a bird, an owl, jolts her into herself. She doesn't know how long it has been. Five minutes? Half an hour? Do they even know she's missing?

She squints down the slope towards the camp. Dark except for the faint outline of the shower block, lit from the other side. And beyond it, through the woods at the edge, where the boys' group is – a flicker of flame. She watches for the beams of torches, but no one is coming. Their fire is still burning. If she listens hard, past the thundering of her own blood in her ears, maybe she will hear them. Singing. Laughing. Or calling his name, because he must have a name. But there is no sound.

They haven't realised he's gone.

She drops the rock, slick as it slips from her fingers. Everything is dark, so dark now, the world reduced to black and white. Too dark for shadows. Even the red on her fingers, thick as a glove, is crude oil in the absence of a moon. She looks down at his face. She waits to feel something. His eyes are open, as if scanning for stars.

The girl looks up. There are no stars.

The silence is punctuated only by the faint, rasping, just-about-something from him. Silence filling the space between each of his shallow breaths, stretching a little longer each time. Her own breath stings in her throat and she tries to remember: was she shouting? Did she scream, before, when he was

when he

when

did she scream? She doesn't remember it. She thinks she didn't cry out, not even when she realised what was happening. His hands on her. Even though she knew what it meant. She is fourteen, she's not stupid.

She brings her fingers up in front of her eyes and what's on them changes direction, slicking downwards towards her wrist, thick as tar.

There's a crack from further down the hill, making her jump. She crouches, runs her eyes across the blackness, but she sees nothing. An animal? But the suddenness of it lights up her mind again – shakes her out of this strange, blinking confusion. *Yes, you must move*, that same ancient part of her says. *Act. Do it now!* There are things she has to do. Wash. Get back. Stay out of sight.

She tears down the hill towards the rectangular glow of the shower block. But she only takes a few steps before her bare toes strike against a rock and she remembers. *The sandal.* She tracks back to where he lies sprawled on the loose rocks. His chest is still rising and falling. His trousers and shorts are halfway down his thighs and his

and his

and

And there, by a miracle, grabbing-distance from his hip, is the sandal.

Right there. He can't reach her. She can move quickly, and he can't. She has to do it. There is no choice. She sets her jaw and dashes in to retrieve it.

In the very same second she snatches it away, he flings his arm out. This time she screams.

From the same direction that she heard the crack, there's a shout.

'Hey!'

Then footsteps.

She flies off down the hill.

'Wait, stop, what's happened?' A man. The man from their camp.

She does not wait. She does not stop.

She doesn't think of anything, of what's happened, because she can't change any of that. Can't control it.

What she can control is what happens next. Who she tells, who she trusts. And it takes her only minutes to make the decision.

She slips unseen into the shower block and stands in the scalding water, scrubbing blisters into her skin, then creeps without a sound into the tent and slips herself back into the oblivious warmth of her family, as if unharmed.

There and then, she makes the promise to herself. She will trust no one.

From this moment onwards, she will fold herself around this secret. She will build a prison around it with no doors and no windows. There will be questions, she has no doubt, but if she has to lie to keep it hidden, she will lie. She will lie now, and tomorrow, and every day until the questions stop, and if they never stop, then she will never stop lying.

As she lies blinking in the blackness, the secret takes its place. It nestles silently, sharp and cancerous against her heart, its claws reaching blindly in.

1

DEE

Twenty years later

Twelve days. Less than two weeks' work. But it's money, and that's why I'm doing it. Anyone can manage a few hundred hours of dealing with other people. A dozen mornings of forcing myself out of bed, washing, eating, functioning. I've done it before and I can do it again. They're not paying me to be chatty, or fun, or sociable. They're paying me to show up with a camera and shoot the bloody thing.

It's only twelve days. And then I can come home and crawl back under my duvet.

Regular as clockwork, minutes after waking, there's Leo's voice in my head. *Come on then. Day's a-wasting. Up and at 'em.*

I squeeze my eyes shut, force him out and turn onto my side. In the corner of the bare room is the suitcase. A ridiculous pink-and-orange thing more suited to a twenty-something on an Ayia Napa bender than a self-shooting TV director on location. But that's what you get when you're renting a room in someone else's house and your own flat is so full of demons that you can't face going back to get your luggage.

So there's that.

I packed last night in under an hour, then spent the rest of the night checking my kit. It's fair to say Tori's priorities were different from mine. Which shirt set off her eyes best? Would three colours of lipstick be enough? Which earrings to take, which to leave? Did I have room for her straighteners? What about the wedges? And how was she seriously going to manage the whole thing without a single stylist?

Bear in mind we're going to be based primarily on a ship, in the Arctic.

My suitcase doesn't contain earrings or mascara, because my job is firmly on the other side of the camera. Always has been. Even when Tori and I first started out as researchers almost a decade ago and it seemed like the whole team spent hours preening and blow-drying every morning in the hope that someone important spotted them and made them the Next Big Thing, my sights were always set on camera-work. I wanted to make documentaries. I wanted the thrill of the investigation, the piecing-together of the puzzle.

And yet, here I am. Self-shooting director for a reality-lite six-parter with a £100,000 prize. Exec-produced by Tori herself and her soon-to-be husband, in their first solo venture. Never mind his non-existent track record; somehow, between them, they've scraped together the cash to fund the show. But everything's tight, starting with the crewing. The original plan to fit out the ship with remotely operated cameras went out of the window as soon as the quote came through, and even though I'm paid to direct *and* shoot, it's still very much mates' rates.

But it's not like anyone else has been beating down the doors to hire me lately.

'Deedee! Half an hour!' she calls from downstairs. Her voice rides high over the state-of-the-art speakers in her kitchen, playing the sort of mindless pop that would make the Tori I met fifteen years ago in the graduate scheme roll her eyes out of her head.

Not that I'm in a position to complain. Her kitchen, her rules.

Her feet on the stairs, a knock at the door.

'Dee! Are you even up? Got coffee!'

The door swings open and there she is.

My best friend – the beautiful, successful, ceaselessly positive Tori Matsuka.

'This is going to be *amazing*,' she says, dancing with excitement the moment the Americano is safe in my hands. 'The actual *Arctic Circle*!'

And this is the thing about her – the reason for her popularity; and her ratings, which broke records from the moment she started presenting and have stayed stratospheric across everything she's fronted. She is *on*, all the time. She is 100 per cent bubbles. Cynicism doesn't reach her. I'm not going to pretend I don't admire it: her ability to be so unendingly optimistic, so apparently bulletproof.

I love her, I do. But sometimes, by God, it is *exhausting*.

Don't get me wrong. Tori deserves everything she has, and without the lifeline she threw me six months ago I'd have struggled, no question. I'd have sunk. It's simply that being the yin to someone else's yang does get old after a while.

She flings my curtains open now, flooding the white-walled

spare room – still not my room, because it's definitely, positively, only temporary – with flinchingly bright daylight.

'Oh God, you're not even packed! Let me help you.' And then the wardrobe is open, and she's on her knees, peering under the bed that I'm only now climbing from.

'I *am* packed.' I gesture loosely to the case, without looking at it.

She laughs, sees I'm serious, then frowns and goes over. She lifts the lid. 'That,' she says, looking from the stacks of folded grey and black fabrics to me, and then back again, 'is not what you're taking for the whole trip.'

'Yeah, it is.' Twelve pairs of knickers, a couple of bras. Thermals, layers, jeans. Two blister packs of Citalopram, the dose checked and double-checked. Last thing I need is to run out in the middle of nowhere. 'It's fine, leave it.'

'What about that blue top? You look great in that.'

'Tore a hole in it.' I'd been trying to customise it for use with a body-worn camera rig, but it went wrong. 'Also, it really doesn't matter what I look like. Who am I trying to impress – the seals?' I go over and snap the case shut. 'At least I'll stand out against the snow.' According to the brief that our researcher Annabel sent over, we'll be spending most of the time in the ship-issue outersuits anyway.

Downstairs the front door opens.

'Tori? Food!'

She's out of the room in three paces. I go out, lean over the banister for as long as it takes to see her locking faces with Will, the fiancé. They've been together for almost two years, but my tenancy here pre-dated the engagement by a few weeks.

Although he still spends most nights in the flat above his Old Street office, there's been talk of selling the house after the wedding in a few months' time. If I don't jump soon, the push is going to come eventually.

Will senses my presence and looks up, waggling a paper bag, rounded by the food inside. 'Bacon butty?' he offers, before taking a bite of his own.

'Are you driving us?' I ask him.

'She means, *could you drive us, please?*' Tori mock-whispers in his ear. 'Also, *no thank you, I'm fine for breakfast, Will, but that's very kind of you to offer.*'

'No thank you, Will, but that's very kind of you to offer,' I yawn.

He laughs, wipes the corners of his mouth, checks the watch that would, on its own, pay the debt that neither of them has the slightest clue I owe. What would Leo make of a watch like that? One that would have solved everything for him, in one go?

'Dee?' Will says, and I blink, caught not paying attention. 'Leave in fifteen, yeah?'

'Fifteen. Yep. No problem.'

I go back into my room and close the door, and am confronted by the mirror hanging from it. I stare back at myself.

Funny how you can spend years wishing to be thinner and, when it's finally granted, it comes as fast and vindictive as a sandstorm. These last months have shrivelled me in more ways than I'd like to admit. I'm thirty-six years old. I could be fifty.

The face in the mirror blinks emptily. *You can do better than that*, Leo's voice says.

I make myself smile, but it's brittle, sad. *Wrong again*, I tell him.

Twelve days. Then I can come back, my bank balance a little closer to the target. A little closer to redemption. Then I can close the door again and drop the act.

And it'll just be me and him and my thoughts again.

2

TORI

And just like that, after the months of planning, the agonising over the contestants, the screen tests, the recces, the endless budgeting woes: we're off. The first shoot of my own production company, Tori Tells Stories, is actually under way. I close the door behind me and head down to where Will's 4x4 is humming into life.

Dee's already in the back. 'You know those shoes aren't going to work, right?' she says, eyeing my wedges. 'On the ice sheets, I mean.'

I waggle an exposed toe as I get in. 'No reason I can't take a little bit of fabulous with me, is there?'

The look she gives me, the shake of her head: it's like she's forgotten that all of this I do – the shiny exterior – is part of the job. Does she not remember those endless nights in our twenties, going over and over YouTube tutorials on walking in heels, contouring, the sweet spot of a good smile? Stuff I'd scoffed at in university before realising, nearly too late, that all the degrees in the world wouldn't get me onscreen work if I didn't look the part. Dee was the one who'd reminded me, right before that big-break audition two years ago, shortly before I met Will, that I wasn't to use any words longer than three syllables.

She knows it's a front. But somehow, these days, it's like it's all she sees.

I film myself clipping on my seatbelt and giving a peace sign, then type the caption: *#FrozenOut: eight leaders, seven Arctic challenges, one ship, one £100k winner! Bring it on!* I follow it with the familiar hashtags, my thumbs flying across the keys almost on muscle-memory alone. #Arctic #£100k #eightleaders.

'House all locked up? Cameras set?' Will asks as I post the video to the socials.

I sigh, annoyed, then open the car door.

'I'll go,' Dee says.

She gets out and Will gives me a look.

'What?'

'Five grand on a brand-new security system and you forget to check it? So you're only concerned about the house when you're actually in it?' Then he frowns. 'You would tell me if there was something going on, right? Like a fan, or whatever?'

I exaggerate an affectionate eye-roll. 'We've been over this.'

It's half true. What we've been over is his assumption that my new-found fame has prompted my concern about safety from strangers.

The truth of it is: strangers, I can deal with.

Will flexes his fingers on the wheel.

'You're not nervous, are you?' I ask him. I poke him gently in the side. 'Not going to miss me so much that you cry?'

'I'll be fine.' There's a lot to do here when we're gone – negotiations about foreign distribution, advertising meetings. Will's got a lot riding on *Frozen Out* too, though for him it's more pride than anything. We'd hoped his family would back it, but when our cashflow issues really showed themselves, his father (not Dad, never Dad) got cold feet. So the money propping up this show is nearly all mine. Not that I'd worry Dee by admitting it.

I lean over and kiss his cheek. 'Your father will be proud, sweetheart. We're going to show him what you can really do.'

From the way his jaw tightens, I can tell that wasn't the right thing to say. And that tiny, niggling question comes to me again. Do I really know this man well enough to marry him?

Dee reappears from the house, and Will turns to kiss me back as she comes down the path.

'Don't worry about me, Tor,' he says. 'Concentrate on you. Focus on doing your best.'

I wince slightly at his tone: we didn't put up that extra shelf in the office last weekend for *his* awards, did we? But I remind myself we're an hour from a big goodbye, and I holster it.

'I'm not worried about anything at all.'

'What you *should* worry about,' says Dee, getting in behind me and slamming the door, 'is that Annabel's already called me five times this morning to make sure we're on schedule.' She belts up, then gives me a look. 'Tell me again why we chose her?'

I laugh and don't look at Will, who insisted that what convinced him to hire the researcher was her efficiency, and definitely not her ludicrously low rates.

'She brings balance,' I say lightly. 'Enthusiasm to counter your relentless apathy?'

'Whatever. A job's a job. Let's go.'

It's a bright day and the traffic is unusually fluid. Will weaves expertly out from my leafy street in Chiswick towards the M4. He finds a lively station on the radio, and I sneak my hand onto his thigh. His muscles tense deliciously under my touch and he takes his eyes from the road to give me that stomach-flipping grin of his. That's what it takes to zip that other, snarky little voice about our relationship, because my God, this *boy*.

I hear Dee shift around in the back of the car and swivel in my seat. She's got her phone out, staring at the screen but not scrolling, not texting. Biting her lip. Meaning it's that guy again. Leo, the one she had the fling with.

'You might as well,' I tell her, making her jump.

She stuffs it quickly away into the pocket of her backpack. 'Might as well what?'

'Text him? I mean, once we're out there, there's no internet, so if you're going to do it, do it now.'

'Tell me about it,' Will says. 'When I was out there XC-ing last year, I hardly got a single message in or out for the full two weeks.'

'XC?' Dee asks flatly.

'Sorry, sorry. XC – cross-country.' He glances up at her in the rear-view. 'Cross-country skiing?'

'Why didn't you say "cross-country skiing"?'

He laughs and looks away, unaffected. Would it be so hard to be nice to him? Given that Will's her boss, actually. Dee meets my glare and gives a small shrug of apology, before looking studiously out of the window. It's the same chill that comes over everything whenever Leo is mentioned. I never met him when

16

they were together, and now I wonder if I ever will. Whoever he is, he cast one hell of a spell.

Quietly I try again. 'Seriously, Dee. Just message him. You could break the ice a bit now, and then by the time we get back maybe he'll be up for a fresh—'

'Can you leave it?'

'Okay, okay,' I say, holding up a hand. 'Sorry. You know what you're doing.'

Except that she doesn't, not really. How long has it been? Almost half a year. Something happened right before she suddenly decided to rent out her flat and move in with me. God knows why it went so cold. I've never known Dee so unhappy. Nothing would shift it, not for months. I'd hoped this job – the chance of a huge change of scene – would make the difference. Take her back to who she'd been, before. It's mad to think that not so long ago, on learning we both had an empty weekend, she demanded that I meet her at the airport with only my passport, my credit card and an open mind. But it's like that adventurous woman I thought I could rely on for ever is . . . gone.

I shift back round and then get out my own phone, feeling suddenly edgy about the lack of comms where we're headed. Despite the show being the kind of format that would usually broadcast daily and semi-live, the whole show has been structured as a pre-shoot, to be edited and broadcast months down the line. It's a decision that was made precisely because we won't be able to transfer the material in time for a daily show. Once we're out there, it's total isolation: just the ship, the cameras, the ice.

We hit the M4 and Will puts his foot down, swinging around

the other traffic and out into the fast lane, his natural territory. I consider calling my dad, but it's been too long to get away with merely a quick goodbye. So I text instead, promising a proper call when I return. I get a message back within seconds. *Love you, sweetie. Your mum would be so proud of you.*

Will glances over. 'Your dad?' I nod. 'Want me to send him updates?'

'God, no,' I tell him. They've only met once, and the last thing I want is for them to start gossiping about me behind my back in my absence. There are things Will could find out from him that could ruin us. Us, this show, my career – everything. So I need to keep them as far apart from each other as I can; at least for now.

I lean my forehead against the cool of the window and watch the airport come into view.

Long-term, I'm going to have to come up with a different solution. I'd hoped I could keep it hidden for ever, but that all changed the moment I got the letter.

3

DEE

It's not her fault. All she's done since my world collapsed under my feet is take care of me. If there's one person I could open up to, one person I could trust, it's Tori. But what would she think of me, if she knew? How would she square the person she thought I was with the truth of what I've done?

The answer is: she couldn't. No one could. And so I keep on putting the bricks in the wall between us, shutting her out.

I stare out of the window, watching the transition from normal-height lamp posts down the central reservation to the stumpy ones they switch to closer to the airport. We're nearly there.

It'll bring me nothing but misery, I know, but I get out my phone again. I bring up the final message I sent him.

Leo, I read. *I didn't mean you to find out like that. I made a mistake. I'm so sorry.*

I screw my eyes shut. I see the minute twitch of his face when I got into the car next to him, the very last time I saw him. I hadn't realised anything was wrong, so I'd chatted away. I asked him about his class that day, and the adult piano student he was tutoring on Tuesday evenings. I didn't know anything had changed. I didn't know that the window I'd had to make everything okay – to give me a shot at spending my life with him – had already closed.

I was going to tell him the truth. I really, truly was.

After he threw me out of the car, I stood out there on the corner for an hour with my phone, calling and calling. So certain that he'd come back. All the messages I sent are still here, unanswered. Would it have made a difference if I'd put it better? Would *I'm sorry I lied* have cut it? *I'm sorry I ruined your career?*

I tap out a message. I don't know why I do it. The hundredth, the thousandth draft of the same thing.

I would give anything to change what happened. Or even just to explain. I know you always said: no excuses, no regrets. But I do have excuses. They're really good ones. And regrets, too. Massive ones; regrets coming out my ears, honestly. I see Leo smile as the words form on the screen.

But he's not going to smile. I let backspace eat it all. This time I write the shortest, the most condensed version there is.

I love you.

And then I delete that, too, and switch the whole thing off. I spend the rest of the journey staring at the back of Tori's beautiful, blameless head, wishing I could tell her, but knowing that I never, ever will.

4

DEE

Annabel, our researcher who's also been in charge of the logistics and crewing, is waiting for us in Departures. Anxiety pulled tight on her face, phone against her ear, sitting on top of a pile of flight cases containing the gear. She sees us coming, fumbles the phone, then jumps up and hurries over, narrowly avoiding a collision with an elderly woman using a walking frame.

Annabel is sweet and she does her best, that much is obvious. But when it comes to people skills? I'm not convinced.

'Really bad news!' she says. 'Poppy and Zach cancelled.'

Tori touches her temples. 'Seriously? On the day we leave?'

Annabel explains that two of our contestants, the husband-and-wife duo chosen partly thanks to their USP of having no fewer than ten children, are now battling an outbreak of chickenpox. The idea was that there's leadership in domestic work, too, that it comes in many forms. I was only present at one of the meetings with the network, but it didn't take me long to see that Tori fought hard to make the show as representative as it is.

Tori turns to me. 'What do we do?'

I put my hands up. 'It's your show.'

She gives me a pleading look. 'That co-producer credit's still on the table?'

'Nope.'

Annabel flutters beside us, digging in her bag for a folder. 'I thought maybe they could come later, when they're better, meet us there? It would only be – what, four, five days? I could get on to the travel people now?'

'We could edit it together if they're not there at the start,' I tell Tori, 'but can the ship wait that long?'

'Oh no, it can't,' Annabel says, screwing up her eyes. 'And the visas would need changing. I don't know if there's time.'

'Let's try to stay calm, all right?' Tori says, forcing a smile to hide the panic. But then her face changes. 'Oh God, seven episodes, eight contestants.'

The show is a knock-out format, meaning that we should be down to the last two standing by the final. If we lose these people, we've got two forty-eight-minute episodes to fill.

'Dee, seriously,' Tori says. 'Help me out.'

The fact is: I owe her. For sharing her house, for hiring me as director of photography when I couldn't even get out of bed for the interview. For her inexplicable loyalty.

'Fine,' I tell her. 'Here's the plan. We go ahead with the six contestants we've got. I bulk it out by giving Craig a bigger role.' Craig is the Arctic guide we're meeting once we're there. He hasn't taken a large group for a while – prefers to spend his time linking green tourism with local environmental work now – but he screen-tested well. Not only that, but he's a former paramedic, meaning we're killing two birds with one freelance fee. 'We build in some one-to-one coaching and character-assessment stuff with all of them, then fudge it by shooting some *before* material when we're back home, and cut that in for the first episode. Start the challenges in episode two.' I count off on my fingers. 'Final challenge ep six, then seven is a round-up. Shoot them all back at home, see them putting what they've learned into practice, that kind of thing.'

Tori gives me a weak smile. 'Okay. Okay, good. Thanks, co-producer.'

'Still no.'

A few feet away, a gaggle of fans is trying to get Tori's attention. 'One sec,' she says to us, and goes over to a chorus of excitement.

'That was amazing,' Annabel tells me. 'Did you just come up with all that – like off the top of your head?'

'Mm-hmm.' I glance around. 'Is there time for coffee?'

'Yes, sorry! Yes, absolutely. One minute.'

'You don't have to—' I start to say, but she's already off. I wonder what it's like to be so keen.

I hear my name and look over to see Will dragging Tori's luggage.

'This everything?' I ask.

He nods. 'Got a buggy coming in a sec. Listen, Dee.' He slips a bag off his own back, a slim fabric, drawstring thing. After glancing over to see that Tori's distracted, he hands it to me. 'Can you pop this in your hand luggage?'

'Is it weed?'

'No, it's not *weed*, Dee.'

'Coke?' I go to open it. 'I've always wanted to be a coke-mule.'

'Stop it,' he says, moving my hand away. 'Don't open it yet.'

I look at him, suspicious.

Will sighs. 'Look. We had a very last-minute change of contestant.'

'I know, the ten-kids couple have flaked out. Annabel already said.'

His mouth drops open. 'This is a piss-take, right?'

I explain how it's not, while he drags his hands down his face. 'But that's not what you were going to tell me?'

'No,' he says, forcing composure. 'The yoga woman's gone too.'

I fail in my attempt not to laugh out loud. 'Right, well, that's that then. Six contestants, I could work with. Five's a joke.'

'No – we're replacing her. New woman. She's kind of similar,' he shrugs. 'She works for this charity. It's all about helping pet owners with substance-abuse issues look after their animals. So there's a lot of counselling and mentoring involved, stuff like that.'

I raise my eyebrows and Will doubles down, folding his arms. 'What? There's leadership in there. Like Tori says. We wanted a broad definition.'

'Kind of tenuous, don't you think?' The premise of the show is that everyone competing is some kind of leader, competing to be voted the best in some of the harshest conditions on the planet. Anyone can see it's a gloss to make it look something more than a rip-off *I'm a Celebrity,* but it has to at least be consistent.

'It's what I could do at short notice,' he says.

'I see. She got a name?'

'Gaia. Strong look, she'll be great. Tattoos, hair about this long,' he says, holding his finger and thumb an inch apart.

'Distinctive. It's exactly what we needed. Don't look at me like that.'

'Just smells like bullshit. I'm sure we could have booked the yoga woman into a salon if it was only about a hairstyle.'

'It's done. All right?' He looks me hard in the eye. 'Try to be positive about it when you tell Tori.'

I raise my eyebrows. 'You haven't told her? Will, you naughty thing. You're scuttling off and leaving me to do the dirty work? I'd have expected better from you.'

He swallows down a flash of anger – he doesn't like being mocked, but he knows he needs me onside. 'Fine. Could you keep it to yourself for a moment, though? I'll call her once you're through Security.'

I don't need to ask why. Their arguments recently have been quite something, and always about the show. We thought we'd had our last change of cast three weeks ago, when Will dropped a perfectly good contestant for someone we hadn't even screen-tested, Helen Greenaway, apparently for the sheer hell of it. There have been problems with budgets, company credit cards not being set up in time – it's been a total shambles from day one. Even so, changing the line-up the morning we start shooting, without telling his fiancée, is a new low.

But I stow the bag like a good girl, and tell Will his secret's safe with me.

One more surely won't hurt.

5

TORI

'He's done *what*?'

Honestly, if I wasn't about to go on the trip of a goddamn lifetime, I could tear the printouts Dee's just given me in half and storm off the plane right now.

Annabel pokes her head through the space between my seat and Dee's.

'What's happened?'

She works hard, despite her inexperience, and she's meticulous, but her jumpiness is getting a little much.

'Bloody Will,' I say, passing the paperwork to her. 'Another last-minute change of contestant.'

'Oh, that,' Annabel says.

'You knew?'

'Of course she knew,' Dee replies. She stows a plastic bag containing her bottle of duty-free rum under her seat, then starts studying the safety leaflet. 'She knows everything about everything. Knew my shoe size without even asking me. She's a fucking encyclopaedia.'

'For the snowshoes,' Annabel says, colouring. 'To be fair, I did kind of guess—'

I hold my hand up. 'I don't care! *Did* Will already tell you about dropping the yoga woman?'

She winces. 'I think he's really doing his best, but . . .'

'And it's a big but,' Dee says, tucking the sheet away. She meets my eye. 'What? We all know he's been winging it right from the start. That's what posh boys do. But we're here now, for better or worse. Let's get on with it. Oh, look,' she says flatly, jerking her chin towards the cockpit where two flight attendants are giggling, wide-eyed, as they welcome the most recent passenger. 'One of yours.'

Coming down the aisle, clad in box-fresh outdoor gear, hair studiously dishevelled, cloud-grey eyes wonder-struck, like he's never been on a plane before, is Wolf Ambrose: television and YouTube survivalist, influencer, model and ex-boyfriend of yours truly. He's holding a small camcorder in front of him on a selfie-stick, talking as he goes, as if to an audience.

' . . . finding my seat,' he says. 'Oh, and here's everyone else!' He turns the camera towards us. 'This is the team; say hello, team!'

I raise a hand and grin before I can stop myself – an involuntary response to the camera. But once Wolf clicks it off, I drop the smile.

'What the hell's that?'

'For my channel,' he says, flopping back into his seat across the aisle, eyes closed, like filming himself is such hard work. He unclips the completely unnecessary mic he's got hooked onto his lapel.

'Why don't you just use your phone?'

He rolls his eyes like I'm an amateur, then reaches across to shake Dee's hand.

'Good to see you,' he says without enthusiasm.

'Wolf,' Dee says with a slight nod. There's no love lost between these two.

He leans forward, craning his neck to find me. 'And like the sunshine behind the cloud . . .' He reaches for my hand, as if he thinks I'm going to let him kiss it.

'Nope,' I say, slapping his arm away.

'I think you have to be nice to him,' Annabel advises in a whisper from behind the headrests.

'Annabel, love, would you mind—' I start, but Dee gets there more quickly.

' . . . backing off? For one minute?'

Annabel recedes, hurt. I give Dee a look.

'She's got a point, though,' Wolf says. 'I am the talent, after all.'

I turn to see Annabel digging in her little backpack, face flushed.

'Bit star-struck,' Wolf mock-whispers. 'Don't worry, sweetie, I get that a lot.'

'I'm not,' she says weakly.

Wolf flashes me a grin, like we're back to sharing in-jokes. He laughs that throaty, million-follower laugh of his and settles back into his seat. 'Shame you couldn't stretch to business class,' he says.

'Shame you're not quite charming enough to be offered it for free,' Dee replies.

He winks at her, then, to me, 'Is she going to be like this the whole time?'

I narrow my eyes at him. 'Don't make me wish we hadn't cast you.'

'Sweetheart, this show wouldn't even have been funded without me.'

Dee is about to retaliate when someone in the aisle blocks Wolf from view. He's broad-shouldered, scruffy in an outdoorsy kind of way. Wide-set eyes, reptilian almost. He checks his boarding pass against the seat that Wolf's in and calls back to the flight attendant.

'Sorry, I think there's a mistake.' A soft Scots burr. Then he looks over and recognises me. 'Oh,' he says, his face clearing. 'It's you. Tori Matsuka.' He puts out a hand.

I'm about to reply when Annabel jumps up. 'John! So good to meet you in person. Wolf, this is John Grandage,' she explains. 'He's a community worker, does a lot of outdoor-pursuits stuff. Proper woodsman! You should get on.'

Wolf raises an eyebrow. 'Proper? Meaning what?'

Dee sighs. 'Don't be a prick, Wolf.' Then, to John, 'Welcome. What happened to the beard?'

John touches his chin self-consciously. 'I thought it better to look smart?'

Wolf, bestubbled as per his wild-man brand, rolls his eyes, never missing an opportunity to take something personally.

Annabel sorts out the seating issue – Wolf was allocated the window, but refuses to move from the aisle.

'I'm nae bothered,' John says convivially, stowing his battered backpack overhead.

'Good man.' Wolf moves aside fractionally to allow John to sit next to him, then closes his eyes.

Dee glances behind us and gestures down the aisle. 'Think that must be Gaia – the late booking,' she says. 'Back there. Crew-cut.'

I get up. The last of the contestants are finding their seats a couple of rows behind us, but right towards the rear is a skinny, shaven-headed woman sliding a case into the locker and taking her seat.

I go straight down, ignoring the couple of gasps of recognition from other passengers. Crouching to her level, I put out a hand, look cheerful. First impressions count. 'Gaia? I'm Tori. I'm working on the show.'

She's late thirties, max, but life doesn't appear to have been kind to her. She nods her hello – as brief as it can be without being rude. Or, if I was being less generous, maybe a little bit over that line.

'Look,' I say, undeterred, 'we're all sitting up there. We could see if there's a spare seat a bit nearer, if you want to come and—'

'No,' she says, her voice tight. 'Thank you. I'll be fine back here.'

A flight attendant darts over, telling me that I need to return to my seat.

'Wait a moment,' I tell her, and then, to Gaia, 'We're not filming yet, just having a chat—'

'I'm happy here, thank you,' she says, firmly this time, eyes on mine. Green and vivid and determined.

I stand, taken aback. 'Sure. No problem. We'll have a chat when we're on the connection then.'

She gives a stiff nod, pushes earbuds into her ears and closes her eyes.

'Madam—' the flight attendant begins.

'Yes, fine,' I snap, instantly regretting it. I follow her back to my seat and she waits as I dutifully click my belt closed. 'Sorry,' I tell her. 'Nervous flyer.'

'No problem,' the flight attendant says tightly, moving off.

Watching the exchange, Wolf gives me an amused half-smile. This is a man who once, quite seriously, considered getting *never apologise, never explain* tattooed on himself. His disdain for my concern about other people's opinions evidently hasn't waned.

Go fuck yourself, I don't tell him. Because much as I resented Will even suggesting that we bring Wolf on board, I know his boast about boosting the viewing figures is absolutely correct. We'll owe half our audience to the relentless curiosity of the glossy mags about what they call our will-they-won't-they relationship. Although, spoiler alert: no, they won't. That ship has sailed, caught fire and sunk.

We start to taxi. Next to me, Dee shakes two pills out of a bottle and swallows them down with some water.

I glance over at Wolf, who's reviewing his footage without headphones, the volume right up. I sigh heavily.

Dee catches my eye. 'And we're not even in the air yet,' she says, pulling a sleep mask down over her eyes.

6

DEE

I wake when the tyres hit the tarmac at Reykjavík. As soon as the seatbelts light goes out, Annabel buzzes around, collecting up the release forms, giving us permission to broadcast what we film. Bags on our shoulders, the five of us from the front section – Tori, Annabel, Wolf, John and me – spill out onto the concourse one after the other. Annabel hangs back for the others.

I shield my eyes against the sun as the wheels of my case rattle on the ground. The air is cold but utterly pure. Conscious of Gaia trailing behind us, I hang back to introduce myself, but she's already making a call, turning her back to me as if I wasn't even there. I catch the others up.

'My favourite capital city in the world,' John says enthusiastically. He's got a guidebook in his hand, the pages thickened with age.

'Been here a few times then?' I half shout over the noise of a passing fuel truck.

'Oh, certainly. Once you get a taste for snow and mountains and all that, you tend to head north a lot. Proposed to my wife about half an hour from here.'

We start walking towards the terminal. 'What did she say?'

He bites back a grin, and I realise my error. 'Oh, right. Obviously yes, if she's your wife.'

Nudging me, he leans in conspiratorially. 'I say daft things all the time. At least *you* won't need to worry about saying them on film, though, given that you're behind the camera. Got to tell you. I've been a little nervous about that.'

Ahead of us, the automatic doors slide open at Tori's approach. John hangs back to speak to Gaia, who's finishing her call. He waves at her to follow, then hitches up his bag and carries on.

I frown, confused. 'You've already met?'

'Just being friendly.' He adjusts his glasses. 'So, you're friends with the big star, hey?' he says, nodding towards Tori up ahead. 'Will mentioned it,' John explains, seeing my confusion. 'So what's she like? What are we in for?'

I'm about to answer, but up ahead Tori beckons me impatiently.

'You'll have to wait and see,' I tell him with a wink.

We find a corner inside and I put down my bags.

Tori stretches. 'We've got an hour to kill before the connection. Shall we get the intros?'

I tell her to give me a sec to set up, and start to unpack the gear. A smartly dressed young woman with impossibly perfect make-up, trailing a small wheeled suitcase, comes straight over to Tori, heels clacking. First thought: am I the only one *not* bringing heels to the Arctic? I hit Record and give Tori the thumbs up in time for her to enter the shot.

Tori glances at the young woman's outstretched hand, shakes it, then yanks her in for a hug. 'Everyone,' she says, turning her to the group, 'this is Nishma Ghosh—'

'Nish,' the woman corrects, immaculate teeth glinting as she smiles.

'Nish.' Tori clamps her arm around Nish's shoulders like they're old mates. They're not. They've literally only met on Zoom. 'Nish is the UK's youngest head teacher. She's an accomplished freediver and occasional concert cellist. Is that right?'

'Yeah, I mean, I dabble.'

'But you *dabbled* enough to play in the London Philharmonic, at one point?'

Nish looks uncomfortable. 'A long time ago. In the youth section. I was fifteen.'

Tori shoots a look at Annabel, who blinks rapidly and consults her clipboard.

'And you entered because . . .' Tori asks.

'I'm always telling my students: aim high. Believe that you don't have limits.' She looks around, making eye contact with everyone. 'Leadership, to me, isn't only about strength; it's about integrity, about respecting the people you lead and only asking them to do things you'd do yourself. So here I am. Pushing myself.'

'Fantastic,' Tori says, beaming. Then she gestures to the older woman seated at the end of the bank of chairs. 'And this is Helen Greenaway.'

I reframe for a two-shot as she stands, takes her glasses off her prominent forehead and snips shut their arms, letting them hang from their chain against her chest. There's no hug this time: I can feel Helen's no-nonsense vibe from where I'm standing, like I've walked into an industrial fridge. But she shakes everyone's hand, making sure to look each of them in the eye and to hear their names. You know she's memorised each one by the time she releases their hand.

Tori cocks her head. 'And you've got a strong leadership background, Helen.'

'I do. I started my first business at eleven, when I went off to boarding school, though it didn't last too long. Turned out to be a little too akin to a protection racket for my housemistress's liking.' She purses her lips and waits for the smattering of laughter. I find myself liking her already. 'But then I abandoned violence, and it was plain sailing from there really. I just floated my twenty-sixth company on the London Stock Exchange.'

'Not in this for the money then,' Nish says.

I come away from the viewfinder and meet Tori's eye for half a second. This tension, from these two women working at opposite ends of the financial spectrum, is exactly what Tori wanted.

'No, I'm not,' Helen says simply. 'I wanted a challenge, and to remind all the young men in the boardroom that there's a reason I've got the seat with the arms on it.'

'I don't remember a Helen in the email,' Gaia says to Tori. 'And weren't there supposed to be eight of us?'

'Helen joined us a little later than the rest,' Tori replies. If she notices Gaia's accusatory tone, she doesn't show it. 'And yes, we did make some last-minute changes to the line-up, so to speak. Thought it would be a neater format with half a dozen contestants – gives us a little longer to focus on your unique stories.'

I hold back a laugh. You can say what you want about Tori, but she's a damn good liar.

Almost as good as me.

Tori gestures towards Gaia like she's presenting a painting for auction. 'Everyone, this is Gaia and – I'm terribly sorry, but I don't know an awful lot about you,' she says apologetically. 'I understand from my brief notes that you're very involved with homeless outreach?'

'Oh, which organisation?' Helen asks, and when Gaia tells her – a small charity dedicated to supporting animal owners with addictions – she nods approvingly.

'Chances are you'll have stayed in one of Helen's hotels at some point,' Tori tells everyone, changing the subject.

'Fairly sure I've *worked* in one,' says another man, coming over. I have to zoom out a bit, so as not to cut off the top of his head – he's huge, easily six foot four, with a buzz cut and sleeves rolled up, to show off heavily inked forearms the size of Christmas hams.

'And we all know this guy, don't we?' Wolf says, slapping him on the back.

Tori gestures towards him. 'Everyone – Marco Tucci. Former captain of England's rugby union team.'

'*Men's* rugby union,' Gaia says pointedly.

'Ha, yes!' Tori agrees. 'And probably our best-known contestant.'

The muscles in Wolf's jaw bulge. 'Big star. Huge!'

Marco tries not to look flattered. 'Rugby man, yeah?'

Wolf wrinkles his nose. 'Keep up with the scores, you know. And those were some serious scores!' The faintest glint of mischief in his eyes. 'Must have been a hell of a fall from all the way up there.'

Helen sucks air through her teeth. You don't have to be a

rugby fan to have heard about Marco Tucci, with the record for shortest-serving captain of the national team. Also one of very few to hold the title without a private education: famously he left school with no qualifications at all. He's been out of rehab for a year, but his catastrophic descent from grace remains a thing of legend. The media couldn't get enough: drugs, prostitutes – even allegations of fraud at the youth foundation he'd set up. More recently, when a tabloid got wind of his new job in hotel security, its comparison of what he earned and owned in his England days versus now was detailed with gleeful Schadenfreude.

I suspect Marco's a bit of a joke hire – his name is too mired in controversy for anyone to see him as a true leader – but Will never said that out loud.

It takes a moment for Marco's face to fall, but Tori doesn't give him time to retaliate.

'And tell us about your leadership style, Marco,' she says, ever the pacifier.

You can almost watch the instincts battle it out on Marco's face: establish dominance over the rival alpha, or prioritise first impressions and let it slide. He blinks and goes with the latter.

'Things have changed, for me. Since the rugby.' He nods, frowning, as if acknowledging it for the first time. 'But I've got my little girls now. No big blokes to order about, so . . . You've got to be gentle, haven't you? It's a different thing.'

There's a surprising vulnerability about the way he's talking half to himself, and Tori does exactly what I'd do and says nothing at all. It's Interview Skills 101, the very first thing you learn: nothing makes people talk like silence.

'I want to show my girls that I'm not that angry bloke shouting through a mouthguard any more. I'd like everyone to see that.'

There's an awkward moment, then Tori claps her hands. 'Right then,' she trills. 'The connecting flight will be here in half an hour. Have a little rest, get to know each other.'

'And I need your release forms before we go any further,' Annabel says nervously. She scuttles straight over to Marco. 'I think I'm missing yours?'

'Didn't get one,' he says.

She quickly digs out a spare, and he sighs and folds it in half. 'No,' she laughs awkwardly, 'sorry. I need it now actually.'

'I'll do it later.'

Annabel glances around. As I pick up some other shots I can hear her cajoling him. 'Marco, it's only a quick form. It'll take two—'

'I fucking said I'll do it later,' he hisses. I look up as John appears, wiping his glasses. 'Air travel plays havoc with my eyes too, you know.' He nods to the form in Marco's fist. 'Tiny print on those things. Want a hand filling it in?'

Marco grunts his agreement, and John produces a pen.

Annabel spots me watching and comes over.

'Not all that . . . friendly, are they?' She's hurt, I can tell – there's a tightness to her voice.

'They're here to win,' I tell her. 'Not to be your mates.'

'Surely it's possible to do both. Do the job, but make friends too?' She gives me a quavering smile that suggests she's not just talking about the contestants.

I snap the lens cap on. There was a time when she would

have been right – working the hours I did on daily or weekly shows, years back, meant that colleagues were bedrock, closer than family. Just look at me and Tori. But it's not like that now. If Annabel knew me better, she'd know to stay well out of my orbit.

'Maybe for some people,' I tell her as I pack up the camera. 'I'm only here for the work.'

It's a long wait, but eventually we're on the second flight – a shared charter flight over to Ilulissat on the west coast of Greenland. A few hours after we leave the runway, we're descending again. I'm sitting next to Nish, whose steely professionalism quickly gives way to a childlike glee.

'Oh my *goodness*,' she yelps, leaning over me to peer through the oval window. 'Mountains, look. Snow!'

It's the Arctic. I'm not entirely sure what she was expecting.

But even I have to admit, it is pretty incredible. We've hugged the Greenland coastline all the way up. Inland to the east, everywhere that isn't black rock is white, as far as the eye can see. Westwards out to sea, icebergs the size of office blocks hang in the water. Tori narrates everything she sees: the dark dots of indistinct vehicles making their way along a white road; the formation of a flight of some kind of Arctic bird beneath us. Every so often there's a village, then the very edges of the town up ahead come into view as we start to bank. Soviet-looking buildings dominate, severe and greyscale, but there are brightly painted houses scattered at their feet like fallen Lego. The airport is little more than a child's model.

It's blinding, breathtaking. It is, as Tori has continuously told me since the day she finally talked me into accepting the contract, the trip of a lifetime.

So why do I feel like I'm making such a massive mistake?

7

TORI

This is where it starts.

Six contestants stamping their feet on a remarkably rickety wooden jetty, looking out into the freezing waters of Ilulissat harbour, in the Arctic Circle. The bright buildings and sloping roofs of the town are behind us, and the wide basin of water is held on either side by rocky cliffs. Maybe a mile ahead of us the fjord opens up into the open, frigid waters of Disko Bay. Hunks of ice clog the harbour waters, from football-sized all the way up to masses the size of caravans, floating companionably among the fishing boats.

Every one of us is shuddering with excitement and cold. And it is *such* cold: rigid and brittle, right across every inch of exposed skin. Divested of the luggage that's being taken to the ship separately, standing here in only the clothes we're wearing, the atmosphere has changed. Anticipation sparkles alongside the fine flakes of snow.

There's no going back, and we all know it.

I'm joined by Helen, who follows my eyeline. 'Big moment for you.'

'How do you mean?'

She nods at the group. 'First show for Tori Tells Stories, isn't it? You got the big network commission, all your people lined up: the ship, the crew.' She gives me a look that falls somewhere between respect and surprise. 'You've made it. Not just a pretty face. A businesswoman, too.'

I'm not sure how I feel about talking about this side of it, but the camera's off, so I shrug. 'I guess I have.'

I've worked my whole life for this. Every cup of tea I made, way back when I was a set runner; every time I had to kiss an exec's arse to secure my foot on the next rung of the ladder. Every low-rent presenting job I took, until I finally got the big-time stuff. Every moment has led me right here. Where I call the shots.

'Good for you,' she says, taking out a vape. 'No one can take this away from you now.'

Making sure Helen looks away before I let my default-smile drop, I think of the words scrawled in the letter I was sent. What they could do to me, if they got out.

'No, you're right. No one can,' I tell her.

And they can't. I won't let them.

Behind us, another off-road SUV pulls up, right on time: Craig Nduka, our Arctic guide and medic. Dee, camera ready, jogs over and catches the moment the door swings open. Craig jumps out – wraparound sunglasses, a quarter-inch of Afro hair, lots of pockets.

I go over, hand outstretched, but he finishes hauling several army-style holdalls from the back of the truck, leaving me hanging. Enough seconds pass for me to suspect a power play, but eventually Craig straightens up and returns the greeting.

'Pleasure,' he says, pressing my hand tightly.

We make small talk about his journey – he's been staying up here with some locals for a month, practising his hunting skills.

'Took a few days out in the open boats,' he says, miming a paddle.

'Must be amazing,' I say, 'having those same skills their ancestors had. I can't imagine what that's like.'

'Aye, well. And how was the private jet?' he asks. His voice is warm, spread thickly with east-coast Scotland, but there's an edge to the question.

I laugh uncertainly. 'It was – quick, I guess!'

Too late, I remember the recurring theme in his CV: sustainable travel, the impact of tourism. Eco responsibility.

'And that's the main thing, right?' He regards me blankly for a moment too long before jerking his head towards the vehicle. 'Let's get this kit, eh?'

I follow him as he picks up a bag to carry it over to where the others are gathered. I try to pick one up too, but it's twice as heavy as I was expecting.

'Ah, leave it, lass—' he begins, but then he stops, impressed, as I get into a squat and heave it up. 'Fair play,' he says, standing back.

It burns every muscle in my legs to do it, and I know I'll pay for it later, but there's no way I'm showing him weakness in the first two minutes of meeting him.

Suddenly there's a roar from the open water. From the main part of the harbour, two small boats are heading towards us. Each has a single crewman and is unladen, the prow nosing high above the water, with a growling outboard at the back end. They're rigid inflatable boats, or RIBs: I remember them from a crime series I presented a while ago with the Met Police.

They slow, the engines dropping to a murmur, then bump against the timber of this jetty, which somehow would look more at home at the edge of Windermere than the Arctic Ocean. One of the crew – a woman, I see now, as blonde as she is sturdy – hops out of her boat, holding a line, and pivots to catch another one that's thrown to her from the second vessel. In a practised movement, she expertly ties both ropes to a mooring post.

'I am Ulla,' she says and then, gesturing to the other skipper, 'this is Stefan.' The whole crew are Finnish, as is the ship – Will got a deal on using them for a few weeks before they go on to their next job – but her English is very good. 'Your ship is just around the fjord.' She points to where a rocky promontory reaches out. 'We take you now.'

The contestants have moved excitedly towards the water, and Annabel comes to the front of the group. 'The ship was meant to meet us here,' she says, looking over anxiously at Dee, who's been crouching for a low shot of the approaching RIBs. 'We wanted to get a shot of it, right, from the land?'

Dee, coming over, makes a dismissive face. 'We'll work around it.'

'But we said,' Annabel complains.

'We can adapt,' Dee assures her. 'I'll cover them getting into these boats here and then when we get to the ship I'll jump out first and shoot them climbing out. No big deal.'

'We shouldn't have to adapt!' Annabel says, plenty loud enough for several heads to turn. I take her firmly by the arm, give Ulla the 'one minute' gesture with a finger and move quickly out of earshot. Behind me, Dee takes the reins without missing a beat and starts directing the contestants into the waiting boats.

'What was that?' I hiss at Annabel.

Her nostrils flare. 'I'm sorry. I want it to be perfect. It's my first job, you know? I don't want things going wrong when I've made the plans right. And I told them we needed that shot of the ship in the harbour.'

'Listen to me. These people need to see us being in control. They need to see professionalism.' I keep my voice low, but my fingers are still gripping her arm, far too tightly. I make myself let go. 'If they don't think we know what we're doing, the whole thing falls apart.'

She nods, mute.

'If something goes wrong, they don't need to know. Rule number one. Did they not teach you that in your internship?'

Annabel shakes her head, and I stifle a growl of frustration. A whole degree in TV and film production, six months on a set in the US, and not a fucking clue. This, here, is a fraction of the bollockings I had in my first job, and she already looks like she might cry.

I remind myself of the thousands we've saved by hiring her over someone with experience, and take a slow breath in through my nose.

'Look, don't get upset. Remember what Dee said – we adapt; it doesn't always go to plan. And we present a united front, okay? Always.'

She nods quickly. 'Yes. Okay. I'm sorry.'

'You're doing fine,' I half lie.

She nods, swiping quickly at her eyes. 'Thanks, Tori. I really appreciate it.'

I release her, then turn back to the group and clap my hands. 'Right, everyone,' I call out as I head brightly over. 'Let's get going!'

8

DEE

We make a 180-degree turn and everyone holds on tightly against the tilt of the boat. The engine hits its speed and we're off. As the boat heads out across the fjord, Nish lets out an exhilarated shout. Even Helen lets her excitement show, and I get a great shot of her pushing her wind-crazed hair from her face and closing her eyes against the blast of Arctic sky. Happy.

Just for a minute, with the cold air rushing through my hair, maybe I am, too.

But then we're past the outcrop and I see the ship. I wipe the spray from my face and lean forward to tap Stefan on the shoulder.

'This . . . that's not our ship, is it?'

He nods without looking at me and my heart sinks.

'Problem?' Marco asks.

I shake my head. 'No, we're good.'

We are not good. The yellow-hulled ship is maybe two-thirds the size I'd expected. It's about the length of a couple of coaches, sharp-nosed and . . . rusty. It looks much, much older than the spec I'd seen back in the production company office.

After a few minutes we pull up alongside it. A taller man,

wiry, with a shirt and tie visible under his insulated jacket, catches the rope Stefan flings to him and ties it off against a post.

Helen goes first. Entirely unfazed by the gap between the RIB and the ship, she steps over and climbs straight up the rungs built into the metal hull, leading to a gap in the vertical panel at the edge of the deck. Once safely on board, she puts out a hand to help Marco as he crests the ladder, but he bats her away.

A little later we're all on board. It was clear from the exterior that the vibe inside was going to be more working ship than boutique yacht, but I hadn't considered how low the ceilings would be, how dated and utilitarian the decor.

We're shown into the saloon, which is panelled in flimsy mahogany-stained plywood and is the size of a very small pub. I give it a higher score for cleanliness than I do for comfort, and note the layout with not insignificant alarm. Built-in benches line the curved bulkhead, with a few more tables in the centre. You get stuck on a certain seat here and you're going to have to climb over people to escape. I give a table a shove – if we can rearrange things to make the room flow a little easier, the shots are going to feel a lot less rigid – but it doesn't budge. It's all bolted down.

From a swinging door, Ulla enters backwards, holding a tray of glass flutes. Without the life-vest, there's a rugged elegance to her.

'Ooh, champagne,' Tori says, accepting a glass from the tray.

Helen lifts hers to the light. 'Close enough,' she says. '*Salut.*'

Wolf's recording himself on his camera again, talking about getting the party started, and tilts a glass to his own image.

'Dee, have a glass,' Tori says.

But I catch sight of the man with the tie, who must be the

captain. I introduce myself, and he puts out his hand. 'Eino Landstrom.'

After we shake, I gesture to the door. 'Can we have a word?' We go out into the passage and I get straight to it. 'Eino, this is a different ship than the one we agreed.'

'No.'

'I'm sorry?'

'I said no. Here.' From inside his fleece he pulls out a small tablet and brings up a document – the booking from the charter company. 'Specifics were changed a few weeks ago. Signed off . . . here. William Ashburton. Executive producer.' He hands it to me. 'Your boss, yes?'

He's right. There's Will's signature, under a scan of a handwritten note. I peer at it, trying to decipher what else he's changed.

'I spoke to him personally to advise against the changes too, but,' he spreads his hands, 'here we are.'

'What changes, specifically?'

He looks at me like I've asked if the ship can fly. 'The original booking was for an icebreaker. Ten crewmen.'

I clasp my hands behind my back. 'So, what's this?'

'The *Skidbladnir*. Ice Class 1A explorer vessel. We were on another charter nearby. Mr Ashburton believed it was a better fit, in his words.'

'But it's still an icebreaker?'

He laughs. I get the sense it's not something he does often. 'What do you think? Ship is only five hundred tonnes.'

'So how do we get to where we're going?'

The captain sighs heavily, leans against the wall and brings up what looks like a map. 'Right now, the water is still open. We move down the coast for your programme. No problem. But two weeks, three weeks? Who knows – ice may form.' He turns down the corners of his mouth. 'But we will be finished by then, no? Twelve days.'

'But . . . what if the ice comes early?' The idea was that we'd slowly make our way down past Nuuk to the southernmost tip of the island over the next week and a half. There was meant to be a challenge a little more than every other day, although the drop in the number of contestants has wrecked the timetable.

'Then maybe we become icebound. It is October,' he adds.

'Icebound?' Even the word sends a shudder through me. 'So how do we get *unbound*?'

'Wait for the tide cycle,' he says, like he's talking to a child.

I don't understand. It's obvious that I don't understand. So I fold my arms and wait.

Eventually Eino gets that I'm not blinking first. He holds one hand out flat, palm down. 'Here is ice, yes? Solid.' Then he brings the other hand up beneath it. 'Water, here. Tidal.' He moves the bottom hand up and down, indicating a rising and falling water level. 'If we become stuck in the ice, we wait for the tide. And the ship is *heavy*,' he says and splays the fingers of the first hand, showing the frozen surface breaking. 'So, tide falls, the ice cracks. With luck we are free, move out to open water, back down the coast. Understand?'

'*With luck?* What if we're not . . . lucky?'

'Then we radio for help. And wait.'

Tori bustles out of the saloon. 'There you are! Ready for the safety briefing?'

Eino nods, and Tori calls everyone out onto the deck. They've already got into their bright-red ship-issue outsuits, apart from Wolf, who insists on wearing his signature green. Nish is fiddling with the neckline – a woman with her eye on the optics, I'm thinking – and Marco's rolling his shoulders uncomfortably.

'This isn't going to work,' he's saying to Annabel. 'Do they have any bigger ones?' She hurries off to find out.

'What happened to the logos?' I ask Tori. She'd mentioned a new sponsor – a marine company, which stepped in with some financing for the show at the last minute. Apparently Will had offered to display their logo on the contestants' clothes.

'Turned it down, for some reason,' Tori says.

The ship engines power up and we start to move, and there's a cheer from John.

I catch Tori's arm. 'Will changed the ship. Did you know?'

She shrugs, trying to make me believe it's no big deal. 'I think there were some tweaks to the plan.'

'It's a completely different ship, Tor.'

'So we adapt!' she says. I open my mouth, but she waves it away and changes the subject. 'How does it feel being back in the saddle? Getting into the swing of the big cameras?'

It used to be a joke between us, after a particularly blokey Director of Photography once told me that it was only men who could use the 'big cameras'. I'd come off a large undercover investigation at the time and explained that my little cameras – the ones I wore hidden in my clothes for secret filming – were the ones that had just forced three MPs from their jobs. The DoP had stood there, fish-mouthing, and Tori and I had fallen about.

But the reminder of covert recording isn't something that makes me laugh any more. I settle the camera on my shoulder. 'Never better.'

While everyone is still occupied with the excitement of moving, Tori leans in. 'Dee. I know it's a big step. Your first job after—'

'I said I'm fine. Let's get the briefing in the can before we freeze our tits off.'

She goes to say something else, then changes her mind. The wide, bright smile comes back and she strides over to where Eino is introducing himself.

He runs through the safety aspects of the ship: the location of the life-vests on the fore and aft decks, the ban on smoking, the gas lockers. There's a demonstration of the use of the lifeboat, hanging from a cradle to the aft.

'Emergency siren is three long blasts of the ship's horn,' he says, 'but we try not to have emergencies, because it is very remote, where we are going. No emergency services for hundreds of miles at a time.'

It's probably meant as some kind of joke, but everyone looks alarmed.

'What he means is, between these guys and me, we'll take care of you,' Craig says, in an obvious attempt at reassurance. Then, to Eino, 'What about weapons, and safety flares? You have your own shotguns, rifles?'

Standing next to me, Nish says, 'Why guns? Why would we need guns?'

'Have you ever met a polar bear?' There's a twinkle in Craig's eye, but we can all tell he's deadly serious.

'We have rifles in the bridge,' Eino says, before going over to a locker built into the deck like a bench. 'Flare guns are here.'

'Anyone know how to use them?' Craig says. 'Nobody? I was told you were a bit of a sailor, Helen, no?'

'A little,' she says, but she's playing it down. I remember an article only a few years ago about her welcoming some mid-ranking royals onto one of her yachts. 'I'm sure we'd rather see it from an expert, though.'

'Fine with me! They're fun,' Craig says with a wink. 'I'll show you.' He snaps open the lid and brings out an orange case, then takes out the gun, chunky and orange like a water-pistol. 'Cartridge goes in here,' he says, as everyone crowds round, 'and then off we go.' He raises it with both arms and everyone stands back. There's a bang, and a vivid arc of brilliant light releases.

'Pretty cool,' Marco says. He appraises Craig. 'Your job's not so bad, is it?'

Eino takes the box from Craig's hands and stores it away. 'I would request that the equipment is not used without permission,' he says tightly, before continuing his briefing. He talks about the new interior security system, how the keycards to the cabins are difficult to replace, so to keep hold of them. Then he mentions the heating. 'The climate-control system is also new, but the old radiators are still in place. If you need to change the temperature, please ask for help, but don't touch the older units.'

Wolf yawns. 'Can we go now?'

'They can be dangerous,' Eino says, louder now. 'Also, do not leave the ship under any circumstances without our knowledge.'

I turn off the camera – we're never going to use this stuff – and Nish comes over.

'What's the deal with this?' she asks, then huffs out a sudden lungful of air. 'It's way colder here, but I could see my breath in Kettering. Here, nothing.'

I tell her I have no idea.

'It's about the aerosol particles.' John, standing close, is looking over. 'The water vapour needs something to condense onto, for you to see it,' he says. 'There's so little pollution up here, or dust. So the vapour disperses differently.'

There's nothing self-satisfied about the way he shares what he knows, and there's a kindness in his quiet, gruff voice that I can't help liking. He's got that stillness about him that I've always admired, that sense of take-it-or-leave-it security in his skin.

Nish drifts away, and John nods at my camera. 'Nice kit. They really do build them for burly blokes, though, don't they? You need a nice little—' He cuts himself off. 'Well, I was about to say ladies' version, but that would make me sound like a total arsehole, wouldn't it?'

I laugh, despite myself. 'I mean, it is kind of true, it's a pretty hefty unit. You're a photographer?'

'Not exactly. Enthusiastic dabbler, let's say. So is it only you filming?'

'Lead camera, and I'm directing. Second camera is Annabel, over there,' I say, pointing to where she's showing Marco a gigantic outersuit, holding it up to his shoulders.

'Ah, yes. Annabel with the emails.'

'She's certainly big on admin,' I agree. Though from what she told me, John, our veteran survival enthusiast and youth mentor, had been harder to get hold of. Off-grid life meant his communication had been patchy, and at one point Will had suggested that we cut our losses. But I'm already glad we didn't. John's the counterpart to Wolf. And Nish, even – there's nothing glossy about him.

'So what's your story then, John?' I ask him, squinting against the relentless sunshine.

His smile flickers. 'How do you mean?'

'Is it like a big ambition of yours to come out here?' I say quickly, conscious that something's changed, that I've thrown him or offended him somehow. 'Or is it more about the prize money or . . .'

'Yes, that. Both!' he says, a little too brightly. 'Nice to have a challenge, at my age.'

The vague inadequacy of it sits uneasily between us for a moment. He's holding something back, but why?

Disappointed by the lost rapport, I try again. 'You ready for this, do you think?'

'Off the record?' He eyes the camera.

I smile, dip the lens definitively away from him. 'Of course.'

He turns towards the towering face of the glacier as we travel past, weighing it up, like he's giving my throwaway question real consideration.

'Honestly,' he tells me eventually, 'I'm terrified. Anyone who tells you otherwise is lying to you.'

9

TORI

With the briefing ticked off, and snow starting to fall, we go back inside to the saloon, where the smell of hot food drifts out from the adjoining galley. Ulla, a tea towel slung over her shoulder, pokes her head out to say dinner will be ready at seven.

Stefan, the other crew member, comes in with a small box. 'Your room keys,' he says. One by one, he starts to call the contestants over, handing out plastic rectangles the size of credit cards, and directs them to their cabins. 'Please be careful to keep your doors closed. They are fire doors. If they are propped open, they will beep to alert you.'

Bringing the box over to where Dee and I stand, he holds up two cards. 'You requested a space to work?' He explains how to find the room we've been allocated to use as a production office, says that our gear has already been taken there. Dee thanks him and then heads down to her cabin.

Wolf ambles over. 'I hear the cabins can be a little poky. Decent room for me, my man?' He gives Stefan a manly handshake, and the Finn looks down. In his hand is a small fold of notes.

'I . . . don't need this,' Stefan says awkwardly, handing the money back and taking two more cards from the box. 'You two, your cabin.'

'No – no, we're not sharing,' I say, urgency overriding politeness.

'Sure we'd find a way,' Wolf says smoothly.

'No, two cabin . . . cabins?' Stefan says. 'Astern, both sides.' He pulls his hands apart, demonstrating two doors, opposite each other. My heart resumes beating.

'Our best rooms, nice and big. Cabin number one for you,' he says, passing a key to Wolf, 'and you, cabin two.' He points us towards the lower passage. 'Best rooms.'

I head down quickly. Below deck, the ship is gloomier than I'd expected, just overhead strip lights in the passageways and plywood-panelled walls. It's not a big ship, but the whole thing is something of a warren.

My cabin is surprisingly spacious. Above the double bed, a porthole glows with the last throes of a pinkish sunset, and there's a shower room, a wardrobe, a little desk.

I unzip the big case that's already been stowed in the wardrobe and choose an outfit. Our time on the *Skidbladnir* is no fancy cruise, but the network made it very clear that I was still expected to give the viewers some level of glamour. I find a full-length mirror inside the wardrobe door and hold a slinky green satin shirt up against me. Will's words from last night, more to assuage his own last-minute nerves than mine, come back to me: 'Don't overthink it. Give them what you're famous for.' I'd thought it was cute, the pep talk he believed I needed, despite me being the big name and him being the brand-new exec. But then he'd ruined it all by adding, 'Tits and teeth!'

The ship gives a sudden lurch and I fling out a hand, upsetting the case onto the floor. In the mess, I see a better plan. I drop the shirt and pull out skinny black jeans and a boxy leather-look top from the upended pile. Wide belt, hair up, cowboy boots with elaborate stitching and – yes, *Dee* – three-inch heels, because I want to.

In the mirror, I pull my eyelids taut one at a time, to apply a thick Winehouse swipe of liquid eyeliner. I arrange my face into a smile, the tried-and-tested flash, jaw just off the midline.

'I'm Tori Matsuka, and this is *Frozen Out*,' I say aloud. I'm the person I wanted to become, and I'm still in charge, whatever Will might think.

He doesn't know me.

As I tidy up the strewn contents of the case, I spot the corner of the envelope, peeking out from underneath it all.

None of them know me, not truly. Except the person who wrote that letter.

There's a knock at the door. 'Matsuka?'

Only Wolf calls me that. 'Can it wait?'

Three more slow knocks in response.

'Christ's sake,' I mutter. I go to open the door, but I don't let him in.

Wolf's showered and tidied his stubble, but his eyes are slightly watery and red. The cashmere roll-neck under his blazer is a deliberate size too small, to make sure no one could miss the impeccable solidity of his chest.

He runs his gaze down my body and back up, slowly. 'Looking good, Matsuka,' he says, leaning on the doorframe.

'You do remember that night when you drunkenly explained

to me how you always use women's surnames because you think it drives them wild with desire, right?'

His eyeline drifts slowly up from its moorings a little below my collarbone. He's already had more than his share of the champagne, I realise. Not drunk, not yet. But considering it.

Wry amusement lifts one corner of his mouth. 'There was a time when you weren't exactly immune to my charms.'

'There was a time when dinosaurs roamed the Earth, Wolf. Why are you here?'

He throws back his head at that and laughs more than it deserves and then somehow he's past me, into my cabin.

'I don't want you in my room,' I tell him.

'Still uptight, huh? Or is it that you're not sure you can trust yourself with me?'

'Uh, no,' I say, scoffing. 'That is certainly not the problem.' But I find myself capitulating anyway and closing the door. Three years on and he still knows how to push my buttons.

He parks himself on the edge of my bed, shakes his damp hair back and fixes me with consciously loose-lidded eyes.

'Hold on, is that the *smouldering with lustful intent* look or the *hidden depths of manly power* one? I can never tell them apart.'

His shoulders drop. 'You used to be fun.'

'By "fun" you mean before willing to laugh off being publicly humiliated?' I retrieve the scattered dresses and jeans and start hanging them in the wardrobe.

'Oh, for God's sake, that was like a whole year ago!'

It's thirteen months, actually, since he went on a national TV chat show to tell the entire sixteen-to-twenty-five demographic of the country all about our long-defunct relationship. The timing, chosen to coincide with the launch of my first prime-time presenting gig, was a particularly nice touch.

'I just don't see why you had to lie.'

From the way his jaw tightens, I know Wolf's in no doubt what I'm referring to. His claim that I was 'cool with being experimental in the bedroom' still crops up in online articles about me. The fact was that whatever we did have, it rarely made it past the safety barrier of our clothes. That familiar shard of shame glints like a blade with the sudden passing of light, as I remember it: how on those rare occasions when he did try to touch me, I shrank from it, the way I shrank from physical contact with everyone else. Plenty of men wouldn't have tolerated it. But Wolf, as it turned out, had his own reasons for not minding.

I go to the door, open it, stand aside. 'See you at dinner, Wolf.'

'Wow, okay.' He gets to his feet, a spark of anger about him. 'I'm beginning to wonder why Will even put me here.'

'Ratings. You said it yourself.'

Wolf pauses before he gets through the door, and for a moment we're wedged up against each other, his chest in my face. But I know how this alpha shit works and I'm not ceding an inch.

'What happened, huh?' he says, deliberate smoothness in his voice. 'We were great together.'

I look at the floor. My baggage aside, I could never understand how he could live his whole life without confronting what was right there in front of him. In front of us. But then it was always his issue to work out. People can say what they like about me: fluffy national treasure or vacuous Botox-fiend, depending on the masthead. But I was never going to go out and shame him.

He dips, trying to hook my eyeline. 'There *was* something, wasn't there?'

'Come on. Let's not do this now.' I open the door a little wider.

He laughs, incredulous, until I meet his eye. Then the laughter evaporates. The smoulder is back, but not the kind he puts on for the cameras. This one is darker. This one is the Wolf I remember – the one they don't show in the final cut. 'What's that supposed to mean?'

The ship pitches again and I stagger. Wolf catches me, sets me straight, and lets go a little too roughly. I fix my feet to the floor.

'Fine,' I say. I glance out into the hall to make sure we're alone, then drop my voice anyway. 'At some point, Wolf, you're going to have to come to terms with who you are. You don't have to be ashamed.'

I wait for it to sink in. And sink in it does, though it takes five seconds, ten seconds, longer. After closing the door again without taking his eyes from mine, he tries to sneer at me, but it slides straight off. And because he's not ready to be honest, all there is underneath it is fury.

'How long have you known.' Flat at the end, like he can't even face asking the question.

I hold his gaze, thinking of the secret stash of porn, the hook-up app, the lube and toys that were definitely never meant for us. 'Years.'

'And you haven't told anyone.'

I nod. But he sees through it.

He draws his chin in, eyes glinting. 'You told Dee.'

I take a breath. Saying it out loud will change everything.

'She's my best friend, Wolf. Realising my partner was secretly gay was—'

'I'm *not. Fucking. Gay,*' he hisses.

'All right, I'm sorry; bisexual then—'

'Shut the fuck up, Tori,' he snarls. 'Shut your fucking mouth, right now.'

I arrange my expression into a delicate blend of composure and submission. 'Look, they're waiting for me up there.'

He's taking these deep animal breaths in through his nose, staring me out, and I don't know whether he wants to cry or kill me. I'm suddenly conscious of how far these two cabins are from everyone else.

'Wolf,' I say slowly, gently, 'you know, you really might be happier if it was all out in the open—'

'Don't you fucking threaten me!'

I don't know why, but it's so far from the truth of what's happening here that I laugh out loud.

The slap, when it comes, is so hard and so sudden that it knocks me off my feet. In one move he's crossed the cabin, looming over where I've landed, crumpled next to the bed.

Wolf breathes hard, pointing a shaking finger at me as he chooses his words, his face twisted with rage. 'You open your fucking mouth, just once, about this and you'll wish you'd never set foot on this fucking ship, you vicious little bitch.'

10

DEE

I raise my hand to knock on her cabin door at the exact moment it swings open. It's not Tori on the other side, though, but Wolf, a look of pure rage on his chiselled face, the smell of booze hanging like a fog.

He flinches in surprise, then storms past me, knocking me into the doorframe.

'Jesus!' I shout, rubbing my arm. He doesn't apologise, of course, doesn't even slow down. 'Maybe brush your teeth before you go back to the bar, mate?'

He doesn't take my advice, striding straight past his own cabin and giving me the finger, before disappearing through the door at the end of the passage.

'Leave him,' Tori says from inside.

'What happened?' I ask as I go in. I take in the rumpled duvet and put a hand to my eyes. 'Tell me you didn't—'

'You are *not* even asking me that. Of course I didn't. He's a bloody barnyard animal.' She keeps her head angled away from me.

'Tor. You good?'

She pulls her hair over one side of her face and grabs the make-up bag from the desk.

'Couldn't be better. Just give me a few minutes to do my face?' she says, ducking into the bathroom, despite the fact that there's a perfectly good mirror right there on the table.

The lock clicks inside the en suite, and Tori tells me to go ahead.

I touch my fingers to the door, frowning. 'You sure you're all right?'

'I said I'm fine. Get some atmos without me. I'll be there in ten.'

I go ahead of her into the saloon so that I can shoot a few bits before her entrance. Craig and the contestants are already there, the conversation bubbling with nervous energy. Every one of them wears neat, practical clothes.

It takes a moment to set up a shot, keeping the wall of faded, dog-eared maps behind me. It's more sixth-form common room than private members' club, which is fine – it's not meant to be opulent – but I wasn't expecting it to be so basic. Shabby. Everything built to last, by people who assumed it wouldn't last as long as it did.

I beckon Annabel over to check what she's shooting, but I can immediately see it's wrong. 'Your white balance is off,' I say, giving her camera back.

'White . . . balance. Okay.'

'You know how to do that, right?'

She flips open the side screen and opens the settings menu. 'Of course!'

I wait a few seconds.

'Do you, though?'

'I . . . I'm not used to this model, it's different from the ones we used at uni.'

'Fine, whatever.' I quickly show her how to point the camera at something white – in this case the centre of the map of Greenland on the wall – and then set the colour temperature from there. I hand it back. 'Just be honest, all right?'

'What do you mean?'

'If you don't know something, say.'

'Oh. Got it. I will. Sorry.'

I wave her away with an instruction to get some wides of the room, without me in them.

As I pick up shots, everyone makes a huge effort to appear cheery and upbeat. Below the surface, though, if you listen to the actual words, they're already wrestling for the top of the hierarchy. Nish appears to be good-humouredly joining in a conversation between Marco and Wolf about rugby.

'Wasn't that the '09 tour?' Wolf says.

Marco sizes him up. 'Yeah. You watch it?'

'I was *there*, mate. Ellis Park game.' He laughs, but not kindly. 'I mean, not your greatest day, admittedly.'

I take a quick swig of water from the bottle by my feet and reframe, as Marco's face falls. John, standing close to me, leans in. 'And now, after mere hours in the new environment,' he whispers, in a perfect Attenborough drawl, 'one of the alphas must establish control.'

It's all I can do not to spit out my water.

I move away to get a bit of Helen regaling Craig with a story about the Trans-Siberian Railway. More smiles and laughter in the few minutes I've been shooting them than I'd ordinarily expend in a solid week, but that's the magic of a couple of glasses of wine and a 100-grand prize, I suppose. We might be talking about the show in terms of leadership qualities, but we all know it's really a glorified popularity contest, especially at the start.

Though I do wonder if Gaia, currently loitering alone like a dateless wonder at a school disco, has realised that yet.

I've got enough footage for now. While I'm watching it back, Helen comes over. I nod to her, but she's making a beeline for Gaia, who is standing a few paces off from where I am and is carrying two glasses of champagne.

'Thirsty?' Helen says.

'I don't drink. They're supposed to know that.'

The annoyance in Gaia's voice, and the fact that Tori and I are the source of it, sparks my attention. I don't turn, but I don't exactly make an effort not to eavesdrop.

'Right, good for you,' Helen says uncomfortably.

I keep them in the periphery of my vision, wanting to hear how the conversation pans out. From the corner of my eye I see Helen lift the glass to her own lips. She swallows and then leans in to mock-whisper, 'Got to say I'm not much of a one for parties, these days. Prefer my own company, if you know what I mean.'

'God, me too,' Gaia says.

Helen cocks her head. 'Kind of begs the question why either of us is here then?' She laughs at herself, puts a hand on her chest. 'Me, I wanted an adventure. All very well running businesses, but there's nothing like a new experience.' She pauses, but when it comes to the art of conversation, it's clear that Gaia's not on the same canvas. 'So what about you,' she asks patiently, 'why are you here?'

Gaia takes so long to reply that I wonder if she's heard. I snatch a proper glance and see her staring off across the room. I try to follow her eyeline – out towards where John stands, talking to Nish and Marco – but then she shakes herself and looks at her feet.

'Same, I suppose,' she says and then, as if she's realised how strange it sounds, she adds, 'I wanted to . . . get some exposure for the charity I work for. That's where the money will go, if I win.'

Helen nods, but something in her expression says she doesn't think this is the whole story. Then she glances over at me and, feeling rumbled, I pick up the camera again and scan the room for another shot.

Getting good material out of Gaia is going to be a challenge – no wonder Will was worried about Tori's reaction to bringing her in.

Over by the window I find Nish, now showing Marco and John her phone. I stay a couple of paces back, and once I frame up, I take my eye from the viewfinder and act casual – it tends to fool people into thinking the camera's not rolling and makes them less shy.

'We did two ceremonies actually,' she says, flicking through photos with the screen angled towards the two men. 'The Quaker one, look, and then the Hindu one, though we couldn't have it at the actual temple unfortunately, because, you know, they don't recognise it.'

'There's a long way still to go,' John says, shaking his head.

Nish passes Marco the phone. It takes a moment for the knot of confusion on his face to unravel, but I can already guess what's happening.

'Oh!' he says, flustered. 'Right, got you. That's your . . . your girlfriend.'

'My wife, yes,' she says patiently. 'Sheena.'

He's nodding far too fast now. 'Sorry, love,' he says. 'I don't know many, um—'

Nish puts her hand gently on his, a delicate sparkle of mischief in her eyes. 'It's all right, Marco. You can say "lesbians".'

He stops nodding, blows out a breath and laughs at himself. 'Lesbians. Okay!' And the two of them clink glasses and giggle together, an unlikely bond somehow sealed.

I can't help but laugh, then I see Tori, hovering in the doorway. I nod to her and she goes back out, giving me the usual ten seconds while I set the shot ready for her entrance. We have a shorthand, she and I. More often than not, she'll know if a take needs another pass, or if a piece to camera isn't hitting the spot, before I even open my mouth.

I frame up, then call out, 'At speed.'

There's a hush as she enters with Craig, Eino trailing behind with all the charisma of a plank of wood.

'Everyone,' she says, 'welcome to *Frozen Out*!' She opens her arms like she's offering a hug that we're all invited to. 'This trip is one I've wanted to make ever since I was a little girl, even though I'll have to admit that I may have thought there were penguins up here, at the time.'

That tiny snip of self-deprecation – I've seen her deploy it so many times, and the outcome is always the same. It's bullshit about the penguins, of course. But between the lines, it's a statement: *I'm not clever. I'm not better than you. I'm not a threat.* Straight away, along with the laughs, shoulders drop and Tori's golden glow spills across the room.

What I wouldn't do for half an ounce of what she's got.

'Now, we're here to work, to show the world what we know about leadership. But more importantly, we're going to learn about ourselves. Craig won't be telling you what the challenges are yet, but rest assured they're going to push you to your limits.'

'Right to the limits of my insurance,' he says, deadpan, raising snorts of mirth.

From under a table, Tori brings out a box. Curious glances are exchanged. 'Now, the first thing we need to do is take away your safety blankets. And for a lot of you, that includes your normal support networks. Real-life and virtual. As you already know, the remote parts of Greenland aren't great for internet access, but as a little extra challenge,' she says, passing the box to John, who's standing closest, 'I'm going to need to take your phones.'

John makes a good-humoured show of reluctance, but any viewer paying attention will see straight away that giving up his ancient Nokia doesn't pose him any difficulty. The box is passed around to an affable chorus of outrage. Tori gives it a gentle shake for effect as it arrives back with her, then closes the lid and puts it on the table.

Then she transitions to serious mode. 'Not all of you are going to enjoy these challenges. Not all of you are even going to complete them. But what we all know, as leaders, is that without a strong sense of a team, there can be no true leadership. We have to know each other, to support each other, if we're going to get through this in one piece.

'Right now, we're all the way up in the Arctic Circle. Our captain, Eino,' she says, extending a hand, 'is going to sail us south tonight towards – where was it, Eino?'

He comes forward, emotional as a robot. 'Towards the islands of Kangaatsiak, where we make first stop tomorrow. It will be cold.'

Craig snorts. 'Don't ruin the surprise for them!'

There is a smattering of nervous laughter, and Eino seems to thaw the slightest bit. 'We make our way down the coast slowly, taking eleven days unless we are impeded by the predicted bad weather, in which case we have provisions for two months.'

There are gasps, then looks exchanged.

'Is that for real?' Marco says, alarmed. 'My kids . . .'

'Course not,' Gaia tells him, standing close. 'He's kidding,' Even I can hear she's not sure.

'Well,' Tori laughs, 'good to know!'

He stonewalls her cheeriness, allows her a small nod, then sits down.

'The format of our competition, as you know, will be of five different challenges. After each one, you'll all get a chance to vote for the best leader among you, and for the person you think is the weakest. And remember, part of leadership is honesty: we're trusting you not to play the system here!' She scrunches up her face and points accusingly around the room, joking but meaning it. 'No voting for the person you think is your own biggest threat, all right?'

There's a ripple of chuckling, and John clutches imaginary pearls in faux-horror at the very idea. Only Nish looks genuinely confused, as if the thought of any such thing would never have occurred to her – giving me the distinct sense that the opposite is true.

Tori beams at them. 'Whoever you vote out can no longer win, but they'll still be a part of the show. They'll be demoted to deckhand – the rest of you will be able to give them jobs, delegate to them. But the deckhands still get to vote: it's about teamwork, all the way through, and every member of that team needs to know they're valued. Once it's all over and we're home in the UK, we'll come to do some follow-ups with you, to see what you end up putting into action from the experience. And you never know, maybe some of you will already be arranging your own meet-ups!'

She pauses as they all look politely around at each other, as if assessing the likelihood of that.

'But that's for later,' she continues. 'At the end of the challenges we'll sail back into Nuuk, and the final vote will decide the winner of the hundred-thousand-pound prize. Pretty good, huh?' she says, to murmurings of agreement.

She fills her glass now and gestures for everyone to do the same.

'By the end of our time on board we're going to be a machine. We're going to know each other better than some of the friends we've had back home for years. And it'll be warts and all – we'll be showcasing our best features, and weeding out our greatest failings. We're here tonight as a group of strangers. But whoever wins the prize at the end, we're going to go home as a team:

strong, compassionate and fearless.' She thrusts her glass high. 'To adventure!'

'To adventure!' they all call back. And just like that, under the auspices of our worshipful leader, the mood is set.

With the show's emphasis on the toughness of the challenge, we wait until the cameras are off before we bring out the luxury, but when the food comes, it is exquisite. A seafood stew bejewelled with olives and served with fresh bread, then a chocolate cake, dense and silky. The wine keeps flowing, and within half an hour someone's put music on and there's a genuine party atmosphere.

I go over to where Helen is topping up glasses for Craig and Wolf. John is there too, but his glass is as full as it was when he joined the toast and I don't think I've seen him take a mouthful.

'I think Stefan's the First Mate,' John is saying. 'But maybe also the mechanic.'

'Small crews, these ships,' Wolf says authoritatively. 'Everyone doubles up. Not like the Navy!' He waits for John to ask him about that, then tells him anyway. 'I spent a month embedded with the Navy for a show, while back. Tough gig, that one,' he says, shaking his head at the memory of it. Then he empties his glass and refills it. 'So what's your background then? What have you done?'

'Ha, well, nothing as interesting as you!' John says, eager to change the subject. 'I hear you've got a book out, is that right?'

'I do actually, yes. Lot of work, that was. A lot.'

Marco, sidling over, nods with interest. 'I remember that, yeah. I did one of them, a few years back.'

A smile plays on Wolf's lips.

'What?' Marco says.

Wolf chuckles, glancing around at the others. 'I mean, I did write mine, so.'

Beneath his deep Mediterranean colouring, you can see Marco blush. 'Did a lot of mine too actually, *mate*.'

Sensing escalation, I tap Marco on the shoulder, lead him a few steps away. We're out of earshot, but I keep my voice low. 'You mentioned your kids.'

'Yeah and?' His nostrils are still flaring.

I make the slightest nod towards Wolf. 'He wants to wind you up. So be the better man.'

Marco holds my gaze for a moment, before his shoulders drop. 'It's cos of them I'm here. Wanted to show 'em I've got uses, you know?'

'I'm sure you've got lots of uses.'

He jerks his chin. 'Yeah, well. Ex-wife wouldn't agree.' He sighs, suddenly beaten, and drops his voice. 'Judge says if I can stay out of trouble for six months, we can go back to unsupervised, but . . .' He shrugs, rubs his face. Grins. 'Anyway. Don't know why I'm telling you that.'

Possibly the booze is what I don't say. 'Wolf tries that again, walk away, yeah?' I tell him. But I know Wolf, and the ways he has of making it impossible to ignore him. It's clear even now that Marco's not going to come off well, if he has to spar with someone like that.

As another half-hour passes, the atmosphere sharpens a little. I pass behind where Wolf is telling John his theories on the armed forces.

'But it stays the same, the military, doesn't it? Same training from one decade to the next, same culture.' Anyone would think he'd done service himself. 'I mean, apart from the madness of letting gay men serve alongside normal soldiers. God knows how the British still get taken seriously.'

He glances right in my direction, then at Tori, who gives him a very slow shake of the head that he chooses to disobey.

'Problem?' Wolf says, holding her with a glare that could burn a hole in the eight-inch hull.

'I don't have a problem with gay men doing whatever they like,' Tori says lightly.

His jaw tightens, but she doesn't flinch. His eyes meet mine, but I don't react. It's his secret, not mine, not hers, and it's his choice if he wants to tell the world one day or die with it.

Nish, who's standing nearby, turns slowly. 'I'm not sure I'd agree.'

'Really?' Wolf says. 'Think about it. You've got a battalion full of buff, sweaty blokes. All cut off from their wives and girlfriends, living in a state of constant adrenaline in the middle of the desert. And then you throw into the mix a whole load of very highly sexed individuals, who are only there for the pecs and biceps? I mean, yes, of course rights are important. But honestly. No bloody wonder the Taliban won.'

Tori looks away.

Wolf pauses for the smattering of awkward laughter, but Marco takes his chance. 'We can do without that, mate. We got a lovely lady here who's married to a girl,' he says, nodding to Nish. 'So less of the homophilia, all right?'

Tori's hand flies to her mouth, but it's not quick enough to hide the laugh.

Marco wheels round, but she corrects it immediately, waving her hand in apology. Wolf, however, is not one to let a good opportunity go to waste.

'I think you might mean homophobia, my friend.' He levels an amused look at the bigger man and swallows a mouthful of wine. Then he goes in for the kill. 'It is a bit of a long word, though, for someone who struggles with them.'

Marco crosses the space between them in one step. 'Fuck's that mean?'

'Now, now,' Wolf says. 'I was just interested in this book of yours. Given how much of a challenge that release form was.'

John clears his throat. 'Let's not start shaming people.'

This, from Marco's expression, is very much the wrong thing to say. 'Shaming me about what? Huh? You want to give me some grief as well, yeah?'

John puts his hands up, appalled. 'Not at all, not in the slightest.'

'Boys, boys,' Tori says. 'Let's play nicely.'

'Back off, Matsuka,' Wolf snaps.

'Whoa, don't talk to her like that!' Marco tells him.

'I'll talk to her any damn way I please.' Wolf sets his drink down, sloshing it onto the table as he does so. He always was unfamiliar with his limits, but this time I'd missed it happening.

Annabel, who's been helping Ulla tidy up, comes over. 'Tell you what, how about I make everyone a mug of—'

'*You* can fucking back off, too,' Wolf tells her. It's a snarl, this time.

'Wolf.' Tori's trying to be diplomatic, her hand on his back to communicate a warning, but it's a mistake. He moves away, but his centre of gravity is drunkenly off and he stumbles straight into her, knocking her to the ground.

John rushes over, offers her a hand up. She ignores it and gets up, not taking her eyes from Wolf.

'What the *hell* do you think you're—' Tori hisses, but before she's had a chance to ask her question, Marco finishes the conversation. His fist ploughs into Wolf's face with a wet crunch and sends him sprawling.

The room goes silent. Wolf gets to his feet, an acid grin on his face, and touches his fingers to his split lip. He looks from the blood to Marco, then to Tori.

'Let's get some fresh air, shall we?' John suggests in a paternal undertone, stepping between them.

'Fuck you, old man,' Wolf says, violence in every syllable.

John holds his gaze. He takes a long breath through his nose, and for a minute I think he's found his limit, too, but then he shakes his head. 'You know what? That's me done. I'm going to bed,' he says. His voice is lit with a quiet fury. 'Goodnight, all.'

No one stops him as he leaves; no one replies. All eyes are still on what's happening in the middle of the room, the tension of it tendon-tight.

Wolf barely notices. He points a thick blood-smeared finger right into Tori's face. 'You brought him here,' he spits at her. 'You fucking muzzle him.' He feints a lunge at Marco, then follows John out.

It takes about a second for Tori to deal with her instinctive reaction and revert to type. By the time she's turned to face the frozen group, the wide smile is already in place.

'Well! It's been a long day. Probably best we all get some sleep,' she says.

Straight away, drinks are drained and goodnights are offered. Within a couple of minutes the room is almost empty. I tell Annabel to call it a night, and she doesn't need telling twice.

'You better get some sleep, too,' I tell Tori, who's staring out of the window. 'Early start.'

She nods slowly, makes as if to leave, then thinks better of it. 'I think I'm going to get some air.'

'Sure,' I say. She sighs and I squeeze her shoulder. 'It'll be all forgotten tomorrow.'

'Will it?'

'Promise. Off you go.'

'All right. Night.' Tori leaves, but pauses at the door, lifting my yellow parka from the hook. 'Do you mind?' she asks, pulling it on. 'Left mine behind, and my cabin's miles away.'

'Sure. See you in the morning.'

I pour a last glass of water from the jug, swallow it down. Behind me, someone clears their throat, making me jump: I'd thought the room was empty.

It's Gaia. Pale, and unable to meet my eye.

'I don't think I can do this.' It's the first unguarded thing she's said the whole day.

I try not to sag, but the last thing I need is a late-night counselling session. 'He'll be fine,' I tell her, as softly as I can manage.

'Really? Because it looked like – I don't know. Both of them looked like wild animals.'

I wrinkle my nose. 'Nah. They'll settle down. First-night nerves. And look, I know Wolf – we go way back.'

Except I remember those outbursts that frightened Tori when they were dating. Some of them bad enough for her to turn up at mine late at night, in tears, determined to end it with him.

Gaia still looks unconvinced.

'Honestly, don't worry,' I say with a smile. 'He's a pussycat most of the time.' I say it with a smile, before leaving the room.

It doesn't matter that it's a lie. All that matters is that we get to the end of the trip without anyone finding out.

11

TORI

Fresh air. If there's one thing I can always rely on to settle my nerves, more than alcohol or cigarettes or the gym, it's a good dose of fresh air.

Right before the exit to the deck is a door marked with the figure of a man and a woman, reminding me that I haven't emptied my bladder for hours. I grab the handle and push, but it only opens a few inches before it hits something. Or some*one*: Marco, standing in the small space in front of the two stalls.

He suddenly straightens up from the surface beside the sink, his fingers flying to his nose, rapidly brushing and sniffing. Right behind him is Stefan, who snatches something off the other side of the sink and shoves it into his pocket in a single movement. It's quick, but not quick enough to disguise what is clearly a baggy of white powder and a credit card. I take a step back, hands up, but Marco grips the door.

'It's not what it looks like.'

I check the passage on both sides, but it's only me here. 'It is exactly what it looks like.'

'Please.' He steps forward, eyes wide with panic, rubbing a finger back and forth against his upper lip. 'My kids.'

'Marco.' He's standing too close, but gets closer.

'My ex – if this gets back to her, that'll be it—'

'*Marco.*'

He falls silent, blinking rapidly.

'Where did you even get it from?'

He jerks round to Stefan, who won't look me in the eye. It tells me everything I need to know; it's not much consolation that the gear belongs to him, but at least it means Marco wasn't stupid enough to smuggle it through Customs himself.

'My boss—' Stefan says.

'Shut up,' I hiss to them both, adrenaline surging like a geyser. 'This show is my life, all right? You do this on my show, I'm taking no fucking prisoners. Do you understand?'

'Yeah,' Marco mutters. 'Okay. Yeah.'

I nod to Stefan. 'Flush it. Do it now.'

He thinks about arguing it for about half a second, then Marco takes over. He forces his hand into the smaller man's pocket, then goes into the stall and flushes.

'There,' Marco says, coming out. 'Done.'

I hold the door open and glare at them both as they file past me, shamefaced.

But Marco pauses in the corridor. 'You won't tell anyone, will you?' he asks in an anxious whisper.

'You should have thought about that first,' I tell him, letting the door close behind me as I go into the vacated bathroom.

When I'm finished, the passage outside is silent, and I make my way towards the exit to the deck. I take a moment zipping myself into the yellow jacket – an ugly thing Dee's owned for years, but which I now discover is unbelievably warm – and pull the cord to fasten the hood around my face. Then I haul the heavy door open. The rush of cold is instant, snatching the air from inside me, bringing tears to my eyes. I blink until I get used to the dark, then shut the metal door.

The sky is completely black, but the vast, immaculate landscape of snow and ice glows like a low-wattage moon. Blue-white, as if lit from within.

And it is, truly, breathtaking. Not only the ice sheet that the ship is moored against, stretching for miles. Or the sheer size of the mountain and the one behind it and the one behind that, their swathes of rockface that have evaded the coverage of snow impossibly black. Or even the endless fathoms of icy water to the starboard side, dotted with anarchic, irregular ice structures drifting silently alongside us.

It's the emptiness. It is oppressive, terrifying, absolute. We've travelled maybe fifteen, twenty miles, but it's as desolate and remote as the face of Mars. White, white, white everywhere, and the mirror-stillness of the water. Nothing makes a sound. I'd imagined fierce weather here, but now there is not a whisper of wind.

It's as if the whole landscape is waiting.

I take a step towards the front of the ship, then another, reaching for the railing as soon as I can. I should not have come out in these shoes. But something draws me forward.

The thought is in my mind before I can barricade it: how there are mere inches of deck between me and certain death beyond the ship. How easy it would be for a body – *my* body – to slip into the water.

There's that dark impulse that goes with vertigo sometimes, what they call *l'appel du vide*, the call of the void. A compulsion to throw yourself off the very height that terrifies you. My face and my gloveless hands are already burning with the cold and I know I should go back. But I can't make myself turn away. There's no raised edge to the top deck, just a double line of cable held up by a series of vertical posts. I lean out over the wire rope and breathe it in.

At the edge of my vision there's a sudden quiver of light. Green, blue, impossibly bright. Flickering like a banner, unfurling endless tendrils of colour that whip across the sky. The Northern Lights.

It breaks the fugue, and I am suddenly elated. I'm a million miles from home, I'm in a different world, a different universe, reborn – clean and perfect, beyond any drug I have ever taken. I can't take my eyes off it. I shout, not even words, into the sky. I am laughing.

The familiar weighty clang of the door behind me. Footsteps, but I don't turn, not until the very last second, when I feel them coming close.

Too close.

The force from behind, against my back, knocks me off my feet. I grasp for the cable but it's not enough, and I am falling, tumbling into the pitch-darkness.

12

DEE

I dress for bed, the ship mumbling and creaking all the while. We've moored up against the ice sheet, with another twenty miles to cover in the morning. I try to put thoughts of tomorrow's tasks – not to mention the atmosphere tonight – out of my mind and relax.

Except you never were very good at relaxing, were you? Leo asks, his voice as clear and vivid as if he was right next to me.

I blink in the darkness, trying to talk myself out of doing the one thing that I know I should not do. But before I've even made the decision, I'm up, digging in my bag for the matchbox-sized digital recorder.

I power it up, get out the cable, link it to my phone, open the playback app.

There are two files on it. The only two I managed to save. The first is four minutes and seventeen seconds long.

It opens with movement, too close to the recording lens to make out what is happening, and a scuffing sound, fabric moving. Ten seconds in, the picture settles.

Leo.

The sight of him loosens something around my heart, like the warmth of his arms holding me. Even though—

Even though.

In the grainy midshot, he sits there in profile on his battered sofa in his Bath flat, reading a newspaper.

Behind the camera, my voice. 'Who even buys the newspaper any more?'

Without taking his eyes from it, he smiles. A lock of his tightly curled black hair hangs over his forehead, and the desire to reach out and touch it, to draw my fingertips down the lazy Saturday stubble of his cheek, thrums in my fingertips.

'People who believe in the beauty of physical things?' he offers. The tip of a foot – my foot – appears at the bottom of the frame then, nudging the paper away. He bats it, but I walk my toes up his jumper.

'Jesus, Sophie,' he says, laughing.

Sophie.

Editorial policy: every undercover job, even just for a single sting, needed a fake identity, an agreed back-story.

He didn't even know my real name. And now these few short video files are all I have left of him.

But I'm sure there's one last recording out there somewhere. The last time I saw him, I left my bag-cam behind in his car. And when the ambulance arrived – called in by a passing motorist, a woman who didn't give her name and was never traced – the bag was gone. The police looked for it, but concluded that Leo could have thrown it out anywhere. There were no witnesses to the crash, no one who came forward who might have picked the bag up. But even now, I feel sure there's evidence out there, somewhere, of his last minutes.

A choke swells in my throat and I yank the cable from the jack and rub the wet from my eyes. I have to get out of here. Get my feet onto solid ground. I pull clothes on over my pyjamas, grab my boots, then look for my coat, before I remember that Tori has it.

The ship at night is like a hall of mirrors. After a few wrong turns, I find the door to the equipment store. A dozen padded jackets hang in a line above the same number of thick salopettes and lines of boots. I slide a jacket out and leave the naked hanger swinging.

When the door to the deck swings open, the drop in temperature almost floors me. Despite the thick extra layer, my skin instantly contracts with the incredible cold.

I hurry along until I come to the ladder set into the side of the ship and pause, with the toe of my boot on the top rung. We're under strict instructions not to disembark, under any circumstances. It's what – one, half one in the morning? We're miles from anywhere. And I'm going out for a walk on an ice floe.

But I'm going anyway.

I'm insane, I realise as I descend. It almost makes me laugh.

The rungs end and I take my first tentative step onto the ice. I place my feet carefully, but both the ice and the ship are far too solid to notice my weight. Earlier, I saw Stefan hammering huge metal spikes into the ice sheet to secure the ship.

My footsteps, their crunch against the covering of snow, are the only sound. Only once I've put twenty paces between me and the ship do I look back. From this vantage point, the silent *Skidbladnir* is the only thing that isn't ice. It looks lost, abandoned. Then, without warning, there's a flash. Above me, bands of neon shift.

I watch the show, waiting for the awe. I'm supposed to feel floored by it. But it's only physics, and my heart remains still. It's like watching it on a screen. All I can think is, *I wish he was here to see this.*

Then I realise there's someone else watching it, up on the ship. I narrow my eyes, trying to make them out, but from this angle and distance it's impossible. They go along the upper deck, right up against the railings. Then a second figure appears.

And it happens so quickly that I hardly know what I'm looking at, until it's over. The second figure crosses the last few steps at speed, their arms outstretched. I don't even have time to cry out before the first person is pitched over the edge, head-first, off the far side of the ship.

I gasp, stunned for a moment. Then I run. Arctic air igniting in my lungs, I make it back to the ship in seconds. Even as I clang up the ladder and around the lower deck I'm unzipping my jacket, ready to dive in, in case whoever it was missed the lower deck and fell straight into the water. I spot a life-ring and head straight for it.

But then I see Tori. Collapsed under a porthole on the lower deck, legs crumpled beneath the thick folds of my parka.

I'm there in a moment and drop down next to her, roll her shoulder back, so I can see her face.

'Tori!' I shout, my heart galloping against my ribs. There is blood in her hair, and even in the light of the aurora, I can see she is not her usual colour at all.

Her eyelids drift open. 'I'm okay,' she breathes.

I let out a sob of relief. But this is far from okay. We're in the middle of nowhere, with eleven people we barely know. And one of them just tried to push Tori to her death.

13

DEE

Tori manages to get to her feet, and I help her inside to the saloon, where it's warm. Ulla is still up and immediately goes to summon Stefan.

'And the medic, too. Craig,' I tell her as she hurries from the room.

I make Tori comfortable and take her hands, my heart doing horrible things against my ribs. If I hadn't found her, if whoever it was had pushed a little harder, what then?

'Did you see their face, Tor?'

She looks at me, blood dripping into one eye from a cut to her head, but blinks and looks away.

'There was no one out there,' she croaks. 'I slipped.'

'What?' I duck my head to get into her eyeline. 'No, I saw it. I saw someone, behind you—'

But then Craig hurries in, and I let him check her over.

I make a loop of the ship to see if anyone else is up. The doors are all airtight, so I can't check beneath them for lights or movement, but I listen at every one. I start at the bottom, where Wolf is, but his cabin is silent. Helen, John, Marco, Gaia, Nish: all of their cabins are in the same long passageway as mine, and there's not a sound from any of them.

I knock for Annabel, and after a couple of moments she opens up. Her hair is dripping and she's wrapped in a towel.

'Get dressed,' I tell her. 'It's Tori. She's hurt.'

I pass Eino in the passage, pulling on a jacket. He's been summoned too and is going out to check the railings, he says, but he confirms my suspicion that there's no CCTV.

When I get back to the saloon, Craig's crouching in front of Tori, who's been covered with blankets. He's flashing a light into her eyes, but gets up as I enter the room.

'She's all right, remarkably,' he says, coming over. 'Bit bruised, and there's a cut above her hairline, which I've cleaned and patched up with some strips. Won't need stitches. There's a chance of some mild concussion. You good to check on her every couple of hours?'

I nod. 'Does she know who it was?'

He frowns, not understanding the question.

'Who it was who did what?'

'Pushed her!'

He glances at Tori, then back to me. 'She says she slipped.'

I go and crouch beside her. 'You must have felt it, Tor. I *saw* someone shove you.'

She shakes her head. 'You can't have done. Honestly, it was a stupid accident.' She seems so certain.

Craig comes back with some biscuits from the kitchen for her. She's still shivering uncontrollably, and the cut has matted her black hair with blood.

To him I say, 'Could she just have forgotten that she was pushed? Like a concussion thing?'

'I didn't forget!' Tori says, to Craig and then to me. 'There wasn't anyone else out there. I'm telling you the truth – if someone pushed me, why would I say they hadn't?'

'What happened?' Annabel asks, rushing in.

'Someone pushed Tori off the deck.'

Tori groans. 'I *slipped*.'

'Fuck's sake!' I sigh, get up, take Annabel aside and give her the summary in a hushed voice.

'You went out on the ice? On your *own*?'

'That's not the fucking headline here, Annabel!'

'Okay, I'm sorry. So – is there CCTV?'

'No, nothing.'

'But she *could* have slipped, right?' Annabel says. 'Maybe there's a loose bit of railing?'

I glare at her. 'How is that your first thought, when I'm standing right here telling you what I saw?'

Annabel swallows. 'So . . . who was it, then, that you saw?'

'I don't know.' I try to replay it, analyse the shape behind her, make it into someone recognisable, but I know I'd be forcing it.

'You're sure?' she asks. 'And no one else saw?'

I throw my arms up, annoyed. 'Obviously I'd tell you!'

There's the briefest flicker in her eyes, but then she goes over and kneels next to Tori.

'You didn't see anyone at all? Or tell anyone you were heading outside?'

Tori meets her eye. For the slightest moment I think she's going to tell. But then she leans away from me, shakes her head and closes her eyes.

'Like I said: I slipped. End of story.'

'What do you want to do? Should we head back?' Craig asks her.

'What? No!' she says, trying to sit up. 'No way whatsoever. We're not turning back for anything.'

'You can't be serious!' I say, looking from her to Craig. 'We need to contact the police.'

Craig lets out a quiet laugh. 'Yeah, no, that's not going to help. Once you're out of range of the closest town, anything goes wrong and your captain is like your king. There are police in Nuuk, and a handful scattered up the coast, but they'd need a helicopter and a bloody good reason.' He dips the corners of his mouth. 'And she's saying a crime hasn't even been committed. They'd laugh you off the radio.'

'Fuck's sake.'

'Dee.' Tori's giving me a look I don't like.

'What?'

She jerks her chin at Craig and Annabel, who throw me a quizzical glance, but give us some space. 'Dee, I don't know why you're doing this—'

'I'm not doing anything. I *saw* someone on the deck.'

I know before it leaves her mouth what she's going to say. 'We've been here before.'

It lands like a punch to the gut. 'This is not like that.'

She raises her eyebrows.

'It was depression,' I say, keeping my voice very steady, my eyes on her. She swore we wouldn't bring this up again. 'I have never suffered from hallucinations. I'm not paranoid.'

The honest truth is that, now, I couldn't swear to the fact that I did ever see anyone outside my flat in the days after Leo died. I'd been living out of an Airbnb in Bath for months, and going back to London jobless and devastated by grief was . . . it was hard. Very. But what I saw, at the time, it was so real: a figure, always half hidden, who'd disappear every time I spotted them. Not only outside my flat, but in the days after I turned up at Tori's place, too. Being there felt safer, though, and it didn't take much for her to convince me to stay at hers for a while, and to rent my own place out until I started feeling better.

But I know that she was worried, even though she wanted me to believe at the time that it was all in my mind. Why else would Tori have installed that alarm system and CCTV? She said she'd been meaning to get round to it, but there was an urgency, even I could see that.

And whether or not I imagined that, back home in London: this, here, is different. There was someone up there on the deck. Tori knows it. And so do I.

She holds my gaze until I look away. I can tell from the way Craig glances at me that he's overheard the whole conversation. I go over to where he's packing away his kit.

He keeps his eyes on what he's doing. 'So you've had some mental-health issues? In the past, I mean?'

I fold my arms. 'I know what I saw.'

He nods, but I can see he's not convinced. 'I'll see you in the morning – remember to check her every couple of hours. Anything amiss, come and wake me.'

Annabel waits for him to leave. 'So,' she says, turning to me, 'what are you going to do?'

'Not much I *can* do, is there? I can't find anyone else up and about, and even if I did, no one's going to come over and say, "Oh hey, by the way, it was me."'

Annabel bites her lip. 'So who do you think it could have been?' I ignore the unspoken part of the sentence, inferred by the inability to meet my eye – the bit that says, *if it was anyone at all.* 'I mean, Tori's not exactly the kind of person to have a load of enemies, is she?' Annabel goes on. 'The whole *hashtag-be-kind* thing? All those TV personality awards?'

I raise an eyebrow.

'What?' she says.

'Annabel. Everyone has enemies.'

She shrugs. 'I don't.'

'Right,' I laugh.

'I don't.'

'Well, believe me, when you get to our age, you will.' If there's one thing I learned from undercover work, it's that everyone has things they'd rather stayed hidden. 'Don't look so shocked.'

'I'm not shocked. It's just a little dark,' she says, with half a smile. 'Even from you.'

I tell her she might as well go to bed. Over on the sofa, Tori is pulling herself upright. She touches her fingertips to the damage to her head, and I think again of the way she covered her face when I went to her cabin before we all assembled in the saloon for the evening.

Wolf's name has already crossed my mind. The vitriol he showed towards her after the meal, and the anger coming off him in waves when he left her cabin earlier on. Had something happened?

It takes no time at all in his company to pick Wolf out as a narcissist. He's manipulative, chauvinistic and goes out of his way to wind people up. But underneath that, he's also someone who would do anything to keep one particular part of himself hidden.

Pushing Tori off the edge of a ship could have made him a killer. Would he really go that far to keep her quiet?

14

DEE

We gather Tori's stuff and go back down to her cabin. Leaving her to have a shower, I take her keycard with me and head out into the passage. There's no way Tori's going to share a room, so if I need to be able to check on her, one of us is going to have to move closer to the other.

Opposite Tori's door is Wolf's cabin. I put my ear to the door – is he snoring? Asleep or not, my knock brings him out.

'Cohen,' he says, slumping on the doorframe. He's wearing nothing but boxers. Behind him there is disorder, his clothes from the evening in a jumble on the floor, and the stale smell of a night of heavy drinking hangs off him like an aura.

But would there have been time for him to go up to the deck, push her and come back down and change clothes?

'Comfortable?' I ask him.

'It's the middle of the fucking night,' he slurs.

'It certainly is. You been outside?' I'm playing for time, peering into his room for clues: wet footwear maybe, or his green jacket hastily discarded in a corner. But even as I search, I know it wouldn't prove a thing.

'What? No. Why?' The look he gives me is pure annoyance. 'What do you want?'

'You were pretty angry with Tori earlier.'

This wakes him up, morphing the annoyance into actual anger. 'Fuck you, Dee,' he says and shoves the door shut. I knock again, wait, but he doesn't return.

Back on the level above, where my cabin is, I tap gently on the door next to mine. John answers straight away, his half-moon reading glasses perched on his nose. His room is lit softly by the bedside lamp. It's the picture of late-night tranquillity. But more importantly, he's *awake*.

The realisation of what this could mean takes a bite out of my composure. But what possible reason could John have for harming Tori?

He sees my confusion. 'Everything all right?'

'Yes!' I say, overcompensating, then remember why I'm here. 'Well actually, not exactly.'

Too quickly I stumble over an ad-libbed version of the situation. Tori's not feeling well, I'd like to have her close to my cabin. 'I hate to ask, but would you mind terribly swapping with her?'

He's nodding before I even finish. 'Absolutely, yes, of course,' he says, whipping the glasses off. His face is all concern. 'The poor thing, though – I hope it's not serious? Can I do anything else to help?'

I assure him that giving up his cabin is more than enough, and leave him to collect his things. 'Cabin two, down a level,' I say over my shoulder.

Back downstairs, I let myself into Tori's cabin and start to get her things ready to transfer to John's. From her nightstand I collect the notebook and a framed picture of Will, then I prepare a few things for the morning. Her clothes are in a case in the bottom of the wardrobe. As I shake a shirt out by the shoulders, an opened envelope falls from between the folds, a letter peeking out from inside it.

Tori emerges from the en suite in a burst of steam, wrapped in a towelling robe. 'What are you doing?'

I put my hands up. 'Only trying to help.'

'Well, could you not?' She snatches the letter, puts it in her pocket, then sags. 'Sorry. I'm not feeling quite right.'

'Not surprised. Anyway, listen.'

'Uh-oh,' she says, rubbing her hair dry. 'Big announcement incoming.'

'Your cabin is the only one that's out this end of the ship.'

'Except for Wolf.'

'Who hates you. And has presumably spent the last three years terrified you're going to out him.'

'Are you . . .' She tilts her head, then gives an incredulous laugh. 'Wolf did not try to kill me. No one pushed me, for Christ's sake!'

I fold my arms. I've known Tori long enough to recognise when her stubbornness puts down its roots and becomes immovable. But what possible reason could she have for lying about *this*? Is it because she can't bear for the show to fail? Simply for the sake of her beloved production company – her reputation? Or is it something else, some deeper thing that she'd risk even her own safety for?

What, though? I've seen her resolute before. I've seen her

stubborn as solid rock. But I've never seen Tori this reckless. No, beyond reckless. Suicidal.

One thing I can see for sure, though – she's not going to budge. Not right now, anyway.

I sigh heavily and throw up my hands.

'Fine. Whatever you say. But I need to keep an eye on you – Craig insisted. So we're swapping your room.'

'Um, no.'

I'm about to answer her when there's a knock at the door. 'It's already done,' I tell her.

She flinches. 'What is?'

'I've got John to swap with you.'

'You've . . . *John*? No. No way.'

'What have you got against John? You were all for having him involved, when we were casting.'

'I just don't need his bullshit chivalry is all.'

I dismiss it with a waft of my hand. 'He's only being kind. Anyway, executive decision. Stick your essentials in there and let's go.'

15

TORI

Pissed off doesn't even come close. I get by with the minimum exchange with John in the passageway, then go to my new cabin. It's immaculately clean, the bed neatly made as if he hasn't even sat on it.

From outside, Dee whispers, 'I'll come and check on you in a couple of hours. If you feel ill, just knock.' Silence. Then, 'Tori? I said—'

'Yes. Fine.' I lean my forehead on the door, wishing I could split in half. Run out there and hug her and tell her everything; but also scream in her face for not leaving me and my secrets alone. I'm rigid with a miserable, unreasonable rage I have no right to. Because I'm not only lying to her. What I said back there, about her imagining things: that's the kind of thing abusers do.

There's a pause before she says goodnight, her voice heavy with confusion and resignation. Then the muffled sound of footsteps moving away, the click of her door opening, to the cabin next to mine.

I sink onto the bed. Of all the things she could have done, it had to be this. Swapping me in the middle of the night with *him*. My teeth squeak against each other as I unzip my case.

The letter is still in the pocket of the damp robe and I take it out carefully, trying to remember which way round I'd slid it back into the envelope last time, and whether there's any chance Dee read it. I know its contents by heart – every venomous word as well as if they were tattooed on my palm. I know who wrote it. So why do I even keep it, when throwing it away would be so much safer? If it got out, it would cost me everything. This entire project. And even more than that. My whole career.

My freedom.

Although it could already be too late, I know what I have to do. I crumple the paper, gripping and crushing it until it's a perfect ball, and I go to the porthole. The latch is stiff but I wrench it free, and a bitter blast of ice-glittered wind rushes straight in. Holding the ruined envelope in my fist, I extend my arm as far as it will go into the wild air outside.

I count to ten. I try to let go.

But I can't do it. I made a promise to myself that I would keep it with me until the danger had passed.

And if tonight has told me anything, it's that the danger is very much still present.

Sleep keeps me on its surface, never letting me fully sink. At three, Dee comes to check I'm still alive, but after she comes back at five, I find myself awake for good.

I deploy everything in my arsenal to disguise the cut on my head, then go up to breakfast as soon as I hear other people moving about. I get started on some eggs and rye bread that looks healthier than it does delicious. When Dee takes the seat opposite me, I meet her eye and give my head the very slightest shake. *Don't mention it. Not here. Please.*

Soon everyone is there. Marco comes in, fills a plate and leaves, without speaking to anyone. There's no sign of Wolf.

Nish starts making small talk with Annabel about the Northern Lights and her hopes to see them.

'I brought a little camera especially – I promised the GCSE Photography group that I'd get some shots,' Nish says. 'Did anyone see anything last night?'

Annabel takes a sip of her juice. 'The captain said they made an appearance very late, but everyone was in bed.'

Not quite everyone, I think.

I refill my coffee and by the time I get back, Nish is telling Annabel and Helen about the exclusion policy in her school.

'Because it's the worst possible message you can send a child,' Nish says sincerely. 'They understand perfectly well what it means. A school kicks a kid out, they extrapolate that society wants them gone. But where to? They don't get to go back home and have a nice time. So when I took the headship I decided: no more. Doesn't matter what they've done – they know I won't exclude. I won't give up on them. It should be what every head teacher does, but I appear to be in the minority.'

Helen sighs heavily. 'Has to stop somewhere though, doesn't it? What about showing the other children that there are boundaries?'

'Right.' Nish lifts her coffee to her mouth, then sets it back down. 'Let me guess. Your children turned out perfectly? Which is nothing to do with their privilege—'

Her attention suddenly on straightening her napkin, Helen replies, 'I don't have children. Didn't want them.'

The air zings with the screech of a touched nerve. 'Me neither,' I say quickly, making it my business to dispel it. 'I think it's a brave choice to stand up and say it.'

Helen pushes her plate away and gets up. 'Better get ready.'

'Starts up a cycle,' Gaia says to the table, once Helen's gone. It takes Nish a moment to realise she's speaking to her.

'Sorry?'

'What you were saying. Self-respect needs a kick-start sometimes. If someone you respect shows *you* respect, it's hard to ignore. Starts up a cycle,' she repeats.

'Exactly,' Nish agrees. 'Do you teach too?'

'No.'

An awkward five seconds pass.

'I think maybe John does?' Nish tries.

Gaia coughs into her napkin. 'I don't know,' she says and then, 'Excuse me.' She gets up to scrape her leftovers into the bin.

Dee calls after her. 'We're meeting on the deck in fifteen. Remember everyone needs to wear swimsuits under their layers, right? And don't ask me why, because it's a surprise.'

Nish watches Gaia go, then leans in and whispers, 'Is she always that – awkward?'

'She'll warm up,' I tell her.

Dee gets to her feet and collects the remaining plates. 'I'm going to set up. See you out there?'

I follow her out and stop her in the passage. 'Thanks,' I say, when we're out of earshot. 'For checking on me. Sorry I was kind of grumpy.'

'No problem.'

'Dee, look – about last night—'

'You remembered something?'

'What? No. I was only going to say: maybe it was one of the lights? I'm thinking about it and there's that big floodlight at the front – it could easily have been a shadow or something you saw.'

'A shadow.'

'Yeah. Crazy, I know, but it's possible?'

Dee waits. 'It wasn't a shadow, Tori.' She takes a step back, hurt. 'Look, you want to insist no one else was there, I can't change that. But you need to be careful. Until you know who it was, you need to be watching everyone. We both do.'

She leaves it there for a moment, watching my face. Then, with a quick, sad shake of her head, she turns to go.

It's all I can do not to run after her. I don't want my friend to be afraid, to have to be mistrustful of everyone. But without telling her the whole truth, what choice do I have? I can hardly expect her to understand that I already know the answer. I know exactly who I have to fear.

I watch her walk away, then realise Annabel is loitering near the saloon door. 'Please don't eavesdrop,' I tell her, and she instantly colours and starts digging in her bag like she was looking for something all along.

I leave her where she is and head outside.

The trick is, I remind myself, not to engage. I don't need to give Dee an explanation. Or Annabel. Just stick to the story – it was simply an accident. She didn't see what she thought she saw.

Outside, I find Craig helping Stefan and Ulla securing some crates on the fore deck.

'What are you guys doing?'

'Getting ready for the storm.'

'What storm?'

He considers me. 'What kind of research did you do – your team, back in London?'

I bristle, defensive. 'We did enough. But,' I allow my tone to become pointed, 'we booked the experts to know what we don't.'

'You know about the storms up here then?'

'A little.'

He nods. 'They call it the Piteraq. It means *that which attacks you*. I've seen it go from still air to almost three hundred kilometres per hour in the space of minutes.'

I laugh. He does not.

'Storms don't do that,' I say.

Craig keeps his eyes on me. 'They do here. Everything needs securing. Anything loose can become a missile.'

Ulla passes us with an armful of thick canvas straps, glancing anxiously at the sky. She unbolts the door of the gas locker and shakes each one of the tall orange cylinders. Where she finds movement, she loops an extra band around to secure it.

'When is it coming?' I ask.

Craig bites a glove off his hand and retrieves a sheet of old-fashioned dot-matrix paper edged with holes from his pocket.

'This is from the Ice Service.' He hands it over, points to a place halfway down, though it's hieroglyphics to me. 'Says the storm will be here in the next forty-eight hours.'

'Okay, good, fine,' I say. The calm in my voice is forced, and he knows it.

'You had no idea what you were letting yourself in for, did you?'

I smile. People don't know it unless they dig deep, but I've done all the journalism training Dee has. I know how to counter a question that I don't want to answer. 'We have our captain, and our expert guide. That *is* you, right?'

He blinks. 'Of course.'

'So if anyone needed to do more research, it's you, right?'

That hits a nerve. 'I told Will there could be storms.'

'I'm aware of that,' I lie. 'But if you knew, and we knew, what's the problem?'

He shakes his head, a barely disguised sense of disgust coming off him. 'You're the problem. Do you not see that? You come here, burning all that fuel—'

'No one made you sign up, Craig,' I tell him tightly. Anger writhes like a snake in my chest: at his criticism of something he could have turned down; at Will for completely failing to mention to me this apparently obvious danger. At myself for trusting someone else to take care of my safety.

'No,' he says. 'But you were coming anyway. If not with me, then someone else. You breeze up here without a single mention in your show, as far as I can tell, of the people who live here, of the fact that the whole place is critically at risk. And you haven't even bothered finding out about the weather.'

16

DEE

I sit in the base of a RIB and film everyone coming down into the boat. We've travelled on again for a few hours this morning and dropped anchor not far from the frozen shore. Slabs of ice float all around and, above us, the sky is alive with colour. We're past sunrise, but apparently it stays like this for hours. Craig recruits a hand from Marco to haul several kit bags down, then gets into the other RIB with Annabel and a few others, everyone but Wolf looking identical in their red suits, including me.

I put a hand on Marco's back and ask him how he's doing, after last night.

'What do you mean?' he says. 'What did she say?'

I frown, confused. 'I only meant, about Wolf.'

'Oh – right. Yeah, I'm used to it,' he says, throwing a glance at Wolf, who's talking to camera again for his channel. 'I'll pretend it never happened, but you're not gonna catch us being mates.'

'This group ready to head off then?' Annabel calls from behind me. 'Meet you over there?'

I keep tight to the eyepiece. 'Yep, sure; who am I waiting for?'

'Just Tori.' I give her the thumbs up with my free hand as I do a slow pan to the ship from the open sea. There's the growl of the outboard and we start to bob as Annabel's boat pulls away.

I get a shot of Marco, who'll be manning the tiller for us, then pull back from the eyepiece as Tori appears on the lower deck and climbs down into the RIB. There's not a mark on her – the miracles of her make-up armoury. With barely a moment's pause, she takes the only space left, beside Wolf, who ignores her. The RIB bobs precariously as she sits.

With everyone settled, Stefan unwinds the line from a mooring ring set into the deck of the *Skidbladnir* and throws it in after us. Then Marco gets to work with the throttle and the idling engine of the RIB crescendoes into a roar. The aft dips, the prow rises and we power after the first RIB across the icy sea towards the frozen shore. I pick a couple of travelling shots as we go: a close-up of Nish laughing; Marco with his meaty hand visored over his eyes against the blinding Arctic morning.

Good shots. Atmospheric. I can see them cutting together already. As we near the ice sheet and the motor slows, I turn to find Tori looking at me.

'What?'

She gives me a look that I can't interpret. 'Just pleased you're here. Looking happy, like you're . . . on the mend.'

I check around me, then drop my voice to a whisper. 'You're serious? After whatever that was last night?'

'Dee, please—'

I put my hand up to stop her and place my eye back to the padded ring.

The other RIB beats us there, but within a couple of minutes we're bumping up against the edge of the ice and I shoot everyone climbing out.

This place. Around every finger of a fjord, it changes. The landscape is smooth here, a flat expanse of white, but in the background of the establishing shot, a little further south, it splits in all directions into troughs and tongues and ridges. The topography of a monochrome brain.

Once we're all on solid land – or ice, at least – and the bags are unloaded, Craig waves us all in. I hold up a hand to stop him, then frame a wide shot of him addressing the group. Annabel moves behind me with the second camera. When I've got the framing right, I give him the thumbs up. 'Speed, and action.'

First of all he unpacks a load of what look like spikes on straps. 'Snowshoes,' he explains, and shows us how to stretch them over the base of our own footwear. Then he straightens up. 'So, welcome to your first challenge. We're starting with a hike.'

I can't see his eyes past his mirrored goggles, but there's a twitch at the side of his mouth that suggests he's enjoying this moment.

I pan the camera across the group. Wolf rolls his shoulders and glances around. If he's feeling any remorse for his drunken idiocy last night, he's doing a good job of hiding it. 'I hope everyone's been training hard,' he says.

Craig gives him a look. 'That's not going to matter.'

'No? Survival of the fittest out here, isn't it?'

'Actually no, not in the way you'd expect.'

There's something Craig does that gets everyone's attention, with the lightest touch. There's no shouting or grandstanding. He's got nothing to prove: he's decent, but doesn't care if you like him or not.

'I used to bring hundreds of people like you – like all of youse – to these sorts of places, doing these sorts of challenges.' He looks each of the contestants in the eye. 'And aye, it's true what our friend here's saying – it's tough, for sure. The Arctic wants you dead.' There's a ripple of uncertain laughter. 'It'll throw everything it's got at you, but it's not physical strength that'll decide who gets their way: it's preparation, teamwork and mental toughness.' He taps both temples. 'If you don't have what it takes up here, the Arctic wins. You die. Simple as that.'

Wolf makes a show of suppressing a grin. 'What – you're saying we can climb up *that*,' he continues, picking a particularly vertiginous mountain in the near distance, 'with our mindset? I don't think so.'

'That's exactly what I'm saying,' Craig replies, with a glance at Tori. 'I have it on good authority that everyone here is adequately fit.'

'Peak physical condition,' she confirms, beaming. 'I wouldn't fancy running a race against any of them.'

I think of the gym in her garden annexe, the way you could set your watch to her 6 a.m. workouts. But this is Tori in a nutshell – never admit anything that might make anyone else feel inadequate.

Craig swings his bag off his back. From inside it he produces a compass on a lanyard, which he holds up. 'I need a navigator. We're going a couple of klicks north-north-east.'

Hands go up: Wolf, obviously; Nish; and the slightest gesture from Gaia. Craig points to her and she comes forward.

'Done this before?'

'I walk a lot,' is all she says.

'Good. We're right behind you.' Then, to everyone else, 'You need to keep in each other's footprints, makes for faster travel. Also, first rule of convoy?'

Marco puts his hand up momentarily, then drops it, embarrassed.

Craig laughs. 'Calling out is fine, laddie, you're not in school. But go ahead.'

'Don't lose your tail,' he mutters, caught between angry and ashamed, which appears to be his usual habitat.

'That's right. Keep checking on the person behind you. Leadership is about keeping the group together – your responsibility is to any of your team who are struggling or slow.'

Wolf does a couple of warm-up squats, grunting, and I cast a glance at Tori, rolling my eyes in his direction. It doesn't raise a smile. The look she gives him, however fleeting, is too similar to what I saw on her face last night. Lying on the deck, her face smeared with blood.

Fear.

But then, ever the professional, it's wiped clean, replaced as quickly as it arrived with a warm excitement.

'Come on then, team. Everyone grab a bag – there's one each. Then let's get going!'

I hang back and film them starting off, then pack the camera away and join the trail behind Craig, who's bringing up the rear. After a couple of minutes we've fallen into pace together, and it becomes apparent that we share that rare lack of compulsion to fill a silence.

Learning to walk in the snowshoes takes time. There is a skill to it, a stamping action, then a powerful push-off. Before

I get the hang of it, every step expends many times more energy than I'm used to, and I'm carrying more than anyone else. Ordinarily I'm bloody-minded about managing my gear alone, but after a few minutes, between the weight and the technique, I'm struggling.

Without a word, Craig gestures for one of the bags. I extricate myself from the strap of the monopod that I brought instead of the heavier tripod and hand it over, thanking him. Freed from its bulk, I'm able to take some freehand shots of the column.

We continue to walk in silence, our footsteps creaking against the compacting snow. Then he points to a spot in the sky, a little way above the grey-white outcrop of rock emerging from the snow cover. 'Whoa. See that?'

I squint. The sun's climbed higher now, but is still only a glow behind almost unbroken cloud.

'Right there. Ptarmigan, you see her?'

I shield my eyes and spot a bird, high up. 'Her?'

'The males have a black strap across the eyes. She's changing to her winter plumage – white for the winter. They grow these sort of feathery snowshoes, too. Fascinating species.'

I quickly ready the camera but the bird wheels to the east, disappearing behind the knuckle of the next fjord before I have a chance to get a shot.

'Next time,' he commiserates. I watch Craig, still smiling at the space where the bird was.

'Really love this place, don't you?'

He gives me a look like I've asked him if he's fond of breathing. 'Well, look at it.'

I nod. 'And it's kind of your home now, right?'

'I mean, Scotland will always be home. Nigeria, where my folks have gone back to now, that should be a close second, the amount of time I spent there as a kid. But Greenland is . . . something else. One of the last great untouched wildernesses.'

'Until people like us touch it, I suppose,' I say, lifting my chin at the party ahead.

'Indeed,' he says darkly. I don't push it. After he'd been confirmed, I spent a few idle late-night hours googling and found some videos of him online that showed him to be more of a diehard environmentalist than Will had made out. A lot of anger, a lot of protests. Even a suggestion – albeit one I hadn't substantiated – that he'd been involved in an altercation with an oil lobbyist.

Picking that particular scab, I sense, would be the start of a conversation I don't really want to have. Since he stopped taking big corporate groups out here a decade ago, his specialism now is small, low-impact expeditions – his website is all about reducing the footprint of tourism. And let's face it, it's not like this show is exactly carbon-neutral.

After a while the silence gets a little thick, even for me.

'How do you think they're going to get on?' I ask him. 'Our contestants?'

Craig moves the extra luggage from one shoulder to the other without breaking his stride and gives my question some thought. When he answers, he does it circuitously.

'It's funny, this obsession with leadership. Being in charge. I spend most of my time here with locals, and every year it gets harder to survive. The ice doesn't form in time, so they can't hunt; and when they can't hunt, they can't trade, they can't survive. Usual story of people of colour bearing the brunt of climate change – people don't think of that applying up here, but it does. They struggle, constantly, but always cooperate with each other. Always. Like this, here,' he says, motioning to my gear. 'Did any of this lot offer to help you? No. But even the kids here will. With my youth group, someone will always get exhausted. But the others will take the weight off whoever's in trouble, without even discussing it.' He shrugs. 'That's not something you can teach. I wish it were. Because some of *this* lot could do with a bit of that.'

'He's not always that bad,' I say, knowing that he means Wolf. I don't know why I'm defending him again. Maybe because I want it to be true, so that I'm not tarred with the same brush.

Craig glances at me, eyebrows raised.

'Okay, sure,' I say, relenting. 'He is mostly that bad.'

He laughs. 'Not only him, though. You watch, when we get this challenge started. It's the ones who've spent their careers being obeyed who're the worst. You throw them into a situation they can't get out of by shouting at people, and you get to see what they're made of pretty damn quick.'

17

TORI

After what has to be at least an hour, Craig calls everyone ahead of him to a stop. The midday sunlight bleeds into a long slick of white cloud, stretching across the mountains.

Nish turns a circle, confused. 'Here? But it's just . . . ice.'

Craig catches up and tells them to drop the bags he's given them. He opens two of them and brings out tools: a pickaxe, some kind of flat trowel, a folding saw like a bayonet. Dropping them, he spreads his arms.

'Right then,' he says as Dee starts to record. 'I want a single hole, yay wide.' He shows the dimensions with his hands, less than a metre square.

'And how deep?' Helen asks.

'Let's say, when you see blue, you can stop.'

Marco breaks into a grin. 'Are we fishing?'

'That would be telling, lad,' Craig says with a wink. 'Off you go!'

Wolf immediately makes a grab for the axe, and the others move in for a discussion – all except Marco.

He sidles up to me and nods.

'Listen,' he says, not making eye contact. 'About last night. It's not a big deal, me and the blow. It's, what's the word, recreational.'

'Forget it,' I hiss. 'But don't do it again.'

But he's shaking his head rapidly now, anxious. 'No, but really. I heard you got pushed or something. I want to make sure you don't think – I mean, it wasn't me, all right?'

I look him square in the face now. I drop the smile that I carry around with me every goddamn minute of the day and I don't give him any chance to misunderstand me. 'Marco. No one was pushed. And no one did any drugs. Right?'

He nods, looks at the floor. 'The hotel, where I work on the door. There's a zero-tolerance policy there, so . . .'

'I said, forget it.'

But when he looks up there's still a manic anxiety in his eyes. 'So, me and you, we're all good then?'

Dee, who's been freehanding the shots of the group, suddenly stands up straight. She looks worried.

'Sure, Marco, we're good,' I say.

I rush over to Dee, who's tapping the air with her finger – a head-count. Then her eyes, round as pennies, settle on mine. She waves me away from the group, out of earshot.

'Where's John?'

Annabel, operating the second camera, looks up and comes over. Dee repeats her question. Annabel glances all round her, like John could be hiding somewhere on a flat sheet of ice. The three of us converge a little way from the others.

Dee glares at Annabel. 'Tell me you didn't leave one of the competitors on the ship. Did I not ask you who I needed to wait for, when we left?'

'I . . . I didn't—' she stutters, and Dee puts both hands to her face and growls.

'Fucking hell. How is that possible?'

'I'm sorry! I thought you'd done the head-count,' Annabel says, on the verge of tears. 'There were the two different boats and I think I must have assumed he was with you . . .' She trails off.

Dee, looking murderous, draws a breath to speak, but I get in there first.

'Okay,' I say, hands up. 'So he definitely didn't get on a RIB?' They shake their heads. 'That's something. But blaming each other isn't going to help—'

'Well, it might,' Dee puts in, unsnapping a radio from her belt. She tries the ship, but there's no answer. She tries again. 'Great. Fantastic,' she says, stowing the radio away. 'Why the fuck didn't John get Eino to radio us? He must have realised he'd been left behind?'

'I could go back,' Annabel says.

'Back in time, you mean?' Dee sighs heavily and looks at her watch, then at Annabel. 'It might work. It's like, what, fifty minutes' walk back to the RIBs?'

'Come on, Dee,' I say, 'we can't possibly send her back on her own.'

But she ignores me. 'Can you operate the outboard? They're not complicated, all you need to do is open the fuel line and pull the cord and—'

'Dee!'

'What? What do you suggest we do?'

'I can do it,' Annabel says in a tiny voice that only confirms that she definitely can't.

I sigh. 'We don't have time. Once we'd gone all the way back, there's not going to be enough decent light left.'

'I'm so sorry, I didn't notice,' Craig says, joining us. 'They all look the same in the suits and—'

'It's not *your* fault,' Dee says pointedly. I can't say I blame her. Anyone can make a mistake, but it's literally Annabel's job to make sure people are where they need to be. Even a runner would have made certain. Not for the first time, I wonder what Will was thinking when he hired her. Cheap isn't everything.

They look to me for a decision. 'Right. Here's what we do. We'll shoot what we can and hope for the best. We'll still have to do the vote tonight, but we'll fudge it in the edit. And then maybe we can find another chance to shoot John's section on its own. Is that doable?' she asks Craig.

'Possibly,' he says, looking doubtful. 'Your schedule's pretty insane as it is.'

'We'll find a way. And we can do it all really tight, so the change in scenery doesn't show so much.'

Dee laughs and looks away, shaking her head. 'Fuck's sake.'

'Right then!' I say, forcing a sanguine tone. 'That's a plan. We'll have to edit around it.'

'I'm only glad I'm not directing the edit as well,' Dee says. 'Oh, wait, I am.'

But with the decision made, off they go.

John's absence has been noticed by the others now. Marco tries to insist that we pause the challenge, but I tell them the plan, like it's the most obvious thing in the world, and although there are mutterings of concern, they go along with it.

It takes an hour to get the hole dug. When they strike the

final chunks through and bottom out the hole to reveal the water beneath, the whole team collapses on the ground to rest.

Craig waits as Dee frames up the wide shot, clapping his hands together for warmth and stamping his feet into the snow.

'You wanted to warm up, maybe you could have helped us dig,' Wolf gripes, wiping sweat from his forehead.

Passing behind him, I pause to whisper in his ear. 'Be. Nice. You're acting like a brat.'

He turns, and there's the same flare of hate in his eyes from yesterday. He sweeps his gaze up and down me, like he's going to reply. I glance behind him, and that's all it takes to remind him there are people here. Witnesses.

'At speed,' Dee says to Craig.

'Right then. Anyone want to tell me what we're doing?' Craig opens the bags one at a time. From one he pulls out an armful of microfibre towels, followed by foil blankets. Another holds a wide, flat package that he opens up to reveal a standing-height pop-up cubicle tent.

Helen rolls her eyes at the theatrics. 'I hardly think I'm in my cossie for a photoshoot, am I? We're going in, obviously.'

Craig laughs. 'Got it in one. We're having an ice dip.'

'We're using wetsuits, though, right?' Nish says, horrified.

'Nope!'

Marco folds his arms and juts out his chin. 'Not in my swimmers – I'm not stupid,' he says. 'I saw a thing about cold-water shock. We've got about ten seconds in there before our organs start failing.'

'Actually that's not true,' Craig says. He hands me a stopwatch. 'Tori, you're recording immersion times.' He appraises the group. 'This is what today's challenge is all about. I'm going to show you how your mindset and your team are what keep you alive.'

They're going to be heading into the water one at a time, he tells them. The group subsides into muttered complaints until Helen steps forward.

'I'll go first.'

She's already zipped off her padded jacket and is unbuttoning her over-trousers. 'I'd rather get it out of the way.'

There's a ripple of admiration, mixed with relief. She wastes no time acknowledging it, or talking to anyone other than Craig, who unrolls a foam mat for her to stand on.

'Do I jump, then, or sort of slide in?' If she feels any kind of shame or embarrassment about the exposure of her stocky, late-middle-aged body to a bunch of near-strangers, not to mention the unrelenting gaze of Dee's lens, Helen does an admirable job of hiding it. She peers, apparently fearlessly, into the blue mirror at the base of the ice hole.

'Either's fine,' Craig says. 'Whenever you're ready.'

The words are barely finished before she hops in, feet together, submerging fully into the freezing water.

'Stopwatch,' Craig reminds me, and I click the button to start it.

There are a few silent moments as the roiling surface closes over her. Then Helen bursts from the blue.

'Christ, that's cold!'

Everyone laughs.

Crouching by the pool, Craig talks her through slowing her breathing. She treads water, her milk-white limbs shuddering at first, but then moving more fluidly as he speaks. 'Mind over matter,' he's telling her, his voice melodic. I watch the seconds tick past, updating Craig every ten seconds before, after a full minute, he stops me with the wave of his hand. He throws down a rope ladder that he's staked into the ice, then lies flat on his stomach to give Helen a hand out. A round of sincere applause greets her as she stands on the mat he's prepared and wraps herself in the waiting towel and foil blanket. She even smiles, for a moment.

She disappears into the narrow tent to change, while Craig unzips another one of the bags and pulls out a flask. The moment she's dressed and out, he hands her a beaker of steaming hot chocolate.

Next in is Nish. She closes her eyes before she enters the water and doesn't open them, or say a word, until she climbs out no fewer than ninety seconds later. Gaia also takes the whole thing extremely seriously. The moment she's out she rushes over to Marco, who's undressing, ready for his turn.

'You need to keep flexing your toes,' she says. 'I just thought about my toes the whole time, and the rest of my body hurt less.'

Marco takes his scowl with him right to the moment he hits the water, but comes up yelling with exhilaration, making everyone laugh, and revelling in the back-slapping when he's out.

'Right then,' Craig says, pulling up the ladder. There's a flicker of mischief in the glance he gives Dee. 'Wolf, my friend. You're up next.'

Knowing the camera is on him, the seasoned star of the outdoor adventure show does what's expected of him, at least to begin with. The clothes come off with speed and panache, the rigid slabs of his pecs flexing as he pulls the final layer from his torso.

'Can a boy get a bit of encouragement?' he asks, grinning as he approaches the hole.

A chant of 'Wolf! Wolf! Wolf!' starts up – even Gaia gets into the spirit. Dee creeps around the edge of the group, collecting detail shots while Annabel gets the wides.

Wolf makes a big thing of psyching himself up with a few sharp breaths, bounces on his heels a few times, then jumps in.

The water swallows him. Seconds pass, and the surface of the water starts to settle. Then he comes up, gasping. His hands flail against the edges of the ice and for a few moments he doesn't speak, can't seem to fill his lungs. No one says a word.

And then the silence gives way to Wolf's shouting, loud and explicit. I catch Dee's eye as she glances up, clearly thinking the same thing as me. He's told us both how his viewers take a coy thrill from seeing the pixelation of his mouth whenever he swears on TV – so much so that he's reproduced the effect on his own social-media channels, where there's no necessity for censorship. Although, to be fair, this doesn't appear to be a pretence. His eyes are wild. Scared.

But he's never been good at differentiating fear from anger. I move over closer to Craig, who's telling Wolf the same thing as he said to his predecessor.

'I can't fucking calm down,' Wolf spits at him. He's shuddering all over, the fibres of his shoulder muscles standing in stiff creases under his tanned, hairless skin.

'Yes, you can,' Craig tells him smoothly, without emotion.

I position myself so that Craig can see the stopwatch. Forty seconds pass. Fifty. A whole minute.

'Throw down the ladder,' Wolf demands. His breath is becoming ragged.

Craig gets to his feet and the whole group exhales, relieved that Wolf's time is up. But then Craig puts his hands in his pockets, leaving the ladder where it is.

'Hands up who knows how long you can survive in water at that temperature? I haven't checked it, but we're gonna guess it's bobbing around the one-to-two-degree mark. Anyone?'

Gaia, unable to tear her eyes from where Wolf is gasping for breath in the pool, raises her hand. 'Two minutes, max.'

'Nope. Anyone else?' He stands in a military at-ease.

'Throw the fucking ladder!' Wolf screams at him.

'The answer is,' Craig says, ignoring him, 'it depends. We talked before about mindset, didn't we?' He kneels by the edge, his eyes on Wolf, but his words directed at the group. 'If you expend all your energy on anger, you're going to struggle. But if you concentrate – if you're thinking about conserving your energy, about doing everything you can to take your mind away from the panic – it can be a lot longer.'

'A minute thirty,' I tell him, in a whisper. Then louder, urgently. 'That's ninety seconds gone, Craig.'

'So, let's try something I do with the kids I work with. Wolf, I want you to sing me a song.'

'Get me—' he starts, but the cold chokes off the rest of it. We get the idea. Wolf wants out. He's got to get out.

Craig remains impassive. 'Just a quick song. Let's try "Happy Birthday", what do you say?'

'Two minutes.' My voice is flat, even though I know I'm in the shot. There's a whimper from one of the women. I glance at Dee for guidance, but her eye is glued to the eyepiece, her gloved hand adjusting the zoom, then moving to the focus ring.

Wolf's trembling intensifies and he goes into full-blown spasm.

And I'm suddenly, horribly aware of my powerlessness and, more than that, even my culpability. Dee and I are responsible for these people. I know nothing about Craig's background beyond the screen test shot by a local producer, and the briefing pack that Annabel put together. Will chose this guy, based on: what? Price? Why was he cheaper than everyone else? Didn't I see; didn't I even point out to Dee last night how Craig and Wolf seemed to lock horns? What if he's some madman intent on killing us all, and we're here, bewitched by the bystander effect, doing exactly as he says because he professes to be the expert?

Two minutes thirty.

Craig is crouching, his focus fully on Wolf. His voice is low, sonorous, aimed only at him. 'Your ego doesn't get you out of this hole. You understand me?'

Even as Wolf claws at the ice, deep and sheer enough that there's no way he's getting out of there without help, his eyes are on those of his tormentor.

'Let me up.'

'I need you to breathe, calmly, enough to sing a song. This is what you're going to learn.'

'*Let me up!*' Wolf's voice is a scrape. He slaps the side of the hole, thrashing with terror.

'Nope, that's enough,' I hear from behind me. I turn to see a scramble of movement, then a splash as Nish throws down the ladder that Craig had put out of reach. She lies flat on her stomach and reaches in, to help haul Wolf up. In another second she's got him wrapped up in a silver sheet.

Then she walks over to Craig. She points a shaking finger in his face, but whatever words she's trying to find won't come out. No one moves, no one speaks, not even Wolf, who stands shuddering on his own, eyes gripped shut.

Helen is the first to act, rushing over and pulling out the flask from Craig's bag for Wolf.

'This is on you,' Nish spits at me, then points to Dee. 'And you. The three of you. Even my Year Sevens know not to bully someone like that!'

I try to take her hands. 'Nish, look, the show is supposed to be challenging—'

'Challenging?' He could have *died* in there.'

'He wouldn't have died,' Craig tells her.

'No? I don't see *you* going in, showing us it's safe. What are you trying to prove?' She shoves him hard in the chest, but Craig sees it coming and stands firm.

Then, as if nothing unusual has happened here, he returns his attention to the horrified group. 'Okay then. Job done. Let's get packed up.'

Five minutes later we're ready to move.

Wolf keeps his distance from the rest of the group, speaking only to a placatory Helen and throwing occasional violent looks at Craig, who is all practicality. Without emotion, he instructs the team on the procedure for the return leg – he'll be leading, Gaia will be at the back.

'We've got a bank of what looks like snow coming in from the south-west now,' Craig tells us, gesturing to a particularly voluminous tower of cloud, 'but if we keep the same pace as before, we should beat it.'

All I can hope is that as well as dealing somehow with the monumental fuck-up of entirely missing out a contestant, we find a way to manage what's clearly become a PR disaster when we get back on board. Because the way it looks now, we're on the verge of a full-scale mutiny.

18

DEE

The atmosphere is so leaden that there's no point even shooting on the way back. I spend the walk trying to make a plan for how we cover the fact that one of the contestants didn't even compete.

Barely anyone speaks. Tori does her best to liven things up when we're finally back at the RIBs, but it's wooden and awkward. The silence on the few minutes' ride back to the *Skidbladnir* makes it feel like an hour.

The ship is coming back into view as Tori steps over and comes to sit beside me in the prow. 'Well, that was interesting.'

'Is that what you call it?'

'We wanted drama, didn't we?' She nods towards the other RIB, out to our starboard side. 'I overheard Nish earlier. Saying how Craig's dangerous, how she doesn't think we should trust him.'

'Pff, he knows what he's doing,' I say, glancing over at him, but finding him staring right at us. I angle myself away, but then something connects in my mind.

'What?' Tori asks, narrowing her eyes.

'Craig. He was talking about the environmental stuff. You

don't think . . . maybe this whole thing, working with us – maybe he's got a score to settle. A grudge that we're even out here—'

She laughs, then stops. 'Wait, you mean it? Dee. Please. Don't.'

'Don't what?'

'Make it a drama. Ruin this whole thing for me. Just try to let it go. Please. For me.'

The nose of the RIB bumps against the ship. I get to my feet, grab the rope from the base of the boat and throw it to Stefan, who's waiting on the deck. Straight away Tori goes over to him, closely followed by Annabel, to find out what's happened to John.

Meanwhile I head to the makeshift production office where we set up our monitors and other kit the night before. We've decided to keep the door unlocked for easy access, and it's ajar when I get there. My yellow jacket hangs on the back of the door, a neat line of stitches where someone – I'm guessing Ulla – has mended it since last night when Tori wore it.

I'm halfway through unpacking when Annabel rushes in, whey-faced.

'It's John,' she says. 'He's not answering the door.'

On the way down, she recounts what Stefan told her. 'He says he had no idea John was still here. They haven't seen him all day.'

I take the steps two at a time. 'So break the door down!'

'I said that,' Annabel replies. 'Stefan said the doors had only been replaced this season.'

'So? Jesus Christ! Did it not occur to anyone that he might be ill?'

We catch up with Tori on the steps down to the cabins. 'Is there a master key?' Tori asks Annabel.

'Eino's bringing it down.'

I pause by the door at the bottom of the steps. 'Annabel, can you go upstairs and keep everyone happy?'

'I mean, I can, but—'

'Great.' I let the door close. I'm not in the mood to manage her feelings right now.

We arrive at the door to cabin two. I knock. 'John,' I say loudly. 'It's Dee here. Can you hear me?'

There's no answer. I turn to Tori, then notice that behind her, mounted on the wall, is a fire extinguisher.

She follows my eyeline, then sidesteps in front of it. 'No. We'll wait for the key.'

Anything might have happened to John behind that door. I'm not waiting another moment. I dodge past her, lift the extinguisher off the wall.

'John, we're coming in, okay?' I give him a few seconds. And then I swing the heavy cylinder back for momentum and crash it, base-first, against the handle.

It takes a few goes, but then the door nudges open. Splinters of wood grind underneath as I push it back across the carpet. I take a deep breath and go inside.

He's in bed, his back to the door.

'John?'

He doesn't move. I can feel Tori close behind me until I cross the threshold, but she doesn't come inside. Alone, I cross the room and touch John's shoulder.

I know he's dead from the moment my hand makes contact.

They hurry in, one after another. Captain Eino, Stefan, Craig, then Tori, whom I sent off to rally them.

Craig goes straight to the bed. He rolls John onto his back, holds his fingers against his neck. Leans over and puts his head against his chest.

No one says a word. I look everywhere but at the sad little scene taking place, which we're all aware will serve only to confirm what we already know.

I take in John's tartan pyjama bottoms, the faded T-shirt from a local music festival of several years ago. The little tuft of greying hair at the curve of the neckline. A pair of reading glasses folded neatly on top of a Philippa Gregory novel in a public-library dustcover, the incongruity of it taking a razor-sharp swipe at my heart. Beside the bed is a small backpack, not yet unpacked, after the good deed he did Tori in the middle of the night without a moment's hesitation.

Craig clears his throat. 'There is no heartbeat.'

Having it confirmed out loud, it seems the whole cabin, the whole ship, shrinks into itself.

John was – nice. He was a nice man.

Craig tries to move John's head slightly from side to side, but it takes some pressure. 'He has been dead for at least four, five, six hours. Muscles are stiffening, you see?' He looks over John's torso. There are no wounds, no blood on his body or the sheets. It's as if he's only sleeping.

Eino goes to the window and opens it. The temperature dips vertiginously. 'Always better to circulate air.'

Craig touches his fingers to John's eyes to close them, but it's clear there's a resistance there, too. 'Rigor mortis tends to peak at twelve hours. He will be . . . softer, after that.'

Tori puts her hands over her eyes and tips her head back. 'This isn't happening,' she says in a voice that threatens to break.

'Any idea what killed him?' I ask.

'I don't know. Nothing external that I can see, but give me a minute.' He gingerly lifts John's T-shirt, and I avert my eyes. The very least he deserves is some dignity, but there is little to be salvaged here, in this poky room, surrounded as he is by near-strangers.

There's something about the way Craig keeps his back to the room as he works that makes me question if something is being withheld. Before I can voice it, though, the examination is suddenly over, a blanket pulled up over John's head.

'Hard to say,' Craig says, looking shaken. 'It's possibly a heart attack, but without a proper post-mortem . . .' He spreads his hands.

'I will contact the police,' Eino says.

'Natural causes, though, you think?' I don't want to say it, but no one else is going to. 'Just that it seems a little out of the blue. More than a little.'

'He's clearly not been murdered, if that's what you're saying,' Tori says sharply.

'Are we sure?'

She flings out a hand towards him. 'It looks pretty peaceful to me. Is there any bruising, Craig, or injuries – anything like that?'

'Well, no, but . . .'

'Then let's not speculate. It could be anything. Appendicitis, stroke, anything. Let's wait until we get a proper opinion.'

I shake my head, confused. 'Aren't you worried? John was fine. What about poisoning – something he ate?'

Craig shrugs again. 'Ask me about field medicine, emergency stuff, and I'm your man. I'm not a pathologist.'

'We wait for the police, please,' Eino says, annoyed. 'We can remove him somewhere secure.'

'Excuse me?' I say, bafflement turning to indignation. 'Is there a reason you don't want us to find out why a perfectly healthy man has died on this ship? *Your* ship?'

Eino brushes an invisible speck of dust from his chest. 'There are questions regarding the gentleman's state of health, which none of us know.'

'Well, that's something I *can* find out,' I reply. 'Annabel has files on everyone.'

Tori follows me out. 'We're keeping this between the people in this room,' she says in the passage. 'Bare minimum.'

I give her a look.

'What?'

'Is that actually your priority? As opposed to, let's say, why John went to bed happy as Larry—'

'He was hardly *happy*—'

'. . . and never woke up?'

Tori sags, and I realise her eyes are shining with the threat of tears. This is her big thing, this show. She's poured literally everything into it. And now – who knows? Can you really continue a show when one of your six contestants is dead?

'I'm sorry,' I tell her. 'Sure, fine. I won't tell a soul.'

I go to the office for the file and get the answer I need in less than a minute. There's a signed disclaimer in there, several sheets of medical questions to which John has ticked 'no' or 'yes' in all the right places.

By the time I get back to the cabin, Eino has gone. Craig has now been joined by Stefan, who's helping to wrap John in a white sheet. They heave the body over, pulling the shroud tight. 'Eino's gone to contact the police, for what it's worth.'

'What does that mean?' I say.

'It means,' Craig says, tucking in a final piece of fabric and stepping back to appraise the job, 'that I know how this works. They're going to tell us to go ashore at the next town where there's a police station, which is days away, and even then it's probably only manned part-time.'

'But there's a *dead body* here.'

Craig spreads his hands. 'I'm only telling you what I know. I mean, maybe if it looked like foul play—'

'Which it doesn't,' Tori puts in.

'And you'd know that how?' I say.

'I'm only saying. John wasn't twenty-five, was he? There might be any number of things that meant he was at risk.'

'Not in his health questionnaire.'

'He might have lied,' Tori says, folding her arms. 'There's a hundred grand at stake, if you'd forgotten. That sort of money could easily have made a little heart condition slip his memory.'

I don't understand what's happening here. A man is dead. On our watch. And no one seems . . . affected. It's like we're talking about a leaking tap.

'We need to do the vote,' she says. 'I'll be up there in five.'

But as Tori leaves the room, I realise two things. First, that she really wants John's death to be a tragic accident. Second, that she knows there's a good chance it's not.

19

TORI

Five minutes. I shut the door of my cabin, set a timer on my phone.

Sitting on my bed, hands on my lap, I take ten slow breaths, close my eyes and get to work.

In my mind's eye, I bring up a picture of last night's spectacle – the swathes of light hanging from the sky – and then I zoom back. I see myself there. I imagine the black shape moving behind me. And then I put the whole image into a box and I shrink it. I do the same with John. His dead body, grotesque even after a few hours. I stand back from the picture of them wrapping him and fold the whole thing up, like it's a model made by a child.

Another box for Wolf, his hand making contact with my cheek last night, the sharp shock of it.

One for Will, and the nagging feeling that something isn't right with him.

One for the money issues, the fact that if this show flops, my house is no longer my own.

In my head, I press these boxes tight, tighter, until they're nothing more than pixels. And then I open my eyes. I uncap my lipstick, open my mouth wide in the mirror, blink through a new layer of mascara.

Big smile!

And, miraculously, everything is fine again. Because it has to be.

In the saloon I find the contestants either heaping food onto their plates from the buffet table or, in Wolf's case, already sitting and eating. The meal looks simple but exactly what's needed: big bowls of chilli, some kind of slaw, hunks of crusty bread still steaming from the oven.

Dee is her usual semi-invisible self, unobtrusively shooting from the edges of the room. I catch her eye once and she gives me a brief, shell-shocked shake of her head, registering her disbelief that we're going ahead with this when there's a dead man downstairs.

But I can't help John now. There's a job to do.

The curtains are open, giving the room a wraparound view of the preternatural world outside. The sky is a solid baby-pink, save for the towering mass of grey-white snow clouds coming in from the south.

Ulla bumps the galley door open with her hip and carries in a big dish of rice, setting it on the long table. Marco, waiting next in line with a serving spoon, immediately plunges in, then suddenly stops.

'Shit, sorry,' he says, abashed. He hands me the spoon. 'Ladies first.'

As I help myself, he leans in. 'So, where's John?'

Nish, behind him, looks over and then a hush takes hold.

One by one the conversations drop off and they all look at me, with the same earnest expression of concern on their faces. Dee lifts the camera off her shoulder and pretends to do something technical.

I have no choice but to improvise.

'He's not feeling too well,' I say sympathetically. 'We'll have to wait and hear.'

'Not too well, like what?' Gaia says, putting down her fork. 'Is he . . . is it serious?'

I glance towards Dee, who studiously avoids my eye. Annabel, who's been perching on the armchair with the second camera across her lap, gets up and takes a clean dish from the stack. 'I'll take him some food.'

'No, he's fine,' I tell her.

'Which is it?' Marco snaps. 'Is he fine or is he ill?'

Before I can answer, Wolf clears his throat. 'What's this going to mean for the vote?'

No one will look directly at me now. It's bad form to be preoccupied with the prize money when someone is clearly in difficulties of some kind, and they all know it – but it's clear that Wolf has just voiced what they've all been thinking.

'Straight after dinner,' I tell them as I start to fill my bowl. And although I'm already regretting it, I add, 'John's in safe hands, he'll be back with us by tomorrow. So let's eat!'

I take a seat next to Helen, but as I settle, Dee comes over and crouches into a low shot at my elbow. She puts her eye to the viewfinder and braces her elbow on the table to steady the shot.

'"Safe hands",' she mutters under her breath. 'What the fuck?'

I pretend I haven't heard her and turn to my neighbour.

'How are you feeling now? Nice to be warm?'

Helen regards me from under her silver fringe as she eats. Then she lays her fork down. 'Tell me about yourself, Tori. What are you like to work with?'

I frown, laughing. 'I'm kind of an open book. I like to look after people, I suppose.'

She waits, her grey, thinly plucked eyebrows raised. 'Do they trust you?'

'I'm sorry?'

She takes another forkful of chilli, takes her time chewing, then swallows. 'What do you know about me?'

Wherever this is going is not a place I want to be. Why did I sit beside *her*? 'Um,' I begin, stupidly. 'You're very successful.'

'What else?'

I sigh. 'You have five hundred people working for you—'

'Six. Go on.'

'And that's even after selling off three businesses in the last two years.'

'Well, that's all very dry. What else?' She waits. 'You can say it.'

I glance around. 'There was a big deal in the press when you'd fired this woman—'

'Not just any woman.'

Do I really have to say this? 'A single parent, for stealing a packet of biscuits.'

'Yes. That's the part the media reported. The whole truth was: she was a shift manager. She earned a good wage.' She smiles. 'And it wasn't about the biscuits.'

'Okay. Hey, how about some wine?'

But Helen won't be distracted. 'It was about trust. It was brought to my attention. I asked her – and if she'd told the truth, she'd have had another chance. But she lied to my face. And I will not work with people I can't trust.'

She leans in.

'Is John all right, Tori? Nothing we need to worry about?' It's as if the room goes suddenly cold. 'You must remember that we're all out here, absolutely isolated. If we can't trust you, who knows what's going to happen.'

20

DEE

I finish the shots of the meal while Annabel gets started taking the contestants out into the passage one at a time to get some soundbite clips of how they plan to vote. She deals with Wolf, Marco and Gaia, then I swap with her and get some material with the others.

Nish is still simmering with anger about Wolf's treatment, but it's clear that won't be enough to get him a sympathy vote. She refuses to say who she's voting out. Helen's got an unapologetic air of confidence about her performance, even stating aloud that she'd vote for herself if she could. For her, it's a clear thumb across the throat for Wolf.

'I mean, no one wants to see a man humiliated,' she says, with the air of a woman describing her favourite thing, 'but he didn't exactly rise to the challenge, did he? And all that posturing, too. I think we really saw what he was made of.'

When we're done, I go in and check that Annabel's collected all the voting forms, then tap Tori on the shoulder to tell her we can get on with the announcement.

We make a plan for the shots, then Annabel hurries over with the results envelope and hands it to Tori.

'They definitely all voted?' Tori asks, taking it.

'Except John,' Annabel says. 'Should I go down and—'

'No,' Tori and I tell her as one.

'We'll edit around it,' I add, though how I'm going to do that now is anyone's guess.

Annabel lowers her voice, her eyes darting over to where Wolf sits with his back to us. 'Wolf, um, did offer me some work when we get home.'

Tori brings her chin in. 'What does that mean?'

'What do you think it means?' I say, polishing the lens. 'He's trying to bribe her to throw the vote. He knows he's fucked.' Then, to Annabel, 'I mean, he *is* fucked, right?'

'I'd certainly think so, after that performance in the hole,' Tori says. 'Ah, here's Craig. We ready?'

Tori waits for me to shoulder the camera, then faces the room and claps her hands.

'Can I have your attention, please?'

It's no surprise to anyone that the contestant with the greatest number of votes is Helen. Sincere-sounding congratulations echo all round the room. She gets up to accept the air-kisses from Tori. It'll edit together beautifully, not least because it's a hell of a transformation: only a few hours ago she was a mottled blue and shivering in a towel and a foil blanket, and here she is now, hair blow-dried and immaculately made up.

Annabel is on second camera, picking up close-ups and cut-aways to blend into my wides. Once the applause has died down, Helen takes her seat again, and Tori lifts her chin and beams at the group, a small gesture that magically silences them. That power she has. That silent force of manipulation. Does she even think about it? Does she even realise what she's got – this ability to hold a roomful of people in the palm of her hand?

'But as you all know,' she says, head tilted in sympathy, 'sadly, when there's a winner, there also has to be a loser. The good news is that whoever receives the most votes for the least-strong performance,' she says, over-diplomatically avoiding using the word *weak*, 'doesn't actually have to leave us, because, well, we're not that many degrees south of the Pole and the only way to get to civilisation right now is by hitching a lift on an iceberg.' She pauses to beam into the mild ripple of nervous laughter.

'But the *Frozen Out* rules say that whoever's the least-popular leader among you is out of the competition. And in here, I have the name of that person.'

She taps the envelope. I look up briefly to indicate to Annabel to switch to the wide shot, then I go close on Wolf.

Tori clears her throat. 'So, without further ado, I have the unfortunate task now of announcing that our first leader relegated to deckhand is . . .'

She makes a big show of anticipation. I go for a medium close-up, shoulders to crown, Wolf's once-chiselled jaw now softened by the first pull of age. For a moment his eyelids flutter shut and then he looks up at her, a canine pleading across his forehead. And I see in his concern the faintest shadow of weakness, of the fear of exposure. He knows how badly the challenge went. He knows how much of a fool he was made to look. And now he sees the reckoning coming, and all he wants is to stop it, to make Tori say someone else's name, to cover his shame. In that short moment between not knowing and knowing – even though, deep down, I know he's little more than a beautiful bully, charming and cruel – I feel sorry for him.

'Wolf.'

The moment she says his name, he puts his hands up to concede, polite resignation on his face. The rest of them gather around to commiserate, and I zoom out and cover the reaction shot of the group, who make out like they're devastated for him.

It takes a good few minutes to die down. I get some words of reaction from the winner and the loser, nice and tight, with the movement of the rest of them in soft focus in the background. The shots are great, everyone smiling; Wolf does a good line in gracious defeat.

But the moment I hit Stop and call it a wrap for the night, he changes. Crossing the room, he's in Tori's face like a shot.

'Tell me you're fucking joking!'

For the briefest of moments it's clear Tori is thinking, or hoping, that his fury is a wind-up.

It's a misstep shared by Marco, standing close by, who snorts his amusement.

'Something funny?' Wolf says.

'Oh, no, sorry, mate.' I've never seen a man's expression change so quickly.

'Didn't think so.'

'Fucking prick,' Marco mutters under his breath, but not low enough that Wolf doesn't hear.

I quickly step in.

'Wolf, look, it's just a vote. One vote each, for the strongest and the weakest. It's that simple. We can't swing it.'

He glares at me, his eyes dangerous. 'I'm not fucking going out on day one. No fucking way.'

'It's a democratic process,' Tori tells him in a low voice.

He turns to the group. Gaia, expressionless, happens to meet his eye first.

'You?' he says to her. 'You voted me out?'

'I wasn't convinced you gave the best performance, if that's what you're asking.'

'So that's a yes, then.'

Gaia walks out of the room without a word. Helen delicately places her near-full wine glass on the table, smooths her hair and goes to follow her. She avoids Wolf's gaze entirely, but as she passes, Tori puts out a beseeching hand for her to stay. 'Helen, please.'

She dodges it, but pauses in the doorway. 'It's not all right for him to talk to her like that,' she says. Then, from the door, she looks Wolf up and down. 'The drinking and the anger are probably the same thing, you know.'

'Oh yeah?' he scoffs, curling his lip. 'What the fuck's that got to do with you?'

The sinews of his neck flex, his nostrils flaring like a silverback's. In the pause, Helen nods once, as if an irrevocable decision has been made, then leaves the room, too.

'Yeah, you run away. You frosty old witch.'

'That'll do,' Tori tells him softly, touching his arm. It's like she's skipped anger and gone straight to damage limitation.

But he wrenches his arm away. 'You tell me what to do one more fucking time and I swear to God, I'll—'

'You'll what?' Tori stays exactly where she is. She tilts her head. 'Hmm?'

Wolf stalks from the room, slamming the door behind him.

Tori slumps into a chair. 'Well, fuck,' she says. It's possibly the first time I've ever heard her swear in front of other people.

Clipping the camera into its bag, I can't say I don't share her sentiment. Drama is fine. Conflict is great. But once you get into the territory of a contestant making threats against the presenter, it crosses a line. You can't go back from there.

One of the people whose safety we were responsible for is dead. Tori could have been killed. Wolf, the star contestant, has all but gone rogue.

And we're only two days in.

21

TORI

I've barely taken my make-up off when there's a knock on my cabin door. Dee, obviously, and she ducks straight past me.

'Come in, make yourself at home,' I tell her.

But she doesn't sit down. With the door closed behind me, she gets straight to the point.

'I think we should abandon the show. No, don't laugh, I'm serious. I don't think we're safe here.'

I fold my arms. 'Dee, come on. Take a breath.'

'One, we've got a dead contestant.' She holds up a thumb, then a finger. 'Two, whatever happened to you last night – and don't say again that you slipped,' she says, holding up the whole hand now to silence me, 'because we're clearly not going to agree on it. But coupled with this? I think we seriously need to be considering that we've got a very major problem here.'

Her assessment hangs there between us for a moment, staring like a spectre.

'I'm asking you to leave it,' I say at last.

She comes to sit beside me and takes my hand. And for a moment I smile until I realise, with a pang of sadness, that we haven't had a close moment like this in so long.

'Listen,' she goes on. 'I know this show is your whole life, right? I know how much you've put into it. But John is *dead*, Tori. I don't see how we can salvage it.'

There's a double knock on the door, and my name, whispered. It's Annabel.

Her eyes are wide as she comes in, shutting the door quietly behind her with a click.

'He's *dead*? John?'

'Anyone ever tell you it's rude to eavesdrop?' Dee says.

'When were you going to tell me?'

Dee gets up. 'Sorry. You weren't exactly a priority.'

'Guys, for heaven's sake,' I say. 'Annabel, I'm sorry we didn't tell you straight away. We're trying to work out what to do next. We'll see what the police say—'

Dee throws her hands in the air. 'We need to get down to Nuuk, get home, and let the insurance take care of it. No one's going to broadcast this now!'

I think of all those late nights with Will, hunched over our desks. Dinners uneaten. Bed cold. Debts creeping up, darkening our every conversation like shadows climbing the walls. Panic revs like an engine at the thought of going back without a show to edit. Without a way of paying back the loans. 'We have to make it work,' I tell her.

'Why? For your company? So that Tori Tells fucking Stories gets to save face?'

'Is that such a crime?'

Dee shakes her head. 'Wow. So that's your priority: your career? Are you serious right now?'

'Can I say something?' Annabel says. 'I think we have to

keep going. The money's been spent. We've promised the network.'

'Oh! Right, I see,' Dee says bitterly. 'So you're only thinking about your own career, too. I thought this was about leadership, for God's sake, not balls-out self-interest!'

Annabel looks like she's been punched.

Dee takes the kind of deep breath that people take when they're trying not to lose their shit. 'We are in danger here. Last night someone tries to throw you to your death, now this.'

'No one threw me anywhere! And this – it's sad, but it's not a *danger*.'

Dee throws me a look. 'You seem to be very sure about this.'

I let my head drop back. 'Can we not try to be optimistic here?'

'Sure, okay. Great plan. Jesus Christ,' Dee says. 'I'm going to the bridge.' And she slams out of the room without another word.

Annabel groans as the door hits its frame. 'Oh my God, what are we going to do?'

I go over and give her shoulder a sympathetic squeeze. I have to keep her onside – even more so now that Dee's being so difficult. 'Don't let her pessimism rub off on you. I can't cope with both of you being like that.'

'And what have I done to her?' Annabel wraps her arms around her torso. 'I've been trying and trying to get to know her, but she's horrible to me. Why is she like that?'

The answer is: I don't know. She's never been cuddly exactly, but she used to be kind, and a steadfast friend. It was Dee who dropped everything when Wolf and I split up; Dee who once even refused to take a DoP job because the presenter she'd have been working with was someone who'd used a racial slur against me years before. When she started her last investigation, something in Bath about falsifying coursework in schools, there was a period when she could have passed for bubbly even – demanding picnics, taking me rowing on the Serpentine one evening. Then the job ended abruptly, and it was like she hauled up the drawbridge.

'She's even like it with you,' Annabel is saying. 'I don't want to speak out of turn, but it's your company, isn't it? I thought you were supposed to be in charge.'

'I am in charge.' And don't I know it. If the show goes to shit, it's on my shoulders. I even let Will convince me to name the company after myself. What was I thinking?

'But Dee's—'

'Just do your job, all right?'

Annabel nods, hurt, and hurries from the room.

I listen to her footsteps retreat. And once I'm sure she won't be able to hear me, I lie face-down on my bed, clamp a pillow to my face and scream.

I run to catch up with Dee as she's entering the bridge. Inside, Eino and Stefan are locked in urgent conversation, which dies a sudden death the moment we're noticed.

'We were discussing the best course of action,' Eino says. 'I spoke to the police.'

'Before you go into that,' Dee replies, 'I need to ask you about access to the bedrooms – the cabins. Who might have gone in and out of them at different times.'

He blinks. 'I do not have that information.'

Dee glares at him. 'No? Kind of convenient.'

'I'm sorry?'

'Starting to look like you have something to hide, that's all.'

He says nothing.

'We need to know who could have accessed cabin two, where John died, before we came on board. Do you have a record of that?'

'No. This is not a prison.'

Dee is running out of patience. 'But were the doors locked before we boarded?'

'After the cabins were cleaned, yes.'

'And what about the keycards, how do they work? They're electronic, so is there a record of who uses each one, and when?'

'It sounds as if you are suspicious of the other guests. And the crew.'

'Can you answer the question, please?'

Eino gives a single shake of his head. 'No. As I understand it, they simply unlock the specific door they are programmed to unlock. No records.'

'As you understand it?'

'The system is new. Installed weeks ago, for your programme. We know the basics, but it's not critical equipment.'

'So we have no way of knowing *when* a cabin door was last unlocked even?'

Eino regards her. 'The dead man had no injuries, and yet you are asking questions as if you suspect he was killed.'

'Is that a no?'

'We don't record when the doors are opened. No.' He clears his throat and goes back to the console, clearly having lost interest in us.

I change tack, and gesture towards the radio unit on his console. 'You were saying the police have been called?'

'Yes. They advised us to move the body to the hold, where the temperature is low and stable.'

'Right. And then?'

'We are to alert them when we return to port. They request that we do this as soon as we are able to.'

'They're not coming?' Exactly as Craig predicted.

'No. They cannot change a man's death. Now, if you'll excuse me.'

Dee turns on her heel and leaves.

I try to sleep, but the ship is an orchestra, even in the middle of the night. It creaks and complains while an endless series of bumps make their way from one end to the other, hunks of ice bouncing against us. Or maybe it's worse than that: some crucial piece of equipment coming loose and being swept out, lost for ever.

Or maybe it's just Dee's negativity, finally starting to get under my skin.

I know why she's so worried. And I wish I could tell her why everything's all right now. But if I even give her a thread of it, she'll pull and pull and it will all unravel. And I can't risk that, not after all this time.

I check the time: 2.49 a.m. Rolling onto my back, I give up on sleep. I watch strands of reflected moonlight dance on the ceiling, crazed like the surface of an antique plate. I concentrate hard, but I last only seconds. The draw of the wardrobe door is too strong, and seconds later I'm lying on my side again, staring at it, sensing the suitcase behind it and, past its lid, the little ball of crumpled envelope and the paper inside, glowing there like a red-hot ember.

One sheet of paper, torn from a spiral pad. Weighing less than a teaspoon of rice. Barely enough to wrap a book, or write a shopping list, or fuel a flame for more than a few seconds.

I push off the covers and retrieve the letter, taking it back to bed with me. It's soft from being folded and unfolded so many times, but in the months I've had it in my possession, all it's done is grow sharper, spiking into my thoughts like that shard of mirror in *The Snow Queen*. Destroying the paper would have been as futile as tearing up a parking ticket. The words had already gained all their power. It's merely my receipt. But now I no longer need to fear the person who sent it to me, it doesn't hurt any more.

I open the porthole again, but this time, when I hold my fist out into the freezing wind, it opens as easily as a rose in summer. I watch the tiny scrap of paper fly off, whirling high out to sea. Disappearing.

22

DEE

I wake early, smarting with purpose. If Tori wants to keep going and pretend everything's fine, I think, as I take the steps of the companionway two at a time, that's her call. She can surround herself with yes-people, put another coat of lipstick on and plough ahead. That's fine. Maybe the world needs people like that.

But if she wants people who'll blindly do whatever she says, without stopping to ask the obvious questions, she shouldn't have hired an investigative journalist.

What I need to do now is go down to cabin two, the room where John died. Properly search it, see if there's anything we missed that might have contributed to what happened.

First stop is the saloon. There's a first-aid kit there that will probably have latex gloves. I tread quietly, so as to not wake anyone, but when I slide the door open, Annabel is already there.

'You're up early,' I say, going over to the green medical kit on the wall and taking it down. I pull out a packet of gloves and slip them into my pocket.

'Couldn't sleep,' she says, sitting up and putting her book

on the table. 'Couldn't stop thinking about poor John. How about you?'

A pang of shame – our last exchange involved me being dismissive, and here she is asking after my well-being. I'm about to apologise, but then I realise what it is that she's been reading.

'Oh, this?' Annabel says, following my eyeline. She picks it up – it's *Lady Sings the Blues*, Billie Holiday's autobiography – and passes it to me. 'You a fan? Have a look. You want some coffee?'

She goes over to flick on the kettle, and I slide the book over. But I don't open it. The answer to her question is: no. I'm not a jazz fan at all. I don't understand the rhythms of it, the disjointedness. But Leo was. And this was his favourite book.

She comes back and puts a mug on the table in front of me. 'You can borrow it if you like. I'm finding it a bit hard going.'

'Not really my thing. But thanks.' I pick up the mug and turn to go.

'Me neither! But this boy lent it to me, so . . .'

'Oh, right,' I say blandly, but she mistakes my comment for interest.

'Yeah. I mean, it's not going anywhere, I don't think. I'm not really girlfriend material.'

'I don't know. Good-looking, great job, you're . . .' I wave a hand, 'fun to be around.'

Annabel gives me a look, and then we both laugh.

'Sorry,' I say. 'Not a great one for small talk.'

'No. You're not.' It's not meant unkindly. Then, unbidden, she says, 'It's that . . . guys my age, you know? It can all feel so superficial.'

'You like an older man then,' I say, and her smile shifts. 'What?'

She wraps her hands around her mug, gives a little shake of her head. 'Doesn't matter.'

'Got it.'

'It's a bit complicated,' she says.

I realise I'm going to hear the story anyway, so I sit down. 'Do you want to talk about it?'

She lets out a long sigh. 'A little while ago there was someone I was – you know, romantic with.'

'Right.'

'It was a really difficult time. I'd left home, come to London, didn't know anyone. And he was, easy, you know? Like some people are immediately really comfortable to be around. Safe. I mean, I still took it slowly, because I thought he was out of my league a bit. He was older, like you said. We'd been seeing each other for a while.'

'How much older are we talking?'

'More than . . . well, quite a lot. He was so cultured, you know? Gorgeous,' she says with a sad laugh.

I nod, but all I can think of is Leo. The way he wrapped me up – the solidity of him. His hands running across the keys of his piano. The shape of his shoulders under his shirts, the droplets of water sliding off his skin when he swam. The deep, soft tenor of his voice. Even now the thought of him thrums, a delicious ache.

'And I wanted to be part of his life, like so, so much,' she says. 'I really thought he felt the same.'

'You're going to tell me he was married, right?'

She shakes her head. 'No. There was someone else, but no, not married.'

'So what happened?'

She shrugs. 'He just dropped off the planet.'

'He ghosted you?'

'I was stupid, expecting anything else.'

'Doesn't sound like you were in the wrong here.'

'Naive, then. Like, I gave my entire heart. Have you ever done that? Like emptied yourself out completely? The problem was that I expected the same in return.'

We drink our coffee. I could tell her about it, I realise. She barely knows me, she certainly doesn't know *him*: I could trust her, open up. A problem shared.

But there aren't words for it. *Grief* doesn't come close. There isn't a description for the intense, bone-deep guilt. It would be like trying to explain colour to someone born without eyes.

Leo has been gone for months. That immediate tsunami of loss has died down into these constant, countless little waves. But what stays with me now is the injustice of it. I would have done anything for those last few moments. Even in the bloodstained horror of the mangled metal and flashing lights and that driving barrage of rain – I wanted to be there. Just to share those very last seconds.

Outside, snow falls like static. Annabel keeps taking these little breaths like she's about to tell me something else, but it never happens.

I finish my coffee and stand up. 'I need to get going.'

The passageways are silent, apart from the tick of the radiators battling the fierce cold outside. But before I get to cabin two,

I have to take a step back to let Stefan pass. He nods without looking at me and hurries away, almost dropping his toolbox in his haste.

'No problem,' I mutter to his back.

I pause outside Wolf's cabin, but it's silent inside. Opposite his cabin is the one that Tori swapped with John. The door is still ajar, the keybox already mended after I broke my way in earlier. Taking a breath, I go inside, switch on the light and close the door behind me.

It's bigger than the other cabins, maybe twelve, fourteen feet in both directions. A faintly familiar smell hangs in the air. Someone has closed the window since I was in here last, but the room is freezing. I touch both heating units, one squat and old, the other a shiny, much newer slab almost flush against the wall. They're both cold. The bed has been stripped right down, but the book and John's glasses are still there next to it. Nothing else of his; no comforts, no photos of anyone he loved.

The rucksack, the one that was next to the bedside table, is gone.

Maybe someone moved it? Put it away in a cupboard? I open the packet under my arm and find the clinical gloves. I snap them on, then get to work.

The double wardrobe contains a scarlet ship-issue weather-proof jacket-and-trousers set and half a dozen dresses. In the narrow chest of drawers beside it I find Tori's hairdryer, a few books, shoes, charging cables. Everything else she'd managed to manhandle into her suitcases when I swapped her room the previous night. I close the door and go into the cupboard-sized en suite, which is entirely empty.

Disappointed, annoyed even, I get onto all fours to see if I've missed anything else under the bed. But there's nothing: some pipework, a fair amount of dust right at the back, but nothing else.

Flat on my front, I shuffle back out from under the bed. I go to stand, but before I do so, I spot it.

I can only see it because my eye level is so low. Under the short, older radiator – which Eino warned us not to touch when we first boarded – a section of the metal pipe running from the base to the bulkhead is . . . incongruous. A couple of inches of bright, new copper, spliced into the older tube with sparkling new solder.

I lie on my side, getting right up close. The rest of the pipe has a thick, ancient layer of dust and grime on top of it. But when I touch the chrome-coloured solder on the new section, it's still hot. It's then that I recognise the smell: it's flux, used to help solder to adhere. I use it when I build undercover rigs.

I bring my hand away, heart hammering, thinking: Stefan. How eager he was to get past me, not looking me in the eye.

Then I see the little pedal bin under the desk. There's a corner of blue paper hanging out of it: that heavy-duty industrial tissue. I tip the contents out onto the floor. More of the paper, smeared with black grease and flux, the sort of detritus you'd expect from plumbing work. And a small piece of copper pipe, the thickness of my little finger. It's a couple of inches long, its ends neatly severed, but with a ragged cut in the middle. I run my thumb over it and it snags: it's been bitten through by some kind of cutter, compressing it slightly before it was wrenched open.

I take it to the radiator, get back down on the floor. This

damaged piece is the exact size of the new, shiny section: it's been removed and replaced.

But that isn't all, is it? I rock back on my heels. I realise what this room is, what it could be. That's a fire door, sealing the room from the passage beyond. Over there, a window built in the Russian High Arctic that will keep out the weather in one of the coldest places on Earth. This is a cabin that can be sealed, absolutely, from the passage outside.

Except that means it's not just a cabin.

It's a gas chamber.

23

DEE

I stop only to get my coat, then I go out into the biting cold.

Fat gobs of snow are falling from miles and miles of unbroken cloud, melting instantly on my face, the threat of the storm still hanging over us. Gripping the grab-rail, I go around the superstructure of the ship until I come to the aft deck and crouch by the hatch to the hold. It's marked with something in a language I can't read – Finnish, I'm assuming. It probably says *No entry*.

It's not locked. I heave it open, climb down, then pull it shut after me. At the bottom of the steep steps I find the light switch and flick it on, thinking of only one thing.

Eino's response in the cabin, when we first discovered John dead. How the first thing he did was open the window.

He knew.

And I'm fairly sure I know how.

The hold is painted a bright white. There are a few feet of open standing room ahead of the entrance, but then it narrows to a central passageway between two banks of floor-to-ceiling cages that run towards the prow. Cases and crates line the walls, but I find what I'm looking for in a matter of seconds.

A moulded plastic stretcher on a shelf at waist height, on top of which lies a long, shrouded object. John's body.

It takes some heaving, but I pull it out by about a foot. I don't need to see everything, but I need to be sure. From a side pocket of my cargo pants I get out my Swiss Army knife and start to cut.

Soon the shroud hangs on either side of his shoulders. There's a slackness to his skin that makes him look unreal, like a model. His eyes are still open. I inhale sharply and quickly place my index and middle fingers on his eyelids, before I can spook myself out of it. The skin feels uncannily rubbery, and though it catches slightly on the drying eyeball, I get the lids closed.

I need to see more of his skin. I start cutting the fabric of his T-shirt, following the line of the side seam. I snip through millimetres at a time: the slightest nick to his skin will be picked up when he finally gets a proper autopsy. But although my eyes are on the job, my mind is elsewhere.

Three years ago I worked on an investigation into a series of deaths at an oil plant. It wasn't a ship, but the principle was the same. An old heating system was replaced around the same time the deaths occurred. I found that the main reason systems like those need upgrading is because they're run straight off an engine – and when you're pumping hot gases around living quarters, sometimes they can leak out.

The deaths were eventually attributed to carbon monoxide. The silent killer. And carbon monoxide, as it turns out, has some quite distinctive signs, post-mortem.

My skin tightens with the cold. When I've made a cut of

maybe eight inches I put the scissors away, steel myself and open the fabric.

I exhale and take it in. The proof I was looking for.

The process of livor mortis has pooled the blood at the lowest points of John's body. But where it would usually be the colour of a dark bruise, here it's a vivid red. All the way down his back, the backs of his arms and – if I chose to look – presumably his buttocks and the backs of his legs too. It's the kind of cherry colour you might see on a person of limited fitness who'd recently exerted themselves. Except that John has been dead for hours.

The death of this otherwise healthy man was down to that damaged pipe in the cabin.

But John wasn't even meant to be in that room. He swapped in the middle of the night, so it follows that he wasn't the target.

I wasn't imagining what I saw on that first night. Someone on this ship wants Tori dead.

24

TORI

Dee doesn't show at breakfast. After I've finished, I knock for her, but there's no answer. She's not in the saloon or the production office. When I open the door to the bridge, Eino is bringing the ship about, following the headland through ice-strewn water. The expanse between the towering cliffs to the north and south of the fjord is frozen solid.

Craig comes in behind me. 'Sleep well?'

I make a face – I slept fine, but what he's asking is whether I could sleep under the circumstances, and there's only one acceptable answer to that.

'Me neither.' He lets out a long breath and shakes his head. 'Poor guy.' After a moment, he shows me a printout. 'The storm's passed just north of us,' Craig says. 'We were lucky, frankly – looks bad.'

His hands on the wheel, Eino looks back over his shoulder. 'We are not, as you say, out of the woods. Look.' He indicates something blotchy on a screen and Craig lets out a low whistle.

'That'll be what, a couple of days?'

Eino makes a non-committal face.

To me, Craig says, 'This might be a problem. Tomorrow,

tomorrow night.' He explains about the pressure, the weather that may or may not cut underneath us as we head south.

'But that's after we get this challenge out of the way, right?' I say, with an optimism I'm struggling to feel.

Eino points to a spot above the ragged peaks, and Craig raises his binoculars.

'Ah. Guides are here.'

He gives me a look and I see two helicopters, one ahead of the other, coming in from the east.

'They hate doing this, you know. Much better to see them in their own environment. Would have made the challenge so much—'

'More authentic. Yes. I know, Craig. We went over it.' In the planning phase he made it very clear how unhappy he was with the amount of carbon the trip was going to burn, many times. But today's challenge didn't fit in the schedule anywhere else. Flying the experts up to meet us was the only option.

As he takes the binoculars back, Dee comes in, flushed and out of breath. 'Can I have a word? Both of you?'

We follow her out and pass Annabel on the companionway. 'What's happening?' I ask, trying to keep up with her. 'Slow down! What's going on?'

'Come with me,' Dee says, leading us down to the lower deck. She digs in the pockets of her combats and passes us each a packet.

'Latex gloves,' she says, snapping her own onto her hands.

'Can this wait?' Craig asks her. 'Our guides for the challenge are nearly here.'

'Put them on, all right?'

She ushers us into cabin two and pushes the door shut behind us.

'We've got a situation. Look.' She crouches down and points to the base of one of the two heating units set against the wall. 'Under there. What do you see?'

Annabel gets on her knees and peers right in.

'I went back to check John's body,' Dee says to me and Craig. 'Turns out there was something quite important that we missed.'

'What am I looking at?' Annabel asks from the floor.

But Craig folds his arms, the muscles at his jaw tensing. 'What? What did we miss?'

Dee glares at him. 'I mean, I say *we*, but really it's you. Because you're the medic, right? You're the one we've paid to look after us. But somehow you missed this.' She takes out her phone, opens the photos.

'Oh good Lord.' I look away, but not in time.

Craig takes the screen from her. 'You see here, and here?' Dee asks him. 'Cherry-red lividity that's called, right? And it's a sign of what?'

Our medic says something inaudible.

'Sorry?' Dee, glowing with anger, inclines her ear to him. 'Say that again?'

Annabel gets back onto her feet. Craig looks away. 'I said, I don't know. I don't know what that is.'

'No. I do, though. I'm not medically trained, but *I* know it's a marker for CO poisoning. Carbon monoxide. And that leads us to two questions. How it happened, and how the fuck anyone with a medical training didn't see it?'

I turn my whole body to Craig. 'Well?'

He meets Dee's eye defiantly. 'What exactly are you accusing me of?'

'Don't waste my time,' she says. 'If you've lied to us, we're obviously going to find out. So which is it? Are you incompetent? Or is it worse than that?'

He swallows. 'I needed the job.'

'Tell me you're joking,' I say.

'He's not joking.' Dee laughs, a note of mania in it. 'You're not qualified. Oh my actual God.'

I look at the ceiling, close my eyes. 'Explain.'

'I was training as a paramedic. I didn't finish.'

I look at Annabel. She might be timid, but she's a powerhouse when it comes to research. 'Did you know?'

She presses her lips between her teeth, doesn't know where to look.

'She knew,' Dee says.

'I told Will,' Annabel says pleadingly. 'I checked with the professional body, and Craig wasn't registered and I told Will that. But he said he'd look into it, that I didn't need to worry. I did ask to see Craig's credentials, but he just brushed me off. Said it was fine, that it was different in Greenland . . .' She trails off.

'Yeah, well, he was certainly right about that,' Dee says.

I don't know what to feel more horrified by: Craig's deception or Will's. He's my fiancé. How could he lie about that to me?

'I did a full year,' Craig says to the floor. His voice is wavering, quiet, nothing like his own. 'And then my parents died. They'd been subsidising everything, but it turned out they were in a lot of debt. I couldn't afford to carry on. So I found a job with a corporate excursions company, and they wanted a guide out here. And they'd seen I'd done paramedic training and assumed I was properly qualified. I didn't correct it.'

'But that's as good as lying to our faces. You know that, right?'

'Yes,' he says, unable to meet my eye. 'I do.'

We're days from the nearest hospital, in one of the most dangerous environments on the planet, and our only medic is a dropout with barely a first-aid certificate. When I open my eyes again, Dee's staring right at me.

'But that's not all. He was also fine to use his bogus medical expertise to imply that I'd *imagined* seeing someone push you, Tori. No, let me finish – and then he, what, doesn't see, or doesn't want to admit, that the man who died in this room died from CO poisoning. Why would that be, Craig?'

'I don't know what you're talking about.'

Dee points again to the radiator. 'There's a fresh piece of pipe there,' she says. 'Stefan did it this morning. It was still hot from the solder – one little piece that was brand-new. He'd fixed it because someone had broken it. The broken piece that he'd removed was in the bin – it had a hole in it.' But when she digs in her pockets, she frowns. 'Fuck. It was right here . . .'

I get down low while she pats down her cargo pants. 'What am I meant to be seeing?'

'There,' she says, pointing to a section of newer piping. 'They've mended it.' She gets back up. 'Listen, someone knew that cutting a pipe under there was going to fill this room with gas. Look, come out here.'

We follow her out to the passage, where Dee opens the door of a narrow cupboard, a few feet up the passageway.

'Tool cupboard. Unlocked,' she says, reaching in and bringing out an old-fashioned cantilevered toolbox. 'First thing you see when you open it.'

When she flips open the lid, there on the top is a pair of pliers.

She turns to face me. 'What happened to John was supposed to happen to you.'

'But the pipe's fine, Dee,' I say gently.

'I'm telling you, the broken bit I found had been wrenched open. There was a gash in it. And it was meant to be your cabin. You do understand the gravity of that, right? And . . . *and* the bag of John's that was here earlier is gone. Why? Who's taken it, huh?'

Craig gives a heavy sigh and checks his watch.

'Look, there's no way we can know, is there? Whether it's misadventure or what. None of us is going to prove anything, one way or another, anyway. And right now we've got two helicopters out there, wondering where the hell we are. So are we going to go out there and do the challenge, or are we not?'

'No, obviously not, because this is slightly more important.' Dee's stare burns right through me. 'I want to get a message to Will and tell him we're coming back.'

I won't, *can't* show her that this is exactly what I want to do. To get him on the phone and ask him exactly what he was thinking, sending me into one of the most dangerous places on the planet without proper support. But what's he going to say? Would an apology make any difference?

If we turn back now, I'll have nothing to go home to.

So I fold my arms. 'No. Nothing's changed. If we want to get paid, we have to keep going.'

Dee shakes her head, incredulous. 'I'm telling you there is a killer on this ship, and they meant to kill *you*. And you're fine with that?'

While I search for the answer, her patience runs out.

'Right then!' she says, bright with sarcasm. 'Let's get on with the morning and hope no one else gets murdered, shall we?'

She walks away, followed by Annabel and Craig. I wait until they're gone, then I lean against the wall, defeated. From out of my pocket, I bring the tiny piece of metal that Dee must have dropped and turn it over in my hand.

It's one thing pretending that I fell on the first night. It's quite another hiding vital evidence that could prove someone tried to gas me to death, and in the process killed . . . *him*.

But if Dee's right, and this piece of metal could help prove an attempt on my life, what happens next? An investigation. Detectives swarming over every moment of my life. Of my past.

Not to mention the end of *Frozen Out*. Defaulting on debts that I'd barely be able to pay back even if the show was a resounding success. So – the end of my company. The end of my career.

Running my thumb over the jagged edge, I know what I have to do. I push the little piece of metal into the inside pocket of my coat and I zip it up, and I'll never tell a soul.

25

DEE

The morning is clear and brutishly cold as Eino steers us alongside the ice. Fizzing with rage, I go outside, allowing myself a single cigarette to get my head straight, ignoring the ban on smoking on deck. Leo hated them, refused to let me smoke anywhere near him. His dad had died of lung cancer when Leo was still a kid. He'd thought it was the worst thing that could happen to a person at the time, he said; but that was before his mum got ill. The cigarette halfway to my lips, the thought of his mother stutters. Her disoriented bafflement at his funeral, clinging on to her surviving child, Leo's sister, like a drowning woman.

All he wanted was to buy her some dignity, at the end, and I took that away.

I grind the butt under my toe and blow out the last lungful in a single jet. A slate-grey sky hangs like a threat over the eye-aching landscape, white and black and unapologetic.

If we want to get paid, Tori said.

It's the only reason I'm here. It was the only reason Leo got mixed up in coursework fraud – because he couldn't afford the care his mum needed. And I can't bring Leo back from the dead, but I can make good on his promise. So until I hit the figure he needed, I'm saving every single penny: from every pay cheque, every bit of revenue from letting out my flat, everything.

The engines drop to a quiet hum and Stefan appears on the lower deck to run out a gangplank onto the sheet. I take the kit down onto the ice and start checking it over. A shadow falls over me and I look up.

'Shall we clear the air?' Tori says, standing beside a shame-faced Craig, who's obviously already been briefed. 'Before we start?'

I screw the lens into the body of the camera and snap off the lens cap. 'Is there a choice?'

She sighs. 'Craig's totally equipped to do what we need him to, in terms of accidents and injuries, right?' she says, turning to him.

Craig clears his throat. 'I'm fine with accidents, injuries, anything you're going to encounter out here involving water, frostbite, any of that—'

I give him a look. 'Except being murdered.'

He gives a curt nod, but he doesn't have an answer.

'Everything is already in place for the challenge today,' Tori says, glancing behind her as the contestants start to climb down from the ship. 'We can make a decision on how to proceed this evening, when we have some time to think.'

I look from her to Craig and back again. 'So we're pretending that John's – what, having a long shower?'

She doesn't grace that with an answer. 'Let's get through the day, yeah?'

Then she walks over to the group. Back in character.

'Everyone, can we have a word?' she calls out, and they all gather round.

I prep the camera and listen in.

'So as you'll notice, I'm afraid John's not feeling any better today. We're obviously not now going to be able to edit around it, so the show is going to be just you five from now on.'

Nish wraps her arms around herself. 'What's wrong with him, though?'

'Possibly food poisoning, but everyone else is well, so we don't know.' Tori is the very definition of quiet concern.

'This doesn't feel right,' Gaia says. She looks at the others. 'Don't you think? Isn't it a bit wrong to carry on like everything's fine?'

'It's either that or forget the money,' Marco says. Then, after a beat, 'I mean, I know we'd all want to pledge some of the winnings to his family or something.'

There's a muted chorus of agreement, except for Gaia, who remains impassive.

'Today's going to be fun,' Tori assures them. Then, calling over to me, 'Are we ready?'

I do what I'm paid to do and frame up. 'Speed,' I tell her flatly.

'Marco, leave those!' She waves Wolf over, pointing to a pile of what look like insulated bags, brought down by Stefan. 'Lunch for everyone, deckhand!'

There's a fraction of a second of hostility before Wolf glances at me. Eye to the eyepiece, I twirl a finger in the air, the universal sign for *camera rolling*. With a miraculously fast change of mood, he laughs good-naturedly and goes over to heave the bags onto the waiting sled.

Marco slaps him on the back as he passes. 'I'll get you a pinny, shall I, mate?'

Without looking up, Wolf extends a foot. Marco trips, tries and fails to correct it and lands on his face. He's barely hit the ground before he's up again, rounding on me. 'Delete that,' he says, indicating the camera.

'I'm not deleting anything.'

He comes right up in my face. I smell the fried processed meat of his breakfast. 'Delete. It.'

Annabel appears at my side. 'It was in the contracts, Marco. I'm sorry, but we do have editorial control.' The way she says it, she could have been offering him a piece of bubble gum.

He leans in like he's got something to say, but then his eyes go to the small camera hanging from her hand.

'Oh this?' she says, lifting it. 'This one's rolling, too.'

Marco runs his tongue over his teeth, then shrugs like it's nothing and walks away.

I watch him go. Annabel tucks her blonde hair into a black beanie, the camera clamped between her knees. The lens cap is on.

'You weren't rolling,' I say.

'Oh, yeah. No. Totally lied.' She grins and snaps the viewscreen open.

Impressed, I give her a slap on the back. 'Very nice.'

A little way off, the helicopters have settled on the ice sheet. Craig jogs over to greet them as the men – I assume they're men – unload their gear.

Tori gathers everyone together for a shot we've planned of everyone walking down the ice towards the guides, *Reservoir Dogs* style.

'Great work,' Tori calls, once it's in the bag. 'We'll be starting in five minutes.' She comes over. 'Look okay?'

'Apart from Gaia continuously looking into the lens.' I run the shot back and show her. 'Call me judgemental, but the woman's kind of, weird, hey?'

It's an olive branch, a sticking plaster, and she knows it. 'You're right. You are judgemental,' she says, smiling. 'It's a horrible flaw.'

'It's not a flaw, it's a *personality*. Who would I be otherwise?'

She smiles, but not all the way, then moves off to speak to Nish and Gaia. I watch them for a moment – Nish's studied earnestness, Gaia's awkward reluctance, both of them utterly fixed on Tori. Off towards the ship, Wolf finishes his job, evidently furious, but then suddenly he's smiling. He stretches languorously, takes his mirrored wraparounds off and perches them on his glossy hair – then I realise he's seen Annabel shooting in his direction.

I scan for Marco and find him apart from the others, struggling with the zip of his too-small outersuit. He glances over at Tori when she throws back her head to laugh at whatever Nish has just said. Maybe it's that he's squinting against the light, but something crosses his face. Irritation? Loathing even?

Someone among these people has the answers. But it could be any of them.

And I can't protect Tori if she won't even accept that she's in danger.

26

TORI

It's Nish who first hears the noise. She squints over across the ice sheet to where the helicopters have landed, maybe a quarter of a mile away, shielding her eyes against the sun.

'Is that . . . a dog?'

'That's a whole fucking load of dogs,' Marco says with excitement. 'Huskies? Is that the challenge?'

Dee moves across us all, picking up the reaction, then pans to where Craig and the guides are approaching.

'Dogs and sleds,' Helen says, happiness creeping across her face. 'Now here's something I can get into.'

A few minutes later and they're with us. Alongside Craig is a Greenlander in his sixties and a young woman of about twenty-five, and maybe two dozen huskies, powerful-looking, but also cute as hell, rolling in the snow.

Craig claps the older man on the back. 'Everyone, this is Pamuk. He's lived here his whole life.'

Pamuk nods, smiling. Wolf strides over and shakes him by the hand, then everyone else follows suit. Pamuk's weathered face speaks of a life outside. He's dressed in a light-coloured coat and a black beanie hat with a sportswear logo. His calf-length trousers appear to be made of animal fur.

He registers Marco's interest and gestures to his thighs. 'Good, yes? Warm.' Without waiting for an answer, Pamuk grasps Marco's hand and pulls it towards his own leg, pressing it into the fur, saying something to him in what I take to be the local language. I make a note to speak to Annabel about logging the footage and getting Craig in to translate, for the subtitles.

'Polar bear,' Craig says as Marco extricates himself, laughing but awkward. 'Killed it himself right down there. Over there, Pamuk?' he repeats, gesturing to the open ice fjord beyond and miming a shotgun.

Pamuk laughs, and Nish visibly recoils. Gaia shoots daggers at the men, but says nothing.

Then Craig gestures to the woman. 'This is Anju – Pamuk's daughter.' She's dressed in furs much like her father, with a heavy synthetic parka on top.

'Nice to meet you all,' she says in impeccable English. 'So today you'll be learning about dog sledding.'

The contestants stand in a horseshoe. Pamuk retreats a little way, connecting ropes to linking rings on the dogs' harnesses, then pulling chunks of what looks like some kind of bloodless meat – animal fat, maybe? – from a sack on one of the sleds and feeding it to them.

While Dee shoots, Anju delivers a crash course in mushing. 'We use the same techniques here that our ancestors used centuries ago.'

Marco looks like he's found God, just looking at her. Even Wolf seems to have cheered up, though it doesn't look like either of them is actually hearing a word she says.

She explains that the traditional Greenlandic mushing

technique is to let the dogs pull as a pack, expressing their own social order.

'Sometimes the hierarchies can shift as the trip goes along. You make a turn and the dog to the right is in the lead for the moment, for example. But in any team there's one constant.' She pauses, mittened hands loosely held together, looking expectantly across the contestants, who glance at each other.

Wolf clears his throat self-importantly. 'The musher?' he offers.

'The musher. Exactly right,' Anju tells him, 'well done. You are a member of the pack. You're the alpha dog, you see?' Then, addressing Wolf specifically, she says, 'Maybe you would like to come and be our first alpha?'

Wolf puffs up. 'Sure thing,' he says.

'Sadly not,' I say. Wolf looks murderous, but I ignore it. 'That's how the competition works, I'm afraid – you'll take part, but you're not competing to win. Anyone else?

All the hands, apart from Gaia's, go up and Anju, unsurprisingly, pounces on exactly that. Gaia shakes her head, but Anju insists. 'Don't be afraid,' she coaxes.

'I'm not *afraid*.'

Anju's gentle smile doesn't shift. 'Great! Who else? How about you,' she says, pointing to Nish.

A light snow starts to fall as Anju gets into the demonstration, which she gives with barely a pause: the commands, voice control, how to hold the ropes, how to turn, how to lean onto the brake-plate to slow.

'Good!' she calls out after a while. 'I think we're ready – it's time for the race!'

175

27

DEE

Craig steps into my shot and I signal to Annabel to get some close ups, while I get wides of the group. But they barely even fill the frame – I'm not even sure I can make this look like a competition.

'We'll be racing in two teams,' Craig calls out. 'Gaia, Helen, Wolf, you're Team A, yes? Nish, Marco, Team B. We've laid a marker all the way back there,' he says, stretching his arm out towards the mouth of the glacier, 'at the half-mile mark. You race all the way up there, you swap mushers, then you come back. I want to see teamwork, control, firm voices.'

If anyone's thinking about the John-shaped hole in this arrangement, they don't show it. I see Tori a little way back, casting an eye over the two groups.

Annabel gets into position by the starting line. 'Whatever you do, keep rolling,' I say to her. 'Don't worry about getting me in shot, I'll cut it out in the edit.'

'Kind of a shame we don't have body-worn cameras for this.' She gives me a bright grin.

I take the camera from my eye. 'What did you say?'

'Body-worn, you know? Like the ones you used for your undercover stuff. So your hands are free.'

Giving the comment a nod, like it's nothing, I remind myself that she doesn't know about Leo, about what happened. Can't know. 'That would make it easier, yes.'

The wind starts to lift the fallen snow. I go over and settle myself at the front end of the smaller team's sled, facing backwards. Nish takes the reins first, standing at the back of the sled with Marco in front of her in a rigid stance.

Anju starts a countdown. Standing back, Pamuk eyes his animals, all standing braced like athletes at the starting block. Annabel quickly steps back and nestles her eye against the viewfinder.

I frame up, hit Record.

And the whistle blows.

Straight away Nish calls out firmly to the dogs and they tear ahead. In my foreground Marco grips his eyes shut and shouts incomprehensibly, which has an immediate effect on the animals. Responding to the extra voice, they lose their synchronisation and suddenly spread out. The sled tips precipitously, but Marco feels it happening and lifts himself to counterbalance.

'Fuck! My fault,' he says, checking behind him that Nish is still on board. The dogs scramble themselves upright and Nish recentres herself.

'Stay quiet!' she shouts back, a savage determination on her face that I haven't seen before. Behind the lens, my first thought is of how I can edit the shot into a sequence about her character arc, once I'm in the cutting room. My second is: what other parts of her personality does she keep hidden?

But before she can restart, the other team flies past, with Gaia gripping hard on the reins. Wolf makes an obscene gesture, and Nish swears under her breath. I grip the seat just in time for Nish to command our dogs again, and this time we stay on track.

The wind streaks past us, wickedly cold, whipping the air from my lungs. Ahead of us, the other team's dogs have hit a rhythm, kicking up clouds of loose snow behind them. We're not far behind. The effort of controlling the animals shows in Nish's face, her teeth clenched hard and her elbows out as she battles the reins. Annabel and the others disappear in the distance.

I swing round for a forward shot as Gaia's woollen hat flies from her head and is whisked away. Up ahead, the marker comes into view – a stout red pole with a pennant at the top. Gaia starts to slow, but too soon, and we gain on her. I twist back to catch the look of pure exhilaration on Marco's face, then tilt up to Nish, who's clearly seen an opportunity. We bank sharply and I realise she's overtaking. We hit the halfway mark several seconds ahead of the others, and Marco and Nish swap places as swiftly as anything.

Marco's already got the reins in his hands by the time Gaia's team comes to a stop. I try to catch it on camera, but we set off again too quickly. My onboard mic picks it up, though – I can clearly hear the other team's dogs sounding anything but calm, and Wolf berating his teammates.

'Get the fuck into position,' he's shouting as Gaia and Helen swap roles. 'What the hell are you doing?'

On our sled, Marco makes a few false starts, but soon we're out in front. Nish calls out encouragement to him, the two of them showing an unexpected fraternity.

I shoot forward for a few seconds, the end coming up three hundred metres away, two-fifty. But then I hear the others. I rotate back, trying to locate them, but in my headphones I hear not Wolf, but Helen, screaming.

'Let go, you maniac! Stop it!'

Marco looks to his right, horrified, then swerves. There's barely time to register what's happening, but then I see it – Wolf has somehow wrestled the reins from Helen and is directing their dog team in a hard left, straight into us.

The impact sends us sprawling. Instinctively wrapping myself around the camera, I hit the frozen ground hard on my shoulder. I get to my feet and stagger over to where the sleds lie on their sides, collided in a heap. Helen is getting up and looking around her, then rushes over to Nish, who's holding on to her ankle and wincing. The noise of the dogs rises to a chaotic pitch, but underneath the barking there's a single, plaintive whine.

Marco advances on Wolf. 'Fuck was that?' he shouts and shoves him hard in the chest.

Wolf staggers back, laughing. 'Come on, big guy, it's only a bit of competition! Or have you forgotten what that's like?'

I jam the camera under my arm and get between them, one arm out. 'Leave it! For Christ's sake!' But then I realise who's missing. 'Where's Gaia?'

I turn in a desperate circle.

'Gaia!'

Then I see her, hurtling across the snow to where the dogs are going berserk. From the other direction, Anju is sprinting towards the animals. 'Leave them! Don't touch them,' she calls.

Either Gaia doesn't hear or she doesn't care. She drops beside the injured animal – the source of the whine – and puts her hand out to soothe it. And in an instant, the whole pack is on her.

28

TORI

Gaia screams like a woman on fire. I catch only flashes of her amid the chaos of canine limbs and jaws and fur, her arms braced around her head, knees up in a foetal ball. Within seconds, everyone is there. Anju and Pamuk run straight in, collaring the two lead dogs and shouting in a harsh staccato of admonition. With the dogs pulled away, Craig clears a space around Gaia. Helen takes Marco out of range of Wolf. Dee stands a way off, trying to console Nish, who's clearly in shock.

I kneel next to Gaia. She's white as a sheet. Craig has stripped some furs off the sleds and has laid her down on them, but she keeps trying to get up. 'The dog,' she's saying, 'is the dog all right?'

'The dog's fine,' I tell her, glancing over to where Anju is sitting beside it. 'They're tough things, you don't need to worry about it. Now tell us where it hurts, Gaia, can you?'

She lifts her hand. There's a puncture wound below the little finger. Blood drips into the snow beside her, but it's clear that it's not badly injured. Craig checks her over carefully. One arm of her jacket is leaking a significant amount of white stuffing, but apart from that, she's miraculously unharmed.

'Thank God for man-made fibres, eh?' he says to her, relief creeping into his voice. 'If that had happened wearing jeans, it would be a very different story. Come on, let's get you back to the ship and clean that hand up, shall we? You good to walk?'

Gaia smiles weakly, nods. Then she sees Wolf and her face crumples. 'What was he doing? He could have killed those animals.'

I put a supportive arm around her shoulder and walk with her like that towards the ship.

Fact of it is, he could have killed *her*. He could have killed any of them.

After a few steps she shrugs me off. 'I'm fine, I can do it.'

Craig nods and I hang back, letting him walk with her. But when she passes Wolf, Gaia breaks away. Before he has time to realise what's happening, she's dropped herself low and tackled him into the ground. His head makes a sickening crack on the ice.

Straddling him, Gaia swings her uninjured arm back and smacks him hard around the face. Hits him again and a third time, before Wolf bucks her off and sends her into the snow.

'You fucking mad bitch,' he shouts at her, ripping off a glove and touching his fingers to the corner of his mouth. They come away red. He advances on her, but then Pamuk is there, pinning Wolf's arms behind him, leading him away.

'*I'm* mad?' she shrieks at his back. 'Me? You're the one ploughing a sled into a group of innocent creatures! Pick on someone your own size, you cunt!'

I run over. 'Take it easy, Gaia.'

'Get your damn hands off me.'

I back off, hands up. 'He's an arsehole, he is. I'm not defending him.'

She eyes me suspiciously, breathing with a primal rage like she's weighing up letting rip. But then she points at me, right up close.

'I was told by your man back home that this would be a professional operation out here. A good way to get some exposure for my charity. Which helps people with addictions care for their *animals,* you understand? Looking after creatures. Not,' she waves a furious hand towards the receding figure of Wolf, 'not *that*. Not endangering them, wilfully.'

'I'll talk to him, all right?'

'No! It's not *all right*! I was told we'd be safe, we'd be looked after. And that's not what's happening.' She turns back to the ship and walks away.

I breathe out slowly, then head over to where Dee is talking to Annabel.

'Can you take them all back, get them some hot drinks?' Dee asks her, and Annabel scurries away. Dee waits until she's gone, then says, 'I talked to Wolf. He basically admits it was a ploy to get himself some more airtime.'

'You're kidding me.'

'Nope. Didn't like being voted out early. It hadn't occurred to him, ahead of coming out here, that he might not be the most popular person in any given group.'

The wind has scoured her cheeks red, but her eyes are fierce.

'I'm sorry I've inflicted him on you,' I tell her.

'What are we going to do with him?'

But if there was an answer to that, we would have found

it by now. We head over to the others, add our voices to the apologies that Craig's making to our horrified guides. He helps them back up to the helicopters, then Dee and I pack up the gear and say goodbye.

The sun is already dropping as we walk back to the ship.

'Craig's doing a good job, though, no?' I say.

'For a medic who's not a medic and doesn't even notice when someone's been murdered, yeah. Not bad,' she replies.

I barely know whether to laugh or cry. For a moment I can almost imagine us walking away side-by-side, laughing at the lunacy of it all.

But then I blink and I see where I am. What I'm trying to hold together. And suddenly the idea of laughter feels a very long way away.

29

DEE

I'm logging the day's rushes in the office with Annabel when Craig knocks softly on the door to tell us that he's dealt with Gaia's inexplicably minor wounds and will be in his cabin if we need him.

I thank him, and when he's gone, I look back to Annabel and blow out my cheeks.

She smiles. 'Well. Certainly a dramatic afternoon.'

'It's not supposed to be quite like this, you know.'

'No? What's it supposed to be like?'

'Boring, actually. People always think of TV production as being this incredible thrill. So much glamour. Is that what you were hoping for?'

She weighs it up. 'I guess I thought it seemed like a cool job.'

'Yeah, well. Is it? You came straight from uni, didn't you? You studied in America?

'Yeah,' she says. 'Film studies. Though I didn't think I'd manage to get on a show like this so quickly.'

Will had said how determined Annabel had been, calling his office every day for a fortnight until he agreed to interview her. Whether she would have got hired if she'd been charging the same rates as everyone else is another matter.

'What about you?' she says. 'You don't usually do this kind of work, do you? Will said you did undercover investigations. That sounds cool. Pretending to be other people all the time? Like nobody knows who you really are?'

I look away, my appetite for small talk evaporating, but she doesn't seem to notice.

'I bet you've got loads of stories from when you were secret filming. Like, how do you do remember all the lies all the time? I mean – sorry, I didn't mean lies,' she says quickly. 'I just meant when you're not, like, being your actual self. And what happens if someone finds out? That you've not been telling the truth?'

'It's not as fun as it sounds.'

Her excitement drops like a rock. 'Oh God, I'm sorry, did I say something wrong?'

I get up, fold my laptop shut. 'It's fine. Long day. I'm going to get some food, all right?' But as I get to the door I think of something. 'Annabel, you did a lot of background on everyone, right?'

She nods. 'Loads.'

'Where is all that now?'

'Will bought that big drive there and transferred everything over,' she says, pointing. 'I didn't know what we'd need, and I knew there wouldn't be any internet, so I thought I might as well bring it.'

'Good. Look, I want you to do me a favour. I need all of the insurance stuff, so we know what we need to do about John—'

'I already started pulling that together actually—'

'Sure, but we need something else, too. Connections, you know? Anything that might link Tori to any of the contestants.'

Her eyes are full of fear. 'You don't think it was an accident? You really do think someone tried to kill her? Who?'

'If I knew that, I wouldn't be asking you, would I?' But the fact remains, I have no idea. Who could have that kind of a grudge against Tori, bad enough that they'd find a way to get into her cabin and sabotage the heating? Would anyone? And how? But given what happened on the first night, what other explanation could there be?

'Could you have a look? It's a long shot, I know. But see if there's a way that Tori's path might have crossed with anyone else here.'

She nods vigorously. 'I will.' There's a pause. 'I'll do what I can. And, Dee, look, I'm sorry what I said. I didn't mean you were a liar.'

I tap the doorframe and go to leave, but then I see the Billie Holiday book tucked into the soft case of the second camera. 'Can I borrow that?'

'Course,' she says, handing it to me.

I leave her where she is and go up to the saloon. It's much too early for dinner, but Ulla's left out a plate of cakes and some fruit. I take an apple and settle in a corner, but after a bit I find I'm not hungry after all. I open the book at random. But I don't read it. I'm thinking of what she said. Because she's right about that. No amount of dressing it up changes the fact that I *am* a liar, actually. That's exactly what I am.

What I was. What I was to him.

'I'd ask if you mind me joining you, but you're not really the sociable kind, are you?'

I look up and find Helen regarding me, a cake on a plate in her hand.

'Be my guest,' I say. It's not like I have any choice.

She comes over, sits next to me and starts eating. Nodding at the book, she swallows and says, 'I don't get that stuff. Bit of rock, Motown, something you can dance to. But jazz?' she wrinkles her nose. 'Doesn't make any sense to me. All – disjointed, you know? I like order.' She laughs at herself. 'Stuffy old cow, aren't I?'

'I don't get it, either,' I tell her, closing the book.

'No?' She angles her head. 'So why are you reading about it?' Before I get to formulate a reply, she leans back, smiling. 'Trying to impress someone, right? The only reason a woman like you would find time to read something she doesn't care about is work, which I'm guessing this isn't, or a love interest.' She waggles her eyebrows.

The right thing to do would be to laugh, but with no warning whatsoever, suddenly I find I'm in tears. I try to make it stop, try to smile, but it's like fighting the tide.

'Oh, goodness,' Helen says softly, pushing her plate away. She touches my shoulder. 'There's more to it than that.' She says nothing for a moment and just watches the sea while I get my breath back. Then she turns back to me. 'How do you feel about whisky, hmm? I have a marvellous Japanese single malt with our name on it. Have a drink with me.'

'Helen, no, it's the middle of the afternoon. I shouldn't—'

'You absolutely should. I don't think I've seen you look happy once since we've been out here. Come on.' She takes hold of my elbow. 'I promise not to ask any questions.'

Five minutes later I'm sitting on the edge of her bed, lifting a mug to my lips. I let the warm fumes, thick as a forest of oaks, sting my eyes.

She watches me drink, then pulls the cork from the neck with a squeak.

'One's probably enough,' I say, vaguely covering the mug with my hand, but she waves the bottle.

'Nonsense. I can't drink it all on my own. Come on.'

So I let her pour. I look around the room and spot a photo tacked up behind the headboard. It's a boy, maybe early teens. I indicate it with a nod. 'Cute kid. Yours?'

She finishes the pour with the accomplished twist of the bottle of someone who knows the value of every drop, then follows my eye.

'My nephew. Lovely boy.'

I take in the goofy expression on his face, his arm slung easily over the shoulder of a woman in her thirties. A woman, I realise now, with the same distinctive nose and steep forehead as Helen. A sister then, but much younger.

She sets the bottle down. Settling next to me, she shifts herself back onto the bed, leaning against the wall. She takes a deep swig of the golden liquid in her glass and exhales, then raises her eyebrows, expectant.

'You did say, Helen, that you wouldn't ask questions.'

'I did.'

I shake my head, smiling.

'Look,' she says. 'It's lovely to have company is all. Lonely old place, out here. Not much action in these old bones any more, so I live vicariously through anyone who'll talk to me. But I do see that you're . . .' she pauses, swirling her mug as she looks for the right word. 'You're a private person.'

It's an understatement that could sink this whole ship.

'Why don't you tell me about who he is. Or she. What do they do for a living?'

'He's a musician and a music teacher,' I tell her, because on paper that was what he did. The tense is the first lie of many, but what's a drop in the ocean?

'Secondary?' she asks.

I take another sip, feeling the rigidity in my spine soften with every swallow. 'Secondary, sixth form, private lessons from home.'

She nods. 'How did you meet?'

I sigh. The thing is, I can't tell her the whole truth – I know it's not possible. But something is happening to me as I sit here with Helen, some kind of loosening, like my chest is an old, seized-up machine and someone has slipped a drop of oil into me.

I can tell her some of it. I can release some of it. And so I do.

It was a drizzly summer evening when I first saw Leo play. It was in a bar I'd never been to, a place that did a roaring trade in the kinds of cocktails people order to show off what they know about cocktails. A grand piano sat beside the vast folding doors that opened out onto the street.

The customers weren't there to listen to music, and nor was I. From one of the whistleblowers who'd contacted the producer about the story in the first place, I'd discovered that Leo played there for extra cash. I'd gone along to establish contact, find a way into what was really still just a rumour, launch the investigation. I don't tell Helen that.

His set started at six, and the place was only beginning to

fill up. I took a small table, close to the piano. I watched him exchange a joke with one of the bar staff, then he came over to settle himself at the stool. Deep-brown arms and a shirt in blue and green. Eyes you could drop into and never find a way out.

He sat and he played. And honestly I know nothing about music. Back then, I couldn't have told an arpeggio from an adagio, but watching him play was like discovering for the first time that birds could fly.

What I learned, very quickly, was that this man was more than a story.

Leo was music. It was his whole life. Everything about him was melody and harmony and sound – it was every spark of his soul, every breath he took. He'd hear a recycling lorry go past as he walked along a pavement and immediately look for the rhythm in it, start accompanying it with an impromptu perfect hum. Once, I found him standing in his kitchen, smoke pouring out of the toaster, utterly lost in a recording of Miles Davis. I didn't understand it. I still don't. I never will, now. But that was who he was.

If I'd known how hard I was going to fall for him, I'd never have gone near. Screw the consequences. Because you can't survive a drop like that. No one can.

30

TORI

I find Dee coming out of Helen's cabin.

'What have you been doing? We need to get everyone up in the saloon to shoot the vote.'

She gives me a look. 'You're not serious.'

I follow her up the passage. 'What do you mean – we have to! We need the reaction after every challenge. It's crucial—'

'No.' She stops outside her door, looking at me like I've suggested we do the next naked. 'You said we'd tell them the truth after the mushing.'

'I didn't. I said we'd talk about it.'

Dee thinks I'm joking, then she looks twice as angry as she was. 'So, what – you want to keep going? Somehow finish the whole trip without them finding out? You might not even survive that long. Has it not occurred to you that if someone has tried to kill you twice, they're unlikely to stop?'

I don't have an answer to that. That first night, I was certain of who had been behind me on the deck. And even then, I'd still hoped that if I could explain myself, make them see I wasn't the monster they believed me to be, I could turn things around.

But that was before the gas. Now, I know what she's saying

is true, but I can't deviate from the story. The consequences of coming clean would be . . . unthinkable. So all I can do is keep going. The only way out is through.

So I sigh like she's being tiresome. 'Don't be dramatic.'

'There is a dead man in the hold!' she hisses.

The engines accelerate and the floor lurches. I grab onto the rail halfway up the wall, and Dee does the same. For a moment our hands touch. She moves away to hold the opposite rail. The ship leans. We lean with it.

'This isn't you,' Dee says with a note of desperation. 'It's beyond unethical, Tor. And what do you think is going to happen when we get back? When the press gets hold of the fact that we blithely carried on making a TV show, when one of the contestants was—'

'We're not blithely doing anything!' I screw my eyes shut for a moment. 'I just need the show to work. I need it to. And so do you.'

Dee goes to respond, but then changes her mind. She won't tell me what that debt of hers is all about, but ever since she moved in with me, she's spent next to nothing. I refused to charge her anything for the room, and she's barely gone out, saving every penny in rent from her flat and selling everything she could. But every conversation about whatever went so badly wrong was simply shut down, until I gave up asking.

For me, though, it's straightforward. I think of the second mortgage, the loans. My name on all the documents. If this show sinks, I sink with it. So, yeah, maybe it is unethical to keep the truth from the others. But I'm damned if I'm going to sign the show's death-warrant myself.

Dee lets out a heavy breath. 'I've got questions for Eino. If you want to come.' She walks off, and I follow at a trot.

'Can we really not leave it until we get back? Once we've got everything in the can?'

She looks at me with disbelief, but keeps walking. 'We're a long way from help out here, Tori. At the very least, we need to be talking about you. Keeping you safe, being vigilant. If we tell them what's happened – only the facts – it means we can start asking questions and—'

'No,' I tell her. 'We're not *investigating*. We leave all of that to the police.'

'But that could be days away,' she says as we arrive outside the bridge. 'You might not give a shit about your own safety, but I still care about you. I'm not taking that risk.'

The moment we enter the bridge, the room falls silent. Eino stands with his hands linked behind his back, having clearly cut himself off mid-sentence. Stefan looks anywhere but at us.

Dee gets right into it. 'A few things, Eino,' she says. 'First, you want to tell me about the pipework in cabin two?'

'Some maintenance was needed,' he says, dismissively.

'So you've done that in all of the other cabins too?'

'No,' he says with an air of dwindling patience.

'I didn't think so,' she says. 'But here's the thing. It looked to me like that pipe had been deliberately broken.'

If you looked up 'impassive' in a dictionary, it would have a picture of Eino's face. 'There was some damage, we fixed it. What were the other concerns?'

Dee cocks her head. 'The pipe was connected to a radiator, which ran off your old system, is that right? A diesel system.'

'The defunct system. It is irrelevant.'

He appears not to even blink as Dee recounts her theory that a break in the pipe could mean the release of poisonous gas. 'And that would, I'm guessing, put you in the frame for negligence, because the system should have been removed.'

Eino doesn't speak for several seconds, but when he does, it's not a reply. 'We will discuss with the police in due course.'

Dee darkens. 'Did *you* have a problem with John, Eino?'

He sighs. 'No.'

'Well someone did, and right now you're not exactly giving me reasons to believe you.'

'As I said. We will speak to the police. Is there anything else?'

'Yes, there is. I'm going to need the bag.'

'What bag?'

'Really? John's rucksack, which was right there in the cabin. Someone's moved it.'

Eino frowns, then says something in Finnish to Stefan, who shakes his head. 'We know nothing about a rucksack. A suitcase was taken to the hold with the body. You are welcome to see it. But no rucksack.'

'Right, I'll make a note of that for the police, too,' Dee says.

'Fine,' Eino says. 'Also, now you're here, you may need to know that we are likely to experience a freeze within the next day or two. This will impede our movements.'

'It's already freezing,' I say.

Dee concurs, sarcastically waving a hand towards the snow that has started to fall outside. There is an odd glow to the sky, a kind of purple, light in colour but with a strange quality to it. Opaque, like it's not air at all, but something heavier.

'You misunderstand.' He moves to a large screen set into a panel of instruments. 'Here, topography.' He changes a setting until the bottom-right corner shows a blurry mass. 'Here, pressure. You see? Our route down to Nuuk has become difficult. There is a storm moving between us, here,' he says, touching the eraser end of a pencil to the screen, 'and the port, there. The temperature will drop. We had planned to move south, but tonight we anticipate the freeze.' He glances at me, then motions to the window. '*This* is snow. This we can move in. But when ice forms around the hull? We cannot move.'

Dee laughs. 'Great. Brilliant! Tell you what, why don't we change the title to *Frozen In*, shall we? Make a feature of it. Fucking *hell*.'

'Can't move for how long?' I ask Eino, trying to stay calm.

'Usually the tide will break it. But if it doesn't – and, you know, it happens, especially this time of year – there's a shipping channel that icebreakers use, not too far out. Worst-case scenario, we call for help, they divert to break us out.'

He's trying very hard to make this all sound like it's no big deal. But there are crystals of ice forming in my veins, shooting out tiny spurs. I'd thought I couldn't feel any less safe, but I hadn't heard the half of it.

'This is madness,' Dee says to the ceiling. 'This was all planned. Months in advance. We had risk assessments.' She turns to me. 'This was supposed to be safe.'

Eino glances back at Stefan, who's pretending to busy himself on a laptop now, and mutters something. Stefan laughs nervously.

'What was that?' Dee asks.

'I said you weren't told it was safe, you were told it was cheap. That's why you've got this ship, and not the one you should have had.'

'So it was about money?' Dee asks me. 'And you *knew* it was the wrong ship for the job, and you went along with it because of the price?'

'Not exclusively, no,' I say. But she knows there were financial issues. Everything in the early stages ended up costing more than we thought and, without my knowledge, Will had over-promised and under-budgeted. The network saw a bargain and pretty much bit his arm off, but it wasn't until much later that he realised how badly he'd messed it up. One night, only weeks before we were due to set out, it looked like it would all fall apart. We'd just put out the social media about the competitors, trying to get the buzz started. But the initial frenzy about Wolf's involvement was quickly followed by the breakdown of re-negotiations over the fee for the original ship. Even with all of the money I could raise with my assets, it looked like we'd have to cancel.

It took twenty-four hours for our fortunes to change. Miraculously, the very next day Will found a sponsor. Some contact of his dad's, he said – they knew of a ship and could help with the costs. But it all coincided with the last-minute decision to take on Helen, who'd contacted Will after hearing about the show on social media; and I was so deep into on-boarding her, coordinating with Annabel, that I didn't pay attention to exactly what the changes to the ship's spec actually were.

I'd thought it was nothing to worry about. Details, which I trusted him to get right. But the way Dee's looking at me now, I know she trusted *me*.

'Is that right, Tor?' she says. 'You knew that we shouldn't be here in a ship like this? And you didn't tell me? You didn't tell any of us?'

'It's not like that, Dee—'

'Isn't it?'

She's right up in my face now. I hold firm, but I can hardly bear the way she's looking at me.

'It feels to me like you can't tell the truth about anything,' she says. 'You're lying about being attacked. You're lying about this. You're even lying to everyone about John, telling them he's fine when he's wrapped up in a bed sheet in the hold, like a piece of fucking luggage.'

There's a gasp from behind me. I spin round to see Nish, standing halfway through the door. She blinks once, then flees from the room.

She knows. And now so does everyone else.

31

TORI

Dee rushes after Nish and I start to follow, but I let them go. It's too late.

I'm going outside. I need to be on my own.

This whole trip – this whole farce – is my fault. Will had started talking about it only weeks after we met, about how he'd always wanted to make TV, how he had these great ideas. And didn't I tell him we'd struggle to do a decent job on the budget we had? Didn't I say we'd need a proper icebreaker, half a dozen camera crew minimum, to make it work? And he bluffed and bullshitted that he knew what he was doing, when all the while he'd been cutting corners and saving costs and turning the whole damn thing into a death-trap.

And this isn't simply an exec on a production that I can choose not to work with again. This is the man I'm meant to marry.

I stop only to collect the outersuit from my room, then head outside. It takes both hands and all my strength to wrench open the door to the aft deck that's almost frozen in place. But as I step out into the vicious cold, my mind goes absolutely still.

In the middle of the deck I take a deep, deep breath, letting the chill spread right into the creases of my lungs, freezing my sinuses, chilling my brain. I sit on a bench overlooking the ice sheet and I let the cold hurt.

The sun is still a way from the horizon, but the sky is an impossible carnival of colour above the glacier. An intense, vivid blue overhead, a band of fuchsia sandwiched between a rope of cloud and the peaks to the west. I get out my phone and shift around to capture the first moments of the sunset that, thanks to the time of year, will last for hours. I angle my head for a selfie, but as I frame it up, I stop.

Instead I watch as the sun moves down towards the mountain, and I admit to myself the other truth about this show. Yes, Will may have come up with the plan originally. But there's a reason I picked it up and ran with it.

I saw an opportunity. I came here for a reason, for something I needed to do – I needed John to understand, to see who I really was. So that he'd finally leave me alone. That letter in my room, the one I could hardly bear to look at before we left: the hold it had over me is little more than a memory now. And no one but me will ever know it existed.

I hear my name and see Craig approaching. Even with the wraparound sunglasses that seem permanently affixed to his head, I can see he's frowning.

'You shouldn't be out here on your own,' he says, sitting down next to me. 'Not with someone after you.'

'I'm a big girl.'

'If you say so.' We both stare out at the glacier. After a minute he says, 'You're lucky to be here. Lucky to see this. It's changing, fast. We're losing all of this.'

It takes me a moment to realise he means the ice.

'Ten years ago you could sled across this whole fjord by October. Solid as a motorway. Last year it was open water at Christmas. People don't realise,' he says, eyes dead ahead.

The shape of something starts to form in my head. 'And then all of us idiots come over and use it as the set for a mindless TV show,' I say. I watch his face, weathered and lined as an old glove from years on this rock that holds his heart.

'Aye,' he says quietly.

'Burning hundreds of pounds of carbon to get here. Melting it before we've even landed. It's enough to make someone who really cares about this place pretty angry.'

Craig takes off the shades, folds them. 'If you've got something to say, Tori, you should probably just say it.'

I say nothing.

'It could have been me, couldn't it?' he asks at last. 'Who filled that room with gas. I mean, I know ships, right? And I've been on the record dozens of times complaining about trips exactly like this one, disrupting the ecosystem. Turning locals into tourist attractions. Maybe I had it in for you because of that.'

He says it casually, like he's positing a theory about a crime series he's watching.

'But here's the thing. That first night, when you fell off the deck? I believed you that it was just a wee accident. I thought it seemed odd – you hadn't been drinking, there was no reason you should have tipped over. But what reason would you have to lie?'

The memory of that blind pitch over the railings replays, the split second of hearing someone behind me, before I force it away, shake back my hair and say nothing.

'But then John died,' he goes on. 'And I didn't want to admit it, but after what Dee discovered, and the fact that you were meant to be in that room, I'm thinking there's no way that's a coincidence.'

'John's death could easily have been an accident. You said it yourself. No one's seen this broken pipe except Dee.'

He rotates his whole body towards me. 'But why would she make something like that up? You should be freaking out right now. Demanding to be taken back home or making everyone swear to their movements. I'd be terrified. But you're not. Why is that?'

'Craig.' I use my most measured voice. 'First, you don't have a clue how I'm feeling. It's literally my job to appear cheerful and calm – you understand that, right?'

He nods.

'And, second, you need to think very carefully about what you're alleging here. You start saying this in front of the contestants, there's going to be all-out panic. And I'm fairly certain there are going to be people who will have plenty to say about being misled about your credentials.'

'See, this isn't the kind of thing that someone who's in fear of her life would usually say.'

I hold his gaze for as long as I can, but Craig wins out in the end and I look away.

'I've given it a lot of thought,' he says, staring out at the sea. 'And there's only two things I can think of. The first is that maybe you've had to work so hard to get where you are that you're refusing to do anything to jeopardise it. Don't get me wrong, I understand that. Me and you have that in common at least, right? Have to work twice as hard for the same outcome, because of the colour of our skin.'

I say nothing to that.

He narrows his eyes, regarding me. 'But that still doesn't seem quite right.'

There's a long pause. Eventually he draws a deep breath. 'The only other explanation is that there's something worse than the danger. That you *were* pushed and you know who pushed you, or you know who killed John – or both. But admitting it would mean exposing something about yourself that would be worse than the danger you're currently in.'

I get to my feet. I make myself smile, spread my hands. 'I don't know what you mean,' I tell him.

But the look on Craig's face tells me that he knows I'm lying.

32

DEE

Before I can stop her, Nish has hammered on every door and brought everyone out. Within minutes the contestants are assembled in the saloon. Tori comes in with Craig, and everyone starts talking at once.

'It's not true, is it?' Helen demands. That calm, powerful demeanour of hers that we all so admired in the last-minute audition tape that Will shot is almost intact, but there's no mistaking the fray to it. 'Please tell me she misheard.'

I touch Annabel's arm, then lean in to whisper, 'Watch them. Their reactions. Closely.'

She nods her understanding.

Nish stands rigid by the window. 'Of course it's true! Why would I make it up?'

Along another bench seat, Marco and Gaia sit a little way apart. Wolf is by the glass door to the deck, hands clasped behind him. Craig's expression is grim.

Tori, looking appropriately sombre, addresses herself to the room.

'I'm afraid that what Nish has told you is correct. Very, very sadly, John passed away.'

There's a collective gasp. I can see Gaia's whole body clench. Wolf casts his eye over the room, his expression unreadable. Helen closes her eyes.

'Oh, wait,' Nish says, all of the anxiety suddenly lifted. She glances around the room mischievously. 'I've been so stupid. It's a challenge! Right? You want to see how we respond—'

Tori shakes her head. She looks exhausted. 'Nish, no. I'm sorry. This is real.'

'When?' Marco says to the floor, fists balled in his lap. 'What happened to him?'

Tori takes a breath. I know for a fact she's not going to give them the whole story.

'We don't know exactly. He was found when we got back after the ice-dip expedition. We wanted to—'

'Yesterday?' Nish cries. 'You lied to us all that time while there's a . . . *dead body* on board? What the actual—'

'Of course she lied,' Wolf snaps, looking Tori up and down in disgust. 'What do you expect? Still think she's the perfect little girl next door? It's all about what's best for her.'

'I asked you What. Fucking. Happened?' Marco repeats, getting to his feet.

Unintimidated, Tori takes her time. 'I'm afraid we don't know. We're in touch with the police already about it, and they've told us to contact them when we're back in port—'

'So they're not coming?' Gaia asks.

'They'd never come all the way out here unless it was a real emergency,' Helen mutters to no one in particular.

'Apparently that's true, yes. And,' Tori goes on, taking care to look everyone in the eye, 'he did die of natural causes, so—'

'No,' I say.

Everyone looks at me. Tori freezes.

But I've had enough. 'I'm sorry. This isn't right. I know Tori is telling you that because she wants to keep everyone calm, but actually it doesn't look like natural causes at all.'

'Oh, now, come on,' Tori says lightly. She tries to laugh, but it falls away.

'What does she mean?' Gaia says.

I stare at Tori. She stares right back. Days ago, literally days, she was the closest friend I had.

The silence is broken by Craig. 'Let's cut to the chase, shall we?'

'Be my guest,' I say tightly.

He clears his throat. 'No one here's an expert, but it looks to us like John died from carbon-monoxide poisoning. Dee believes she found a damaged pipe under his radiator. Although actually it happened in cabin two, which was meant to be Tori's cabin. The two of them swapped, the night before.'

'Why?' Nish and Gaia say together.

Tori gets in there quickly. 'Because I had an accident. I went out late, I'd had a couple of glasses of wine,' she says, rolling her eyes at herself like it's a tale of silly drunken antics. But when her gaze falls on me, she's challenging me to contradict her. 'And the Northern Lights suddenly started, and I wasn't looking where I was going and I had a bit of a fall.'

'So I suggested that she sleep closer to Dee, who could check on her,' Craig says.

I say nothing.

'And then sometime overnight, we think, John passed away. Apparently the radiator could have been the source of it.'

I wait for Craig to say the rest of it – about the sabotage. But his eyes go to Tori, who's staring daggers at him, and then he looks at the floor.

I clear my throat. 'I think it might have been deliberate,' I say.

There's a stunned moment. And then there's chaos.

'He was *murdered*?' Marco shouts. 'By who?'

'What on earth are you saying?' Helen wants to know. 'What's the evidence?'

Gaia's got her head in her hands and, standing next to her, Marco is shaking his head.

It's Nish, though, who makes the connection. 'But if John was in what should have been Tori's cabin . . .'

'Then it follows that someone was targeting *her*,' I finish for her. 'That's what I'm thinking, yes.'

Tori makes her voice heard over the others. 'It's important you understand that what Dee's saying is an opinion.'

'That's it.' Helen folds her arms. 'I want a helicopter sent up here right now. I'm going home.'

'That would mean abandoning the show,' Tori tells them. 'And the prize. We're not quite at the point where—'

'Young lady, I don't care where you are. I am *here*, and I don't wish to be. I'm not staying a minute longer than I have to.'

'There's going to be a delay with that, I'm afraid,' Craig tells her. To an increasingly agitated audience, he explains about the conditions. The ice, the storm.

'So we're talking about the quarterdeck,' Marco says, interrupting. 'And there's only one other cabin on that section, right?' He raises his eyebrows and fixes his eyes on Wolf.

'Got something to say?' Wolf asks, drawing himself up.

Marco gives him a slow shrug. 'Just seems a coincidence,' he says casually. 'You two, with your history, and you weren't exactly friendly that first night.'

'Yeah?' Wolf rounds on me. 'Bit of a coincidence for you as well, Dee, from what I hear.'

My blood runs cold.

'Word on the street is there was a death on an undercover show. That was you, right – maybe six months ago? You making a habit of that now, are you?'

Everyone is looking at me. Tori's gaze burns into the edge of my peripheral vision like a laser beam, but I hold his eye. 'I don't know what you mean, Wolf.'

'No?'

'I have literally no idea.' I say, unbothered, like it's nothing. 'I haven't worked undercover for more than a year.' If he really wants to pit his wits against me, knowing as he does that I am literally a professional liar, that's his problem, not mine. 'What undercover show?'

'I don't know the details,' he blusters, the wind visibly going out of him.

I force a laugh. 'Okay, well. Makes two of us.'

Annabel clears her throat. 'And there was a bag, right?'

I can't acknowledge the lifeline, but I could kiss her for it. 'Yeah. John had a bag, like a rucksack? About this big.' I show it with my hands. 'It was in the room, but it's gone missing. So we need that back.'

Everyone looks at each other. No one gives anything away.

Nish laughs. She sounds close to hysteria. 'Well, someone must have it!' Silence. 'Oh my God. Is this really happening?'

I know I should comfort her, but I have nothing. I'm so out of my depth that I want to cry.

'No, I've had enough.' Helen stands. She brushes invisible dust from her trousers, shakes her hair back. 'What kind of a show is this? You're saying someone wants to kill your presenter? I demand that we abandon this farce immediately. Get off this ship. If you're saying there's *gas*, how do we know we're not all next?'

'I checked that with Eino,' Craig says. 'The old system connects only to the quarterdeck. No other cabins could be affected.'

'You seem to know a lot about it,' Wolf says darkly, sitting down.

'But you're saying it wasn't an accident,' Gaia says to no one, her voice quavering.

'I think it's possible,' I tell her levelly. 'Anyone can have an enemy.'

'For example,' Marco says, gesturing to Wolf without looking at him.

Wolf explodes from his seat. Craig crosses the room in two steps and puts himself between him and Marco. At the same moment Eino comes into the room. He scans the faces for a moment, then nods.

To me, without emotion, he says, 'They all know?'

There's a collective moment of silence.

'I see. I would like their keycards, please,' Eino says to me, like he's asking for breakfast orders.

Wolf scoffs, incredulous. 'Not a chance,' he says and leaves the room.

Eino watches him go, then faces us again, hand outstretched.

'Your keys, please. I will conduct a thorough search of the cabins for the missing bag.'

Even Gaia stiffens, suddenly engaged. 'On whose authority, exactly? We're private citizens.'

'On mine,' Eino says coldly. 'We are on the water, outside of Greenland.'

'Greenland's jurisdiction extends twelve miles from its coast, last time I checked.' Helen throws out an arm towards the window. 'Does that look like twelve miles of water?'

Everyone turns. Though the flatness of the water makes it hard to be sure of the distance, anyone can see we're nothing like twelve miles from the coast.

Caught in the lie, Eino pivots on his heel. He leaves the sense of a shift in the room – a solidarity borne of the common enemy.

'Everyone, listen,' Tori says softly, addressing them all. 'This is for the police. I'm sure they'll want to talk to all of us. What we need to decide is what we do next. The question is: can we keep going?'

33

TORI

It's touch and go, but I talk them round to going ahead with the vote. Dee and Annabel are a well-oiled machine getting a few words of pre-vote material from everyone, though from the faces Dee pulls when she brings them back in, one by one, from the passageway, I'm guessing it's not exactly BAFTA-winning. Then we quickly set up to shoot the main event before anyone changes their mind.

We get it in one lightning-fast take. I coax some kind of atmosphere into it for long enough to get it into the can, but the moment the results are announced – Nish as the winner, with Gaia relegated – we call it a night. Nish asks to delay shooting her post-win debrief, a set-piece shot we'll need for each episode, and I'm hardly in a position to refuse.

In my cabin, I start getting ready for bed. But everything is mechanical: brushing my teeth, seeing to my face, finding my pyjamas, starting to brush my teeth a second time because I'm not even thinking about what I'm doing. I put the brush down, spit and stare at my reflection.

A death on an undercover show. That's what Wolf said. It would explain Dee's collapse after her last job and her flat-out refusal to tell me what had really happened. But if there's any truth to his rumour, the worst of it is that she chose not to trust me. Wolf is the absolute king of industry gossip, so it's no surprise that he would have heard, but I can't help feeling hurt and humiliated that he knew and I didn't.

I blink in the mirror and look away, realising the hypocrisy of it. Because I'm hardly in any position to complain about someone keeping a secret.

Sleep keeps its distance for hours, baiting me, and when I wake up I barely feel I've closed my eyes. Still stuck on the same thought-loop, the first thing I do when I climb out from under the covers is get my jacket from the wardrobe and pull out my phone. I go to look up what I can find about any fatalities that fit the description Wolf gave, before remembering there's no signal. Then I think of Annabel, how she transferred all the production files to drives before we left. What if there's something in there?

It's still early in the morning, barely six, but I take a quick shower, dress, leave my pyjamas folded on my bed and go to the office.

As I approach it, I hear a low voice. I peek around the corner and see a glow bleeding out from there – the desk light. And leaning casually against the doorframe, with his back to me, is Wolf.

I hang back.

'. . . haven't really got to know each other,' he's saying.

I strain hard to hear the other voice, but although I miss the odd word, from the mousy pitch I know in a second it's Annabel.

He's making small talk about his YouTube channel. 'I'd been hoping to get some shots of the Northern Lights, got this great idea for editing them into a title sequence.'

'I already saw them,' she says weakly. 'They're . . . pretty.'

It sounds almost like she's trying to flirt, but it's like watching a child do it.

'And they're not the only pretty thing around here, are they?'

Keeping out of view, I steal another quick glimpse around the corner, in time to see Wolf lift a hand from his pocket and rub it lazily across his chin.

'Neat as a pin, aren't you?'

There's a short pause. 'I – I do my best.' That fawning tone: I almost cringe myself inside-out. Annabel's surely not going to fall for his flattery, when he so obviously wants something from her?

'So listen. About the keycards,' he says, right on cue. 'There's that spare cabin, where the married couple who dropped out were going to be? I could do with a little extra space. Get started on editing the content, you know? I thought maybe you could do a boy a favour. Yours is a master key, right?'

There's a pause.

'Wolf, stop—'

He's taken a step into the room. There's a thump, things falling from the desk.

'I just want to borrow it,' he's saying, but I can see Annabel too now, pulling back on his hand. After a brief tussle he lets go, shakes back his hair.

'Mine only opens my cabin!' Annabel says. 'I don't have any more access than you do.'

'No? But you can get me a master, can't you?'

'I'm sorry, Wolf. I think you should go.'

'I'm sorry, Wolf,' he mimics, nasty now. 'Look at you. Tits on display one minute, head girl the next. Make up your fucking mind.'

I duck back around the corner as he comes back towards me and then, because there's no way of avoiding him, I start walking towards the office, nearly bumping into him.

'Watch where you're fucking going,' he growls at me, pushing something into his pocket.

The office door closes as I get there. When I pull it back open, Annabel gasps, obviously expecting Wolf again. She's fastening the top button of her shirt.

'Only me,' I tell her. 'What did he want?'

'Nothing, just saying hello,' she lies.

'Gloomy in here,' I say, flicking on the overhead light. I pull out the single chair. 'What are you up to?'

She's got her laptop connected to one of the drives, but there's something guilty about the way she angles the screen away from me.

'I wanted to see if I missed anything about John—'

I get behind her and read over her shoulder. It takes me a moment to realise that what Annabel's reading isn't about John at all. I feel her deflate in her chair, and she gets up and closes the door, with no option but to come clean.

'It's what Wolf said,' she sighs. 'About a coincidence, with Dee? He reckoned something happened on another show she worked on. I wanted to see if there was a record of . . . any of it.'

'You were spying on her.' Seems we both had the same idea.

'No, it's not like that—'

'Yes, you were.'

She looks away. 'Sorry. Yeah. You got me.'

'So what did you find out?'

She gestures at the drive. 'I wanted to see if there was any-thing on her employment records. But I think Will must have password-protected them.'

I bring up the dialogue box. 'This one?'

She nods. I put in a password, the one Will uses for everything. 'All yours.'

As she searches through the documents, I busy myself with swapping over some camera batteries. Anything to distract from the fact that if Dee saw what we're doing here, she'd never forgive me.

But the fact remains that Dee's my friend. However hard things have been for the last few months, we've got a history. We've always been there for each other: I opened my home to her, never asked for anything in return. I don't want to be here, scrabbling around for the scraps of Wolf's gossip like an animal at a bin. I want her to—

'I think this is it.'

Annabel shows me the screen and stands back. I lean in. 'What am I looking at?'

'Dee doesn't have an agent, but she got a lawyer to look over her contracts. It's an email from the lawyer, to Will's – to *your* – HR guy.'

'*To confirm,*' I read from the screen, '*Ms Dee Cohen was under contract with SyncHole Productions until earlier last year, but the production was halted before completion, due to . . .'*

I look up at Annabel.

' *. . . the death of the target of the covert investigation.'*

34

DEE

Day four. But it feels like I've been out here for weeks.

I get out of bed and go to fill a beaker from the tap. It spits, the pressure pathetic, and when I knock back my pills and swallow, the water tastes bitter, metallic. In the mirror above the sink, my face is pulled tight with anger.

I've slept on it, what happened in the saloon last night. But rest hasn't blunted a thing – I could still kill Wolf.

How he knew about Leo I have no idea, but dropping it in like that, in front of everyone? I could wring his fucking neck.

I'm not just furious, I'm jittery as hell. I think of the bottle of rum I bought at the airport, currently lying unopened in the bottom of the wardrobe. But where would that end? Half a bottle down, a whole one? I can tell you exactly where: with me in a ball in the corner of the bed, watching those clips of Leo over and over again. Just me and the biting grief, and then a hangover.

And he'll still be dead.

And it'll still be my fault.

The cogs spin and spin in my head – what I need is something to jam them. I get down on the floor, settle my feet at hip-width and start a set of crunches. After twenty I switch to leg lifts, then up for lunges, then squats. Repeat.

Pretty soon I've hit a rhythm, my thoughts taking on a liquidity that makes them less easy, less appealing to hold on to. I replay the conversations with Tori and find them already robbed of their power.

Then, with no trigger, as I straighten from a squat, the image of John's body floats up again. Blotchy, cold, the eyeballs dried. Everything collapsing slowly into itself.

I sink onto the floor, elbows on my knees, head in my hands. I sit there watching the sweat dripping from my forehead onto the carpet tiles, my heart banging loudly in my throat.

I need to talk to Wolf. Because, yes, he might be a narcissist, but is he violent? Tori never said so, though I know his temper can get out of control. And if it takes us days to get back to civilisation, I need him to cooperate. We all do.

I weave through the ship towards his cabin, but the door to his passage is locked. I peer through the circle of glass set into the metal. On the other side is Ulla, running something that looks like a vacuum cleaner over one spot on the carpet.

I rap on the glass, startling her. She comes over, but rather than letting me though, she comes out to the stairs and closes the door behind her.

'What's going on?' I ask. 'Why's the door locked?'

'Sorry, madam. It's the carpet. Best to keep guests away when cleaning. Man in cabin one is already up,' she says, gesturing to Wolf's door, 'so I clean now.'

'But why does the carpet *need* cleaning?' I'm not feeling patient.

'It is . . . dirty. Dirtied?' she tries, uncomfortable, like there's more to it.

'What kind of dirty? Where?'

She sighs. 'Come,' she says, then opens the door and beckons for me to follow.

In the passage there's a strong scent of industrial cleaning, and the air is heavy and humid. The patch on the floor, dark with whatever fluid she's been using, is right outside cabin two.

'What was it?' I ask. I bend to touch my fingers to the patch, sniff them. There's a faint sourness that I can't instantly place.

She puts her hands in her pockets. 'We find it when we were at anchor. When you are out with the small boats,' she says, meaning on our ice-hole trip. 'Before you come back to the ship, I am down here and find the smell. Someone has tried to clean up, but not good. Not well? But then—' Her eyes drift to the door of the cabin. 'The poor man was found and everyone here so . . . But now I do the full clean.'

'What was on the carpet, Ulla?'

She rubs her chin, searching for the word.

'Spilled food?' I offer. 'Coffee? Mud? What?'

She's flustered now, but she makes a gesture, moving her hand from her mouth to demonstrate. Making a face like gagging.

'You found *vomit*?'

'Yes,' she says, serious. 'Yes, vomit.'

'Outside the room where we found a dead man?'

She nods.

But John was lying in bed, with no sign of any sickness. So it follows that if there was vomit outside his room – and someone had tried to clean up – it must have been someone else's.

Someone who knew what was inside.

35

TORI

I slouch on the stool. I don't understand what I'm looking at.

Annabel lifts the laptop out of my hands. 'Do you want me to?' she says gently, and begins to read.

'*As we understand it, the subject in question had developed a personal relationship with Ms Cohen during the process of the filming. Ms Cohen had no involvement in the death, which resulted from a road-traffic accident north of the city of Bath. While admitting that the forming of relationships such as that between Ms Cohen and the subject when working undercover poses ethical concerns, Ms Cohen and the production company were cleared of any involvement in the death. Therefore this should not interfere with her future employment—*'

'Okay, all right,' I say, and she stops.

Neither of us speaks. After a minute Annabel gets up, digs in a bag at the base of the single cupboard in the corner and brings out two cans of cola.

'You didn't know,' she says, handing me one.

I pull the tab, take a sip, set it down carefully. I line the label up just so. 'I did not.'

'I mean, it *said* she had nothing to do with it.'

I meet her eye. It takes me that long to realise what she means. 'Annabel, Dee didn't *kill* this person. For goodness' sake.'

'No. Sure. But I mean, under the circumstances—'

I realise what she means and I laugh out loud. 'You're saying, what: Dee killed John? Give me a break. What possible reason could she have? And also, no. There's no way – don't be absurd. She's the one trying to convince everyone it's foul play in the first place, isn't she?'

Annabel nods. 'But it's a big secret, isn't it? A big thing to keep back from—' She cuts herself off, leaving the implication to leak out of the severed end of the sentence. *From you*, she means. From someone who's supposed to be her friend.

Part of me wants to tell Annabel to go screw herself. Who is she to sit there and judge me, judge our friendship? This woman, this *girl*, has been around us for a matter of months and, what, she's qualified to tell me what Dee and I should or shouldn't tell each other?

But the other side of it, the bigger part, is that she's absolutely right.

She finishes her drink, crushes the can under her foot and drops it into the bin. 'I can imagine Dee keeping something like that quiet, actually. She's very – secretive. Isn't she?'

I almost laugh. 'You could say that, yes.'

'Was she always like that? I mean, before it happened. Did she not tell you about the work she was doing at all?'

'All I knew was that it was an investigation. Something about a school.'

*

A memory bubbles up. We'd met for a drink after Dee had got the job, I remember now – the kind of spit-and-sawdust place she always seemed to suggest. Wine list of red or white. I'd waited at a corner table for twenty minutes before I realised she was already there, laptop open, but almost unrecognisable from when I'd last seen her a few months before. New hair, different kind of clothing. Professional-looking, cool but mainstream – a long way from the threadbare black jeans and buttoned-to-the-neck checked shirts that off-duty Dee tended to favour. I didn't even have to ask what it was in aid of.

'The new undercover's started then,' I said, pulling out a chair and placing my dishwasher-dulled glass of room-temperature Sauvignon Blanc on the beer mat.

She rolled her eyes as I air-kissed her cheeks and sat down. 'So what do you think?' she asked, inclining her chin this way and that to show off the chic new pixie cut. 'This is Sophie. Sophie is a teaching assistant.'

I raised my glass to toast her. 'Nice to meet you, Sophie.'

She told me only the most skeletal details about the investigation. It was a private school, a local one. Some suspicion that there were teachers there who were writing assignments on behalf of the students – essentially, exam fraud. And then what did we talk about? It was soon after I'd started getting Tori Tells Stories off the ground, so I would have talked about that. About Will, probably. I remember that when Dee looked at her watch, saying she had to leave, it was still kind of early.

I bored her, I realise now. I bored her by talking about myself, back when she trusted me enough to talk about an undercover investigation. Even though she'd have been fired for telling me about it, she would have done so. But I barely asked her a thing.

The next time I saw her, a couple of months later because we'd both been so busy, something had changed. There was a colour to her. We literally bumped into each other in a bathroom at a jazz bar – I was with Will and his friends, Dee was about to leave to meet someone else. The conversation lasted a minute, two.

'Anyone handsome?' I'd asked about her date. She had broken into a shy, one-sided smile.

'Might be. I mean, it's kind of work, so . . .'

She told me his name – Leo.

And then the thing I remember most: she got out a lipstick. And Dee never wore lipstick.

'Is this a Sophie thing?' I asked her as she dabbed a smudge from a tooth. And it was somehow not the right thing to say, because Dee was flustered after that. She promised she'd call, and then she was gone. The next time I saw her, months later, she arrived on my doorstep with little more than the clothes she was wearing, rain-soaked and inconsolable. And Sophie was little more than a memory.

'You all right?' Annabel asks.

I look up. Blink. 'Give me that email again.'

She passes it over and I read it through. And it's like a path of lights illuminating a runway all of a sudden – a path between two things that I hadn't thought to connect.

This Leo. This death that happened during Dee's investigation. They're the same thing – the same man.

There's a click behind me and then I'm shoved forward as the door crashes open.

'Shit, sorry,' Dee says, 'I didn't know you were here.'

My heart skids. I silently will Annabel to angle the laptop away, but she does nothing but blink, frozen.

'I was just going to speak to Wolf,' Dee's saying. 'But the passage was locked off. I got Ulla to let me in and she was steam-cleaning vomit off the carpet. Someone had been sick outside John's cabin. It wasn't there when you swapped, but Ulla noticed the smell the next day, before we found him dead. So someone might have known he was—'

Then she stops.

I follow her eyeline.

'What the fuck is this?' She picks up the laptop. 'This is confidential.' Her voice is low, dangerous.

'Dee, look, I was only—' Annabel starts, but Dee shoves the computer, hard, towards her. It makes contact, and Annabel gasps and staggers back.

I get up, hands out, conciliatory. 'Stop it. Stop. Let's talk about it like adults—'

'Really? Adults who go around digging through the private information of their colleagues? Am I a fucking suspect here? Is that what this is? You two squirrelled away up here, trying to find shit out about *me*?'

She's close enough for me to smell the damp of her wool sweater.

'We wanted to know what Wolf meant. About a coincidence.'

'Right. Great!' she says, throwing her hands up in furious sarcasm. 'And it didn't occur to you to, I don't know, *ask me*?'

And I know I should try to be kind, try to be compassionate, but the way she's looking at me now, with nothing short of hate – it breaks something in me. And for the first time I can remember ever feeling like this about her, I want to hurt her. I want to hurt her back.

'It's not like you've been exactly behaving rationally, Dee.'

'*What?*'

I don't want to lie. But it's out of my mouth before I even realise what I'm saying.

'This broken gas pipe, or whatever it is. That no one else can see. And it's not the first time, is it?' Dee shakes her head, warning me, but there's nothing I can do to stop it. 'You know when you were convinced someone had let the air out of your tyres? Or that someone had broken into your email?'

She takes half a step back, her eyes flicking over my shoulder to Annabel. 'Tor, don't.'

'Or when you didn't go out for two whole weeks because you insisted someone was following you?'

'Someone *was* following me.'

It's my turn to laugh now. 'But why? No one even knows who you are. No one knows where you live. Isn't that how you like it? Hiding behind these fake names? Pretending you're someone they can trust, when secretly shit like this happens and you don't even tell your *best friend*? I know you haven't been well, but you're supposed to trust me! Why didn't you just say someone had died?'

She holds my eye for a moment.

'You want to talk about trust, Tor? Really? You've done nothing but lie since we got here. You went in there last night, in front of a room full of people who are here *because of you*, and you lied to every one of them. You've even lied about me, because – no, I'm saying it – we both know you were pushed that first night. You want to keep running this show like that? Fine. I'll shoot it, because I need the money. But that's all I'm doing. Here on out: you're on your own.'

36

TORI

With Dee gone, a horrible silence descends in the room. I close the laptop, but I've got nothing to say. It feels like something pivotal has happened. Something final.

'Maybe I should go and find out who it might have been who was sick?' Annabel asks quietly.

'Yep. Sure. You do that.'

I close the door behind her and get started with logging some footage. It's Annabel's job, but it's an excuse to stay in here. Today is a travel day, and Dee's going to be ticking off a list of shots and interviews with the contestants; though I'll have to get out there later, right now I just want to keep out of her way.

I get lost in the job. Hours go past, and then Annabel returns with a plate of food, saying that Ulla was clearing the last things away. I start to pick at it half-heartedly, then there are excited voices in the passage outside. Annabel opens the door as Nish hurries past, followed by Craig.

'What's going on?' Annabel asks.

'The glacier,' he says. 'We're getting up close, hoping we might see some calving.' He leans in. 'Thought it might give them something to take their minds off . . . you know.'

'Where's Dee?' I ask Annabel.

'In her cabin. She's been shooting with the others, one-to-one stuff. I mean, I can go and get her if you want, but—'

'No, we'll manage.' Her expression tells me it's not been a comfortable day. I reach down and pull out the second camera from under the desk, check the stock pocket, then slide open the drawer where we keep the blank data cards.

'You'll be okay to shoot it. Big clean GVs.'

'Right. And by "clean", you mean—'

'Without people,' I explain. 'GV – general view? Like an establishing shot. Did you not cover this on your course?'

'Maybe the terminology is different in the States,' Annabel says vaguely.

'Yeah, whatever. Think of the stuff Dee would get, and do that.'

I hear my voice like I'm listening to someone else. Flat and robotic. Annabel takes the camera, and I get to my feet.

And by the time I'm in the passage I'm transformed. Full-beam, absolute presence.

Out on the front deck, the atmosphere is alive. We're a few hundred metres out from shore, on a sea littered with ice. Everything from huge, jagged hulks as big as the ship – bigger – right down to the much smaller chunks that Craig tells us are called *bergy bits*. The whole expanse is vivid with reflected light. But even with the distance, the ice still towers where the glacier meets the sea.

Right at the V of the prow, Craig is standing with his back to the spectacle, waving insistently with both arms above his head to whoever's up in the bridge.

'Back, back!' he's shouting. 'We're too close!'

I hurry over. 'Everything all right?'

'I've explained what's going to happen.' His face is creased with worry. 'That thing'll easily drop a hundred tonnes of ice into the sea in the space of a second.'

I stare at the precipitous end of the glacier. In the weeks before we came, Annabel printed out a load of satellite images of Greenland, eager as she was to learn remotely as much as she could about our route. The whole island is a giant bowl of ice, pushing out its glacial fingers into so many jagged fjords and estuaries that the coastline measures more than the circumference of the entire Earth. But although pictures of the ice from the air show an immaculate expanse, seemingly smooth, from where we are on the water it's a different picture entirely. The exposed edge is riven with cracks and fissures, the whole thing looming top-heavy as if waiting to dive. Dark streaks of dirt stand out against the glowing mass of white.

'That sounds . . . fun?' I say.

'It's not going to be *fun*. It's enough to knock a ship like this sideways.'

'So why isn't Eino moving us back?'

I look up to the bridge above us, but it's Stefan, not Eino, peering through the sloped glass. There's no one else up there.

Craig shouts for everyone to hold on to something, but right at that moment the engines engage and we start to reverse. There's a good-natured groan from the spectators.

'Thank fuck for that,' Craig says. Then he suddenly points to the cliff of ice. 'There, look. It's going to go!'

When it starts, it's just a small slice slipping into the water below, spraying white all around it. Seconds later there is an almighty crack.

No one speaks. With the base of the glacier's face gone, a huge facet of ice jolts diagonally. There's a pause, then it collapses almost in slow motion into the sea, sending up violent sprays of water. An avalanche of smaller pieces follows with a thunderous rumble. Immediately a semicircular ripple warps its way across the surface of the water, growing higher as it does so.

'Hold on to something!' Craig shouts.

Everyone joins in a call of anticipation, rising as the crest of the wave approaches, like I used to with my dad at the cricket during a Mexican wave. When it hits, everyone cheers.

I go up behind Annabel to suggest running up for a high-level shot of everyone on the deck, but before I can, Wolf sidles up to her.

'Looks like something's cheered her up,' he says to her, nodding towards Gaia, eyes narrowed, a nasty half-smile on his lips. He hasn't seen me. 'I have a feeling we're going to learn a little more about that one sometime soon.'

'I'm shooting, Wolf,' she says, staying tight to the eyepiece. 'With sound.'

He makes to move away. But before he does so, he goes up close to her and says, 'Thanks, by the way. It'll be our secret.'

She takes her eye from the camera, but he's already walked off.

I stand beside her. 'What was that about?' I ask her.

She frowns, shaking her head. 'No idea.'

Whatever it is he's up to, I already know I don't like it. But from the way she watches him go, I can see that Annabel likes it even less.

37

DEE

I'm not paranoid.

It's not paranoia.

It's real. Someone killed John. Someone tried to kill Tori – someone tried to throw her into the water, and then tried to gas her. She would have died if I hadn't stopped them. It's not about me.

It can't be.

I sit on my bed, knees bunched under my chin. I can hear them all out there, their footsteps directly above me. I can hear their voices even over the rumble of the engine. Bonding over some mutual experience. I can't go up. I don't want to.

Tori doesn't believe me, and so neither will anyone else. And I shouldn't have said what I did, but what Tori was saying – that stuff she was bringing up – was like being stripped naked, like having someone rummage around inside me and pull out the very worst things. I wanted to hurt her back.

But it's more than that. Without even looking, I reach over the bedside table and pull out the little black unit with the material from my undercover rig – the two files I have left. I link it up to my phone. Choose the second one. Press Play.

The dashboard of the car – his car. Leo's car. The car that, three weeks and two days after this footage was shot, will be reduced to a wreck of mangled metal. The car into which he will bleed to death, alone.

But that is for later. Right now, on the screen, Leo is talking to me. To *Sophie*.

' . . . kids need more encouragement than others is what I mean,' he's saying.

'It must be tempting to give them a bit of a leg up, where you can,' I say clumsily. There's a pause.

The next thing he says is the single line that we needed, to make his school the official target of the investigation. Until that point I'd been following up on leads about coursework fraud at six different places. I needed only a single, clear admission of guilt on camera to get the go-ahead from the lawyers to broadcast.

'Sometimes it's more than a temptation,' he says. There's a pause before he makes the confession. 'People will pay a lot of money to give their children a better chance.'

'And everyone likes a lot of money, right?'

He laughs. 'I don't care about it. No, it's true, I don't. But my mum . . .' He sighs. 'She's getting worse. Carers already cost a lot. Like, a whole lot. Way more than I can afford on just—'

Suddenly the whole ship lurches to the side, then there's a cheer from above. I'm missing out on whatever's making them all so animated out there.

On the screen, the car stops and we get out. I hit Fast-forward: the rest of that afternoon passed without me getting a chance to be alone with Leo to continue the conversation of the journey.

When the scene changes, it's dark. We're walking down a busy street in Hampstead. We're about to go for a drink together. I pull the duvet around my legs and curl up around the viewer, wishing myself back there.

I still had the brakes on things at this point, only a couple of weeks into knowing him. I was still professional, I was still ignoring those heady vibrations of desire whenever he gave me that look. He was the teacher, I was the assistant. Or, from the other side of the lens: he was the target, and I was the journalist.

It wouldn't last long.

I speed through the footage, waiting for the right frame. After dozens of times watching this – scores of times, maybe hundreds – I know the words of this conversation by heart.

The whole thing is shot from the height of my chest, where a pinhole camera was set into a shirt button. So even when we're standing at the bar in about five minutes' time, Leo's face is missing. Right now it's just a bumpy tracking shot of a high street – shops closing up and pubs filling. But then we take a side road. We keep walking, take a left, cross the road.

I press Play.

' . . . absolutely tone-deaf!' he's saying, midway through a story about a boy in his Year Seven music class with a burning urge to play the trombone. I close my eyes and let the sound of Leo's smooth, bassy voice wrap me up and hold me. Then he stops suddenly and looks behind him.

'What's up?' I ask, stopping too. I take a step back, and he briefly comes into the frame. The orange light shining on his close-cropped head. His eyes flitting, anxious.

'Someone behind us.'

The shot pans. 'There's no one there.'

He laughs, but without conviction, then carries on walking, the anecdote forgotten. We move in silence, until eventually he says, 'Have you ever had that? The sense someone's on your tail?'

Now it's my turn – Sophie's turn – to laugh. 'Big bloke like you, jumpy about being followed?'

But he doesn't laugh back.

There are another two minutes of dead air before the scene changes again.

I hit Stop, run it back, listen again. We talked about the same thing, three or four times. How someone had followed him home, more than once – he was sure of it, was certain they'd even got into his flat. But he had no proof. And when he told the police, they just looked him up and down – all six foot three of him, all sixteen stone of him – and asked him if he really, honestly needed to report it.

And when he told me, I'd scoffed. *Sure you're not imagining things?* I asked him. *Sure you're not watching too many scary films and getting paranoid?*

He hadn't laughed then. And now I know why. It's not a great feeling – not being believed. I can hear Tori up there, laughing. The glittering, immaculate on-camera version of her.

The tears break over my cheeks and I rub them angrily away, then push the player back into the cupboard. I get up and go to wash my face.

But before I twist the tap, I stop, suddenly aware of a sound in the passageway. On tiptoe, I go back to the door. There it is again. Whispering, outside my cabin. I try to make it out – a male voice. Two voices. Then a mechanical sound, a click and silence.

Someone has gone into Tori's cabin, next door. And it's not Tori.

I go out into the empty passageway and knock on her door. 'Hello?'

Nothing.

I try again. 'Is someone in there?' I put my ear to the wood.

Then, from above me, I hear a noise. Banging, like a hand on a door. Then voices. It starts with a polite call.

'Excuse me!' someone is saying.

'Hello? *Hello?*'

And then louder, more indignant. Fists on steel. 'They've locked us out!' someone is shouting. 'Can someone please let us in?'

38

TORI

I hammer on the door, shouting, my breath blooming in clouds against the freezing atmosphere.

'Can someone please open this door?'

Dee appears in the glass panel, confusion on her face.

'Can you let us in?' I say, pointing urgently at the handle.

'It's not budging,' comes Dee's muffled voice. She looks up, then points. 'There's a padlock! Wait a minute.' She disappears, to groans of frustration behind me.

'What the hell is happening?' Helen shouts at no one in particular. 'Why are we locked out?'

I cup my hands around my eyes and peer through the window, steaming it instantly with my heat.

'They're making a search,' Craig says suddenly.

'What do you mean?' asks Annabel. 'Search for *what*?'

He gestures to the door. 'People's cabins. Eino wanted our keys, right? We said no. And now we're locked out.' He shrugs. 'So I guess he's invoking his rights as captain.'

'He can't do that,' Annabel says.

'Well, it looks like he is.'

Dee takes for ever, but when she returns she's got Stefan with her. He doesn't look at us as he opens the door, but Dee's staring daggers at him. Her eyes are rimmed with red.

Wolf elbows his way to the front of the group. 'Are you fucking joking?' he says to Stefan as he pushes past him. 'Locking us out in the middle of the Arctic Ocean?'

'I'm sorry,' I tell Stefan, who watches Wolf go. 'It's nothing personal.' Then, turning to everyone else, 'Let's go in and see if we can find some coffee, shall we? I'm sure it's only a misunderstanding. A mistake.'

Dee waits for the others to file inside, then says to me, 'It's not a mistake. They're searching the rooms. I think someone's in yours.'

I reach my cabin, the first after the corner of the passageway, just as Eino is coming out of my door. He has a keycard in his hand, and a faint righteous look about him.

'That is a private room,' I tell him.

'This is my ship.'

'A *charter* ship that we have paid for. We have guaranteed privacy to these people. How dare you invade their personal—'

'We have located the bag belonging to the dead man.'

39

DEE

On the console of the bridge is a small rucksack. Grey and green, the straps worn, a handful of embroidered patch-badges – Helvellyn Youth Hostel, the Snowdon Mountain Railway – neatly sewn on. It's John's.

'Is there a first-aid box in here?' I ask Stefan, who's loitering awkwardly. 'We need gloves. Who else has touched this?'

From his pause, I infer that the answer is several people, and none of them covered their hands first. But he brings out a plastic box and hands me a packet of sterile gloves.

'Where did you find it?' I ask him. The room has filled up – Helen and Wolf, Gaia at the back, Marco. I don't know where the others are and do not care.

Eino turns to Wolf, his eyebrows raised.

'You had no right to go into my cabin,' Wolf snarls.

'No, I do,' the captain corrects him. '*My* ship. I keep telling you all this.'

Wolf spreads his arms, addressing everyone now. 'You want to maybe ask me about it? Huh? Explain that I was literally just about to bring it to your attention? Or is that not how this works? Rather go straight in and hang a man before he even gets to—'

'Why was John's bag in your room then, Wolf?' I ask. 'You want your chance to explain, here it is. Explain.'

Wolf glares at me. 'It was in Gaia's cabin. Under her bed. I went in after you told us the bag was missing.'

'What?' Gaia blurts. 'No, you *didn't*! What possible reason could *I* have for taking it?'

'Sounds like bullshit,' I say.

'Maybe it does, but it's not,' he says simply.

And although it's not often that I take something Wolf says at face value, I believe him. But then I realise what it means. 'How did you get in there?'

'Annabel left me the key.'

'*What?*' Annabel laughs, a single note of incredulity, but then the seriousness of what Wolf's saying hits her. 'I didn't. Honestly, I didn't!' she insists.

'You fucking did! Slid it under my door.'

I watch her shake her head, colour blooming on her face even as she does so. 'I did not.' To me, in a pointlessly low tone, she says, 'He came to see me in the office. He flirted with me.'

'Oh, did I?' Wolf slides his eyes disgustedly over her in a way that makes me thankful Annabel's looking away. 'Don't think I was the one waving my cleavage around. There's another side to this one—'

'Shut up, Wolf,' I tell him, a warning finger in the air. I keep my eyes on Annabel. 'Tell us.'

In a quiet, halting voice she explains how Wolf found her in the office and tried to get her to help him look for John's bag.

'But I swear I didn't give him anything. My card's only for my cabin.'

'Except it's not, is it?' Wolf snarls. 'And when it turned up in my room, I guessed what it was. I got to work. I'm not ashamed of that – someone had to take some action, rather than pissing around waiting to see what we're *allowed* to do.' He squares his shoulders. 'So I started looking.'

'Where is this card now?' I ask Wolf.

Wolf folds his arms, defiant. 'I destroyed it.'

Helen clears her throat. 'Convenient. But Annabel denies giving a keycard to you.'

'I absolutely do,' Annabel says quickly. 'I don't have a master key. Never have.'

'I do, but I've had it with me since we left,' Stefan says, pulling a lanyard from inside his sweater. A plastic rectangle with a hole punched in one corner hangs from a ring. 'There is only one.'

'That we know of. And there's the rub,' Helen says. 'Without knowing how you got it, Wolf, we don't know how long you really had this key for. Maybe you've had it all along.'

It's like everyone in the room suddenly breathes in.

'What?' Wolf says. But then he looks around the room, as if suddenly aware of the implications of what he's done. 'I had nothing to do with John *dying*! *She* gave it to me!' he shouts, flinging an arm towards Annabel. 'And I didn't even have it until after John was already dead.'

'Oh, for goodness' sake,' Helen says. 'It's perfectly straightforward, from where we're standing. You get yourself this card, go and kill John for some reason—'

'Wait, we don't even know whether there was any foul play at all,' Tori says.

I resist the urge to point out the glaring inaccuracy of that. 'Or that John was the intended victim,' I add.

'But why?' Wolf says, with all the finesse of a drowning man scrambling onto a log. 'What possible reason could I have for murdering anyone?'

'I don't know – something to do with your fragile ego?' I say. Because it was Wolf who fought with John and was on the same passageway as him that night.

And if I'm right, and John wasn't the target anyway – it's still Wolf who's got enough proven enmity against Tori to push her off the deck. And when that didn't work, who's to say he wouldn't have sabotaged her cabin too, to finish the job?

'Fuck you, Dee,' he says, but his righteous rage is crumbling into open panic as it becomes apparent that no one in the room believes him. I almost feel sorry for him.

Eino is watching everyone lose their shit, like it's boring him.

'Have you any idea how Wolf got this key?' I ask him.

He rolls a hand towards the computer system. 'No. He may have programmed it himself. I don't know. As I mentioned, the system is new.' He clears his throat. 'Here is my decision. We are not the police.'

'No, you're damned right you're not,' Wolf puts in.

'But,' Eino continues, talking over him, 'people are concerned this man may be a danger to us. So he will voluntarily confine himself to quarters until we pass him to the police as soon as we are able.'

To begin with, Wolf thinks he's joking. Then his face falls. 'You're locking me up? Are you serious?'

'Give us a good reason why not.' Marco approaches him, chest out, gorilla-stance.

I cast a look across the room. There's a dangerous energy here, a sense of mob justice. I don't like where it's going.

Speaking low, I say, 'Come on, Wolf. Do it for this evening, all right?' With my eyes, I'm telling him something else. *This could get nasty.*

And it works. With the slightest grunt of defeat, he steps back. Eino says something in Finnish to Stefan, who nods and goes over to the door, gesturing to Wolf to follow him. As swiftly as it started, the confrontation is over. The air in the room is still tight with it.

'That's fucking right,' Marco says, his aggression needing somewhere to go, as Wolf crosses the threshold.

'That'll do.' I touch his shoulder. 'Let's all . . . have some time to ourselves, yes?'

I step over to where John's bag lies on the console. Eino puts out a hand to stop me, but I take it anyway. 'Anyone wants me, I'll be in my cabin.'

As I pass Tori, I meet her eye. 'Now would be an excellent time to admit you were pushed, by the way. Just to clear the air.'

She blinks back at me without a shred of emotion. 'How many times do I have to tell you, Dee? There was no one else up there. Exactly like there was no one outside my house.'

Then she looks away, as if I'm no more than an irritating stranger.

40

TORI

Everyone files out of the bridge, but Eino gestures to me.

'A word.'

Outside there's another rumble as the glacier, half a mile from here, sheds another face into the hungry sea. I wait until the door has closed before I speak to him. 'I wish you'd asked me, before you decided to go into everyone's rooms.'

'I did ask. Before. They said no.'

'But if you'd come to me, personally, I mean. We could have worked something out.'

He waves a hand dismissively. 'It's done now. But let me ask you a question, Tori.' He goes back to his console desk and opens a small drawer. Then, between his finger and thumb, he lifts up the piece of broken pipe from cabin two.

In the moments that he appraises me, I try to formulate a reason for having it. But I've got nothing.

'You were keeping this a secret,' he says, without urgency.

I shake my head.

'Yes, you were.'

'I just . . . These people are my responsibility, Eino. You must understand that, as a captain?' He remains unmoved. 'All I was doing was trying to prevent anyone from panicking.'

'Including your colleagues.'

'What about you then, and Stefan? Dee said that piece was in the bin – why did you hide it there?'

He sighs. 'If we had wished to hide it, we would have hidden it. Not left it in the bin.'

We stare each other out for a moment. Any faster and my heart would burst from my chest and gallop away. But I make myself laugh.

'Eino, it's nothing. I wanted to wait for the police investigation. I was going to give this to them.'

'Good. I'll be sure to do that for you.' It's obvious he doesn't believe a word of it. 'My question to you is: knowing what we know now, why are you insisting there has been no sabotage? Why are you so eager to dismiss it?'

'Honestly I'm not!'

'Like you were keen to dismiss the suggestion that someone else had a hand in your accident on the deck.'

I go to argue it, but he raises a hand.

'So maybe it is the same person behind both incidents. And, for some reason, you are covering for them.'

I give nothing away. If Eino believes I'm not concerned, that I'm not checking behind me every moment, that simply means I'm hiding it well. But the fact is that I know it can't be the same person. Because the person who pushed me is already dead.

'No one pushed me, Eino.'

'Ah, yes. You fell.' After a moment he sighs. 'I'll pass on to the others that the pipe has been found, yes?'

'Please, Eino.' I put my hands together. 'Can we keep this between ourselves? I don't want to worry people.'

'No. That's not it. You think that if you admit what we both know, your television programme will have to come to an end. Which is a problem for you. All that money gone.' He leans back on the console. 'And we all need money.'

I realise what he's asking.

'But maybe there is a solution,' I say. 'Maybe you never actually found that . . . piece of metal. And maybe your fee wasn't quite right, given the circumstances. I'm thinking—' I swallow, remembering the precipitous figures that we already owe. 'Twenty per cent, on top of what was agreed.'

He looks at the hand I'm holding out for the pipe, but he doesn't give it to me. He slides the box back into the drawer, locks it.

'Forty, Eino.'

He raises his chin, but still says nothing.

I want to cry. 'Fifty.'

'Good. I accept. But I will keep the pipe here. It is my insurance.'

There's no choice but to agree.

'We will complete the next phase of your journey as quickly as we can, in order to beat the storm. Today we continue south as planned, for your next challenge in the morning. We will complete the tasks and your filming. I need to be paid in full within a week.'

Eino remains expressionless. I understand the blackmail very well. But we could be discussing an afternoon stroll.

I clear my throat, and from somewhere I pull out a smile.

He might have me completely cowed, but I don't have to lose my dignity.

'I'm on your side, Eino,' I tell him.

'You are. Very much so,' he says, as I leave the room on shaking legs.

41

DEE

I brace myself when I go into my cabin, but my digital recorder is exactly where I left it. My laptop is still locked in the case under my bed. There's nothing else in the room that either Eino or Wolf could have seen that tells them anything I don't want them to know. I've never kept a diary – who needs that hanging over them? My secrets stay safe in my head where they can't hurt anyone.

Or anyone else, at least.

Putting John's bag down on the bed, I empty the water from the glass on the desk and unsnap the seal from my duty-free rum. I take a neat, burning mouthful, and mumble a quiet apology to John for the invasion of his privacy. Then I pull his rucksack towards me and get started.

It's good-quality but small, with padded shoulder straps and a waist support: the kind of rucksack a serious walker might take for a day-long hike.

In the outer pocket I find a passport, boarding passes and a printout of an email from Annabel. There's a battered leather wallet containing some bank cards, fifteen pounds in notes. His driving licence has no endorsements and is one year from renewal.

Somehow it's this that drives home the reality of what's

happened here. I can't get the picture of John in that cabin out of my head. A room small enough to cross in a few strides, behind an airtight fireproof door. A single window the size of a tea tray, the white world beyond it warped by two-inch glass. A thousand miles from home, among absolute strangers.

What a place to die.

I put the licence back in the wallet, followed by the money, but then I feel something lodged in the lining. It's a small plastic sheath no bigger than a credit card, stuffed with folded paper. I grab my tweezers from beside the sink, then sit back down and pull the contents out carefully and lay them on the bed. The first object is a photograph, the plasticky film on the front of it peeling off with age. Passport-sized: the kind you get in a booth.

The image is yellowing, but it shows three faces, close up, laughing. A dark-skinned woman with big sunglasses and a 1980s perm, holding a plump-faced mixed-race baby girl next to her cheek. And, on the other side, John, much younger. His hair thicker and darker, wearing un-ironic ombre-tinted glasses.

I look back at the picture, studying the happy family. Except that John lived alone, didn't he? So somewhere along the way, the happy family got broken.

I go back to the transparent wallet, containing a yellowed fold of card. I ease it out and smooth it onto the table.

It's an order of service for a funeral. The oval-shaped photo on the front shows a young man, Caucasian with dark hair. Underneath the image is the name Kelvin Pearce, and dates that would have made him seventeen when he died in 2001.

Inside are detailed some prayers, the titles of hymns and readings. The exit music is given as 'Have a Nice Day' by the

Stereophonics. On the back page there is a short obituary of a boy who played sports, who liked expeditions with his youth group. Though there's no mention of family, there are a couple of unusually acerbic lines in there that suggest they have been written by someone still in the anger stage of grief:

Every day without you is a day without sunshine. You had your whole life ahead of you. You loved your Scout group more than anything, but the man who should have looked after you let you die. May God keep you safe, and may He help us to forgive.

I leave it flat on the duvet, thinking: Scouts. Was John a Scout leader?

Digging back into the bag, my fingers close over something coin-shaped. But when I bring it out, it's not currency, but a medallion of some kind. The word *Recovery* is embossed along one edge; a triangle, with a large V in the middle.

There's a knock at the cabin door. I pick up my glass and go to open it.

It's Gaia. 'I was wondering how you were.'

'Were you? Why?' I frown and put the rum to my lips.

'There are better ways to deal with it, you know.'

'Deal with what?'

'Whatever you're using that for.'

I hold her eyeline as I swallow again, drawing my lips back from my teeth as it burns on its way down.

'Yeah, but this is quicker,' I say, raising the glass towards her. 'Tempt you?'

With barely disguised contempt – more for the drinking

than for me personally, I think – she lets her eyes drift over my shoulder into the room. I close the door between us a little more.

'What can I do for you, Gaia?'

'Just wondered what you're doing with that bag. If you're keeping it safe.'

It's more than she's said to me this whole trip. Then something occurs to me – something that she and John had in common was work related to substance abuse. For him, it was a guiding principle in his work with young people: to keep them clean. And Gaia specifically helps people with addictions to look after their pets.

I put the glass on the floor and show her the coin.

'This is your kind of thing, isn't it?' I say, holding it up, one side, then the other. 'Drug rehab stuff maybe?'

She puts both hands in her pockets, doesn't even look at it. 'Maybe you should leave it all where it is. For his family. Did you consider that?'

'Sorry, Gaia, did I say something—'

'Doesn't it feel rather grubby?' Her voice is tight, the sinews in her neck rigid. 'Going through a dead man's things. Oh, you too, huh?' she says as Tori appears from the passageway. Gaia moves to let her pass. 'I'll leave you to it. Have another drink, why don't you. Make it a party.'

'O . . . kay,' Tori says. 'Goodnight, Gaia! Sleep well.' She turns back to me, one eyebrow up. All friendly. 'What was that about?'

'I have no idea.' I go back into my cabin and Tori follows without invitation, nudging the door shut behind her with her foot.

'Annabel's asked around about that mess you mentioned,' she says, like everything's fine. 'Someone being seasick?'

'Oh, that's what it was? Seasickness. Glad you've been able to diagnose that, rather than – oh, I don't know, poisoning, or someone throwing up after seeing a dead body or committing a murder, or something.'

It goes hard in the space between us. It goes black.

'Okay, Dee. Fine.' Tori lets it drift off, then nods at the bag. 'You find anything?'

'Picture of him with a baby.' I tell her about the order of service, but all she does is shrug.

'Weird thing to keep.'

It's more than weird. But I'm still so angry with her that I barely know how to keep the conversation civil.

'What do you want, Tor?' I unzip a side pocket of the bag.

She brings her arms from behind her back. In one hand are two stemmed glasses; in the other is a bottle of champagne.

'Peace offering?' She waggles it seductively, trying to make me laugh.

And I want to, I do. I want us to crack it open and talk shit and scroll through the Instagrams of people we hate, and just be Dee and Tori again.

But the woman standing here now, trying to pretend that she hasn't spent the last few days setting fire to our friendship: she's not the Tori I used to do that with.

I don't know how, and I've no idea why, but that woman is gone for good.

People's lives are at risk here, and not only hers. So whatever this is, here with the bubbles and the silly grins, it's not enough.

42

TORI

It's not enough. I can see it's not, and I can feel it. I have to fight hard not to cry – that look Dee gives me, like I'm no one to her. I want to throw my arms around her, or shake her until she's kind to me again.

But I don't do any of those things, of course. I toss back my hair and get to work on the champagne foil. I can't afford to get distracted by what I want. What I *need* is to know what's in that bag.

'Now's not really the time,' Dee says, watching me.

'I think you'll find now is *always* the time for Veuve Clicquot.' I get down to the bare cork and twist it, gripping the bottle with my knees, until it's ready to pop. '*Achtung!*'

The cork fires, missing Dee by inches. I laugh. She doesn't.

'Could you be careful, please?' she says, gesturing to the bag in front of her.

I make her glass do a little dance as I slide it over. She ignores it. I drink mine before the bubbles have settled, briefly setting my sinuses on fire. When I've blinked it away, I give myself a refill and try again.

'Look, I'm sorry we fell out.'

'*Fell out.* Right.'

I line the glass up between my fingers. 'I mean it. I was unkind. I shouldn't have brought up any of that about your . . . the mental-health stuff.'

Dee flinches at the words. 'I was *fine.*'

She wasn't fine. She was catatonic, for days. She wouldn't speak, wouldn't eat. Once I found her at dawn, blue with cold on a deckchair in the rain. Scrapes and cuts had appeared on her skin. A deep burn to the forearm, which could only have been deliberate. And though I don't know what I'd call that, *fine* is definitely not the right word.

But I know her well enough to sense when the direct approach isn't working. As casually as I can, I say, 'Gaia didn't look too cheerful.'

'She's never cheerful.'

Like someone else I know, I think, but don't say. 'Shame, really. I thought she was starting to show a lighter side.'

Dee picks up the glass and drinks it in one, like it's water. 'What makes you say that?'

I shrug. 'She popped in earlier on. Asking about the next challenge, saying it was a shame about John.' Then I realise what's happening. 'Come on. There's no way she had anything to do with it. What could she possibly have—'

'But we don't *know*, do we? We don't know any of them. Especially her.'

'Look,' I say, 'can we not just have a drink and forget it for a bit?'

'Someone wants you dead, Tori! I'm telling you, that pipe had been sabotaged. Whoever it was knew exactly what they were doing.'

There's a crack in her voice. And I want to go over and tell her I love her. Tell her the whole truth. But where would that end? It wouldn't just be the show going belly-up. It wouldn't even be complete financial ruin for me and for Will.

I would lose *everything*. I picture the airport, full of reporters. John's coffin being unloaded in front of his horrified child maybe. Nish's wife, Marco's kids, a tearful reunion on the concourse. And for me? Reporters. Flashbulbs, microphones, shouted questions.

Police. My lawyer. And no one believing that I didn't kill John, because if I tell them the truth, I'll be the person with the motive. A squad car there waiting for me, a hand on my head as I'm taken away. The image of it across every front page in the country within hours. And then every detail of my life – what I've done, what I did – pored over for anyone to see.

'There's no evidence,' I say. 'That's the problem.'

'I know that! Look at this. Look!' She waves her hand at the bag. 'This is all we've got, right? After all that – after Eino searching the ship for it – here it is.' Flushed with fury, she fights with the fastenings and undoes the top, then flips it, holds it from the straps at the bottom and shakes the contents onto the floor. 'A washbag. Some clothes. That's all we've . . .' She trails off, her attention suddenly elsewhere.

'What?'

She peers over the pile. 'I didn't notice this before,' she mutters.

I see what she's holding. An invisible hand takes hold of my throat.

'Some kind of medical tag,' she says, turning it over. It's a thick silver chain with a no-nonsense clasp. An elongated oval of the same metal sits at its centre, with the distinctive design of a snake climbing a staff. 'What do people have these for? Diabetes?'

By the time she holds it out to me, I've arranged a neutral look of vague interest on my face. But I don't take the bracelet. Can't. Even with my arms folded, I can feel the shake in my hands.

She holds it up to her face for closer inspection. 'Is this John's? Or someone else's? I wonder if there's a name.' She squints at the back of it.

There won't be a name. But there will be a number.

And for the first time since we left dry land, I thank God and all the saints for the lack of an internet signal here, so that the number doesn't lead her any further.

43

DEE

We wake on the fifth day to a dirty white sky, the glow of a half-hearted sun leaking out from behind it, without any interest in breaking through. As I dress I peer out of the porthole and see a tiny settlement, hemmed in between hulking hills of rock that rise out of the snow like monstrous fists. The bright buildings are scattered in the white like a dropped handful of Lego, providing the only colour against the endless ice. From here, every building seems to have the same square base and pitched roof, but each is unique in its colour: vivid blues and reds and yellows. The exact opposite of the endless stone and brick and concrete of London.

When I go up to the saloon, where the others have already started breakfast, the atmosphere is taut. Tori comes over, and I discover why.

'It's happened then,' she says grimly.

'What has?'

She nods to the window on the opposite side of the saloon. Where there should be open sea, there is only ice. A shallow geometric mess of it, angles pointing upwards like a badly iced Christmas cake.

'We're frozen in,' she says. 'Icebound.'

'Shit.'

'It is not an ideal situation, no,' Eino says, coming up behind us. He stands at the glass, hands behind his back. 'I am hopeful that when the tide drops, the ice will collapse.'

'Hopeful,' Gaia echoes.

Eino nods. 'I have established radio contact with another ship, an icebreaker. She is several hours away, if we need assistance.'

'Good. Great!' Tori says, then addresses the worried group. 'You see? All normal. We can do our challenge today, and by the afternoon we should be on our way again.' She looks to Eino for confirmation, but all he does is clear his throat and leave the room.

Annabel finishes up a conversation with Nish, then walks over. 'I've asked everyone about the vomit. No one's admitting to it.'

'Seriously?' I lift my hands and drop them. 'Well, someone's lying. You didn't pick up on anything, no one being cagey or—'

She opens her hands, apologetic. 'Sorry,' she says feebly. 'But listen, Dee. I wanted to say, I'm sorry about the thing yesterday. With your files. I shouldn't have—'

'Don't.' I fix a smile. 'Let's forget about it, okay?'

'Morning, girls,' says Craig from behind us. I toast him with my coffee cup, glad of the distraction. To Annabel, he says, 'You find out who threw up then? No takers?'

She shakes her head. 'I asked everyone. I don't understand it.'

But Craig is dismissive. 'You're on a ship with half a dozen landlubbers, lass. Be a miracle if you didnae have someone boak at some point.'

'It's more the lying about it that's the concern,' I say.

The contestants start to leave, and I pull the medical bracelet from John's bag out of my pocket and show it to Annabel. 'Any idea what this is?'

She takes it from me, inspects it. The chain meets at a thin, elongated disc, like those pennies you can roll into flat ovals in a machine at a fair. 'It's an epilepsy thing. Or diabetes? Like, to identify you if you have a seizure or a hypo, or something. I'm not sure. Where'd you get it?'

I tell her, and she frowns. 'Can't be John's, though. It would have been in his notes. Maybe his kid's?'

I wrinkle my nose. 'Kind of a weird keepsake, though.'

I task Annabel with asking Ulla to take some breakfast down to Wolf, and go out onto the deck. The wind has a hard bite to it, and the seabirds are conspicuously absent from the sky. We're caught in a solid sheet of white, about halfway between the sea and the settlement where we're doing the next challenge. The ice has bound a small flotilla of dilapidated boats close to what must, in summer, be a harbour edge, where a small wooden jetty protrudes from the village.

As Eino patiently explains again to the others about the tide breaking up the ice, Craig studies the village with his binoculars. But when I ask to use them, I quickly notice what's not right about this place. Several of the roofs have collapsed. The only two-storey building, maybe a school or community place, leans at a slight angle. And the uppermost section of what appears to be a communications mast has completely folded onto itself.

'There's no . . . people,' Nish says, hand visoring her eyes. She turns back to us from the prow. 'Why are there no people?'

'It's a common pattern, unfortunately,' Craig says. 'Places like these need subsidising, but to get the money they have to show they're sustainable. But these days the young people don't want to stay.' He shakes his head, evidently sad about it. 'Without young people, there's no investment and the community dies.'

Just then my name is called, and I look round to see Ulla striding over.

Haltingly she explains that she's been collecting bed linen from the bedrooms. 'And I also take dirty laundry, from baskets? We talk before about,' she pauses, uncomfortable, 'illness?'

'Oh, you mean the vomit? You found something?'

'Yes.' She checks around her, then leans in. 'Cabin six. Lady there. Clothes, bottom of the basket. Very dirty.'

I take a breath, realising what this means.

Cabin six is Gaia.

I go straight down with Annabel and knock. Gaia, wrapped up ready for the ice in her padded outerwear, opens her door an inch, already suspicious.

'Gaia, was it you who was unwell outside cabin two?'

The muscles in her jaw bulge. 'I was seasick.'

'Right.' I give that a moment, waiting for her to explain, but that's all she's giving me. 'When?'

She hesitates. 'I don't . . . I don't remember.'

'Before or after the ice hole?'

'I told you, I don't remember.'

'I see.' I turn to Annabel, who's hovering, and unshoulder the tripod. 'Take this, set it up at the base of the gangway. I'll be there in a minute.' She does what she's told, struggling under the weight of it and throwing Gaia an anxious, suspicious look as she leaves.

With her gone, I turn back to Gaia, whose defiance appears to be faltering.

'I'm sorry, but that doesn't make any sense,' I tell her. 'You *must* remember whether it was before we went out or not.'

She rolls her eyes and sighs, making a big deal of recalling it. 'Before. And all right, I should have said—'

'When Annabel asked you a direct question about it, yes, you should.'

'But I was embarrassed. I did try to clear it up.'

'See, that doesn't add up, either. This was right outside the cabin where a man died. What were you even doing there? Your cabin is at the other end of the ship. I'm not pointing any fingers – I've got no idea what's happened. But if there's something you need to say, now is the time.'

She folds her arms and looks away. 'Why can't you people leave me alone?'

This is more than I have patience for. 'Because you're on a bloody television show! The whole point is that you talk to us. Why did you even sign up?'

Without warning, tears spill across her face. 'Because he was—'

Her face crumples, and she clamps a hand over her mouth.

'Because what, Gaia? *Who* was *what*?'

But she closes the door again, and no amount of hammering will make her open it.

I go straight to the office and pull on the yellow coat hanging from the peg there, while I wait for the laptop to power up.

It sings its readiness and I get to work. Because the more I think about it, the more it's been staring me in the face all along. What if the reason Gaia has been so reluctant to be involved is because she never wanted to be on the show in the first place? What if she came out here – somehow circumvented the audition process and got Will to give her a last-minute place – because she wanted something else? Something to do with John?

It would explain her interest in his bag; enough for her to come to my cabin last night and ask me not to go through it. And it would explain why she was outside cabin two – but how would she have known John was in there? And, more importantly, does this mean that he might have been the target after all?

I lay my fingers on the keys. The bracelet in the bag was too small to be John's. What if it was Gaia's?

Linking up the drive with all the contestants' background documents on it, I type *diabetes*, get nothing back. I try *epilepsy*.

One result. I raise my eyebrows, click on it. Read it through. But it's from Tori's file; a footnote that she'd had the condition as a kid, though not severely. I kiss my teeth and close the file, minimise the portal.

What I want is a bloody internet connection, but I go over anyway to the email icon and open it up. The last message to load was days ago – and this is the main production account. I search for Gaia's name, and it comes up with hundreds of messages. But one thread catches my eye.

It's twenty-six messages long, marked with a red flag for urgency. The title: *Nicola Reese: Risk Assessment for Arctic*. It's an exchange between Will and Hugo, the contact at the insurance company.

I click the thread, confused. *Reese.* There was never anyone involved in *Frozen Out* by that name.

I'm sorry, bro, Will's saying in this email, *but we need to push it through somehow. Do we even need to mention the change of name?*

I scroll back up through the thread, tracking the conversation.

It's the nature of the crimes that is the issue, Hugo says. *It's because it's drug-related, and that stint at Pentonville in '98 for ABH (local radio star, lol). She'd supplied Class As to him at one point, then it got weird apparently; she followed him and kept turning up at his house, until she eventually turned violent. Might cause problems on the border – I've asked around, but don't think we're going to be able to push this through without a much pricier package now, mate.*

Will again. *Thing is, we're already maxed out and we need her.*

And, after another week. *All fine, got it agreed – finally! So do you want the policy under Nicola Reese then or her new name?*

New name, Will says. *Gaia Lakshmi.*

I snatch my fingers off the mouse like it's grown teeth.

Gaia's a convicted criminal. And worse than that, worse even than the fact that she changed her name so that we didn't find out, is the profile of her victim. The person she assaulted – the person she stalked – was a celebrity. A celebrity with a secret history of drug use.

What all of that adds up to is one hell of a red flag. If Tori thought she wasn't in danger before, she's going to change her mind now.

44

TORI

It is bitterly, miserably cold on the deck, cold enough to take your breath away and numb your exposed skin within minutes. But I hold everyone there while Annabel sets up the tripod on the ice. The wind is picking up, and the first few flakes of snow are not so much falling as launching a horizontal assault. While this landscape has never been welcoming, right now it feels actively hostile. Eino insists that we should be free of the ice within a few hours, but there's nothing comforting about being held firm against the coast. For the first time I believe what Craig said about the Arctic wanting us dead.

The contestants are all zipped up like toddlers in their scarlet suits, indistinguishable from each other, apart from the black or yellow vests Craig has given them to wear over the top. He's handed out spiked overshoes for them to wear on top of their boots as well.

Marco comes over. 'Do I really need this on?' He flaps the yellow vest. 'It's too small.'

'You do really. It's so that people can see which team you're on. Kind of like with the rugby.'

He glares at me. 'This shit is *nothing* like rugby.' He gives up getting the vest over his clothes and starts trying to tie it around his arm.

Then Dee appears, weighed down with all her camera gear. I go straight over.

'You seen Wolf today?'

'He's fucking furious about being kept inside, but he's cooperating.' She looks around her. 'Listen, I need to talk to you about Gaia.'

'Later, okay? We need to get started.'

'It's important.'

But we don't have time. 'First thing when we're done, okay?'

'No. Now. This is serious, you need to hear—'

'Dee! Tori,' Craig calls. He's beckoning urgently, and we go down the gangway to where he's standing with Eino on the ice.

'What's going on?' Dee asks them.

'That,' Craig says, pointing up and to the south. In the distance is a thick grey-white mass of cloud.

'What is it?'

'It's the storm. It could be here any minute.'

'Not any minute,' Eino counters. 'You can do your filming. You have at least an hour, maybe two.'

Craig goes to speak, then stops, hands together in front of his lips, holding back from an outburst. He takes a breath and tries again. 'It could be much less. And when it comes, you've got no time at all to get back inside.'

But we can't wait. Eino's already said that the police expect us to get John to them as soon as we can. So delaying this would take such a big bite out of our time that we might as well cancel the show.

And not only that, but staying here any longer than we need to means whoever it is that filled that room with gas has a little longer to get to me. We have to get this challenge in the bag, today.

Reading my mind, Dee says, 'It's not worth the risk, Tori.' No *Tor*, not any more. 'The network will understand. And there's no way I can get all the shots in an hour, anyway.'

Except Dee doesn't have everything she owns riding on it. I'm not going back to the network empty-handed. 'Then we cut it down. You shoot one team, Annabel does the other. Dispense with the stuff on the deck – let's go straight over now. Eino, do we definitely have an hour?'

'Yes.'

'No!' Craig says, aghast. 'Maybe, but not definitely. It can't possibly be worth it.'

Dee growls with frustration, then kneels next to the assembled kit. 'Give me two minutes.'

She starts to brief Annabel. 'We're going to use the radio mics. Each camera has two audio channels: we're going to have the onboard mic linked up to one of them, and the other will be on a radio-clip mic. We'll give one of the radio mics to Tori and the other one to Marco.' To me, she says, 'Come here, I'll mic you up.'

I let her move me around, twisting to hook one of the transmitter units onto the back of my belt, then threading a wire up under my jacket. She attaches the clip-on mic to my collar.

'Keep your distance from Gaia,' she says straight into my ear.

I turn, follow her eyeline to where Gaia is standing alone on the deck. 'What? Why?'

'Just do it, okay?'

Then she shows Annabel where the inputs go, and discusses how to change the sound levels if the wind starts interfering. After that, the two of them start shooting: Dee gets down low to capture the contestants coming down onto the ice, and Annabel gets ahead to pick up some GVs. Together, we move out towards the village. I'm about to call out to Annabel to get closer to the group – we need the frame filled with movement and shot from the back, to disguise the fact that no one's smiling – but before I do, she's moved into the exact position I'd have suggested. There may not be many positives right now, but she's come a long way.

I head over to where Craig has unfolded a plasticised map on the ground. 'This is madness. You do realise that?'

As clearly and calmly as I can, I lay it on the line. 'If we don't shoot the material, Craig, we don't get paid. Understand? None of us.'

He laughs, incredulous. 'At this point I'm rather more concerned about survival that remuneration.'

Right then Dee comes hurrying past, her spiked overshoes crunching into the snow.

'Something weird about the sound levels on this one,' she says without stopping, holding up a radio-mic transmitter. 'Getting the spare – I'll be quick. Annabel's ready to shoot Craig's intro,' she shouts behind her.

Craig folds up his map. 'I hope you know what you're doing.'

Annabel, joining us, looks defensive. 'Tori always knows what she's doing.'

Then, as if in disagreement, a sudden furious gust of wind takes hold of the sheet in Craig's hands and whips it directly upwards. He watches it hopelessly as it flies out towards the mountains.

Annabel jumps up and sprints after it, but after about twenty metres she can see it's futile.

'Let it go,' Craig calls out. When she's back in earshot he asks her, 'Did you have those satellite pictures of the village anywhere?'

'On my phone, I think—' She pauses to dig in her pockets. Then, frowning, she spreads her hands. 'I thought it was here . . .'

'When did you last have it?'

'Yesterday, in the office?' she says vaguely, checking the camera bag now.

'Nae bother.' Craig gets to his feet. 'We're winging it anyway, right? Who needs maps?'

But she's still searching every pocket, with increasing concern.

'Forget it, Annabel,' I tell her. 'It'll be on the ship.' None of us has used a phone in days – I'm surprised she'd even meant to bring it with her.

Still unsmiling, she gives up and balances the second camera steadily on her shoulder. 'I'm ready when you are.'

I give her the thumbs up, and a few seconds later she raises a hand.

'At speed.'

For a second Craig just stares at me without emotion. Then he shakes his head and addresses the assembled crowd, with the trapped ship looming in the background.

'Right, guys!' You'd never know he was anything other than 100 per cent pumped and ready. 'Let's head over to the village for your next challenge!'

45

DEE

I race back to the ship, almost knocking over Stefan on the deck as he tightens the RIBs to the ship's side with ratchet straps in preparation for the storm. I go straight to the office. But the mic I need isn't in any of the drawers. I stand for a moment, panting, trying to place it. Precious seconds later, I think of the camera Wolf's been using for his stupid channel. It's not perfect, but it's a workaround.

With Wolf locked in, I need a key. I go back out and grab Stefan, explaining the situation on the way down to Wolf's cabin. He lets me in, but waits outside.

Wolf jumps up from his desk as I walk in. His eyes are red, like he hasn't slept at all, and his hair is wild. 'Dee! I need to talk to you.'

'I don't have time,' I hold up the mic. 'You've got one of these, right? I'm having trouble—'

'That doesn't matter,' he says, going over to his desk. I spot his kit and start digging for a spare before he can stop me.

'You want to tell me about SyncHole Productions?'

I miss a heartbeat. 'What.' It comes out flat, a whisper.

'Ah.' He wafts a hand at me, signifying my whole reaction.

'That only confirms it. Aren't you supposed to be this brilliant liar? What happened to the poker face, huh?'

My breath trembles in my throat, refusing to come out.

'See,' he goes on, 'when I mentioned something going tits up on an undercover job, and you said you didn't know what I meant, you overdid it. I wasn't sure it was even you that was involved, previously. But the *way* you denied it?' He gives a slow heave of a shrug. 'That's what gave you away.'

All I have to do is open my mouth and tell him it's not true. *Just say it.* But I can't.

'Not like you not to have an answer,' Wolf says. I want to hate him for that, but for once there's no malice in it. The man looks desperate, sure, but he's not enjoying this. He stands there, watching me.

I find I have laid the mic on the desk. Without looking at him, I say, 'It's nothing to do with you. That stuff is all over now.'

'Maybe for you. No, don't go yet. Listen. I need you to hear this.' But then he stops, points at the mic. 'Is that . . . Can she hear us?'

'What? No, she's—' I start to tell him that Tori's wearing the other unit, but stop myself. 'What difference does it make?'

'Because you don't know her. She's not what you think she is.'

I laugh. Always this. In the handful of times our paths have crossed since they split, he always finds a way to go off about Tori. The big-name girlfriend that Wolf let slip through his fingers, as if his own fame was never enough. '*You're* the one who doesn't know her, Wolf. I've got to go.'

He looks up at me, like he's about to laugh, but he doesn't. 'I think people need to know who they're working with. You need to know about her. What she's actually been doing all this time. Just like we need to know about you. Sophie.'

It takes a physical effort to keep my knees from buckling.

No one knows about Sophie. Afterwards, when it all blew up, I was only ever referred to as 'the investigator'.

But Wolf knows.

'So what is this then? You're blackmailing me?'

'No, look. I'm on your side, all right?' He's being serious now, aiming for sincerity, like he cares. 'I've found something you're going to want to hear. But I need you to tell them it wasn't me. John – it wasn't me. All right, Dee?'

I swallow. 'Say your piece, Wolf.'

'Not unless you back me up.'

I let out a laugh that I don't mean and go to the door. He advances on me, but I get there first.

'Tell it to your fucking channel.' I shut the door and Stefan, waiting in the passage, darts in to lock it, then leaves without a word.

Hammering on the door, Wolf shouts after me. 'Dee. *Dee!* You're going to want to hear this. *Dee!*'

I grit my teeth against the hot prickle of tears, but I don't pause, not even for a moment. Leo's voice sounds in my head, as clear as if he was standing beside me.

Sophie. Sophie.

Mechanically I check the new mic as I mount the stairs. Check the battery, check the levels. Replace the protective case.

Remember why I'm here and do the work.

46

TORI

On arrival in the village, the contestants gather on what remains of the steps of the biggest building. Ahead of them, across a hundred metres of ice, is the ship, bound to its sheltered spot beside the rocky toes of the fjord.

Hauling a huge ring of coiled red rope over his shoulder, Craig gets to work setting up. He starts unspooling it to create a dividing line down the middle of a central emptiness – what must have once been a market square or a playground.

I call out to Annabel that we're nearly ready to get started, but she doesn't move from where she's crouching. I make my way over to where she's staring off in concentration, listening, one hand pressing the cup of the headphones to her ear. When I tap her on the shoulder, it makes her jump.

'Sorry!' She flips up the cans. 'Didn't hear you.'

'Are you ready? We need to start as soon as Dee's back.'

'Sure, okay.' She gathers her things and gets up, getting a few more shots of the ghost village before we begin.

The wind is picking up by the minute. I squint out towards the ship and soon I see Dee hurrying back towards us. Out of breath as she comes to a stop, she calls Annabel over and takes the camera from her to un-jack the receiver that's linked to the faulty one. But then she suddenly freezes.

'Did you hear any of that?' Dee asks.

Annabel looks up. 'Any of what?'

'I was . . . singing to myself, on the ship.'

I frown. Dee never sings.

'Hope you didn't hear it, through the mic.'

Annabel shakes her head, amused. 'Didn't hear a thing.'

Obviously hiding her relief, Dee calls Marco over and mics him up before we get into position for the briefing. Then she frames up and shows me the shot: red-clad contestants milling in front of an abandoned village of maybe two dozen dwellings. The bright paint of them against the virgin snow should be picturesque, stunning. But the snow is already whirling more thickly now, interfering with the light.

'It's the best I can do,' Dee says. 'Can't guarantee how it'll cut together.'

I know what she means – the whole thing is just wrong. Four contestants, instead of the eight we were meant to have originally. Everyone preoccupied. And a dead man on a ship, with, very possibly, a killer among us. What are we even doing here?

Nish comes over. 'This doesn't look safe,' she tells me. 'What's the plan if the storm gets worse?'

Dee cocks her head at me, eyebrows raised.

I put my hand on Nish's shoulder. 'Truth is, this wasn't going to be today's challenge, but with the weather like it is, we've decided it'll make it all the more . . . challenging.' Nish goes to argue it, but before she gets a chance I turn to Dee, beaming. 'Okay then! Are you ready?'

Dee snaps her headphones back on. 'As I'll ever be.'

She signals speed and, with Craig standing beside me, I summon a massive smile and spread my arms wide.

'Welcome to the game! It's exactly like you might have played as a kid. Except this time we've got the added element . . . of the *elements*!' I raise my arms to signify the weather, but it doesn't even elicit a good-natured groan.

Nish folds her arms and looks at the ground.

'The line down the middle delineates your territory,' Craig says, saving me. 'Each team has one of these,' he says, holding up two large flags, one yellow, one black. 'You can choose a place in your sector to stake it. Then all you've got to do is be the first team to successfully steal the other team's flag. The leadership qualities we'll be looking for in particular are to do with strategy as well as communication. Who's going to be your spy? Who's going to guard your flag? When do you change tactics? How do you play to your strengths?'

He pauses to check over his shoulder, out towards the direction of the weather. Then he glances back to me. The stony set of his eyes says it all. The snow is getting worse: we're running out of time.

'Right then!' I call into the wind. I take the air-horn canister Craig is holding out to me, raise it up above my head and release a powerful blast of sound. 'You have half an hour to capture the flag!'

47

DEE

The yellow team is just Marco and Helen. If there were four on a side, the way we'd planned it, they'd have been able to really get into the teamwork – defence, sneak attacks, decoys, subterfuge, loads of great material. As it is, I've got visibility dropping by the second, as many crew as competitors. Once it's layered with voiceover and moody music, maybe it'll be passable. But what I'm looking at through the lens right now doesn't look fun. It looks futile.

I follow them round the back of a row of houses where they search for somewhere to place their flag, and try to concentrate on what's ahead of me. But after what I've just heard from Wolf, it's hard to keep my mind focused. From the way Annabel looked at me when I came back with the mic, I'm certain she heard me talking to him. The connection had been glitching and the signal would have been weak. But she could have heard.

It's bad enough her knowing about SyncHole. But if it gets out about Sophie too – about what I really did to Leo – that's more than I can contain.

There's a shout from behind me, Marco calling to his team-mate, and I make myself do what I'm here to do. I have to walk backwards, keeping my back to the blowing snow so that I don't have to constantly wipe the lens. Even with snowshoes gripping the icy earth, I'm unsteady on my feet, relying on my locked core to stop me overbalancing in the ever-shifting wind. Behind the houses, great ethereal drifts of snow are blowing upwards and away, like the ghosts of waves rising over the hills.

'Here's good,' Marco calls, pointing to a pile of ropes, his voice loud and clear in my headphones. He brushes the worst of the snow off with a gloved hand and gestures for the flag from Helen.

'The place back there was better!' Helen shouts back over the wind. I can pick her up only vaguely on the onboard mic, but I'll find a way to edit it. I start imagining whether this discussion will work with subtitles, but then Helen concedes. 'Could we please get on with it? I don't think we should be out here at all.'

I tighten up on their faces as they settle their flag – even with the eyewear she's got on, the anxiety is clear to see.

They move off and I un-shoulder the camera and run into a different shot, looping around the back of where Helen's standing guard. From here, I can frame the red dividing line and Helen at opposite sides of the same shot, with Marco and the sheet of ice behind.

But even in the minutes it takes me to reset, things have changed. The weather is accelerating. It's got a noise all of its own now, a constant howl, as if it's angry, or in pain. Both. The snow is coming in so fast and fat that it's like watching the world through a filter. I try to keep the camera trained on Marco as he calls something back to Helen, but even with his radio mic in my headphones at maximum volume, I'm struggling to make him out now, let alone her.

Marco makes a bolt across the no-man's land in the middle. Almost immediately I see Nish and Gaia – identifiable by their black vests – coming the other way. One of them stumbles, grabbing on to the other as they try to run into yellow's territory. Marco sees them and sprints across to get in their way. I go closer to capture the action, but before I zoom in, my eye is drawn away.

To another shape, much further back.

I take my eye from the viewfinder and squint into the whitening distance. Visibility is dropping by the second. But even in flashes, it's unmistakable: the vivid green of Wolf's jacket.

He gets closer, lumbering across the ice, the weather bearing down on the space in between us like static. My heart thumps with deafening rapidity in my ears. Why is he here? How did he get out?

'. . . over there?' I hear someone say. I turn, flip one of the headphones away from my ear and realise it's Craig, calling me from the centre line. He's only twenty, thirty feet away, but he's almost inaudible through the fearsome wind.

'What?' I shout back.

'I said we need to get out of here. Can you see Tori over there?'

A curtain of snow sweeps past me, so thick that I lose sight of him until he reappears by my side.

'We need to get to shelter!' he shouts, pulling on my sleeve, trying to drag me with him towards a building.

I shake him off and tuck the camera under my arm, pressing the earphones hard against my head. From Marco's mic I can make out the sound of Wolf's voice.

'Where is she?' he's saying. But I still can't see him.

There's a huge roar of wind, and a bombardment of white comes at me like a solid mass. For half a second the snow clears enough for me to see Wolf, a blur of green, moving off. Fast, northwards, towards the other side of the village.

Then I'm running. I can hardly see where, but I have to catch him up. I try to keep him in my sights, not even thinking about the camera now, barely hearing Craig behind me, screaming.

I crouch by the side of a building, clutching the camera to my chest. It's not only the snow, turned ballistic by a wind that must be beyond fifty miles an hour. It's the debris – pieces of board, a torn sheet of corrugated iron, plastic stuff that flies past so fast I can't even identify it. I try crying for help, but I can't hear my own voice. Nothing but white noise in my ears. Eyes gripped shut against the onslaught of snow, muscles spasming with cold. Except this isn't snow. Five minutes ago it was snow. This, now, is a risk to life.

A noise cuts through the howl of the storm, an irregular rumble. I open my eyes long enough to see something huge, blue, bouncing towards me. In the same second, I recognise what it is – a plastic barrel, easily as big as I am – and duck.

I'm not quick enough. Blinding, dense pain slams through my head and almost out the other side. And then, suddenly, everything is still.

And I'm outside Leo's flat, back in Bath, six months ago.

I see him in the car, where he'd told me to meet him. I see it all, like a film. Street light fragmenting in the puddles by my feet. His face lit blue by the light of his phone.

I make that split-second decision about the camera in my bag, which I no longer want to be carrying. Something makes me reach in to turn it off, because what we have now is private. Not something I'm going to hand over for use in an edit suite. Not something to be broadcast. It's our love affair. Me and him.

My hand falters on the remote to pause the recording, but then he looks up, sees me.

And I know there's something wrong.

So although he doesn't see the camera, I'm still rolling as I climb into the passenger seat next to him.

Still rolling as he shows me the email he got, telling him who I really am. From someone anonymous, tipping him off about SyncHole, the investigation – the fact that I have lied about everything.

Still rolling when he tells me I'm nothing to him. That he never wants to see my face again.

That I've ruined his life.

And even after I've finally done what he's screaming at me to do and got out of his car, the camera is still rolling as he drives away, because I've left the bag behind.

'Dee!'

A hand on my shoulder. My leg. Someone I know, yelling my name.

'Jesus Christ, Dee!' It's Tori. 'She's here!'

'Get her up!' Another voice. A man. Craig. Marco. John.

No. Not John. I don't know.

'Dee, get up!'

Definitely Craig, and then Tori's voice too. 'Leave the camera, come on!'

I force myself to my feet, but my knees buckle.

'Leave it!' Tori implores.

But I can't let go of it. And I can't see – not a thing – but I let them lead me. I have to kick my boots to excavate them from what must be a drift of snow, fallen in what can only have been minutes. With someone's guiding hand on my back, I feel my way along a wall with one free hand, utterly disorientated, the white-out so complete that when the solid surface ends and I come to empty space, I can hardly tell if it's the corner of the building or a doorway into it.

'In here!'

I'm pushed inside, and I drop to my knees as the deafening storm shakes the ground beneath us.

48

TORI

An hour later I let myself into Dee's cabin and kneel next to her.

'How are you doing?' I whisper. Her eyelids move, but she stays asleep. I hold her hand, knowing she won't let me once she wakes up again. Her hair clings in damp cords across her forehead, despite my best efforts to rub it dry after we got to safety.

Outside the storm is still slamming us with everything it's got, picking up again after the short window of reprieve that allowed us back onto the ship. And despite Eino's reassurances, the ice around us hasn't budged. We're still stuck.

Dee was knocked out for only a moment, but came round when the three of us – Marco, Craig and I – got her into the abandoned house where we were sheltering. And it's thanks to Craig that we got out of there: he saw when the break in the weather had come and knew, almost to the minute, how long we had before it started again. I wince in shame as I think of him, and the way he hasn't even mentioned whose fault this is, even when he was getting ready to head back out.

Because not everyone got back safely. Wolf is missing.

There's a soft knock at the door. It's Annabel, with tea.

She's pale, almost colourlessly so. The mugs rattle on the tray as she sets it down and passes one to me, and then her eyes go to Dee. 'She'll be all right, won't she?'

'Sit with me,' I tell her. I put the steaming mug on the floor beside me. 'She's going to be fine, she only needed to sleep.'

Annabel pulls out her phone.

'You found it then?' I ask, pointing.

She smiles, embarrassed. 'It was there all the time, in the camera case. I don't know how I missed it. But here's the thing. I asked everyone what they saw, to try to work out where Wolf might have gone,' she tells me, scrolling through her notes. 'They're all saying the same thing. They couldn't hear him. Helen didn't see anything, nor did Nish. Marco thought he saw Wolf turning back this way.' She stops, raises a shoulder, drops it. 'But if he did, he didn't make it.'

'And you're sure you didn't see where he was going?'

'No. But—' She looks away, awkward. 'I heard him. On the mic. He was looking for you.'

My blood goes cold. 'Why? What did he want?'

But she doesn't answer the question. She leans forward, her skinny forearms resting on her legs. 'Did he find you?'

A dark mass gathers in the pit of my stomach. 'Nope,' I say, careful not to look away, 'he didn't.'

'You're sure?'

'Uh, yes? Why are you asking me like that?' I try to laugh, but it dies on its way out. Because Annabel's not laughing.

'You and Wolf. The two of you have been hostile to each other this whole time.' She twists her hands together in her lap, not meeting my eye. 'Everyone's noticed it. And when I saw Wolf coming out looking for you, it was . . .' She lets it trail off and sighs, as if every word is painful. 'It was like he wanted a fight, you know? And now he's missing, and I'm not saying anything happened,' she says, speeding up, 'I'm only asking the question. Whether anything did.'

'Nothing *happened*, Annabel.'

'Okay,' she says, but she doesn't seem satisfied. 'Oh, also, I think someone picked up my camera?'

'Craig. He brought both of them back when we evacuated.'

'Right. So. Someone should check the footage.' She makes herself look at me. 'I think it should probably be me.'

So she can see if I'm lying, she means. See if she or Dee caught footage of me hurting Wolf. She's only doing her job. She wants to do the right thing. But I hate her for it. A switch flicks in me.

'Why don't you come straight out and say it, Annabel? Huh? Have the guts to say what you think. That I *attacked* him, is that it?'

'No! That's not what I'm saying. I just thought . . . for the others. For transparency. If I could tell them there's nothing there, they'd know they can trust you.'

'So, wait, is it *them* wanting to see the footage or you?'

Right then there's a groan from the bed. It's Dee, waking up.

'The camera,' she says.

Of course it's her first thought. 'It's fine,' I tell her.

'Where – we're back on board?' she says weakly, her own survival evidently an afterthought to the safety of the material. 'How?'

'You don't remember?' Annabel says, looking from her to me, alarmed.

'Craig said she might be groggy,' I tell Annabel, then give Dee

282

the potted version of how we got back. Craig, with the makeshift stretcher he made for her from a plank because she was too weak to walk. How Eino used the ship's lights to guide us back, and Craig organised the rest of them to hold onto the length of rope, so we could get back to the ship if there was another whiteout.

'Everyone?' she asks.

Annabel meets my eye. But it falls to me to say it out loud.

'Wolf is . . . We don't know where he is.'

'No.' Dee immediately struggles to sit. 'Out there?' I try to stop her, but she's blinking the drowsiness away. 'No. *No*. We have to find him.'

'Stop – you have to rest. Craig and Stefan are out there now. Stefan said Wolf was hammering on the door of his cabin to be let out, said it was an emergency.'

'What emergency?'

I spread my hands.

'We're going to find him!' Annabel says, her eyes shining with tears. 'People are up there with binoculars looking for movement, it's not like we've *left him—*' Her voice cracks and wells up, and she presses her lips between her teeth.

It takes her a minute to compose herself, and then she glances at me. I know what's coming. If I don't tell Dee, Annabel will. So I take a deep breath. 'Apparently Wolf was looking for me, when he came out in the storm.'

'Why? What did he want?'

'I don't know.'

She doesn't believe me. She pulls a hand out from under the covers and rubs it across her forehead. Colour is starting to return, but so is everything else. Suspicion. Distrust.

Dee clears her throat. 'Annabel, could you give us a minute?'

'Oh.' Her face flashes with hurt. 'Sure. Sorry.' Then, to me, 'So shall I get the cameras now or—'

I give her a look she can't misinterpret.

'Right. Later then.'

Dee watches her go, then turns to me. She's not smiling.

'Tor.' She takes a breath, studying me. Dread tightens like an iron band across my chest. 'You know I came back to the ship, before we started?'

I nod. 'For the mic.'

'Yeah. Well, I spoke to Wolf.'

I keep my eyes on her.

'And he had something he wanted to tell me. About you, I think.'

I keep my face mild, interested. On the inside, every alarm I have is firing.

'He said there was something you were hiding.'

I cock my head, my smile mild, but inside I turn myself to stone. Wolf can't have known about me. About me and John. No one knew. I was sure of it. But what if I've taken too many risks? I see the end of the lie coming into sight, like the light of an oncoming train.

Dee raises her eyebrows, giving me one last chance, but it's not a chance I want to take.

I clear my throat, give her a *search me* look. 'I don't know what he meant, Dee.' I get up, go to the door. 'I have no idea.'

'You don't have to tell me,' she says. 'But I'll find out.'

And as I head into the passage, I know that somehow, she will.

49

DEE

I make myself get up and take a long shower, but I can't thaw out, not even when my skin is red and swollen from the hot water. I dry off and get into thermals, jeans and three sweaters. I'm still shivering when I leave my cabin.

As I enter the bridge, Tori hurries over. 'What are you doing up here? You look awful. You need to be resting.'

'I'm fine,' I tell her and go over to the angled window. Every floodlight on the ship is pointing inland towards the village. The effect is ghostly, the snow uplit against a violet-black sky as it falls, the ruined houses casting long shadows into the hills.

The captain sets his binoculars down and speaks to Ulla, who's saying the same thing over and over again into what I'm guessing is the radio. He asks her something in Finnish, to which she replies with a shake of her head.

He sees my expectant glance and draws a deep breath that tells me it's not going to be good news.

'The tide has peaked, but we are still icebound. I have asked for urgent medical evacuation, but no one can fly to us in this weather.'

'But the other ship, the icebreaker, it can help us out, right?'

'We have been unable to contact them in the last hour. Our communications are still online, but they're not responding. It's not only us – coastguard has been unable to contact them, either. It may be that they have been damaged in the storm.'

'So what do we do?'

'We keep trying.' He glances at his watch. 'Stefan and Craig should be back soon.' Although they'd been forced to wait until the storm was a little calmer, the weather is still appalling. It was agreed they'd go out for no more than forty-five minutes, but that time is nearly up.

'They said they'd send one flare if they were delayed but safe. Two is a call for help.'

I scan the ice, but there's no sign of them. No flares. Nothing.

Ulla slams her hand on the desk in sudden frustration, and Eino spins round to reprimand her. 'Keep going,' he says in English. 'It's all we can do.'

I swallow and make myself ask the question that no one wants to ask. 'How long until it's . . . until he's not going to be okay, do you think?'

He takes such a long time to answer me that I think he hasn't heard. Just as I'm about to repeat it, Eino clears his throat.

'He will be okay.'

'I mean, yes, we all want—'

'There,' he says suddenly, pointing. 'There, over there!'

And I see them too. Two figures, heads bowed, leaning into the wind at an almost impossible angle. Impossible until I see that, behind them, they're dragging the stretcher. And on the stretcher is what looks, from this distance, like a thick bundle of fabric. Dense and inert. It can only be Wolf.

Eino has already dropped his binoculars and is zipping up his outer jacket and pulling on gloves. As he races from the bridge he shouts something to Ulla, who crosses the room in three steps and disappears too, following him.

I watch as another figure – Marco, I think – runs out from the ship to meet the others. With the weight spread between more people, their pace increases and soon they're hauling the stretcher up the gangplank.

Following Tori, I get to the saloon – the closest properly heated room to the main deck – just as Wolf is lifted by Stefan, Craig and Marco onto the table. Snow shakes onto the floor, melting instantly where it lies. Annabel is there, too, deathly white. Nish comes in and immediately leaves, shouting behind her that she'll bring blankets.

'Oh my God,' Tori is saying over and over.

Craig tears off his outersuit. 'Anyone who doesn't need to be here, get out or stay well out of the way.' Marco leaves, and I steer Tori over to a seat by the door. I glance round and notice that Gaia's nowhere to be seen.

'Annabel, hot water in bowls, please,' Craig says as he hurriedly removes his backpack, unzips it and digs inside.

I ask him what happened.

'We found him behind one of the houses, face-down,' he says, pulling out a small torch. He stands to lean over Wolf, trying to open his eyes to shine a light into them. 'Possible head wound, judging by the blood on his face, but I haven't investigated. We had to get him back before the frostbite got any worse.'

'Do you know what to do?' I ask him.

'The basic stuff,' he says, waving me out of the way. 'Annabel! Water and towels now, or get out of here!'

'Yes, got it,' she says, blinking. 'Towels.'

I stand there speechless, trying to make sense of what I'm seeing. Wolf is barely breathing. His face is the colour of wallpaper paste, but his nose and ears are blueish and waxy with frostbite. His eyes are rolled back, his lips parted. There's a thick swathe of blood across his jaw, but it's not clear where it's coming from.

Ulla calls from the passage and I take an armful of tea towels from her. When I carry them back into the saloon, Craig is finishing cutting away the hood of Wolf's coat. He jerks away, the back of his wrist going to his mouth as he realises what he's looking at. And then everyone else sees it, too.

A gash in Wolf's head, right above his ear. No, not a gash. A hollow. A cavity, thick with blood.

Something else showing through. Pale.

'Fuck,' says Stefan.

50

DEE

Within minutes, the saloon has been transformed into a make-shift hospital. Helen has shepherded everyone out, and now it's only Craig and Stefan in there.

I stand in the passageway, waiting silently for news, flanked by Tori on one side and Annabel on the other. I'm shivering still, and my head feels like I've just woken up after two pints of gin and a street fight.

'He's going to make it, right?' Annabel whispers.

I don't have an answer. She repeats her question to Tori, but then the door swings open and Craig comes out.

'I need some air for a minute,' he says, not making eye contact. He snaps off the latex gloves, which aren't as white any more. I immediately look away from them.

'Did he say anything?' Annabel asks him. Craig keeps walking, but she follows, so Tori and I do the same. 'Did Wolf say what happened?'

'No.' He goes ahead of us and opens a window an inch. Immediately the passage fills with icy air. 'Groans, nothing else.' He closes his eyes and leans back against the wall, breathing deeply.

'Nothing at all, even when you found him?'

'I said no,' Craig tells her, irritated. 'Does it matter? Poor bastard's brain's exposed in there.'

'We're only worried,' I say for her.

'Aye? Well, I'm fucking worried too.' The muscles are tense in his jaw. 'I'm really fucking worried.' He lets out a ragged breath, wiping his forehead with the back of his arm. 'Man needs a hospital. Now. A bloody good one.'

Tori can't quite look at him. 'So what happened? Did he trip or . . . ?'

'How am I supposed to know?' Craig snaps. 'Anything could have happened. I mean, these *people*. I wouldnae be surprised by anything any more.'

'I think you might, actually,' I tell him. They all look at me. 'Not here,' I say.

We go down a level and I usher them all into the office. I check the passage before I click the door shut, then I cross to the heavy desk under one window and open up the laptop. The three of them crowd around me as I open the tabs.

'It seems that Gaia isn't quite who she claimed to be.' I glance at Tori, knowing how badly she's going to take this latest lie from Will. I explain briefly what they're looking at.

Craig leans in, and I take my hands away from the trackpad. He reads, the others craning, crammed in behind him, to see the email thread I found earlier about Gaia, her history.

'Holy shit,' is Craig's assessment.

'Wow,' says Annabel. 'ABH? That's – wow.'

Tori takes a step back, her expression unreadable.

'And then there's the details of it,' I say, scrolling down. 'The person she assaulted was a radio personality. Minor, but still; they were well known, at the time. But not as well known as you, Tori. Not as well known as Wolf. Apparently the victim had been followed for some time.'

'Shit,' Annabel breathes, her eyes drifting towards Tori. 'She *stalked* a celebrity.'

It sounds ludicrous, but I think of that figure approaching Tori on the first night. Could it have been Gaia?

'So let me get this straight.' Craig pushes his hands into his pockets. 'She's got previous for assaulting someone who happened to be small-town famous. Might be relevant, might not. But then we have our *properly* famous presenter falling suspiciously from the ship. And someone dead in the room that everyone thought was Tori's. And a few days later our *other*, actually really famous guy – who Gaia laid into only the day before, if I need to remind you – loses the side of his fucking head.'

'After he drove a pack of dogs into her,' Annabel says. We all look at her. 'Well, it's true. Gaia's charity is there specifically to help addicts with their animals, remember. And you saw what happened when the huskies went for her. She only went over there because one of them was injured.' She folds her arms. 'Maybe she wanted revenge on Wolf for that.'

I get up. 'I'm going to ask her about it. Nothing to lose.'

Craig growls in frustration as he goes to the door. 'This is without a doubt the most fucked-up thing I have ever been a part of.'

We follow him out into the passage, where he heads off in the direction of the saloon, back up to Wolf. 'Tell me what she says, right?' he calls back. 'Straight away.'

The three of us make our way in silence to Gaia's cabin. She answers my knock immediately, like she's been waiting for us.

'Hey.' I make my voice soft. 'Can we come in?'

She reads our faces one by one. 'Why?'

'We asked you about your criminal record,' I tell her. 'You told us it was clean.'

Gaia folds her arms. 'Will knew.'

I go at it another way. 'Did you have anything to do with what happened to Wolf, Gaia? Or is it *Nicola*?'

She goes to close the door, but I'm expecting it and push my foot into the gap. 'You can either talk to us now,' I tell her, 'or you can explain it to the police.'

From behind the door she releases the pressure, and in the second that I'm unbalanced she pushes hard. The door clicks shut.

Tori, Annabel and I share a look. I jerk my head and they follow me to the end of the passageway.

'Someone's got to stay and talk to her,' I say. 'Tor, can you do that?' Annabel looks crestfallen, but this is no time for massaging egos. The girl couldn't coax the skin from a banana.

'I'm going to go back and see Wolf. I'll return in a bit.'

Tori nods and goes back to Gaia's cabin, but Annabel follows me up the companionway. When we're out of earshot, she stops. 'Dee. Did you see anything, out there? When Wolf came out in the challenge?'

'I blacked out,' I remind her.

'There must be something useful on one of the cameras. I can totally do that job – go through it all, see if we shot anything? Tori said Craig had them, but—'

Right then, Ulla appears, looking for us.

'Come. He is trying to speak.'

I follow her at a run, calling over my shoulder for Annabel to get Tori.

In the saloon Craig stands stony-faced, arms crossed. As I come in, he and Stefan take a step away from where Wolf lies supine. The room is overcrowded with spare free-standing heaters, and there is a smell of something awful in there, something solid and metallic, inhuman. Dishcloths hang over the lamps.

'The light was bothering him,' Craig says quietly, seeing my confusion.

Wolf's green jacket lies eviscerated, reduced to a pile of rags and reddened wadding, in the corner of the room. They've made him as comfortable as they can. What half an hour ago was a dining table is now a bed, padded with duvets. The pillowcases under his head are sodden with red.

I swallow. The person I approach, his once-lustrous hair matted with blood, looks ten, twenty years older than the Wolf I last saw. His skin is the colour of roadside snow, and waxy.

He was beautiful.

He's not beautiful now.

By some psychological sleight of hand, I manage to look only at his face, and not see the horror that I already know is bulging out from between the blood-streaked wounds beyond his hairline. It takes every ounce of courage, but I touch him on the shoulder. I say his name.

Wolf opens his eyes a fraction and looks right at me.

'Hey,' I say softly. Dropping into a crouch, I take his hand.

But although I move, his eyes don't, staying fixed on the space above my head.

Opposite me, Craig is gazing into the middle distance, holding three fingers to Wolf's wrist. But then he looks down at me. He carefully places Wolf's hand on his chest. He gives me the slightest shake of his head. There are tears in his eyes.

I stand, walk over to the window, vaguely aware of voices behind me, Tori crashing into the room. A wail. Craig's voice, low and susurrant beneath it.

He's dead.

Wolf's dead.

There are two dead men on the ship.

51

TORI

I skid into the saloon, but straight away I can see something is wrong. No one's rushing around, no one's talking. Dee's staring out of the window, Craig's standing with his back to the room, head tipped back.

'What are you all doing?' I say, rushing over to Wolf. 'Hey. Hey! It's me, I'm here. It's Tor.'

I take his shoulders, give him a gentle shake. He's just sleeping. Resting.

Dee is by my elbow now. 'Tori, stop.'

One of his hands swings off the side of the table. The fingers are curled, lifeless.

Someone puts an arm around me, tries to move me, but it's like there's a thick band of elastic keeping me tethered to him.

Come on, Tori, someone is saying. *Come and sit down.*

I'm holding his hand, but his skin is ice-cold, unresponsive. And I let them lead me away.

Sit, come on. Drink this. Here. Blow your nose.

A mug of something hot on the table next to me. A hand on my back. Watching people who don't even know Wolf talk about what they're going to do, how they're going to move him. Talk about it like he's a broken-down car.

Someone brings a folded pile of towels. Someone lifts his head, someone else wraps it. They fold the sheet around him. They count to three and then lift and then he's gone.

He was my man for five years.

Once, he filled all the kitchen cupboards with balloons to make me laugh. He secretly loved K-pop and *Warhammer*, and he was scared of frogs.

He was angry, a lot. When he cried, he did it in secret.

He didn't bother coming to the airport to see my dad off with me, when he moved back to Japan.

When I decided to stop using coke for good just before my thirtieth, he said I was boring. He bought me a gram for my birthday, then called me a mad cunt for flushing it.

Every morning he ate the sugary cereal he'd eaten as a kid, unable to kick the habit, in a world of sourdough and kefir. He ran every single day, counted calories religiously. Sometimes, if he overate, he'd make himself sick, though he'd never admit it.

Once, when the dishwasher broke down and I blamed him, he threw a plate at me. Another time, one winter night when he'd passed out after being obnoxiously drunk, I opened all the windows and left him there, out of sheer spite.

His grandmother died, and I held him when he cried himself to sleep because he hadn't called her enough, hadn't visited and couldn't forgive himself.

And worst of all, he spent his whole life ashamed, lonely and in hiding. Closing the door on true happiness, on finding real love, because he was so afraid of what would happen if he came out and told the world who he was.

He hurt me, and he loved me, and I did both of those things, too. We were friends. We should have been kinder.

And he's dead now. And it's because of me.

52

DEE

I sit with her for a long time. I make her tea, give her tissues. I sit until the shuddering subsides, and I smooth the hair from her face.

She did all of these things for me, not so long ago. But I never did her the kindness of telling her why. Tori didn't even know that my pain was grief, too.

After a long time I give her hand a squeeze and let it go. I make sure she has everything she needs, then tell her I'm going up to the bridge. I want to see what the state of play is with the storm and make a plan to get out of here.

Tori sighs and turns to me. 'I don't understand it. What was Wolf even doing out there? What did he want?'

'I don't—' I start to say, but then I cut myself off. Because maybe there's a way of finding out. What I said the last time I saw Wolf, safe and well on the ship, sounds in my head. *Tell it to your fucking channel.*

When I get to the bridge, Eino is hunched over a screen with Stefan, who straightens up when I walk in. I ask Stefan for access to Wolf's room, but he shakes his head in apology.

'I was just looking for the keycard, the master,' he says. 'It was around my neck when I went out on the ice and I must have lost it.'

'Is there a spare?' I ask Eino.

'No.'

'So make a new one,' I tell him, exasperated. It turns out, however, that it's not as straightforward as it sounds, and Eino struggles to get his computer to locate the external device that programs the keycards.

'Do none of your team know how to do this?' he asks me irritably, the blueish screen reflecting in the lenses of his glasses.

'No, why would we?'

'Because it's your specification. We had it installed at your request.'

This is news to me. 'What do you mean?'

He types something, swears in Finnish and straightens up. 'Do you people not communicate with each other at all?' He waves me over to another machine, taps something in and brings up his email. He searches for 'keycard' and a whole thread emerges.

'Here. I had been in contact with William – Will. Everything agreed, all booked, months ago. And then, much later, he got back to me about security. Said there was someone on board concerned about safety.'

'Did he say who?'

'No. But he wanted a specific system installed.' He gestures to the black box sitting beside the console. 'I explain that I cannot afford to have this done on the money he wishes to pay for it, and then . . . Wait.' He scrolls down the emails fast until he lands on one and flashes a hand at it. 'Here. Will says he will pay personally.'

I lean in.

'*Not to worry,*' Will's email says, '*we can sort that. I've got a fitter lined up for you who happens to be in Helsinki next week. Can you give him a call to coordinate? It's a guy called Ian, from HG Marine Services.*'

The date is from a month ago. I remember it because it was crazily busy that week. Tori had started the social media for the show and had put out posts about the confirmed contestants. They'd started to field the press: a woman with a tell-all about a liaison with Marco at the hotel where he worked on security; someone claiming Nish was an illegal immigrant. And the predictable resurrection of gossip about Wolf and Tori's relationship.

But I don't remember a thing about security on the ship.

'Ah, finally!' Eino says. 'The card update is coming now, see?' He points to the screen, but there's a progress bar and it's moving very, very slowly. 'Leave it with me. As soon as it's done, I'll bring it to you.'

I'm about to head down to ask Tori about this email from Will, when Eino calls me back. He goes to a slim cupboard and pulls out a khaki-coloured jacket. The style worn by men going fishing. Lots of pockets.

'This was left behind by John. He came up on the first evening – he was interested in the navigation systems.' He holds it out. 'Would you like us to put it with his corpse or . . . ?'

I flinch at the word, but take it from him. 'No, that's fine. I'll keep hold of it.'

The first thing I do is to check the pockets. There are two on the chest, both empty, and another pair at the hip. In one there's a packet of boiled sweets, and the other contains nothing but some old receipts and lint.

I don't see the inside pocket at first glance, but when I fold the coat over my arm I can feel something rigid in there. Eino's gone back to one of his screens, so I go to the empty end of the long desk and lay the coat out. Zipped up in a concealed pocket there's a clear plastic sleeve the size of a postcard. The kind I've used to keep maps dry, when out hiking. However, inside it isn't a map, but a cutting from a newspaper.

It's from a Scottish local publication, and it's old, dating from when I was barely into my teens. The headline announces the death of a young man: Kelvin Pierce. The same boy from the order of service in John's bag.

I start to read:

The death of seventeen-year-old Kelvin Pierce has been ruled accidental, according to documents released yesterday by the Sheriff Court of Aberdeen. While high levels of alcohol were detected in Pierce's system when he was found dead at a campsite near Glenmore in September, the inquiry concluded that the death was accidental and was caused by head trauma. The autopsy recorded signs of recent sexual activity, but police investigations failed to identify the other party. The teen, who had been on a camping trip with Explorer Scouts from Dunbar, had been looking forward to beginning his studies at Cambridge University. His mother, Mrs Carole Pierce, has publicly blamed the Scout leader in charge of the trip. She told The Aberdonian yesterday that she will not accept the sheriff's ruling. 'My son had his whole life ahead of him,' she told reporters, 'while the man who put him at risk gets to walk free. I don't know how he sleeps at night.'

But it's the next line that makes me inhale sharply:

Group leader John Grandage was not available for comment.

John. He was in charge when this child died.

I read on – about the football team the boy played for, his hopes to be an engineer. There are a few comments from people in his home town, but then I drift back up to the name of the place where he died.

Glenmore. Why is that familiar?

It takes me a moment, but then it swims up from my memory. Years back, Tori and I and a few others went to a Hogmanay near Inverness to support a friend playing a gig up there. I owed Tori a birthday present, so instead of travelling back down with the others, I booked us a night in a place out in the Cairngorms – Glenmore.

Except that when I told her where it was, she flat out refused to go. She wouldn't tell me why.

I read the rest of the article, but my mind is already racing ahead. Because if John really was responsible for a group of kids, and one of them died under his care, what does that mean? The fabric-soft sheet I have in my hand says it was ruled an accidental death, but the fact remains that this was someone's son. I check the date again: 2001. A contemporary of his would be a little older than me. Siblings could be younger, but late twenties if they were to remember it happening. And Kelvin's parents could be any-where between – I do a quick calculation – fifty at the youngest, seventy at the top end? Anyone here might have known Kelvin – meaning anyone here might have blamed John for his death.

Behind me, I hear the door opening, clicking shut, but I concentrate on the words on the page.

Witnesses recall the group returning from a canoeing trip on Loch Morlich.

'What's that?'

I startle, turn and find Tori standing right behind me. She reaches out, but I angle myself around to finish the article.

'Dee,' she says. 'Give it to me – what is it?'

I keep reading:

'They seemed in high spirits, but I'm horrified something like this could happen when my daughter and I were on holiday,' said one camper, teacher and father-of-one, Graham Matsuka.

I clutch the sheet to my chest, adrenaline galloping in my blood. She was there. A boy died, and John was there, and so was Tori.

'What?' she says again, her voice reedy now, desperate.

But when I turn to face her, I can see that she knows.

53

TORI

I make an immediate bolt for the door.

'Tor. Stop. *Stop!*' Dee is saying behind me. But I don't stop, even though I barely know where I'm going. Down the companionway from the bridge, along the central passage. Away. Away from her. Away from all of it.

She catches up with me at the metal hatch to the aft deck. Through the thick circle of glass I can see the storm is still blowing. But she's right behind me – all the questions I've run from, for twenty years, queuing up on her face. I'm cornered. So there's only one place to go. I twist the handle down hard and lean into the wind.

Dee cries out behind me as the blast of ice blows in. It cuts instantly through my double layer of fleece and the thermals underneath, but I grab onto the handrail, dragging myself further from her.

'For Christ's sake, stop!' she shouts behind me. 'You'll die out there!'

I don't care. I can't talk to her. I can't give her the answers she wants. I can't even hear the questions. The vicious cold bites into my skin and still she follows me, grabbing my sleeve, pulling me back.

'You knew him!' she screams at me, her face screwed up against the wind. 'All that time, you knew him, and you didn't tell me! What the hell did you do, Tori?'

'Get away!'

Barely able to see what I'm doing or where she is, the muscle-memory of my years of self-defence classes kicks in and I twist myself from her grasp. Dee staggers back, falls. Then she's on her feet again, launching herself at me.

She takes hold of my fleece. 'You brought me out here!' Her eyes are savage slits, bright with rage. Snow clinging to her lashes, her cheeks, her hair. 'You brought all of us out here! You brought him out here, and lied to everyone about why.' She shakes me, her frustration coming out like a scream. *'Tell me!'*

Suddenly she jerks back, upwards almost, but doesn't release me quickly enough. I crash forward, my knees hitting the gritted metal deck. The pain knocks the air out of me, but I spring back up. Quick enough to see Marco dragging Dee backwards into the open doorway. A second later he's back, hauling me up too, moving me ahead of him through the door. Back into the ship, where there are people who will want answers. I struggle, but he holds me firm.

And I see it as clearly as if it were a physical thing right there in front of me. The thin line of a lie that has trailed around with me, with every step, every passing minute and day and year, since I was fourteen years old.

I've tried so hard to keep it from tying me up. But I'd always known there would come a time when I became so tangled in it that I couldn't get free. It looks like today is that day.

Marco swings an arm out towards the passageway. 'Get in the saloon, now. You need to warm up. Fuck's sake!'

'No.' I get to my feet. 'Dee, let's go. My cabin.'

'I don't think so,' Marco says, herding us along. 'We're sitting down and having this out.'

He ushers us angrily through the door. Nish and Helen look up from where they're sitting, behind mugs of tea.

Marco plants his feet and folds his arms. 'Go on then. What were you doing, fighting in the storm of the century?'

'It's hardly the storm of the—' Craig says, coming out of the galley and drying his hands. The room is back to the way it was, the cloths and sheets and cut-up clothes nowhere to be seen.

'What's happening?' Craig asks, sitting down wearily.

'Tori's got something to tell us,' Dee says over me. 'About John.' She hasn't looked at me once since we got inside.

There's a long, long silence. The heating ticks. But I've run out of road.

So I take a deep breath, choose a spot to focus on in the middle of the room. And I tell them.

'Look. John was . . . he was someone whose path I'd crossed before. It was once, decades ago. I was camping with my family, and somewhere else on the site there was an accident. A boy, a teenager, got hurt. Really badly, a head injury. He didn't survive. It was nothing to do with me: the police interviewed everyone who was there, and they let us all go. But it was still horrible, knowing this kid had . . . died. But I didn't know him. I didn't even know who he was. So I tried to forget all about it. And then a year or so ago, it . . .' I search for the right phrase. Take my time. 'It reared its head. There had been a man there, at the site, who'd been in charge of the boys.'

'John,' Dee says. I can feel her eyes on me. I don't meet them.

'John. Yeah. And I remember seeing him, remember him talking to the police when they were all there. His face – I mean, you know what he looked like, he was distinctive. So years later, when I saw him at an event I was doing, I recognised him straight away.'

When it happened, I was already on the stage. Hosting a live panel about women in the media industry. I'd opened up to questions and the microphone was being passed back to someone in the crowd. And I saw him. Staring straight ahead, not smiling. It lifts the hairs on my arms even now, thinking about it.

And as whoever it was started asking their question into the microphone, my world gave way. This confident adult persona I'd spent years curating and polishing and turning into something people believed in, something even *I* believed in: somehow, it splintered.

And suddenly I was fourteen years old again. Standing on a hillside, exiled from my childhood without warning, without help.

How I finished the event I have no idea. But I did my job, relayed the questions. Worked and smiled and engaged with the audience the way I always do, gave it everything. But seeing John made me realise that it wasn't a matter of *if* any more, but *when*. My secret wasn't going to stay a secret. It was too big. And the fear that I'd managed to suppress into a low rumble all these years became a cacophony again. The fear that I'd be found out. That everyone would know what I did. Who I really am.

'I thought, to start with, that it was a coincidence – it

wouldn't have been that impossible to cross paths again after decades, like that. But then he just stared at me, like . . . I don't know.'

I do know. It was like he hated me.

I take a deep breath and go on.

'And then I knew it wasn't a coincidence. John was there for *me*. I was a bit alarmed, I suppose, and I looked out for him after the event, but he was gone.'

Helen clears her throat. 'Goodness me, that hardly seems like something to fight about—'

'It's not,' Dee says. 'It wouldn't be, I mean. The issue is,' and now she lifts her head, drills right into me with her eyes, 'the issue is that you hid it. And you insisted on having him on the show,' she says. There's a pause. 'And now John's dead.'

'Okay.' I lift my hands, drop them, defeated. 'Okay. Fine. He came back. Two other live events, I saw him. He wanted me to see him. Made it so that he was right there in my eyeline. It was a threat.'

'A threat of what?' Dee asks, incredulous. 'What did you think he was going to do?'

'I didn't know. But pretty soon I found out. He sent me this letter.'

'Saying what?'

I see the words in my mind in their thick, blocky capitals as clearly as if they were written on the wall in front of me.

'It said, "*You killed him. You're going to pay.*" And shortly after I got it, there was his application to the show, too, on the desk. John was trying to get close to me. And now he had his chance.'

'So you thought he wanted you dead,' Dee says, menacingly

calm. 'And rather than go to the police, you engineered a way to spend two weeks with him in the middle of nowhere?'

'I know how it looks,' I turn to Dee. 'I do. But I thought – I know you won't believe me, but I thought I could change his mind. That we could talk about it.'

I don't tell them how I'd spent the weeks and months leading up to the expedition wondering whether I'd survive it.

Dee closes her eyes. 'So you *were* pushed then. On that first night?'

I can't look at her.

'And you didn't want to say, because you knew who it was. You thought if you admitted it was John, all of this would come out.'

'But you said you didn't hurt this kid,' Craig says. 'So if that's true, why didn't you go to the police in the first place? If you had nothing to hide?'

'Because that's not what happened,' comes a voice from behind me.

Gaia, looking drawn and pale, is standing in the doorway. Eyes on me.

'Wait,' Dee says, hands up. '*You* knew him, too? John?'

But Gaia ignores her.

'What you're saying,' she continues, 'about John wanting his revenge on you? Sending you some note? Pushing you over the railings? That couldn't be further from it.'

I swallow. 'You don't know what you're talking about.'

'I do, actually.' Gaia comes in and takes a seat against the wall, crossing her legs.

'You changed his life. But not in the way you think.'

54

GAIA

It was the end of a long meeting, a year ago, give or take.

Late summer, at the Methodist Hall, Southville, where I'd been coming to meetings for a decade, since I was twenty-two and fresh out of prison. By pure coincidence, three members had reached their two hundred days sober in the same week, so we'd had a lot to celebrate. There were maybe a dozen regulars that night, plus a few floaters. And then that one guy, who'd been coming for maybe a couple of months. Older guy, well turned out. Clean always, the kind who takes care of his well-made but unflashy clothes. And never spoke a word: I hardly even saw his eyes. He spent the meetings with his head bowed. Could have been asleep. Some of them are like that. That's their choice.

I was helping stack the chairs when I noticed that he was taking his time over buttoning his coat. You do these things as long as I have, you learn the tells. So I went over.

'You've been coming a while,' I said.

He nodded. Didn't make eye contact. But didn't leave.

I put my hand out. The look he gave it, like I'd offered him a tentacle, made me laugh out loud. And that wasn't something I did very often back then. I dropped the hand, tried again. 'I'd introduce myself, but you already know my name.'

The tiniest nod, over in a second. 'John,' he said. I didn't believe him, not at first. A lot of them start off as John. Trust takes time.

But he wanted to trust me. His scarf was already wound up around his chin, his gloves were on. There was no other reason to stay behind.

So I said I was going to have a walk. Asked if he fancied coming. That time of night, the cafés are all closed, and what you don't do after a meeting is go to a bar, however long you've been sober. And he seemed like a nice guy, but Lord knew my instincts had been off before: no way was I inviting him to mine. So what was there to do but walk? First just a loop down to the city farm, past the allotments, back round. Then, the following week, we did it again.

It became a ritual. Meeting, clear up, walk. Scraps of conversation, never about anything important. What we never said out loud, of course, was that this was an extension of the meeting. Which meant that eventually whatever dark thing kept pushing him through those doors, week after week, would come out. I'd assumed it would happen a little at a time, a trickle into a stream into a river. But it wasn't like that. One night, without any kind of build-up, the dam simply burst.

We'd been following the river path out towards Portishead, the lights of the suspension bridge a bar of stars across the swollen River Avon. Late enough into the year for our breath to fog out in front of us. Then, once we were out into the quiet, he pointed up at the rocky gorge. Started telling me about the youth group he'd taken up there a while back, climbing. How one of them had got stuck, and two more had got into trouble trying to rescue them. A comedy of errors, and he was happy to cast himself as the hapless ringmaster, trying to help, but making things worse.

'And so we had a dozen blokes from the Fire Service scratching their heads, and three of these teenagers up there – *wailing*, mind you,' he said, 'before they admitted defeat and called Mountain Rescue.'

The passing of time had made it acceptable to laugh, and by the time he'd finished the story, I was practically crying with it.

When we were silent again, I realised something. 'You remembered all their names. The kids.'

John's hands went into his pockets as we walked. 'I remember all of them.' He stared straight ahead into the white fog of his breath. And then he stopped. 'I need to tell you what happened.'

We found a bench. And we stayed there until he'd got it all out.

He'd always been into the outdoors. Camping, caving, climbing, hiking – you name it. Had got into it through a youth group that took kids out of the worst bits of Glasgow and into the countryside. It just lit something in him that never went out. By his twenties he was taking groups of kids out most weekends.

Life was good. He met the woman of his dreams, had a daughter, moved to the coast. He'd got into some tech thing early and made what he needed to feather the nest. He wasn't interested in being rich, but there was enough to live comfortably without working himself to the bone. They had a little boat, a caravan, holidays. Friends over for weekends on the beach. He thought it would last for ever.

By the time they realised that his wife's headache wasn't simply a headache, she had weeks left. And when the sun went down, it didn't come back up.

He'd always liked a drink, he said. He was from a community where a lot of men and women were slaves to it. Thing was, even though John thought he knew what the pit of alcoholism looked like, from seeing other people down there, he didn't realise how slippery the sides were. How you could be sitting on the edge of it, marvelling at what a long way down it was – how you'd never be *that* bad. But then, before you knew it, there you were at the bottom.

And that's where John was when he took a group of boys to the Cairngorms one weekend in October, a little into the new millennium. His daughter was off exploring the world by then – couldn't leave home fast enough, not that he blamed her. It meant there'd been no one at home for a while, for him to moderate his drinking for, and he was . . . well, things were bad. He couldn't tell me how he'd been able to carry on his work with kids. High functioning, he supposed. Good at hiding it. But when his second-in-command dropped out of the weekend trip, he chose not to mention to the boys' parents that he'd be in sole charge. The group went anyway.

The first night was fine – he had a few beers around the campfire, found a way to make himself stop. The second day they hiked, took the canoes out. There was a bit of a scrape, someone got into trouble on the water, so when they got back to the tents, everyone was in high spirits. Relief of disaster averted, or something like that.

And he did hear the boys mention a girl, while he was building the fire. Three of them came back laughing and slapping each other's backs, from where they'd been gathering fallen branches for the fire. Black hair, this girl they'd seen. East Asian, mixed-race. Bit of a knockout. The way they talked, it was like she was older than they were. A woman.

Turned out that wasn't the case at all.

After the meal, things got a bit rowdy. These boys were six-teen, seventeen, and they talked John into giving them some booze. He let them facilitate his drinking – he knew what he was doing. But at the time, he convinced himself it was a good thing. That they'd be doing it somewhere else, unsupervised, if it wasn't for him. Except that then he got the keys to the van and drove the few miles to the local shop. Filled the boot with strong lager. Shared it out. These kids loved him anyway, but that night made him a legend.

John said he didn't know how long this one boy, Kelvin, had been gone, when he realised he was missing. But he went looking for him straight away. It was pitch-black, maybe two in the morning, and cold. It was the cold that sobered John up, too. He checked the woods, the shower block, the whole of the campsite. He was walking back to the other lads, reali-sation dawning that things were getting serious, when he saw movement a little way up a hill on a slope of scree. He went over, calling as he went. And what he thought in the darkness was one shape was actually two. First thought – and his face crumpled with shame when he told me this part – was that the lad had got lucky with this girl. But something about the motion made it look . . . wrong.

Even from down at the bottom of the hill, he saw how it

ended. Kelvin rising up, but then collapsing suddenly, after being struck by the other figure. He didn't realise it was a girl there until he saw her tear off down the hill. John tried to stop her, but she was fast, and then she was gone.

You have to remember that he was a father. That he had a daughter.

By the time he got to the boy, he knew what had happened. His trousers were still undone. John wasn't a doctor, but he could see the injury to the kid's head wasn't going to be survivable. There were rocks and stones everywhere, but one, right next to Kelvin's head, was bloody. Even as he nudged that rock closer with his foot to make it plausible that Kelvin had fallen – slipped while going out to smoke or piss or watch the stars – he knew what he was doing was a crime. John always carried a clean handkerchief in his pocket, so he found a puddle from the afternoon's rainfall and wet it, then looked the other way as he wiped the boy down, cleaning off the evidence as best he could. He even pulled his sleeves over his hands to get the boy's trousers back up, talking gently to him as he did so, in case he could still hear him. He owed him that much, at least.

He said there was only a minute or two before the breathing stopped altogether. Nothing he could have done would have saved that boy. The girl, though – her life was already in pieces before she did what she did. It wasn't her fault.

John was thinking clearly by then. He started shouting, and the others came tearing out of the tents. It had exactly the effect he wanted: everyone all over the whole patch of ground, disturbing everything with shoes and knees and hands. If the girl had left a mark, it was already long gone.

So when the police arrived, the entire rocky area around the boy was scuffed up, where John had tried to save him. It was hardly surprising they couldn't be sure that Kelvin hadn't just tripped, cracked his head. And if no one came forward as a victim, who was to know a crime had been committed?

He saw the girl the next day, being questioned outside her tent, her family a few steps away. Their eyes met only that once and then she looked away, and he knew that his decision was the right one. He never mentioned her. Not to the other boys, not to the police, not at the inquest, not to the dead boy's relatives – nothing.

The family laid the blame squarely at his door. The organisation he'd given up weeks and years of his life for quietly asked him to leave. But that was as far as it went. What little physical evidence there was pointed to an accident; and he was someone with an immaculate, decades-long record of youth work by then.

Except that wasn't the end of it for John. The way he saw it, all that girl did was hold the rock. What he told himself, what he believed every single day of his life afterwards, was that *he'd* put it in her hand. *He'd* given that boy the opportunity to do what he did. For John, if anyone was responsible, it was *him*.

I tried to say it wasn't true, but he didn't want to hear it. If he hadn't bought those boys the alcohol, trying to impress them, none of it would have happened. The girl would have been safe.

John just hung his head after that. Sat there for so long that I thought he'd finished.

We watched the silhouette of a fox trot along the opposite

bank, until it was out of sight. John said then how he'd heard that Kelvin's mum had died, not so long ago. An eating disorder – in and out of hospital for years and years, but she got too weak in the end. Faded away. And though he'd moved hundreds of miles away by then, he went back up there, went to the funeral. Heard about how her life had been one long black night since she lost her son.

There was no doubt in his mind that what happened to her was his fault, too. More blood on his hands.

He hadn't had a single drop since that night on the campsite. Then after that funeral he found himself in the corner shop, hardly knowing what he was doing. Got as far as asking the guy to pull a bottle of vodka down from the shelf. And then he put his hand in his pocket and found a reminder.

He brought it out to show me – he carried it everywhere. It was a silver medical ID bracelet. He'd found it next to Kelvin. It was hers; he didn't want anyone to find it. He'd used it to keep his resolve, remind him why he didn't drink any more. So although he left the shop with his sobriety intact, he realised how fragile it was. And that's when he started coming to meetings.

He told me the whole thing, then all of a sudden he got worried. He wanted to know that I wasn't going to blab about what he'd told me.

Though I couldn't blame him for wanting to be sure, I asked him whether, in the months we'd been walking together, I'd ever talked about anyone else's business?

Because the fact was, I didn't. I never have. Gossip blackens you. The moment someone tells you someone else's secrets, you know what they'll do with yours. And I'm a person with a past I'm not proud of. I know the value of confidentiality.

John took a deep breath, nodded to himself like he'd made a decision. And then he told me about how he'd found the girl. He'd worked out her name from the inquest – there hadn't been that many people camping, and her dad had been interviewed at the time. And he'd never tried to locate her or anything like that, had stayed well away; he'd done enough damage as it was, he said. But then a few months after the boy's mum died, the name of that girl found its way back to him.

I was confused – I thought he meant she'd tracked him down. But he said it wasn't that. It was more that she became kind of hard to avoid.

When he told me her name, I laughed. I genuinely thought he was joking.

But he wasn't. And after he'd seen her once, he started watching all her shows, scrutinising them for evidence of whether she really was happy, healed. He went to every public appearance she made. Once she even met his eyes, and he thought for a horrified moment that she recognised him. But her gaze slid on past, her smile not wavering.

John wanted me to understand that there really wasn't anything creepy about it. He wiped his eyes as he said it, repeated it – it's not like he was weird. He didn't want anything from her. He didn't mean her any harm.

I told him I understood, that I knew he only wanted to know she was all right. So that he could forgive himself.

And I thought even then how different his life could have been, at all those junctions. If his wife hadn't died. If he'd been sober when he'd gone on that trip. If that boy had just gone to bed, instead of deciding to do what he did.

Or if the girl whose secrets John had covered up hadn't been Tori Matsuka.

55

TORI

When Gaia finishes, she turns to me.

'He told me about applying for the show, all about the auditions and the rest of it. He was thrilled to get to spend time with you. But then he got cold feet and wanted to drop out. A week ago he'd decided it was too much. He phoned me in the middle of the night, so choked that I could hardly hear what he was saying. His anxiety was off the charts: worried about seeing you, about the fact that there was alcohol on board, that he might not cope.'

'And that's why you're here,' Annabel says. She looks at me. 'Makes sense. The last-minute change of contestant.'

Gaia confirms it with a nod. 'He told Will he'd only come if I could come, too. An ally, for support. I didn't want to do it—'

'Yeah, that much was obvious,' Dee says.

'But I agreed to come along, for John. Because I could see how much the closure meant to him. What happened that night on the campsite broke him.' Her voice wavers now, for the first time. 'And all he wanted, in order to be able to forgive himself, was to meet you and prove to himself that you were okay.'

Dee lets out a long breath. 'So that's the real reason you were sick outside cabin two. You found him.'

'I didn't know what I was doing,' Gaia says. 'I went over to see him, to check he was all right. He never slept well, always awake by four. And so I went in, and I found him. I was there only seconds, but—'

'Wait,' Dee says. She tents her fingers in front of her, eyes closed. 'You went into his room at four o'clock in the morning?'

'Yes.'

'How?'

'I had his keycard.'

Dee raises her eyebrows. 'Right.'

'After he swapped rooms with Tori, John came to my cabin to tell me what was happening. We walked back to his together, he let himself into the room, then gave the card to me.'

'I see. And he did that because?'

Gaia sighs and looks away. 'I think maybe if you haven't been an alcoholic, you can't really understand the way the stuff drags you in. Look around you.' She gestures to the drinks cabinet. Inside are maybe two dozen bottles of spirits.

'But it's locked,' Craig says.

'Sure, but it's flimsy. We were told the booze would be out of reach, and this is what we got.' She goes over and gives the cabinet a shake. It's clear to anyone that getting into it without a key would hardly be the heist of the century.

Dee folds her arms. 'But he could always have got *out* of his room, right? He wasn't locked in.'

'But giving the key to me meant if he came out, he couldn't have got back *in*. It would have meant sitting up here until someone found him. And this is a man with pride, you understand. He'd been at the bottom. He knew what it was like. He didn't want to go there again. He was putting as many obstacles between him and *this* as possible,' she finishes, dismissing the bottles with a hateful hand.

Dee goes to look out of the window. There's only the reflection of the room in the glass. We could be anywhere.

From her perch on the armchair, Nish clears her throat. 'I'm sorry, but why did you lie about it? I mean, right up to the minute you couldn't sustain it any more? And it was hardly like you were traumatised. You joined in the next day like nothing had happened.'

All eyes go to Gaia. She wraps her arms around herself. 'I was . . . I didn't know what else to do. I didn't even want to be here.'

Craig clears his throat. 'It makes sense.'

'Oh, you think?' Nish trills, rich with sarcasm.

He ignores her. 'Gaia has secrets of her own. She knows she's going to struggle to keep them after someone's died suspiciously on a TV show, right?' He glances over to her and she gives him a tight nod. 'So between that and – I don't know – shock? Fear? She just bottles it up.'

'I saw it all unravelling,' Gaia says quietly. 'Everything I've done to try to get my life back. I loved John, you have to know that. But that day when we were out on the ice, I realised what would happen once it got out that he'd died on this show, and that I already knew him. The police would be all over everything – the media.'

Dee holds up a hand, realising something. 'So you did take the bag. Like Wolf said you did.'

Gaia sighs. 'I did. I'm sorry. Once we were back from the

ice hole, I waited until you all left his cabin and I went in and took the rucksack, in case something in it gave me away. It was stupid, and selfish. I'm sorry.' Gaia gets up. She comes over and drops into a crouch. Puts a hand on my shoulder.

I shrink from her. 'Don't touch me.'

She rocks back onto her heels. 'All right. But look. John never told anyone else what happened. He kept your secret because he didn't think it was his to tell. And I'm sorry for what you went through. I truly am. But what you're saying about him: that he meant you any ill? I can't have you say that. He was a good man.' She stands up, makes eye contact with everyone in the room. 'He was a good man,' she repeats, 'and he was my friend.' She shakes her head, expressionless. Lost. And then she leaves the room.

For a moment, no one speaks.

Then Dee gets to her feet. 'Well, I believe her. But someone here isn't telling the truth.' She looks around. 'Anyone else want to get anything off their chest?'

'That's not helpful,' I tell her, quietly.

'Is it not?' Craig looks up. 'Because actually I agree. I think it is. See, even your story doesn't add up, Tori. How do we know it wasn't you who sabotaged that cabin? You had the opportunity,' he says, counting on his fingers. 'You had a motive, as it turns out.'

'And previous, by the sound of what happened to that boy,' Helen says.

I can't bring myself even to meet her gaze, but I can feel her stone-cold judgement on my skin.

Craig folds his arms. 'And from what I understand, Wolf

came out looking for *you*, right before he died. So what happened?'

I don't have an answer to that.

'Come on,' Annabel says to me, standing. 'Let's get out of here.'

'You can't just walk out!' Craig calls after us.

But that's exactly what I do. She walks me back to my cabin and she sits me down, gives me a glass of water. Beyond the porthole the night folds itself around us, thick enough to hold in your hands.

'Do you want to talk about it?' she asks.

'No.' There is little in the world I want to do less.

'Fine. Listen. That, back there, must have been horrible. But we have to deal with something that's here in front of us, right now.' I've never heard this blade in Annabel's voice before. 'Craig thinks someone on this ship killed Wolf. We need to know who – or any of us could be next.'

'Okay.'

'I need to see that footage. From the challenge. It's the only thing that might prove what happened to him.'

'It's with Dee. Craig gave it to me to give her. I'm sure she'll look it over.'

'No. It needs to be me.'

I don't understand. 'Why?'

She gets up. 'Can you get into her cabin?'

'No, but I can just ask her.'

'We can't. I'll have to find another way.' Seeing my confusion, Annabel says, 'Dee doesn't trust you, which probably means she doesn't trust me, either.'

'Wait.' I go across and catch hold of her fingers. 'They all think I might have killed him. Wolf, I mean. And John.'

'Possibly.'

'But I didn't.'

'I know.' She extricates her fingers and gives me a nod.

But then something feels off. 'Why haven't you asked? About – what really happened? My version?'

Annabel gives me a look like she wouldn't have considered it. 'It's your business,' she says, going out. 'There's plenty of time for that.'

56

DEE

I leave the others in the saloon and go down to my cabin. It's a long shot, but maybe there's something on the footage of the challenge that could shed light on what happened to Wolf.

But when I pass Tori's cabin, I pause. That story Gaia told: every word of it was new to me.

All those times Tori counselled me through break-ups. All those nights knee-deep in red wine, barely watching whatever film it was we'd chosen. Talking about everything, sharing everything. Work stuff, crushes, stories about our families, our childhoods. How she missed her mum, how she felt guilty for not seeing her dad.

The whole time she'd been holding this back. And when it all came bubbling back to the surface for her – the one time she needed me – what did I do? I simultaneously swamped her with my misery and pulled right back, refusing to treat her like a friend.

I made a bad situation a hundred times worse.

I knock. It takes a few attempts, but Tori answers the door and I follow her in. Her eyes are red, swollen. I've never seen her look like this. I doubt anyone has.

'It wasn't me, Dee. I didn't hurt anyone.'

'So why the hell did you bring John out here?' From the moment we found him in the applications account, she was dead-set on having him in. Beyond normal casting instincts even. John was qualified, certainly, but so were many others. 'You actively chose him. Why?'

It's plain from her face that she knows how incredibly reckless it was. 'I thought: he's going to come for me anyway. He's following me around – so what if I'm safer where I can see him?'

I shake my head. 'But why would you do that, if you thought he was a danger to you?'

'Because I wanted John to see me. I wanted him to spend time seeing who I am. That I'm . . .' She rakes her nails into her hair. 'That I'm a good person, even though I killed that boy. That I deserve to be forgiven. I thought: if I can just show him that, then maybe . . .'

She trails off, but I know how the sentence ends.

'You could forgive yourself,' I say quietly. But she doesn't say anything to that. 'You could have told me, Tori.'

She laughs.

'But you *could* have,' I say. 'I would have listened.'

'Dee, I love you, but that's simply not true. The day I got that letter through the door, you know what you were doing?'

'No. Obviously.' I try not to bristle at what I suspect is coming.

She glances at my forearm, the angry burn scar the size of a toddler's hand, immediately below my elbow. The grief was so thick back then that I barely remember doing it to myself. I pull my cuff down to cover it.

'That,' she says, indicating it with the slightest jerk of her head. 'Those hours we spent waiting in A&E for them to dress it properly, check for nerve damage? I had that piece of paper in my pocket, the whole time.'

Hot shame rises in my face, but something in what she says glints at me, like a coin in river silt. 'Wait.' Everything starts to feel very slow. 'I was there? At your house, when this *message* came? You're sure?'

She shrugs. 'Like I said. You weren't exactly in a state to be supportive about it.'

'Do you still have it?'

'No.'

It takes a force of will to keep my voice steady. 'Do you have a picture of it?'

'Why, Dee? What difference does it make?'

'Did it have your name on it? Like, was it addressed to you, specifically?'

She throws up her hands. 'It was sent to my house. *You killed him – you're going to pay*, it said. Who else—' she starts, but her voice breaks and she puts her fingertips to her lips. Buds of tears burst at the corners of her eyes. 'Who else was it going to be for, huh?'

I'm saved from answering her question by a knock at the door. It's Eino.

He holds up a white card. 'Did you still want the key to Wolf's cabin?'

57

TORI

Dee takes the card from Eino and disappears off down the passageway, but he lingers by the door. 'You may want to come with me,' he says.

I follow him out, not even asking what he wants to show me. I can barely keep my thoughts in order. In the space of a few days, everything I've worked for has just . . . disintegrated. And I'm utterly out of my depth. I don't even know what the procedure is for a death on location.

I'm no closer to knowing who's responsible for John's death than I was when he was found. And that piece of pipe, which I stupidly, *stupidly* put in my pocket, will only convince people further that it was me.

At the time I didn't care who killed him. At the time, deep down, I was glad he was dead. But if Gaia's account is right, everything I thought I knew was wrong.

But what difference does it make? By the time I get home, none of it is going to matter.

As I go into the bridge, Eino and Craig are talking heatedly about something on a screen.

'What's going on now?' I ask, the door swinging shut behind me.

Craig takes an at-ease stance, awaiting the explanation with raised eyebrows. 'Go on. Tell her.'

'Tell me what?'

'We have a couple of problems,' Eino says.

The first, he explains, is that the ship he'd made contact with doesn't appear to be diverting. He waves an arm towards the rocky claw of the fjord. 'We are tucked in, so it's possible they are unable to find us here. We've lost contact with them. It's been several hours now.'

I blink, then laugh out loud. Even I can hear how unhinged I sound.

'I'm afraid I am not joking,' he says, as if I needed telling. 'Stefan is outside right now trying to boost our radio signal, but it is a serious concern.'

'Good. Great! And what's the other thing?'

Eino lifts a hand to the console. 'It's the keycards,' he says. There's something unusual about his posture, a sheepishness. 'While I was programming the key earlier, I came across an . . . anomaly.'

'Like what?'

He clears his throat. 'From a few days ago.'

'On the first night,' Craig says.

Eino coughs again. It's the first time I've seen him looking anxious. 'Late on your first night on board, it appears that someone programmed an all-access keycard.'

'Because *someone* failed to log out,' Craig says darkly. 'Which kind of makes the security system slightly obsolete, hey?'

I stare at Eino. 'As in, a key that could have given them access to John's room?'

'Yes.'

'The key that Wolf got hold of somehow?'

'Yes. Possibly.'

'So? Who was it?'

Eino goes back to the monitor. 'I do not have that information. It tells me when it happened, but that's all.'

'We thought maybe Wolf programmed it himself,' Craig says. 'But the timings – basically it doesn't add up. You saw how much wine he drank, he could hardly stand by the end of the night. And this,' he says, rolling his hand disdainfully at the monitor, 'is not a simple system.'

'So who then?' I ask. 'You're saying it can only have been someone who knew their way around how it works.'

'Which these clowns do not,' Craig says tightly.

'What about you, then?' I say. My enthusiasm for mediation has worn so thin I could make stockings out of it. 'You've probably been on a ship like this before. How do we know you didn't do it? You don't exactly have a reputation for honesty.'

Craig glowers, eyes raging. 'Are you fucking joking me right now?'

'You wouldn't have to know ships,' Eino says.

'What?' Craig and I ask in unison, turning to him.

He shrugs. 'The gentleman who installed it told me it's a common system on land. Hotels, conference centres.'

From the look on Craig's face, he has the thought the same time as I do. *Hotels.*

Marco works in hotels. And after what I saw on the very first night on board, he also has more than enough reason to try to keep me quiet.

*

We find him in his cabin. He answers the knock straight away, barely decent in a towel and nothing else. He's chewing, holding a duty-free-sized chocolate bar.

'Need a word, my friend,' Craig says, unsmiling.

Marco swallows, his face falling. He retreats and sits on a corner of the neatly-made bed. We remain standing.

'Go on then,' he says, elbows on knees. 'What have I done now?' He glances at me, and I know he thinks this is about the drugs. But I'm in no mood to put anyone's mind at ease.

Slowly, diplomatically, Craig explains the issue. Eino says nothing. Me, I just watch.

'And we – Tori and I – recalled that you yourself had worked in hospitality,' Craig finishes.

There's a moment when Marco figures out what he's being told. He clears his throat. 'So you're asking me if I programmed that card.'

Craig spreads his hands. 'It's the question I'd ask anyone, in the circumstances.'

For a minute, from the way the deep flush rises from his neck into his face so suddenly, it looks like Marco's going to hit him. His jaw tightens and he looks between the three of us and lands on me.

'Didn't I tell you we were all good? But you still think I'm, what? Some fucking murderer?'

There's something so hurt in his expression that I immediately want to take it all back. I glance at the others, but they're not seeing what I'm seeing.

Marco drops his head into his hands. 'It wasn't me,' he says to his feet.

'And that is something you can prove?' Eino asks bluntly.

Marco mutters something none of us hear.

Craig crouches. 'Sorry, my friend, what was—'

'I said I can't read.' He lifts his head, but his eyes are gripped shut. When he opens them, they're wet. 'All right? I can't read, and I can't write. It's why I was so fucked off with Wolf, that first night. Giving me grief about the book I worked on, and that release form. Course I didn't write a book. I can barely write my kids a fucking birthday card.' Bitter shame glows in every word. I have to look away. 'I couldn't have programmed shit. So there's your alibi. That okay, is it? You happy now?'

Craig winces, then stands. 'I'm sorry, big guy.' He slaps Marco on the back. 'Nobody's perfect.'

'He knew,' Marco says. 'John. Went out of his way to help me. I didn't even thank him.' He rubs the heels of his hands into his eyes and pretends he's not crying.

'I didn't know,' I tell him.

'Course you didn't know.' He laughs, but not really, then sniffs hard. 'Not your fault. But I've got to say, I do like the way the three of you fuckers hear *hotel* and go for the meathead bouncer,' he says, jabbing a finger into his chest, 'rather than the millionaire owner of a whole bloody chain of the things.'

58

DEE

The green light on Wolf's lock chirrups and the door clicks open.

I go inside and take it all in. The dresser covered in expensive-looking cosmetics with minimalist, masculine packaging over-compensating for their contents. Two ring lights of different sizes, a state-of-the-art laptop, trailing cables to drives. And, lying awkwardly on the floor, a compact top-of-the-range HD video recorder mounted on a tripod.

The place reeks of him – a fragrance he's used ever since I met him. He was that kind of man, seeing himself as a brand even before he was one, needing a signature fragrance, a catchphrase. All these identical combat trousers, too, folded and waiting. The curling tongs, off but still plugged in. He had a uniform: everything down to the tone of the highlights in his hair, the length of his stubble, the square cut of his fingernails.

I never felt sorry for him. But now pity is like a ball in my throat.

He was the first celebrity who'd bothered to speak to me. It was a Christmas party at my first production company – I'd been there a couple of weeks, just work experience and still in that awkward phase of being given tasks I barely understood, by people who had neither the time nor the inclination to explain them to me. I'd almost not gone that evening, but they'd needed someone to set up. I was going down for a cigarette when Wolf buzzed to be let in. Right from the off, he was rude, abrasive. Funny. I didn't like him. I'm not going to pretend that I'm heartbroken by his death.

But the truth of it is that by mistrusting him, I have missed something crucial. What if he needed listening to, without me constantly pointing the finger, oscillating between laughing at him and despising him? Even that last time Wolf ever properly spoke to me – especially then – I wouldn't even let him finish.

I go to the corner of the room and set the tripod onto its feet. I release the camcorder from the plate, clear a space to sit on the bed and power it up. It's massively over-spec for what he used it for, bulky and professional and, if I'm not mistaken, worth a couple of grand even without all the add-ons. I switch it from record mode into playback and it tells me the memory card is full, with a little over thirty-five minutes of footage, thanks to the insanely high resolution he'd set it at. I run it backwards about five minutes, then hit Play.

On the flip-out screen, there he is. Dishevelled, exactly as he was the last time I saw him alive: the manic eyes, the man-bun falling out.

The shot begins with his face huge and looming as he starts the camera rolling. The he sits back, his eyeline drifting to the right, watching himself on the flip-out screen. He clears his throat. 'You wouldn't hear me out, Dee, so here it is on tape for you instead.' The anger from our conversation is clearly still fizzing.

Then the screen is obscured by something too close, out of focus. Blocky.

'Know what this is?' He brings the object closer to his face, grinning darkly.

It's a phone, nondescript, black.

He turns it over, tilts his head. 'See, I thought something was off. You know how you do sometimes? Meet someone and think,' he creases up his face, the universal expression for *not quite right*, 'something weird about them. But I thought it could be me. Maybe I'm not such a good judge of character. Certainly had Tori wrong, didn't I?' He laughs as he says it, but it drops straight off. 'So anyway I went to see her.'

'Who?' I whisper aloud, exasperated. But as I say it, I realise something about the phrasing. Whoever he'd wanted to talk to me about, it wasn't Tori.

'And it was something she said about the Northern Lights. How pretty they were. And I knew straight away, that's not right.'

He punctuates what he says next with the phone, using it like the jab of a finger in the air.

'Because I've been trying to get a shot of the light show for the channel since I got here. But, nothing. So I asked the captain, and he told me they'd been visible on the first night, really late. But apart from that, the conditions hadn't been right. Now, Tori saw them that first night, when everyone else was in bed, right?' A manic grin splits his face now, and he shakes his head. 'Except not everyone *was* in bed. Because here was Annabel, saying she'd seen them, too.'

I find my breath has gone very shallow.

Annabel. It's Annabel's phone he's holding.

He waggles it, then moves it out of sight. 'So I got hold of this. Just sneaked it off the desk in your office when she was distracted. And I had a little look.' He lifts the screen again, and this time it's lit up. 'And I found some very interesting things. Pictures. Bit hidden, but like I said: I had time.'

But he doesn't open the gallery app. He taps something too quickly for me to see, then again a couple more times. When Wolf faces the lens again, he shakes back his hair and leans in, half twisted towards the camera, like he's sharing selfies with a friend.

'Here, see? They go back months. Tori at her house. You at Tori's house. The two of you at a bar. Tori's *back garden*. Look.'

I do. I sit very still, my mouth suddenly arid, and I look. He pauses on each photo for a second, not even long enough to read the captions that Annabel has written underneath each one. Time, date, place. He flicks back and back and back. In every single photo is either me or Tori, or my car, or Tori's house. Every single one. And there are dozens. Hundreds.

Time reverses on the screen. My hair gets shorter as the pictures get older. Wolf pauses on one image and sighs as he looks at it. It's me, leaving a building.

'Now this one, this one made me worry.' He expands it until my face fills the screen. I look – awful. Haggard. Thin, pale, years older than I am. He zooms out again and I see the red neon sign above the door I'm coming through.

SyncHole Productions, in west London. And a caption underneath the image, two words: *Sophie's work?*

I remember that day. Maybe a week after Leo's death. A meeting with the lawyers, the execs. The decision to terminate my employment there. Not that I cared. It was only mid-morning, but I was already several drinks in. I laughed in their faces, and they asked me to leave. They didn't know, or didn't care, that I'd already sworn blind I would never, ever shoot a single frame of undercover footage again as long as I lived.

He flicks back and back. Me at the shops, me going into Tori's house in London again, Tori getting out of my car.

Rain. Me in my yellow coat – the one I'm wearing right now – standing at Tori's door.

This is the day I arrived at her home.

Wolf keeps flicking, then lifts his finger to tap the X, closing the file. 'That's the end of the Tori ones—'

But I lurch forward. Hit Stop on the camera, scrub back. I don't even breathe as I play it again, at quarter-speed. Because there on the screen, right before he closes it down, is a picture of me outside Leo's place in Bath. Getting into Leo's car.

Beneath the image is a caption, but this time the freeze-frame gives me long enough to read it. Just a single name, and a time of day.

Sophie 8.38 p.m.

She was there. Annabel was there. And less than an hour later, Leo was dead.

And I put it all together. It wasn't Tori she was following at all. It was me. The pictures of Tori were incidental – she was only at Tori's because I was there, too.

I close my eyes as it falls into place. When Tori was pushed, she was wearing my jacket, the hood right up. From the back, we're the same.

It was never supposed to be Tori who fell. It was meant to be me.

That letter Tori got – it wasn't for her. It was nothing to do with John, nothing to do with the boy at the campsite. It was from Annabel. For me.

I leave the image quivering on the screen. The picture of me and Leo on the phone, Wolf's face caught in freeze-frame next to it, his eyes half closed. I find I'm on my feet, walking away. I turn back, already at the door, watching this horror with my hand over my mouth.

How was Annabel there? I don't understand. She was in America; she said she'd been in America for the last year. We did checks, references. She couldn't have been in those places, flitting between Bath and London, following me.

Except, she was.

Don't I know – aren't I the one person who should know – how easy it is to pretend to be someone else? To lie about your past? To reinvent it?

Here is the evidence that Annabel did exactly what I did. Not for a job though. And, not exactly like me, either.

No. She did it better.

She's not what you think she is. The last thing Wolf ever said to me. I thought he was talking about Tori. But I was wrong.

I trusted what Annabel told me. I even trusted her more than—

My shoulders drop.

I trusted her more than Tori. Annabel told me that Wolf had come looking for Tori out on the ice. It was only her word, against everything I knew about Tori. And I'd let all those years of friendship, all that loyalty, just evaporate, and had taken Annabel at her word.

It takes a force of will to go back. But when I reach up to restart Wolf's video, my hands don't shake. I hit Play. I don't look away.

'But there's some video files too,' he's saying. He moves out of the folder and into another one. 'Loads, here. I mean, I haven't watched them all. But look, take this one.'

His camera struggles with the autofocus on the phone screen, and it takes me a moment to work out what I'm looking at.

A busy bar. Low light. The bassy thrum of music, overtones of people talking, the brief familiar sound of a cocktail being made, ice knocking against the shaker. Then there's a high, light laugh, and I recognise the glossy black veil of Tori's hair, a couple of tables from where the shot is taken. And next to her, me.

'See?' Wolf says over it. 'Fucking obsessed! But you didn't want to hear me out, did you?' There's a part of him, I realise now, that's enjoying this discovery. Righteous indignation glints in his eyes as he scrolls down the thumbnails of videos. Tens of them fly past at a time. He hits another one, but the screen is angled too far now. I can't see what he's looking at.

But then his face completely changes. It shifts to confusion, to concern, to horror. Under his breath, he mutters, 'What the fuck?' He seems to forget what he's doing.

I hear the muted sound of another video playing, but I can't see a thing. And then the shot changes: Wolf's up, the fabric of his shirt filling the screen.

His voice, further away, is oddly high. 'Fucking hell!'

Then everything is movement. He's too close to the lens to

see properly, but I can just make out him pulling on a coat – that bright-green coat – and zipping the phone up inside. For a moment he pauses, his breath panicky and loud, and then he leaves the frame. The shot totters, swings to the side and crashes down.

Out of shot, he hammers on the door. 'Stefan. Stefan! Are you there? You need to let me out! *Stefan!*' He keeps that up for a little under a minute. There's a pause, a clunk of the lock, then Stefan saying something I can't make out. Wolf's shouted apology, as his heavy footsteps thunder away; Stefan's pleas for him to return. The door clicking shut. And that's it.

I scrub forward, double speed, four times speed, eight times. I watch the empty, sideways shot of the patch of carpet beside his bed, willing something else to happen, for Wolf to come back. I pause, listen, restart. There's nothing. The time-code rolls on and I run it even faster, fitting together what would have been happening. The final challenge getting under way. The storm bearing down on us.

By the time the tape ran out, Wolf would have been struggling out across the ice, driven out by a desperation to tell someone something. Maybe only minutes later, he was dying in the snow – the secret of what he wanted to say, and what happened to him when he tried to say it, dying with him.

Then I'm on my feet.

Because maybe there's a way to find out, after all.

59

TORI

Halfway to Helen's cabin, there's a crash outside. Eino, Craig and I rush over to the exit to the deck as Stefan comes rushing in.

He's wearing a welding mask, but he flips it up and starts speaking urgently to Eino in Finnish, before turning and sprinting back out the way he came.

For the first time since we boarded, Eino looks shaken. He pushes past to a store cupboard, pulls out a red outersuit and throws another one to Craig, who puts it on without question. 'There's a fire. We'd moved the backup generator before the storm – Stefan forgot it was there on the lower deck. And the sparks from the welder—'

'Fuck,' Craig says. 'Petrol?'

Eino nods once, and then they're both running the way Stefan went.

'What do I do?' I call after them, grabbing an outersuit for myself and pulling it on.

'We'll get it under control,' Craig tells me from the door. 'Keep clear of it for now, all right?'

Down the passage, Helen's door opens.

'Tori. What a pleasant surprise,' she says, without pleasure. She stands aside. For a moment I consider going out to the deck, but I go in.

Her room is as neat as a cloister, as if she has only just arrived. The only personal items are a folded pair of reading glasses and what appears to be a leather-bound album on her nightstand.

Helen sits on the edge of her bed, hands folded serenely on her lap. I have no doubt at all that she knows exactly why I'm here.

'Do you want to tell me about the keycard, Helen?'

She watches me, head cocked. It's meant to unnerve me, and it's working.

'That was quite some story Gaia told. Quite a lot to understand.'

The room feels too small, all of a sudden. 'I'm not going to talk about that right now,' I say.

She takes her time. Her hair, usually pinned up in a careful French pleat, is loose.

'You *are* going to talk about it,' she says. 'You're going to tell me the whole story.'

I glance at the door, my heart slamming against my ribs. 'Look, Helen, someone programmed a—'

'That's not important.'

I open my mouth to tell her that yes, it's actually very important, but then for the first time I see – really see – the shape of her face. The particular dent under her nose. And the words dissolve.

She takes her eyes off me for a moment to pick up the thick book beside the bed. 'We talked before, didn't we? About children. How I didn't want them. You told me you weren't interested in having them.'

'I did,' I say, my voice tight. A blister of memory pops: the way she looked at me when I tried to save her from an awkward moment with Nish, about having a family. Then, days ago, I only half saw it. Now I see there was something black in that look. Something – jealous. Angry. Hurt. I need to steer the conversation back, steer it anywhere else, but it's as if Helen's taken hold of the wheel.

She holds the book – a photo album – in both hands. . 'My sister died, a year or so ago. Twin sister. No – don't,' she says sharply. 'You don't get to say you're sorry for my loss. You don't get to say anything of the sort.'

It's two steps to the door. I could make it in a second.

'Do you want to know how she died?'

I don't. I definitely don't.

'Anorexia,' she tells me, conversationally. 'I mean, it took her a while. Decades. Thought she'd beaten it in her teens, then . . . Well. She didn't beat it, in the end. And I'll have to admit, those last years were hard. People don't know that about me – that I'm a caring person – but I am. I loved her so much. And I might not have had a kid of my own, but by God, I loved hers. My nephew. He was special.'

All I hear is the *was*.

I find I am on a stool now, but I don't remember sitting. Helen comes over and kneels in front of me.

'Family, you know? You'd do anything for them. But I don't suppose you know that, do you?'

She waits for me to answer, but I can't. I can't put the words in order. Can't think of anything but the set of her forehead, the way it bulges a little too much above the eyebrows, the narrow set of her nose.

Those features that I have seen on hundreds of people since him, and which I have forced myself to learn do not indicate menace. Do not mean a person is unkind, or bad, or evil. Do not mean that I need to fear them.

Except here she is.

'He was the world, to my sister. And to me. I used to bring him to the office, when I'd just started my first business. Had him in his little playpen.' Half a wistful smile drifts across her face, before her expression hardens. 'All this time I'd blamed John. And when he turned up at my sister's funeral, hidden in the back like he thought we wouldn't notice, I couldn't take it any more. I'd always believed – she did, too – that he'd got away with murdering my sister's beautiful son. And there he was, gloating.'

She opens the album on her lap. I see only a flash of a photo, but it sends a sickening bolt of shame and revulsion and hate through me.

His face. The black-haired boy from the campsite.

'But all along,' she says, her voice sharp as claws, 'it was you.'

60

DEE

I crash into my cabin and drag the cameras out from under my bed, and power up Annabel's first. But the batteries die straight away. I go out, racing up the companionway two steps at a time, heading for the office.

Inside, I find the spare power bank and click it into place, then pull on a pair of headphones and switch it to playback.

The scene opens in the abandoned village. I skip through the establishing shots – the incredible landscape, footage of the whole group, set-ups panning across all their faces. And although I didn't give it my attention at the time, all the while that dense, concrete-heavy bank of cloud is getting closer overhead. Heading straight for us, like the menace of death.

I keep spinning forward. Even at speed, I can see the storm building in the footage. People lean more and more steeply into the wind, the snow travelling too fast, heavier with every minute. Then the shot changes. I switch back to normal speed.

It's a big, wide shot. The foreground settles – the edge of a dilapidated building – in time for Craig to come around the edge of it, passing through the frame from left to right in a couple of seconds. The white closing in, thickening like a fog. But the shot lingers, and every few moments there's a blink of a view all the way out to where the promontory that edges the fjord claws at the ice. Beyond that, the yellow-and-white shape of the *Skidbladnir*.

And in front of that, flashes of green. Wolf, coming slowly but determinedly towards the camera. The shot shudders for a while – Annabel is running with the camera on her shoulder. Then she stops, right behind a building. The camera is put down, the view tilting, the bottom half obscured now but snow right up to the lens, and then immediately I see feet – hers – pass the shot. Then there's nothing.

Obviously there's nothing. Growling in frustration, I close my eyes, concentrating hard on the audio. Though the noise of the wind almost obliterates everything else, there are thumps and thuds too. A voice shouting – Craig, I think – then only the wind again.

But here, faintly, is another voice. *Where is she?*

I open my eyes. There's nothing on the screen – the shot's filling up with snow – but it's unmistakably Wolf. I run it back, adjusting the playback setting to try to clear some of the ambient noise. Things are made worse by a crackle on the radio mic – the same issue as with the one I replaced immediately before the challenge. I remember a detail: when I came back out after replacing that mic, after seeing Wolf, how I'd thought for a moment Annabel had overheard my conversation with him. How relieved I'd been to realise I was wrong.

But what if I'd been right? What if she knew what he'd found on her phone?

That he might be about to spill her secret?

With the settings adjusted, I hit Play again and this time the sound is much clearer. Cutting through the noise of the storm is Wolf's voice.

Where is she? he's saying.

I open my eyes. He says it again, yelling it into the wind. And then, straight afterwards, he says something different.

Where's Annabel?

A hand on my shoulder makes me jump. I whip off the head-phones and turn. And there is Annabel, standing over me, head tilted. Watching me with a cold glare.

61

TORI

The air has gone solid in my lungs. There's a hollow thud from below the water line and the ship moves, settles.

Helen turns the album to me.

'That's it,' she says. 'You look at him.'

Staring out from the photograph is a young man. Suspended in time, exactly as he was, except this version is the person that any aunt, any mother or father or teacher would be proud of. Hair styled for a formal photograph. Eyes that look straight ahead, confident but not cocky – not eyes that would drift suggestively down the length of a girl's body and lazily back up.

Strong arms beneath shirt sleeves, which could surely only be honed for rugby or cricket – not to pin a person down. Hands neatly folded: impossible to imagine them clamped across someone's mouth.

'And now you're going to tell me why. Because I've spent far too long not knowing. I came all the way out here believing I knew exactly what had happened.' Helen's voice gives, just a crack, and I see the pain in it. The realisation of what she's done. The fact that the game is well and truly up.

She intended to kill John all along. The gas was never meant for me, it was meant for him.

'You knew we'd swapped cabins.' My voice is a whisper as I stand, slotting the pieces together. She must have heard us discussing it in the passageway and somehow got down there ahead of us. 'But how did you know what to do, with the gas?'

'I've been on boats since I was a little girl. Sailing, motoring – all kinds. They're my weakness. I asked for the spec of the ship, saw an opportunity,' she says. 'I wasn't going to come all the way out here without a plan, was I? And obviously I needed *some* concessions, given how much I was paying.' The bewilderment must show on my face. 'He really didn't tell you? Will?'

'Tell me what?'

She rolls her eyes. 'Now *this* is why you shouldn't go into business with a man. I asked him to keep my sponsorship from you, keep a lid on the whole thing, but I have to say, I'm impressed he actually did it.'

The sponsor that Will found. The person who saved the show from going under. The person who sent the fitter for the new security system. HG Marine Services.

Helen Greenaway.

'But I got it wrong, didn't I?' she says. 'Got the wrong person, after all that.'

I have to get out of here.

I go for the door, but she's there right behind me, grabbing hold of my sleeve, pulling me back. I stumble, take a step back, but I don't fall. She's heavier than me – much – but those hundreds of self-defence lessons have left their mark on my brain. I think of the concern on my dad's face as he dropped me off, week after month after year at the same classes, over and over, honing the same skills. His patient endeavours to get me to open up to therapist after therapist, his desperation to find out where his easy-going, happy little girl had gone. He'd been a widower for a decade by then. What must have that been like, with no one to share the worry with?

I kick out behind me, unbalancing her, and twist from her grasp. She cries out in pain, but I don't look back. Outside in the passage I don't even think which way I'm turning. It's not until I hear her feet pounding up behind me that I realise the way to the stairs – to the saloon, to people, to safety – is the other way. Behind me.

It's already too late to go back. So I keep going, towards the prow of the ship: a thick metal door right onto the deck.

There's no choice but to go outside. The cold hits me like a physical blow, ripping my breath from my throat. The storm has blown itself out, but the wind is still enough to whisk the settled snow into a shifting carpet on the pack ice beneath us. But although I can't see its source, the smell of burning is unmistakable. The door bangs shut behind me, impossibly loud. I glance back and Helen's there. She crouches for a moment and, when she stands, she has an iron mooring stake in her hand.

The only thing to keep me from dropping off the edge of the deck is a length of cable stretched tightly between metal posts. I'm backed up against it as she comes towards me. There's nowhere to go.

'You killed my sister as well as my nephew. She died, because of what you did. And I don't know why you did it—'

'Yes, you do.'

My breath is ragged, but I make myself feel it. The swell of my lungs, the brittle feeling of the cold, all the way down. The white, perfect scentlessness of the air. I look beyond her, beyond the deck, the ship. The mountains around this wild, immaculate island rise up, encircling its frozen heart. And I am just a speck, out here at its edge.

Helen, who has spent so many years full of rage and hate, stifles a sob, then gives up, lets it out. She wipes quickly at tears.

She is the same as me, I see now. Tiny, frightened. Sad. Pretending to be brave. And the truth of what happened turns its face to me. It demands that I speak its name.

'He raped me, Helen.'

Something gives way inside me. It is an ancient tree falling at last. A cliff collapsing into the sea. The burst of a bomb.

I am barely loud enough to reach her, but from the crumple of her face, I know she hears me.

'No.'

'Yes. I was fourteen years old, and he raped me.'

'No.' Her voice creases. Then she straightens. 'No,' she says again, bolstering it with a certainty I can tell she doesn't truly have. 'He didn't.'

I don't look at the metal bar she's raising above her head. I look only at the woman behind it, damaged beyond recognition by a crime she never knew had been committed.

'He did, Helen. And you know I'm telling you the truth. I'm sorry he died. I didn't mean—' I take a long, shuddering breath and I let it out. 'I didn't mean to kill him. But he raped me, and I was scared, and he wouldn't stop. And it wasn't my fault.'

I tell it to her and then I say it again, to myself. To the girl I was twenty years ago, who built that wall around her. Who started lying and never stopped.

'It wasn't my fault.'

62

ANNABEL

I wanted this trip to be beautiful. I had a plan. It was going to be the start of something incredible for me, the end of always having to try so hard, of always losing things, of having everything go wrong. There was something Leo said, not long after I met him. My third piano lesson, maybe. *If you want to excel, just relax. Allow yourself to be you.* I'd tried to do what he said. But somehow I always ended up messing up.

I think of my tiny life back home. Of all the choices I've made. Leaving my home town after the mess with my mother and her boyfriend. Not a single text from her when I went. Not a single message from a friend. That resolution I had, to make something of my life.

But I wasn't good enough for anyone, even when I completely reinvented myself. Lost all the weight, whitened the teeth. New hair, new everything. I became – someone. Saved enough money to learn the piano in lessons after work. Met the man of my dreams. And look where that left me.

I close the door behind me. I know Dee's found the footage, from the way she snaps the screen shut. Backing away, she flips open the cartridge and takes out the card.

'I was coming with some news about Helen,' I say, watching her tuck the card into her back pocket. 'But maybe you've got something to tell me, too?'

She glances behind me, her eyes darting like she's a trapped animal. I shouldn't laugh, but I can't help it.

'Looking a bit nervous there, Dee.'

She wets her lips. 'You want to tell me why you lied about Wolf? Why you said he was looking for Tori out there, when he was looking for you?'

Shrugging, I pull the stool over and sit down. 'I don't remember what he said, if I'm honest.' I pick up an open can of Coke on the desk, give it a little shake. It's half full, with a trace of Tori's deep-red lipstick under the opening. Watching Dee over the rim, I touch my tongue to the smear and take a long drink of it.

I swallow, stifle a burp. It's a funny thing, this sense of calm. All this time, all this effort that went into getting here. Getting Will to believe the references I created for myself, finding a way to make him hire me. Sleeping in squats and hostels to stretch out the pathetic scraps of pay on this discount *I'm a Celebrity* train wreck – all leading up to this. Because after that first night, after that stupid mix-up on the deck when I mistook Dee for Tori, the game should have been up. This is a woman whose entire job is about finding things out that people don't want discovered. Wheedling her way into their lives, fishing out their secrets.

I saw how she did it. I learned from her. Turns out she's not the best in the game, after all. She's not even the best in the room.

Dee nods at the phone in my hand. 'You want to tell me where you found that?'

I glance at it. 'This? Oh, it turned up in the camera case.' I put it in the side pocket of my combats – the ugly, utilitarian things that I only got to flatter her, make her think I was following her shitty sense of style. 'Like I told Tori.'

'I don't think that's true.'

'No?' I pluck at the ring pull of the can. Enjoying the little ripples of discomfort it sends through her. Ding-ding-ding.

'No,' she says. She clenches her hands, like it'll stop me seeing them trembling. 'I think Wolf had it. And I think you knew he had it, because you heard him talking to me when I went back in for the spare mic.'

I don't say anything to that, just sit back, watching Dee pretend she's not scared shitless. Watching her fail.

When I first met her, I expected to find that she had some incredible force of intellect, that she was blisteringly funny. Magnetic. Something that would explain the hold she clearly had over the man I loved – the man who should have been mine. But I never found it. All I found was this sulking, buttoned-up chameleon who could barely hold on to a friendship, let alone a love affair.

With her back against the wall, she doesn't take her eyes off me. 'You knew Wolf had found you out,' she says. 'You knew he'd discovered something on that phone. Something even worse than all the pictures. Bad enough for him to go out into that storm to confront you.'

'Is that right?' I say.

'Yeah. And now you've got it back, and Wolf's dead.' There's the hint of a quiver in her voice. 'So what did you do? What did you use, to do *that* to his skull?'

I'm not going to tell her. I can't say I enjoyed it – I'm not a psychopath – but I remember the dull surprise on his face, and I can't help but smile. I finish the can.

Somewhere in the ship, a siren starts to wail. Dee's frightened eyes go to the door.

In the second that I'm distracted, she twists out from under me, gets to the door and grabs the handle. I launch myself towards her, snatching at the back of her jacket, but she kicks back and connects with my shin. I howl as she turns into the passage, heading for the exit onto the portside deck.

I catch up with her as she wrenches open the heavy-duty door. I hook my leg around the front of her ankle and she trips, face-first onto the metal. Before she gets a chance to even start getting to her feet, I twist my hand into her hood and drag her along the deck.

Her hands go to her strangled throat, her feet scrabbling on the icy deck. If she's trying to scream, to shout for help, she can't do it. With one hand Dee claws at my ankle, but I plant every step with a conviction she can only imagine, a boiling determination that I've cultivated for months now. I grit my teeth as I pull her towards the hatch to the hold.

At the other end of the ship, I can hear a commotion. Marco's voice, Helen's, over the shrill scream of what can only be a fire alarm. I ignore it all. There is only forward. Every inch of my skin trills with the exhilaration of it, this last scene that I've fantasised about over and over again for months, finally being played out in real life. It's happening.

I keep a good hold of Dee's hood while I get down and drag the bolt back, then swing the hatch open. The cover clangs on the deck.

For one second I let her see what's about to happen. Horror registers on her face and she tries to cry out.

'*Tori!*' she rasps, but there's no air behind it.

And then, with one almighty heave, I swing her round and drop her into the hold.

63

TORI

The smell of burning intensifies. Around the other side of the ship I can hear bursts of pressurised gas, shouting – but as Helen raises the iron bar, I close my eyes.

I wait for the impact.

And in the split second that remains, I see some things.

A girl, one autumn afternoon, making a den with a new-found friend. A girl who often believed she was a radical young woman, but who was still only a kid, unburdened with guilt or shame. Concerned only with the *right now* and the very next moment. Walking into that woodland, thrilled at finding those perfect fingers of hazel.

My dad, trying his best, year after year, as his little girl drifted out of sight. Sitting by the phone table in the hall. Dutifully dialling my number every weekend, resignation on his face as he speaks into the voicemail yet again. Getting older every time.

Myself. Versions of myself, at eighteen, twenty, twenty-nine, onwards. Walking with my keys in my fist. Cutting runs short with the dimming of the day, like someone in a vampire movie. Always scared. Every single day.

And myself again, curled in different beds, at different times, recoiling from the touch of good men and not-so-good men alike. Rigid against walls, teeth gritted in showers, on sofas, the back seats of cars. Playing a part, wanting it to be over, always. Mourning the fabled thrill of sex that I'd never experienced, wondering if it would ever happen. If I'd ever trust any of them.

It was a quick thing, this crime against me. Minutes long. But even though I left him on that hillside, bleeding, I didn't win. He followed me. He still follows me now.

'It's over, Helen.'

She lets out an agonised shout of frustration. Then the metal bar drops from her hand, clattering onto the floor. She crumples, her arms dropping first and then the rest of her following like she's a dress falling from a hanger, until she's kneeling on the deck.

From around the other side of the deck comes Craig.

'They're here!' he shouts. Then he seems to see what's happening.

'It was her,' I tell him. 'She killed John.' I kick the mooring stake away, sending it spinning. But anyone can see that Helen's spent, the fight entirely gone out of her.

Craig takes her by the arm. 'It doesn't matter now – we've got to get off.' He marches Helen away, giving an urgent jerk of his chin as he passes me. 'Come on, let's go!'

And when I follow him, I understand.

Half of the starboard side of the ship is on fire. I run out to the fore deck, where I find Gaia and Nish crowding around Eino, shouting for information, while Ulla hands out red outersuits to those who don't already have them. Craig disappears down the side of the ship and then reappears a little way off on the ice around us, where Marco is strapping one of the RIBs to some kind of frame, like a big sledge.

Eino cups his hand around his mouth and calls for calm.

'We haven't been able to make contact with the icebreaker,' he says, 'but we can see it.'

He raises an arm and everyone looks out towards the sea. Between the ship and the open water is maybe a hundred metres of ice sheet, pinning us tight. Beyond that, there is a mess of white: the flat, irregular polygons where the edge of the sheet has broken up. Eventually, the fractured ice thins out and gives way to the undulating grey of the North Atlantic. And in the distance is a huge red-hulled ship.

'If she knew we were here, she would have diverted. But she's keeping her course.'

'They'll see the smoke, though, surely?' Gaia says, horrified.

Eino shrugs. 'That doesn't appear to be happening. And our attempts to put out the fire have so far not been successful. It's now preventing access to the bridge, and it is spreading.'

Gaia covers her mouth with both her hands and turns away, gripping her eyes shut in terror.

'Stefan, Ulla and I will continue to fight it and try to save the ship,' Eino shouts over the alarms, 'but I am giving the order for all non-crew to evacuate now, using one of the RIBs. It will need to be taken to the edge of the ice, and then Craig will pilot you towards the icebreaker and hope to catch up with her.'

'What about you?' Nish asks. But then realisation hits. 'What about – John? And Wolf?'

Eino falters, just for a moment. 'We hope to save the *Skidbladnir*, but if we also must abandon ship, we will meet you there. We will bring the—' He swallows, searching for the word, 'the cargo, if we need to also leave.'

I hear the words he's saying, but I can't make them make sense. *Fire. Abandon ship.* On the ice below, Marco calls up that he's ready. And then, led by Nish, the contestants – my contestants, the people I brought out here – climb down to join him.

A door to the side of the superstructure slams open and Stefan, in a ventilator mask, staggers out. A dark cloud of smoke blooms out around him and he bends double, coughing intensely, a pitifully inadequate extinguisher hanging from his hand.

This can't be real.

'*Tori!*' Suddenly Annabel is standing right in front of me, hair dishevelled, a wild look in her eye. 'You need to get on that boat, okay?' She takes hold of my arm and steers me towards where Craig is ushering people through the gap in the lower-deck gunwale and down towards where the RIB sits waiting to be hauled over to the water.

I climb down, then spin round. 'Dee – where is she?'

Annabel leans over from the lower deck. 'She won't leave. She says she needs to get the cameras.'

'What? But the ship's on fire!' I grab the rail to go back up, but Annabel comes halfway down, blocking my way.

'I *know*,' she says, exasperated. 'She wouldn't listen. But I'll get her, I promise.' The stench of smoke intensifies.

'That everyone?' Craig asks from the ice, doing a quick head-count.

'Dee's still on the ship,' I tell him, trying again to get past Annabel.

From the ladder, Annabel explains again. 'She said you should go. That one of you needs to be there with the others.'

Craig growls in frustration. 'We have to go, now! We can't lose any more time.' He shields his eyes as he looks up at Annabel, 'You get Dee, and you do whatever Eino does. All right?'

Annabel nods solemnly and turns to go, and Craig jogs back over to where Marco is already starting to drag the RIB towards the open sea.

I call up to her again, 'You promise me you'll get Dee to come? Straight away?'

'I promise,' she says. But as she turns to go back up to the deck, I swear I see something on her face.

Something I don't trust.

Something like a smile.

64

DEE

Pitch-black.

My head screams, the pain so intense I can barely form a thought through it. I bring my fingers to my scalp and they come away wet.

I try to cry out, but something in my throat is wrong, crushed. Every breath drags. Shifting my weight comes with a blinding white burst of pain: my leg, right above the ankle. I move my fingers down. I touch bone.

A minute passes, another. The pain doesn't subside, but I make myself breathe slow, bitterly cold mouthfuls of air. I move, a fraction at a time, unfolding myself out of the crumpled heap I landed in. I can't see them, but I know from coming down here before that I must have fallen ten, twelve steps, so steep they're more like rungs. Eight feet at least, an almost unbroken drop, straight onto the bare metal of the empty aft hold.

Not quite empty. I give a shudder, remembering what – who – else is down here, only feet from where I'm huddled.

But I can't think about that. Because I can hear footsteps overhead, the thud of people on the ice and, now, the muffled rumble of an outboard a little way off. They're evacuating, but not all of them.

Voices. I listen hard.

' . . . said I'd stay behind with you and get the equipment.' It's Annabel's voice. Every word brimming with synthesised concern. A flawless performance.

I try again to shout, but it's useless. Even slamming a fist into the thick steel of the hull barely makes a thud.

'You should have gone with the rest of them!' Eino says above me.

I scrabble about blindly, looking for anything I can use to bang against the side, but there's nothing.

' . . . have to find her,' Annabel is saying to him.

There are footsteps again, moving away. One pair. Eino's voice is indistinct, then shouts, 'Signal to abandon is three blasts.'

A few seconds of silence, then the screech of an unoiled metal hinge. A column of light streams in and Annabel climbs down, flicking on the strip light as she does. Thick red streaks cross my vision as she closes the hatch above her. I try to scramble back, away from her, but pain explodes in my ankle. She crouches next to me. Touches her fingertips to my cheek.

'I did wonder how it would end,' she says, tilting her head, her voice soft. 'I suppose I had thought it would be . . .' She rolls her hand at the general area. 'More special, somehow. But it's fine. As long as we get to have our chat.'

I spit into her face. A bubbly glob of it trickles down the side of her nose before she wipes it away, disgusted.

'You know when I first saw you, I thought you were

incredible. I was coming out of his building, after a piano lesson, and you were just going in. And he forgot even to say goodbye to me.' She laughs at this, like it's a fond moment we're sharing. 'Because he was watching you. Captivated, like you were some – I don't know – goddess.' She rocks back onto her heels, looks me over.

It takes everything I've got, but I manage three scratchy words. 'Who. Are. You?'

'Me? I'm the one who told Leo who you were,' she hisses, her eyes narrowing, hateful. At his name, something in my chest gives. 'You never saw me, did you? I saw you, though. I worked it all out: where you lived, the office you'd go to, your favourite coffee shop. Americano, an almond croissant, but only on a Friday. You never noticed me. I was invisible.'

Except she wasn't. I remember her. I gasp, seeing it now, a slight woman in the queue behind me, hood up, eyes averted, nervous fingers ticking at the edge of a phone as I went to leave. I *saw* her. More than once. I assumed she was a regular.

Because I was so used to being the watcher. It never occurred to me that I was being watched myself.

'I wanted to see what was so special about you,' she says. 'See if I could be that, too. But the more I looked, the less I could see it. You were . . . nothing. Basic. And *devious*. Sneaking around, pretending to be someone he'd actually like. When all the time you were lying to him. Digging up nasty little stories about him. So he helped a few students with their coursework. That was worth losing everything for, was it? A bad enough crime to have some sneering little bitch like you following him around, filming him. And *fucking* him, too?' She waits.

I breathe short, hard breaths through my nose, not looking away.

She raises a hand, and before I know what's happening she swings it flat against my face. 'You didn't even like him. Did you? You destroyed him, and you didn't even give him a backward glance.'

It's not true. I try to say it, but I can't, and this time it's not because of the pain. It's because it's what Leo thought, too, once he realised who I was. He thought I didn't care about him at all, that all he was to me was a mark for a show. He wouldn't listen that it had become more than that. I didn't have time to tell him.

She took that all away from me.

Outside, the siren screams. There are voices again, and Annabel leans over suddenly, clamping a hand over my mouth. I bite her instinctively and she pulls back, then grasps my throat. It hurts so much that I retch, and she shoves me away.

'I played nice, you see,' she says now, swiping indignantly at tears. 'I was polite, kept my distance. I worked out where he went, what he liked to do. I had a plan, you see. People like *me*,' she says, but a sob breaks over her and she pauses, takes a breath, comes back angrier. 'People like me have to work differently, when we want someone. But I would have got him. I knew everything about him.'

A memory surfaces, faint at first. A walk home from a bar, Leo's jumpiness. *Sure you're not imagining things?* I asked him. *Sure you're not watching too many scary films and getting paranoid?*

He wasn't, though, was he? He was right. It was her.

'And that's what isn't fair. You got him, even though you

didn't deserve him. And then when I told him who you were, it was my turn, but I didn't get a chance. All because of you. He died, because of *you*. He was driving too fast that night, because of what *you* did.'

I meet Annabel's eyes now. I blink, the weight of what she's just said settling on me like a blanket of silent snow.

He was driving too fast.

She can't have known. There were no witnesses. I was the last person to see him alive – that awful confrontation in his car. Leo throwing every ugly accusation at me: that I'd lied to him, that I'd tricked him. And then, after he'd demanded that I leave and I stumbled out into the deserted street, he'd driven off.

The next anyone knew, he'd skidded off the road and, when the police got there, he was already dead. It was the rain, they said. *Adverse weather conditions.* And my bag – the bag with the recording unit running – was nowhere to be found.

Except: someone called the ambulance. Someone was there.

I meet her eyes and make myself speak.

'What. Did. You. Do?'

65

ANNABEL

I'm struck by how old Dee looks, all of a sudden. Pale and beaten. The flesh around her neck already sagging. Her eyes puffy with that thin, shiny skin that people get when they're past their best.

He chose *this*, over me?

There is a bang from somewhere else in the ship and a sudden lurch, and the strip light overhead flickers and goes out.

I don't care. I navigate on my phone to my video folders, click into the right one, bring the volume up, so we can both hear it. I sit, pushing in close to her, close enough to smell the blood oozing from the wound on her head. The screen the only point of light.

'Let's have a look, shall we? Here.' I tap the white 'Play' triangle and the still image moves. I had to drop the resolution to get the whole file on my phone, but it's clear enough.

She lets out a broken moan and stiffens.

'Oh, yeah, you recognise this, don't you? No, don't look away. You'll want to see it.'

But Dee scrunches her eyes tight. I reach out and rest the tip of my finger on the smashed mess of her ankle.

'Watch,' I tell her.

And she does.

It starts on a wet street, rain, the orange of street lights. Georgian buildings in a suburb of Bath. Shot from the other side of the street, the angle low because the camera was concealed inside Dee's shoulder bag, the lens glued against a tiny hole in the side. The top corners of the shot are rounded off, where the vinyl of the bag obscured it. Even so, it's cinematic. I can't take that away from her – she certainly knows how to take a good shot.

A white car sits, engine off, outside a handsome town house. It is night. Inside the car is a man behind the wheel, looking down. His face lit blue by an unseen screen.

Beside me now, Dee's breathing slows.

Leo Adeyemi. The most beautiful man I've ever met.

The shot shifts jerkily across the road, dipping in time with the sound of footsteps. Dee's footsteps. For a second as she moves off the kerb, another car is visible – just the headlights and a few inches of the bonnet of a red Honda.

My car. Not that she would have known, then.

She crosses the road. A hand emerges to the right of frame, takes the passenger-door handle, pulls. The interior light comes on – the man has been sitting there for a while, though she didn't know that, either. He turns, and although the shot loses his face almost immediately, there is a moment when you can see his eyes. Wet. Harrowed.

The sound of the street shuts off suddenly as the door is closed. She settles the bag on her lap, turned towards him.

Hey, she says. And Dee, this six-months-older version of the same woman, whimpers beside me.

Off-camera, her voice is easy, relaxed. She starts to ask him about his day, then about the adult piano student he was teaching on Tuesdays – the student who happened to be me. It takes her a while to respond to the fact that he's not answering. *Hey,* she says after a pause. Then again. *Hey, what's up?* Worried now. *What's going on?*

He shows her the phone he's holding. The writing is illegible in the shot, but I know what it says. It's an email, and I know every word. There is a pause as she reads. The only sound is the rain on the roof.

Is it true? He asks. *What she's saying. Tell me.*

It is not his usual voice. It is not the voice Leo used with me in our evening lessons after he'd finished his school day: encouraging and calm and joyful. It's not how he sounded when I met him for coffee, the one time he agreed to meet me outside the lessons. That time was different – he was so careful with every word, making sure he said the things that he knew he was supposed to say. That he couldn't continue the lessons, if that was the way I felt about him. That it would be best for me to find another teacher for a while, though I knew that, deep down, he was only saying it because he felt he had to. Even then, I knew that what he was really asking me to do was prove myself to him. It would only be a matter of time.

The silence breaks.

Leo, look, she says. *It was . . . I was going to tell you. It started off as work, but this is – oh God – what they're saying there, it's not like that.*

No? It isn't? What is it like then? Explain it to me. Are you doing an investigation about me? Is that part true?

They start talking over each other now. She starts to answer – *it's not only you, it's* – but he interrupts her.

I know all the lines. Under my breath, I mouth every word.

I took the money from those parents because of my mum. Do you understand? Those students would have passed those assessments anyway. And now my career is over. It's all gone! Because of you. Please, don't.

The shot shifts as she leans over, tries to touch his arm.

He flings her off. *Don't. You have ruined my life. Do you understand that, Sophie? Or whatever the hell your name really is—*

Dee. It's Dee.

He laughs, but it's a horrible thing to hear. *I don't care. You're a liar, that's what you are. I cared about you. You made me think it was real. But it was nothing.*

It wasn't nothing. It's not like that. I love—

He shouts over her now. *Don't! You don't. Get out. I don't want to see your face ever again. You understand? Get out!*

There's movement, a scuffle. The door opens, the distant noise of a police car somewhere. She protests, but the door slams and then the shot drops, the bag in the footwell now, angled upwards. Just the edge of him rotated awkwardly in the bottom of the frame. He fumbles the phone back into the cradle beside the wheel. He sobs. A hollow, awful, desperate sound.

Beside me, Dee holds her breath, and I know why. Beyond this, every moment of his life is new for her.

The engine starts. Beyond the driver's side window, the scene changes. Beneath the rumble of the car and the windscreen wipers working at full speed against the rain, you can hear him crying.

The things you see when you watch it the first time are not the same as the things you see on the tenth watch, or the twentieth, or the hundredth. But what I see is that he is not wearing a seatbelt. That his sweater is ruched at the back, so that it shows half an inch of flesh. That on the fingers of the left hand, which rests on the wheel – fingers that can play the lower half of a Prokofiev concerto with such delicious dexterity that you would watch them and never want them to stop – are nails that are bitten to the quick.

I see it all. I see every detail because I loved him. He was all I thought of. I was his guardian angel, watching him, making sure he was safe, showing him the truth when he was deceived.

On the deck above us now there are noises, something mechanical. Shouts in Finnish. Dee struggles, tries to get up.

'No,' I tell her, pulling her down.

'We have to go,' she says, her voice an ugly scrape, every word an effort.

'Not yet. You're going to see this.'

Three loud blasts of the ship's horn sound.

'We have . . . to go,' Dee says in a whisper.

So I make good on the threat. When I grasp her ankle, there is both a softness and a sharpness to it that are not meant to be there. The sound she makes is not even human.

On the screen, the street lights space out.

When Leo drove away, I followed him. He didn't know, not until later. But I was there, watching over him even in his last minutes. We drove out together away from the city, in the relentless rain. As I drove I grabbed my phone and rang his number. All I wanted was to talk to him. To tell him I was there for him, right behind him. It rang and rang, went to voicemail.

I got closer. We were doing fifty, then sixty, along the mirror-wet, unlit road. I wanted him to slow down – I was crying, shouting his name at the back of his head on the headrest. And he couldn't hear me, of course he couldn't, but he must have seen me. So I drew up tighter, matched his speed. I felt the pull of him, urging me forward, until our bumpers were almost touching.

I flashed my headlights. He swerved a little, and my heart jumped – he knew it was me. I remember taking my hands from the wheel and wiping the tears away because I thought he was slowing down. That maybe this was the start of everything: me and him, together. I rang the number again, let it ring and ring.

That's when it all changed. Suddenly he was accelerating faster than I could match. I flashed again, sounded my horn – did he not know it was me, after all? I cried out as he streaked away from me.

And then he swerved, the smallest jolt to the right. Overcorrected to the left. Too much.

The car lights lifted, arcing upwards. I braked hard, watching, open-mouthed. One side of his car lifting impossibly, before coming down again on the side. And, like that, it skidded further and further away, the scream of metal against road until it struck a tree. Wheels spinning sideways against the empty air.

I got out of my car and I ran to him.

66

DEE

The hold is filling with smoke. Lightning sparkles at the edge of my vision, threatening to shut it down. I grip on to consciousness through the pain in my ankle, my head.

I summon enough breath to speak. 'Please. They're leaving. We need to go.'

But Annabel simply brings the screen closer to my face. 'You're watching this. You're watching it to the end.'

And I can't move.

The video – my video, from my bag-cam – shows a car filling with the light that can only be headlights from behind. Somewhere in the car a phone rings, but Leo ignores it. He squints, eyes going up to the rear-view mirror. He's not angry. He's scared.

Back off, he's saying under his breath. He says it again, blinking against the brightness. *Back off – what the fuck?*

The phone rings again. He glances at it, and then his eyes flash with a sudden fear. He looks back at the mirror. Terror and recognition. Illuminated in another flash, he lets out a cry.

You, he says, to the empty car. *Oh my God. Oh my God, it's you.*

The engine growls. He leans forward, gripping the wheel. Accelerating. Faster. Too fast. There is the sound of a car horn, impossibly close, then a moment of silence as the sound of tyres against tarmac disappears. He braces, arms locked, eyes gripped wide with impotent horror.

For a moment he flies. The shot changes, swings uncontrolled, flashes with light, then goes completely black – chaotic movement making no sense as the bag cam is thrown around. There is a deafening, grinding sound, rending metal, the crunching of glass. His scream stops. The movement slows. I can't make sense of what I'm seeing: everything is broken, reordered in a nightmarish jigsaw. Something wet in the foreground moves. Twitches.

The smoke in the hold thickens, burning against my eyes. The horn blares again, three long notes. They're abandoning ship.

Barely breathing, I glance at Annabel. Her head is tilted, a thin changeling of a smile as she searches my face. 'You did this,' she says. 'You killed him. And now you're going to pay. Just like I said in my letter.'

She shoves the screen right up to my face. A rhythmic, laboured sound starts up, livid enough to hear over the smoke alarms. A wet sound, choking. Leo, trying to breathe, but unable to.

Then there's a voice. Female, breathless.

I'm here, it says. *I'm here, my love, I'm here. It's me.*

It's her. It's Annabel.

Leo crashed because of her. Not me. He's dead because of her. The woman who called the ambulance. It was her.

And then I realise something else, too.

'Wolf,' I croak. This is the video Wolf found. Annabel knew he had her phone when I spoke to him in his cabin. Knew exactly what he'd said to me, because I was carrying a radio mic.

She grimaces, like it's bothersome. An inconvenience.

'What was I supposed to do? He wasn't going to give my phone back and pretend he hadn't seen it, was he? Oh, don't look at me like that. It was a rock to the head. Wolf wouldn't have felt a thing.'

Except that he did. She knows that, she saw him suffer. But she doesn't care at all.

I see a chance. With the video still running, I take hold of the phone in her hand and wrench it free. Holding it in my fist, I slam it against the side of her head, knocking her sideways. She roars, and I grab her hair and propel her head as hard as I can back against the metal bulkhead.

The ladder steps are directly behind me. I turn, haul myself up with one foot and wedge the knee of the bad leg above the next rung. She launches herself at me, but I grip hard, use the good leg to kick and connect with her abdomen. With every ounce of strength, I climb. Hand, hand, foot, knee. Hand, hand, foot, knee. I don't look down. As I reach for the final rung I feel Annabel's grip on my uninjured foot. Howling wordlessly, she pulls, but I twist out of her grasp.

I duck my head, put the weight of the hatch across my shoulders and heave it open. With my knees finally on the painted steel of the deck, I crawl away. I gulp at the air, blinking against the sudden overwhelming light.

It's like a scene from a war movie. Flames coil out of doorways, smoke billows from glassless window frames. Against a drift of soft snow, I cry out for Eino, Stefan, anyone, but there's no sign of them. Forcing myself forward, I grab hold of the cable barrier above the gunwale, get up onto my one good leg and stagger past the gas locker to the fore deck. Just ahead of the cage, running crossways, there is another locker, one I remember from the safety briefing.

'Dee!'

Annabel is emerging from the aft hold. She climbs out onto the deck, but then she stops, crouches. When she stands, she's holding what looks like a discarded handle from a winch – steel, one foot long, weighty. I don't hang around to find out what she plans to do with it.

Faster now, I limp right to the peaked fore of the deck. She shouts my name again, her voice wild with rage.

There is a boom as something explodes, something high up. I fling my arms over my head, but the rain of glass misses me. Annabel screams, hits the deck. Looking up, I see the blind, glassless gallery of the bridge belching smoke, lit from within by fire. But as I look away, something catches my eye.

Beyond the broken-up edge of the ice sheet, heading out into the open water maybe a quarter-mile away, is the second RIB, its wake a wide white V.

I try to shout, but my voice is a hoarse nothingness.

'They can't hear you!' Annabel shrieks, getting to her feet. Blood and dust cake her face – even from here, I can see a piece of glass glinting at her cheek. She closes in.

But I know what I have to do. Turning from the prow, I stumble back towards the locker on the deck. I flip the lid and pull out the orange case, open it up. I take out the orange pistol, the way Craig showed us in the briefing, load it with a cartridge. I lift the gun high and fire the flare high above me.

Two seconds, three, four. Nothing happens. The RIB holds its course, getting smaller by the second. I glance back to see Annabel hobbling forward, the whites of her eyes bright against the slick of red across her skin.

Still the RIB doesn't deviate. *See me*, I tell it. I scream it in my head. *See me!*

Then the apex of the little boat's wake curves left. Keeps curving. They're coming back.

Another explosion sounds, but this time it's inside the main superstructure of the vessel. Deep, thunderous, enough to rock the whole ship. Annabel is knocked off her feet. She tumbles over the rail of the upper level and falls, crumpling down against the lower deck like a dropped doll.

Close enough to hear now, the RIB closes the gap. Its nose rides high in the air as it bounces across the sea and navigates a path through the maze of ice. When it bumps to a stop at the water's edge, Stefan and Eino jump out onto the solid ice and race out across it towards me. I drag my leg behind me and get to the top of the steep steps to the lower deck.

Annabel is only metres away, lying on her back. Unmoving, shielded from their view by the bulwark. She might be breathing. She might not.

A wave of flame erupts from the portside door. The side of my face ignites with blistering pain, and I smell burning hair. Burning meat. I fall back, the flames now blocking my path – and her path – to the ladder down.

Eino gets to the ship first. He calls out again asking if I'm alone, where the hell I've been. He holds out his hand to help me climb to safety.

I could leave Annabel where she is. They'd never know.

But who would I be, then?

I pull myself along, crouch down beside her and shake her by the shoulders. 'Come on,' I tell her, my voice just a scrape in my throat against the scream of the alarm.

Her eyes fly open. She scrambles to her feet, and I stagger back on the narrow strip of deck.

'Quickly!' Eino shouts from the lower rung, reaching out his hand for either one of us to grab.

But Annabel doesn't grab it. Her face contorted with rage, she flies at me, swinging her arm back, the metal handle in her hand. It glints as she brings it in a high arc.

Time slows. In the same moment that I drop, my arms going instinctively to my head, Eino reaches up and grasps hold of her wrist. Unbalanced, Annabel loses her footing. It could be the weight of the metal in her hand or the pull of Eino's grip that drags her over, it's impossible to tell.

But when I lean over the edge of the ship, she's on the ice. Face-down, a stain of blood blooming from her head.

67

TORI

One month later, London

I wipe the shower steam from the mirror of the beautiful en suite and lean in. My towel-dry hair hangs in messy tendrils around my shoulders, in need of a cut. It's something I'll get to. I think of Dee, just before we left for the Arctic, telling me how good I'd look with half of it shaved off. I'd feigned horror at the time – Tori Matsuka with an undercut! Imagine my agent's horror. But now I lift it up, angle my head to the side. Maybe an undercut would be fun, for a little while. It's only hair.

Back in the bedroom, I choose a pair of jeans, a white shirt, a thin chain necklace that I always liked. A present from Wolf, years ago, that I never felt I could wear around Will. But things have changed now.

The house is quiet and the curtain in the long window billows full of air as I dress. In one of the gardens beyond it there are some children playing. There is birdsong. It's a shame I can't stay here: it's a nice house. But it's only a house. Dee's flat will do fine, until I get back on my feet.

The clasp of the necklace is tricky to manage on my own,

but once it's done I go downstairs. In the hall the last of Will's boxes stand against the wall. I wanted it to be amicable, but the moment we got back, it became apparent that he didn't share the sentiment. There was a nice story on the front page of a national rag before I'd even got off the plane, written entirely around an interview with him, all about my supposed fixation with Wolf. Will had even hired a lawyer to find ways to limit his own responsibility for the production's debt. It's fair to say the wedding's off.

I fill a bottle of water, pull on my trainers and go outside.

The bike ride to the hospital is as quick on two wheels as it would have been on four. I don't miss the Discovery really. I don't miss much of anything, as it happens.

But I do miss Dee.

I lock up the bike, spend a couple of quid on some unopened dahlias from a stall outside and head inside. That particular combination of antiseptic and canteen cooking greets me, newly familiar. I keep my sunglasses on, disguising myself out of habit because these days when people recognise me, it's not because they want selfies, but because they want to ask questions. What were Wolf's last words? Is it true I was sleeping with Marco? Did I push Annabel?

Just as nature abhors a vacuum, so gossip abhors the absence of fact. But between the things I can't talk about yet and those I choose not to discuss, there's little for me to tell them.

In the stairwell, my phone rings: my agent. I let my finger hover over the red button. I've been stalling for time, but I owe her a decision. I lean against the wall, looking out through the wide window, and accept the call.

She tells me the woman from the publishing house has a ghostwriter all lined up, that she's desperate for an answer. 'They're saying it'll be five, six interview sessions, max, and they'll do the rest. Honestly, Tori, you'd be mad not to take it. Under the circumstances.'

The *circumstances* are really only one circumstance, which is a seven-figure deal for the book. *Death in the Arctic*, they're calling it.

'It's going to be their lead non-fiction title for the spring,' she gushes now. 'I mean, obviously it is! It's the story of the year.'

But that's exactly it – it's not really only *my* story they want. Wolf and I were never going to be close again, but we were once, and I don't want to do wrong by him. I'm still working out how it feels that he's gone. Gaia has visited a few times, and from our tentative steps towards friendship over cups of tea from a Thermos by the Serpentine, I'm getting a sense of who John really was. Both Marco and Nish have told me privately that they want to forget about the whole sorry affair, and Helen's trial won't even start for months yet. And while I'm expecting Annabel's memorial service later this week to be crowded out by reporters, I still don't really know who she was. Why she did what she did. Maybe I will one day, but right now I can't say it really feels like my job to tell her story.

What people want is the pain. The victimhood. They want the secrets. They don't just want Tori Matsuka; they want John Grandage and Annabel Trent and Helen Greenaway. They want Kelvin Pierce. They want every moment, from the outbound flight to the real story behind the viral video of us bobbing in the waves in the shadow of that massive icebreaker, the burning ruins of our ship barely visible in the distance. They've already decided on how it goes: the triumph over adversity, the brave survivor, rising strong. But I'm not there yet. I can't give them something I don't have.

So I give my agent my answer, and tell her I want to clear the slate. No to the book, no to the 'final offer' from another network for me to go back to 'tell the true story' of *Frozen Out*. I tell her I'll be in touch, and then I tell her that honestly, I might not. Then I drop my phone into my bag and finish the climb to the second floor.

The nurse is coming out of the room when I get up there. 'A little groggy from the operation still,' she says, placing a warning hand on my arm. 'But I'm sure she'd like to see *you*.'

Dee switches off the TV as soon as I go in. The left side of her face is bandaged – her second skin graft – but I gingerly kiss the right. 'Hey.'

She smiles, winces, then smiles again, but more carefully. 'Hey. Tell you what, if they ever offer it to you, I think on balance I'd recommend keeping your face-skin on your face, instead of replacing it with skin from your—'

'Okay, thank you,' I say over her, laughing. 'Painful, huh?'

'Kind of. You think I'd be used to it by now.' She pats the bed and I sit.

Work on the flat is going well, I tell her: some fresh paint, new shelves and a big order of houseplants coming to fill them.

'You really didn't need to,' she says, wincing as she moves.

I look her in the eye. 'I really did, you know. And I need to do a whole lot more than that.'

'Tori, seriously, it's fine. It's forgiven.'

Dee puts her hand, palm up, on the bed and I slip mine into it. For the first week, while we were waiting in Nuuk to bring her back, she wouldn't return my calls and asked me by text not to visit her in hospital. Everyone else flew home, but I stayed there, just waiting. I thought it was all over, that she'd never talk to me again. Because what I did – lying to her, gaslighting her, knowing that she and the rest of them were in danger, but burying my head in the sand – I can't truthfully say I would forgive that, if the tables were turned.

But after a week Dee called me in. She listened to everything I had to say. About how I'd got so blinded by fear of the show failing, and my desperation to keep the secret I'd built my life around, that I stopped doing the right thing.

We agreed then and there what we would both do. It hasn't been easy and it's far from over, but what I know for sure is that shame is a mould, an infection. Without exposing it to the light, without scraping it out and calling it by its name, it will spread and deepen until it is all you are. We made a plan, and it started with a promise of honesty.

'Oh, the interim payment has just gone through,' I tell her, to save her asking. It'll be a while until the dust has settled on the financial disaster that was the first and last Tori Tells Stories production, but at least it's looking like Dee's insurance payout will be higher than we thought.

Dee reaches for a beaker of water. She mimes a toast, watches me as she drinks, then holds up a finger, knowing what I'm going to ask. She swallows. 'Don't! I've made up my mind. Every penny of it goes to her.'

'But what will you live on?' I ask her. Once she's transferred the money over to Leo's mum, she'll have barely enough to survive.

'I'll work something out.'

I let it go. Truth is, I know how it feels to be indebted. Though I never asked for John's silence about what I did to Kelvin Pierce, and what he did to me, by keeping my secret, John made a sacrifice that changed the course of my life. I wish I could thank him for that now, for doing what he thought was right. What fourteen-year-old Tori Matsuka would have wanted him to do.

Except that now I've brought the whole thing into the open, I understand that it would have been better all along if John had simply come out and said what he saw. Or if I had come forward. Because despite all the uncertainty, and all the fear of what might or might not happen now, I've never known relief like I felt on walking out of Chiswick police station after being questioned on our return from Greenland. All I can do is wait, but my lawyer is quietly hopeful that a sympathetic Crown Prosecution Service will let sleeping dogs lie.

'Fact is,' Dee says, smoothing the sheet across her stomach, 'money's not going to pay the debt, is it? There's more to it than that.' She glances at the clock and nods. 'Talking of which . . .'

I gather my things and lean over to kiss her exposed cheek again. 'Good luck.'

In the corridor outside, I pass two women approaching the nurses' desk. One is elderly, her frail hands gripping the bars of a walking frame, but the other is the spitting image of the photos Dee showed me. Tall, slender, with neat cornrows ending in a burst of loose salt-and-pepper hair. Cheekbones that I'd happily walk over hot coals for. Leo's mother, and his sister. The nurse directs them to Dee's room, and I pause for a moment to watch them knock, go in.

Outside the sun is doing its thing. I leave my bike where it is and walk for a while, unable to shake the picture of Dee in that bed. The redemption she's hoping for might never come, but she's opened the door.

I stop at a bench, pull out my phone. I dial a long number. There's a pause as the international line connects – a sound I haven't heard often enough, for a very long time. I listen to the silence, seeing in my mind's eye a bright thread wrapping halfway around the world.

Dee is in there now, opening a door. So I open my own.

'Dad? It's Tori. Listen, I've got some things to tell you.'

ACKNOWLEDGEMENTS

As I understand it, some books are born smoothly into the world. They make the transition from the author's mind to the printed page as effortlessly as a frog squelches out its spawn.

This was not one of those books. This was the sort of drawn-out, screaming, expletive-laden birth that could traumatise our young people out of continuing the human race.

I exaggerate a little, of course. I also understand that no one wants an acknowledgements page full of increasingly inelegant references to breech, contractions, and fourth-degree tears. But this is my book, and that's exactly what you're going to get, so strap in.

After a rather lengthy delivery, there are many people I need to thank for their patience as much as their input.

To begin with, my gratitude to my principal midwife, Therese Keating, for her faultless stewardship. Without her confidence that we would have a book at the end of what at times was a medieval hell-fest of primitive forceps and biting down on sticks, I may have receded into a cave and awaited the end. I am being dramatic, but that is literally my job. Enormous thanks also to Ward Sister Miranda Jewess, who correctly diagnosed an earlier phantom pregnancy and patiently sent me home to try again. (At the time, the words, 'Why don't you try something completely different? A locked room thriller?' filled me with terror, but as it turns out . . .). Thanks also to my matchless agent/doula Veronique Baxter whose no-nonsense advice and enthusiasm aided every stage of gestation, and to everyone at David Higham for their championing of my slippery and blood-spattered offspring.

Fortunately for the reader, my personal experience of childbirth is now a distant memory, and I can't remember the roles of the labour ward well enough to ascribe one to every person involved in this book. But suffice it to say that the team at Viper have all been crucial, and not a little fabulous. Drew Jerrison, Alia McKellar, Mandy Greenfield, Emily Frisella, Sam Johnson, Flora Willis, Rosie Parnham, Angana Narula, Claire Beaumont, Sian Gibson, Anya Johnson, Elif Akar, Lisa Finch, Robert Greer, Sarah Ward and Louisa Dunnigan: my gratitude to every one of you. If I could give this book middle names, yours would be among them.

Huge and serious thanks to the inspirational Craig Mathieson of the Polar Academy, which offers life-changing polar expeditions to young people. Also to Matt Spenceley of Pirhuk Greenland Mountain Guides, Nicolai Christensen of the Greenland Police. My boaty chum Admiral Sam Rabin helped with maritime queries, as did Captain Clare Devonport – though mistakes are mine and mine alone.

Glorious gas-and-air was provided by my dear writer friends, in the form of first reads, endless encouragement and general good humour. Thank you Rachael Blok, Trevor Wood, Harriet

Tyce, Jo Furniss, Niki Mackay, Susie Lynes, Danny Marshall, Garry Abson, Jen Faulkner and the Criminal Minds crew – you lot are the absolute bollocks. Mum, Dad and Faye, thank you for being there.

In what is now fast becoming a rather overcrowded delivery room, it would be easy to miss the smaller people – namely Mo and Sid Kennedy, my actual children. Thanks for understanding when I had to prioritise this needy younger sibling. You two being proud of my books makes everything worthwhile.

As with all massively overstretched metaphors (don't worry, I'm nearly done) there are some aspects that really don't work. In this genre, the husband is usually an astonishing wrong 'un who'd just as likely sneak in a visit to the pub or his mistress while I was screaming for an epidural. Tom, not so much. Thank you, mate, for your friendship and your kindness. You'll never find yourself in a book of mine because you're frankly just implausible.

ABOUT THE AUTHOR

Kate Simants was shortlisted for a CWA Debut Dagger for her first novel, *Lock Me In*, and won the UEA Literary Festival Scholarship to study for an MA in Crime Fiction, where she graduated with distinction. Her second novel, *A Ruined Girl*, won the Bath Novel Award. Her third novel, *Freeze*, was a *Sunday Times* Book of the Month and a *Times* Book Club pick. Before writing full time, Kate worked as an investigative undercover journalist for Channel 4 and the BBC. Her experiences undercover partly inspired the plot of *Freeze*, as well as her expertise behind the camera. She lives near Bristol with her family.

AVAILABLE NOW

The immersive, heartrending thriller and
Winner of the Bath Novel Award

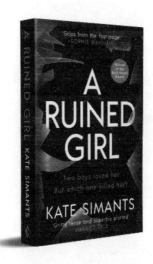

'An emotionally engaging whydunnit'
Sophie Hannah

'Gritty, tense and superbly plotted'
Harriet Tyce

AVAILABLE NOW

The #1 Kindle bestseller

As seen on *Lorraine*

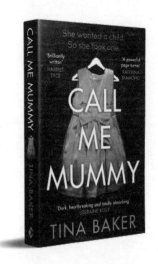

'Beautifully written'
Harriet Tyce

'Heartbreaking and totally absorbing'
Lorraine Kelly

AVAILABLE NOW

The *Sunday Times* bestseller and
Waterstones Thriller of the Month

'Dazzlingly clever'
The Times

'A modern Agatha Christie'
Sunday Times

AVAILABLE NOW

The *Sunday Times* bestseller and
Richard & Judy Book Club pick

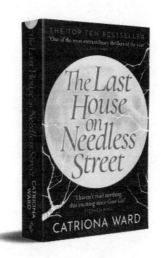

'Extraordinary'
Daily Mail

'I was blown away'
Stephen King

AVAILABLE NOW

The inspiration behind the hit TV series
American Horror Story: Delicate

'Tense and thrilling'
Heat

'Shockingly real, twisty and dark'
Independent

AVAILABLE NOW

The darkly funny and compulsive debut,
introducing your new favourite serial killer

'Refreshingly original'
Clare Mackintosh

'Delightfully shocking'
Janice Hallett